# *JUMP*

MARIANNE ACKERMAN

McArthur & Company
Toronto

This Canadian paperback edition published
by McArthur & Company, 2001

Copyright © 2000 Marianne Ackerman
First published in 2000 by McArthur & Company
All rights reserved

Canadian Cataloguing in Publication Data

    Ackerman, Marianne
      Jump

    ISBN 1-55278-133-X (bound)    ISBN 1-55278-184-4 (pbk.)

    I. Title.

    PS8551.C33J85 2001      C813'.54      C00-930255-7
    PR9199.3.A34J85 2001

Composition & Design by *Michael P. Callaghan*
Cover Illustration by *J.W. Stewart*
Cover Design by *Mad Dog Design Connection Inc.*
Typeset at *Moons of Jupiter, Inc.* (Toronto)
Printed in Canada by *Transcontinental Printing Inc.*

McArthur & Company
322 King Street West, Suite 402
Toronto, ON, M5V 1J2

10 9 8 7 6 5 4 3 2 1

The publisher wishes to acknowledge the financial support of the Government
of Canada through the Book Publishing Industry Development Program (BPIDP)
for our publishing activities.The publisher further wishes to acknowledge the
financial support of the Ontario Arts Council for our publishing program.

*for* Gwyn

# QUESTION

# I

◆

September, a phone booth on the corner of Woodbine and Queen St. East, a windy day in Toronto. Myra is away from Montreal on a networking trip to the city that counts. Moved by an impulse as deep as instinct, she is calling her long-lost husband in Calgary, and everything is about to change.

"Could I speak with Jack Grant please?"

A brisk male voice says Mr. Grant isn't available.

"Well, his secretary . . . ?"

"He doesn't have a secretary. She's back in the pool. May I refer you to someone else?"

Seems strange, a lawyer without a secretary. Then the man says he's sorry but he'll have to put her on hold and Myra says, "Wait a minute, I'm calling long distance and I've been trying to reach him for days but all I get is a machine. Could you make sure he gets a message?"

"You're a friend of his?"

His wife, she almost blurts out, but decides not to confuse a man who happened to walk by a ringing phone, a man who, like the rest of the Calgary office, thinks of Mrs. Grant as a tightly packaged French-speaking woman named Paulette. A legal secretary who first slept with Jack 15 years ago when the glue of family life was coming undone in Montreal, Paulette is a Québécoise pure laine with no use for clergymen of any stripe. So in due time, they formalized their union aboard a Caribbean cruise ship. Jack took great delight in telling how a sea captain blessed them with champagne but he acts fully married to Paulette. So Myra falls back on a simplified form of the truth.

"Yeah, a friend. Is he on vacation?"

"Well, no, actually, it's medical leave."

Granite Jack, sick? He's never sick. "How long has he been off?"

"Let's see, I guess about two months now."

Her legs are numb. It's been ages since she's had reason to think about Jack. Then a few days ago an old photo turned up, the two of them standing in front of Niagara Falls, looking misty and young, and now his face won't disappear. Smooth, high forehead, fine nose like a statue of Cicero, John Lennon glasses. Someone is waiting to use the phone but the glass walls are melting.

When she asks what's the matter, she can hear the man in Calgary breathing. His answer sounds almost human. "We don't actually know. You'll have to call him at home."

Ah. Home.

She hangs up the phone, steps into the wind, and a cloud of dust swirls round her ankles. Two young grease-balls huddling together outside a mean little milk store on the corner, a stubby dog dragging an old man by a chain:

these are the signs of life she registers, crossing Queen for a streetcar heading west, on her way toward Union Station and the train back to Montreal. The wind is sharp, the pavement floats. She holds her position against a wave of panic, a gut-deep feeling she did not know back in 1980, when things were falling apart.

The streetcar pulls up and a few minutes later she's in the middle of Toronto, walking south toward the trains, wondering what to do about Jack. Straight ahead is the Royal York Hotel, a ritzy mausoleum where they spent their one honeymoon night. It's on the way, so she goes inside. All that plush carpet, dark wood and leather luggage makes her think of gin and tonic and how it might be wise to have one, because impulse can easily be confused with instinct and you leap into action, then later, see so clearly how a little reflection would have saved much grief. She is on her way out the revolving door to look for a cheaper bar, some place where the situation can be mulled over calmly, when she sees a wall of phones, and stops.

A youthful Japanese man is holding a receiver with his shoulder, twisting a newspaper in both hands. The words "referendum," "Quebec" and "Parizeau" pop up in 14-point bold amid the brush strokes of his native language. There is urgency in his voice, he is selling peace of mind, long distance, trying to convince Tokyo it's perfectly safe to do business with Canada. This referendum is no real threat to stability, all the opinion polls say the Non side is ahead by a comfortable margin. Quebecers do not want to break up the second largest country on earth. Suddenly, he slips from Japanese to English, "It's a ritual. Nothing will change."

Myra stands beside him, picks up the receiver, puts her card in the slot and watches as he disappears into the crowded lobby. *Nothing will change.* At this precise moment, dialing Calgary, she desperately wants to believe him and in the space of three rings, considers hanging up the phone but her arm won't move. Then a flowery voice on the other end sings, "Allô?"

Jack and Paulette met at a seminar on tax law. She was taking notes for her boss, a partner in the biggest francophone law firm in Quebec. He was hiding out from the howls of Saturday morning, waiting till the kids woke up from their nap and it was his turn to play parent, take them to a park while Myra worked. After that, they bumped into each other on the street and stopped to chat. Then it happened again, outside Paulette's office. The third time, Jack was with Myra on the corner of St. Catherine and Bleury, three of them standing side by side, waiting for the light to change. He met her eyes but neither spoke. The next day they went for coffee.

Technically speaking, nothing happened until the ultimate blow-up got Jack into his own room. Then Myra sold her first magazine piece to Saturday Night and he started staying over at Paulette's. A profile of the Canadian Reader's Digest, headquarters in Westmount, Quebec, the piece took months and a godawful amount of work and by the time it was finished and she came up for air, Jack had given up his phoneless room to move in with Paulette.

On one point, he and Myra have always agreed: under no circumstances would Sally and Mitch be allowed to feel they have anything less than two able parents on the job, and as all the books agree, that means good communication. They kept in touch but if Myra called at the wrong time, or too often, or for no particular child-related reason, Paulette tended to stage a scene. Amid flying cutlery, he'd put the receiver up against his bathrobe and growl, then come back to Myra with splinters in his voice, promise to call back, keep his promise, and the next day, take her out to lunch. It was a lot easier being Jack's absent wife than it had been living under the same roof. Paulette's jealousy helped. Her tantrums made their alliance look flimsy and gave Myra the incentive to appear cool, which she did, with the exception of one or two memorable incidents, until gradually the appearance of cool turned into a habit.

Then one day Jack announced he'd been offered a great opportunity in Calgary with the government. In Alberta, I'll pass for perfectly bilingual, he joked. Myra wanted to ask, what about Paulette, then he said something that implied she'd be going too, and they left. He got a secretary and a professional mailing address, so there was no more need to call him at home. Until today.

Paulette's voice is unnaturally cheerful. "I'm so happy to hear from you. I was going to call. Jack's been sick." He must be standing nearby, her voice bubbles over with conspiracy. "He's much better now than he was a month ago. Aren't you, chéri? It's Myra, phoning from Montreal. Are you in Montreal? Hurry up, it's long distance, she wants to talk to you. Just a minute, he's in the middle of making a pot of tea, and oh my god, what a mess. Jack!" She sets the phone down and has a conversation with the sick man that sounds like a woman talking to a cat.

Finally, the line rustles and Myra hears a tiny, fragile hello.

"Jack, what happened?"

"I had a breakdown."

The sigh of his voice makes her mouth go dry. "Why didn't you call?"

"I did call. Got the fax machine."

"Sorry, it's one of those ones you turn on, and I keep forgetting to turn it off. I mean, when I'm not . . ." Parched, no juice in her throat for the word home.

"How are you?"

"Oh, I'm better now, " he says, a tiny smile in his voice.

"But, how did — what happened?"

"Don't know. Woke up one morning and started to sweat. Time I got downtown, didn't remember a thing. They picked me up."

"Who?"

"Police."

And that's when out of the blue Myra hears herself say, "I'm coming out there."

"You are? Here, just a minute then." There is more muffled conversation as Paulette picks up the receiver.

"Allô? It's me again. Jack, your tea is on the counter. Don't forget those pills, hein? Tu les prends toutes." She cups her hands around the mouthpiece and whispers, "He's gone back into the kitchen. Mon Dieu. It's bad, did you notice his voice?"

"He sounds smaller," says Myra.

"He is! He lost 30 pounds in that hospital. What an ordeal. The first few weeks were the worst. His mother said, don't bother the children, they'll worry, men go through this. Jack's strong. It's not true! That woman is méchante. You wouldn't know him, he's so much changed. Mon Dieu. Oh, he's coming back. Viens ici, chéri."

Myra is chewing the ends of her hair. In the dead space between conversations, her mental image of the misty man by the Falls is suddenly sharper and more dear. *You wouldn't know him.* Her chest aches, and the tightness in her throat dissolves into a powerful urge to cry. Why didn't someone call me? She is about to ask this question when Jack comes back on the line.

His voice is stronger. "I've got the Air Canada flight schedule. Where are you?"

"Toronto."

"Is that right? Where in TO?"

"The Royal York."

"I thought big splashy hotels weren't your style."

He leans on the word "style" just hard enough to summon up an ancient grudge: their single honeymoon night, Jack's father's gift inspired a tirade from Myra about the perverse tastes of people with money. A tearful night, not worth revisiting. "I was just taking a short-cut to the train station and saw a phone."

Jack has already moved on to his plan, page two of the schedule, and a flight to Calgary at 12:05. "If you go out the door right now, you can catch an airport bus and still have time for a coffee. Oh! Bring me cigars, could you?"

In the background, she hears Paulette wail against smoking. A teacup falls, Jack says see you, and the line goes dead.

The airport lounge for the Calgary flight is buzzing. Seats fill up with suited men and polished women bearing briefcases packed with deals. Since it's Friday, most are on their way home, eager to be airborne and start the weekend. The heaviness of calling Jack is beginning to lift, and Myra remembers how long it has been since she stepped on a plane. No time, no money. An hour ago her mind was foggy with a premonition of disaster, but the festive mood is contagious.

In the excitement she almost forgets that nobody at home knows about this impulse. Mitch isn't there when the phone rings, so she leaves a message saying she won't be back today as planned. The truth thus far is not something to be left on an answering machine for an 18-year-old boy-man. Then she calls Sally but before there is time to say more than hi, it's me, the phone card runs out, and she has to call back collect. A mechanical voice announces, you have a collect call from MOM. To accept the charges please press one. The voice on the other end sounds faintly annoyed.

"Mom, what is this?"

"My card ran out. Didn't think you'd be home, anyway. I'll pay you back."

"You don't have to pay me back. But, you know, collect calls cost more. There's no discount."

Sally is her father's daughter, careful with the details. Her turf is her mother's turf, the Plateau Mont-Royal, a mongrel mix of immigrant enclave and yuppie chic, east of the Mountain and up from Sherbrooke. But lately she has begun to stake out new borders. Her old bedroom at home, on Esplanade, is empty. She lives a few blocks away, on Henri-Julien. On weekends, she slings beer on the Main to pay for a ground-floor apartment shared with three friends. When she moved out last spring, Myra stayed out of sight, determined not to be seen crying. Since then, Sally's life has filled up with independence. She pays scant attention to her mother's movements.

"Where are you?"

"Toronto. The airport. I'm on my way out to Calgary."

"Oh." Her voice drops into a foreboding key and with one word Myra knows the crisis in Calgary is not news to Sal.

"How did you know?"

"What do you mean?"

"Sally!"

"Daddy wrote me some kind of weird letter about sweating and not knowing where he was."

"When was this?"

"I don't know. A few weeks ago. Didn't he talk to you? He said he was going to call. I told you to get that fax machine sorted out."

As Sal lectures, Myra makes notes: a wired world, so much information falling into a black hole. Story idea? Could have magazine potential. But another part of her brain is processing Jack's breakdown. Everybody knows, they thought she knew too, but no. The news is a colourless, odourless acid on tender skin.

Sally's voice stays in the low register of someone holding back. "You're going out there?"

"Yeah."

"Why?"

"Well. Jack had the flight times. And, I spoke to Paulette. . . . You don't think I should go?"

"I'm just wondering if he needs the two of you right now, in the same room."

She was prepared to reassure Sally everything will be all right, daddy's fine, the world as we know it is not going to change, don't you worry. But the known world has already changed, the centre is moving. When the steward calls out her row, Myra heads toward the aircraft. The floor beneath her quivers with the weight of footsteps.

# II

◆

An empty wheelchair and a lady with a sign are all Myra sees as she walks through the arrival doors at Calgary International. The sight is startling. She hurries on by in search of a taxi stand, but a thin man in a pale grey sports jacket grabs her arm and for a split second she doesn't recognize him. He seems smaller, his hair is wispy, longer than before, parted slightly off-centre, left to hang over both ears. He says, "You were supposed to be on the noon flight."

"It was overbooked," she replies. "They were giving out $300 vouchers to people who'd wait for the next one."

He arches his eyebrows, and she says flights cost a fortune when you don't book ahead. "If I'd known you'd be waiting — "

He lets go of her elbow, takes a step back. "I said I would."

She says, "I'll pay you back."

"You don't have to pay me back." He sighs.

And thus they say hello.

Jack and Myra haven't seen each other since the last time he came East two years ago. When they kiss on both cheeks, he feels her body rigid. She thinks, his skin is loose and soft. He's still wearing the same John Lennon glasses he bought in university, the ones he wore in that picture, by the Falls.

He slings her backpack over his shoulder, and as they walk towards the car, he thinks, how strange to see her here, as if a character from one movie has suddenly walked into another. She hasn't changed. Still dressed for comfort, flat sandals, a jean skirt and black cotton sweater, as always, lugging a ton of books and newspapers. A little more grey in her long brown hair. Still babbles when she's nervous, the Rockies, airplane food, bloody referendum. Same questioning eyes that won't leave you alone. They have known each other forever, she is present in the farthest corners of his mind, he would like to crack that presence, or reconfigure, at least, understand. Ever since the day he woke up downtown in a fog, he can't seem to stop himself from crossing lines, provoking situations, and now Myra is in Calgary.

By the time they get to the parking lot, they've run out of easy things to say. Jack throws her pack into his 1973 Buick Electra convertible, the kind of car he dreamed of having all through law school. Except that now it's an antique, lovingly restored, and rolls like a luxury hotel suite on wheels. Black leather seats, whitewall tires, sleek body painted a high-gloss yellow that could almost pass for gold. He opens his door and waits for her reaction.

"You've lost a lot of weight," she says, getting in.

"Yeah, well, I was too fat. Breakdown's good for the waistline."

They glide through the flat expanse of country toward a city of skyscrapers, familiar from magazine stories about booms and busts. Calgary lives up to its media rep. Clean and unabashedly prosperous, downtown is humming with construction, acre after acre of glass, the streets crawling with new cars, no potholes. For a while this ride seems like the beginning of an assignment, and she's tempted to look for a story.

Jack slips k.d. lang into the CD player and a clear-water voice fills the air. The wind whips her hair into a tailspin. They can't talk over the combined rush of music and motor which is just as well since the impulse that set her in motion is pretty well spent. Without a top, the car seems to be moving awfully fast, which may or may not contribute to the rush of vertigo. Her stomach feels queasy, she remembers she hasn't eaten yet today, leans back on the seat and gazes up at the sky, as blue as a calendar photo and there's so much of it. How do people keep their eyes on the road ahead?

The Buick noses into a landscaped neighbourhood and the houses get bigger, row after row of large, frame two-storeys, surrounded by shrubs and flowers. She holds her beat-up leather purse in her lap and thinks that luckily, the return ticket is completely flexible, departure is possible any time. Glancing over at his profile, she realizes she was wrong about his glasses. They're still wire-rimmed, all right, but they turn into sunglasses when he hits the outdoors. The leather case says Gucci. She has landed in a foreign country.

For a good part of the last dozen years, the Calgary Grants have existed for Myra as a kind of private cartoon strip. In the beginning, Paulette's jealous outbursts established the tone: cutlery flying through the air and lots of exclamation marks in the conversation balloons. Once, before they left Montreal, she saw them walking down Sherbrooke Street, a reformed hippie striding along beside a small, brightly feathered bird, teetering and twittering on impossibly high heels, flaming red hair, a lot of jewelry. When Mitch and Sally started spending holidays in Calgary, it didn't take them long to figure out what kind of souvenirs to bring back: domestic details, to be doled out at the dinner table, amid giggles and groans. They argue all the time, said Sally. She has weird hobbies. Loud, said Mitch. She laughs at silly jokes. Bowls of candies all over the house. Quite a lot of pink. Jack hangs out at malls on Saturday afternoon. Paulette's taking singing lessons. Every summer, more stories. Kitchenette, steakette, rockette, lifette, Paulette. But the chief source of information was Jack. From the beginning, when they used to meet for lunch in Montreal to discuss the kids, he made the whole idea of Paulette seem vaguely temporary. Getting over stuff, on the outs with her large, French-Canadian family, she was, Jack hinted, having a rough time. The centre of the storm was elsewhere.

"I don't know, I just don't know anymore," he'd say, staring off into space as if his inner turmoil rendered such details as who he was sleeping with quite insignificant.

As they wheel into the yard, Paulette is standing on the porch, wearing a lavender pantsuit, her strawberry blonde hair cropped short and neat. She waves, calls out something inaudible. They live in the upscale neighbourhood of Kensington, in a vintage frame house, ancient for

Calgary, with grey siding and white trim, a wraparound sun porch and lawn. Mitch had mentioned they'd moved when he went out there last summer, but he said the house was run down. Sally hasn't been West in four years. She prefers to spend time with Jack and his money visiting the art galleries of New York.

Jack is about to get out of the car when Myra catches him by the arm and says, "Wait, I thought — I thought you had a breakdown?"

"I did."

"But?"

"I'm still off work."

"I know, they don't seem to know what you're doing at the office. It sounded serious. I mean . . . Didn't you tell them anything?"

"Less said, the better. Avoids rumour. You know how people gossip."

"But, you seem . . ."

"What?"

"Well, fine."

"Mad people often do," and he throws his mouth open wide so a goulishly wicked laugh fills the day. As he snatches her backpack out of the back seat, Myra sits there, staring out ahead, and Paulette comes clicking down the sidewalk.

"Bon Dieu, es-tu allé à Montréal la chercher?"

He rolls his eyes. "She took a later flight."

"Ah bon. Hello. How was the trip?"

"Fine," says Myra, her mouth completely devoid of moisture.

Paulette is beaming. "Jack says you've never been West. Comment ça?"

Naturally, Myra answers in French, something like she's never had any reason to come to Calgary, but Paulette answers back in English, "I'm surprised you don't want to see your country." Myra looks around at the acres of suburbia and feels no trace of country.

The double living room is large and painted pale orange, with creamy wall-to-wall carpet, antiques and a few quiet modern pieces, a flowered sofa, real Inuit art and sunflowers by Cézanne, Mozart for background. Something sweet-smelling wafts from a distance. Paulette hurries off into the kitchen, and Jack takes the backpack upstairs, then goes down to help with snacks.

The guest room is large and flowery with pink and green brocade wallpaper, its own bathroom, emerald walls above cedar wainscotting. A terra-cotta jar of cattails fills a corner of the room. One entire wall is mirror, head to foot. Myra washes her face with a guest washcloth. It smells new, but the wall of mirror is irresistible, she is fascinated by the reflection, jean skirt so old it hugs her bum and a cast-off sweater from Sally, feet spilling out of last summer's sandals, no makeup, wild hair. As if a shaggy-haired reporter has wandered by mistake into a feature article in Better Homes and Gardens.

She flops down on the double bed and kicks off her sandals. Strange turf. She does not like being a guest. Minutes tick by, she knows the more time that passes the harder it will be to go downstairs but she closes her eyes anyway, sinks into a dizzy image of her own face, flowers and cattails, and suddenly she is thinking of Port Hope, high school, St. Mary's, and a bumpy side road that leads to the lake, past a marsh full of cattails. Floating pictures, one strange sight after another, like clouds in the calendar sky. She opens her eyes and is momentarily lost. Then the flowers come back into focus. Wallpaper. Calgary.

Downstairs, Jack and Paulette are sitting beside each other on the Bauhaus sofa, an open bottle of wine and a feast of delectable snacks stretching out in front of them. Myra says she's sorry, must have fallen asleep. Oh, that's fine, they say, as she sinks into a wingback chair. Paulette hands her a plate, Jack fills her glass, and the story begins.

A complicated litany of incident and opinion, it all started with the death of Jack's father, Phil, on an Ottawa golf course, which prompted his wife to relocate to Calgary, the better to be near her only child. Two of her former neighbours in Rockcliffe had come West the year before and took her into their bridge club, but still Edith did not adjust to the move, decided she didn't want to live in a house any more, she wanted to live in a hotel, like some woman she'd read about in a book, although that was New York. After talking about it for a few weeks, she got up one morning and cleaned house. Hundreds of un-opened moving boxes were sent to the Salvation Army. Then she checked into a room in the Palliser.

As Paulette tells the story, chronologically, but with many reversals, asides, and corrections, Jack nibbles away at high-fibre crackers spread with goat cheese and salmon paté, popping the occasional black olive. When she gets to the part about Edith breaking her hip, he drains his glass and pours a fresh round. After spending two months in hospital, the doctor made it clear Edith could not live alone. When they gave her the news, she balked, blamed Paulette for talking Jack into putting her away. In the ensuing scene, it came out that she had sent every bit of memorabilia from Jack's childhood to the Salvation Army. He managed in his panic to buy back a baseball glove and a copy of *The Red Badge of Courage*, inscribed by his late father, Christmas of 1960, but otherwise, all was gone. She had completely divested herself of the past. The liberation, and Jack's badly disguised anger, seemed to take her mind off resistance; house empty, she agreed to go quietly.

When the move was over, Jack and Paulette checked into the Banff Springs Hotel to get a little perspective. The following Monday he started back to work, and freaked. Six weeks, raving mad, a psychiatric ward, refusing to eat. He had to be restrained. Didn't know anybody. Drugs. Talk of shock therapy. Finally, the sweat passed. He stared out the window for a long time, then got up and called home.

As Myra zeroes in on the marinated shrimp, she can't help imagining the whole exhaustive confession as an afternoon on Oprah. Jack nods at crucial moments, laughs out loud once or twice, but generally seems to regard his breakdown as something quirky that happened to somebody else. When Paulette catches up to the present day, she points out that the wine bottle is empty. As if on cue, Jack leaves for the kitchen. When he's out of earshot, she leans forward, whispers in a conspiratorial tone, "Maybe you think I bullied Edith, but she hates me. Every maudit step is a blow-up with her. It looks like I caused all the trouble, doesn't it?"

Myra has a history with the indomitable Mrs. Grant so it doesn't take much effort to come up with a matching story: the day of their wedding, Edith presented two dresses she'd bought and demanded a choice. Myra had no opinion, but that wasn't an option, so she blinked, pointed at one, and Edith wore the other.

Paulette covers her face with her hands, "Mon Dieu! Oui, oui, ça c'est Edith!"

By this time Jack emerges from the kitchen with another bottle of wine, but he can't find a corkscrew, so she goes looking and then it's Jack's turn to whisper, "She and my mother don't get along."

Myra looks him straight in the eye: "You don't look sick to me."

"I'm not."

"What happened? Was it your father's death? Or your mother moving out here? All your childhood stuff gone, that's rough. Still, she's been after you to go through those boxes for years. And she moved it all the way to Calgary?"

He eats another shrimp and ponders. The far-off voice returns. "It isn't the stuff."

"What, then?"

"I don't know. Does everything have to have a cause?"

When Paulette returns from the kitchen with the open bottle, she brings a plate of chocolate brownies dripping in a hot cherry, chocolate and wine sauce. She is still giggling over the dress saga as she pours a 1994 Châteauneuf-du-Pape, and hands out a fresh round of napkins. This wine is noticeably better than the first bottle, causing Jack to raise his eyebrows at the label. It goes down like liquid velvet, and as the conversation turns to Calgary, what there is to do and see, Myra settles back and drifts, persuaded that her fears were unfounded, she can let the evening unfold. They will sink into the colour-magazine spread, drink fine wines and become pleasantly loose, then maybe go out to a great restaurant, steer clear of politics, tiptoe around the past and make conversation until it is time to roll into bed and live happily ever after. This is, after all, the bourgeois life. Superficial, painless, sometimes a great relief. While the light talk flows, Myra thinks, Jack's right. I'm way too intense. Things just are. Not all causes have effects.

But they do not get to the restaurant. A short blurry while later, she wakes up to find her cheek resting on the cold ceramic bathroom floor, the vase of cattails lying right beside her, little furry fingers rolling in what looks and smells like a mixture of puked up cherry brownies and vino. She lifts her aching head off the tiles in time to see a pair of moccasins enter the room. Jack is wearing the moccasins, and wondering if she's all right.

"What happened?" she moans.

"I think you, ah, threw up."

"Ohhh, no. Alcohol poisoning."

He bends down and hands her a wet washcloth which she uses to wipe a foul-smelling streak off her cheek. "This used to happen to my mother. It's because I didn't eat. Hits you, like thunder. Ow, my head."

As he helps her up, she catches sight of the mirror. A new picture of Jack and Myra, but this one isn't misty, it's all too sharp. A middle-aged couple, one pale and bemused, the other flushed, looking like she's about to meet death by embarrassment.

Jack laughs. "Hey, wash up and come on downstairs. There's a CBC special on the referendum, about to start."

She whispers, "I can't go down there."

"Why not?"

Because her only skirt is smeared with a mixture of red wine and shrimp, because she smells like fish and feels like garbage. Mainly because a long day has suddenly crashed into blind night. Not at all what Myra had in mind when she flew to the rescue of Eternal Jack.

# III

◆

So the three of them are sitting side by side on the Bauhaus sofa, Paulette curled up on her bare feet, Jack in the middle with the channel changer pointed at a 50-inch TV screen, Myra clinging to the other end, feeling tender and humbled in a borrowed bathrobe, fluffy pink and smelling of perfume. Both Radio-Canada and the CBC have preempted regular programming for a special broadcast on the referendum. Jack flips back and forth between the French- and English-language channels.

In the first few weeks, the campaign inspired a great collective yawn. Politicians mouthed the usual arguments and attacked each other with rote vitriol. Without passion in the streets, the status quo has a huge advantage, but now a new poll has just been released showing a dramatic rise in support for the Oui option. If these numbers hold, the Parti Québécois could end up with a mandate for independence. Myra can't believe what she's hearing, on the edge of Jack's sofa, the other side of the planet. All the old familiar media and political faces look out at her from the screen, bigger, more colourful than reality. Their politics may be transparent and diametrically opposed, but both French- and English-language journalists are ecstatic. The CBC is covering the apocalypse; for Radio-Canada, it's the birth of a nation.

"I take it you're voting Oui?" says Jack, flipping back to Peter Mansbridge, who is wearing his fate-of-the-nation frown in Toronto's CBC headquarters. Myra is still floundering for an answer when Paulette jabs him with her elbow.

"People in Calgary can't vote, chéri!" In the silence that follows, she realizes the question was not addressed to her, and leans forward to peer around Jack, as if to catch a better look at the strange beast wearing her bathrobe.

"Tu vas voter Oui?"

All Myra can muster is a combination shrug and affirmative nod of the head.

"Why?"

"Well, a lot of reasons."

"But you're English."

"I definitely am not English." The bite in her voice sends Paulette reeling back into her nest of pillows, but she won't let the question drop.

"Quoi donc? . . . Were you born in Quebec?"

"I was born in Port Hope, Ontario."

"Mais oui, c'est ce que je pensais. Alors?"

There is another pause until Jack says, "She's Irish," as if that settles the matter.

"Not exactly Irish. My great-grandfather was a Callaghan, from County Cork. His family emigrated during the potato famine, in the winter of 1848. Montreal, Griffintown, to be exact. His parents and sisters died of the flu, so he went on alone, got a job as a lumberjack near Madoc, Ontario, when he was 14. My mother's people came north from Boston shortly after the American Revolution. They were political refugees."

"United Empire Loyalists," Jack interjects. "They skipped out on the war and got a free farm in the Gaspé."

"It wasn't a farm," says Myra, "It was a rocky woodlot in New Carlisle. Some of them stayed in Quebec, some didn't. My grandmother always claimed we're cousins of René Lévesque. Guess there is a bit of a resemblance."

As she sketches the family tree, Myra manages to subdue the edge in her voice, except for a trace of irony behind the Lévesque connection, which is not lost on Paulette. That an English-speaking woman from Ontario, an anglophone to boot, could be a blood relation of the great PQ leader, St. René, the man who launched the first referendum and died too young thereafter — well, this information is surreal.

René Lévesque is a god in Quebec. When she was a teen-ager, Paulette used to watch him on TV, a famous face reporting all the big stories. Then one day he stopped following the news and started making it. His footsoldiers included her father, a lifelong union man, card-carrying CSN militant, who was in the crowd at the founding congress of the Parti Québécois in Quebec City, 1968. He came home from the event in a jubilant mood, turned off the TV and ordered his six kids into the beat-up old Chevy. Slowing down as they passed the front of their parish church, he said, take a good look mes petits. Independence was declared the new religion; they never went inside a church again.

Paulette's mother was aghast, but didn't protest. She prayed in silence for his immortal soul, and when she wasn't praying, cheered for her weary man, intoxicated by history. Five boys and a girl grew up on politics, some for independence and some against, but all of them deeply marked by the chain-smoking little man who died before the dream could become reality. Eventually, the endless arguing among her brothers made Paulette want to run away to a clean quiet place where people talk about good wines and weather . She ended up in Calgary, beside Jack.

Now a woman who lives far away but takes up a lot of space in their life is sitting beside Jack. Paulette wants desperately to be calm and polite for however long this surprise visit takes, the point being to show Myra how happy they are. But, a cousin of René Lévesque?

She looks at Jack, who flips back to Radio-Canada, where an excited young blonde is interviewing Premier Jacques Parizeau, Lévesque's successor in the cause. She shakes her head. "Je comprends pas!" As she fetches a bowl of peanuts from the dining room table, portly Parizeau is looking pleased but cautious in his tailormade London suit, explaining his faith in the democratic process. Paulette offers Myra the peanuts, and a question: "Who looks like René Lévesque in your family?"

Declining the peanuts, Myra says, "Uncle Pat. Doesn't he, Jack?"

"Well, he smokes a lot, and he's short. The nose. Guess he could be . . ."

Paulette takes a position in front of the TV. She wonders if anybody would like a Scotch or anything, and Jack says, "You're darn right we would," and leaps up to get it.

"So, Lévesque is your cousin? That's why you're going to vote Yes in the referendum?"

Vote *Yes*? Myra senses a wall of incredulity around these questions. Until now, she has found it hard to find anybody who wanted to argue about this referendum. People who were once fanatics are either cynical or bored. But Paulette's response to a simple question calls forth the old passion. She is looking forward to defending her position, looking forward to winning. She takes her time with the answer, careful to keep a smile in her voice.

"No, I am not voting Oui because my short, smoky uncle might be a blood relative of one of the finest leaders this country has ever produced. That thinking is so . . . well . . . symptomatic of all that's sad about Quebec today, as opposed to 15 years ago when the independence movement meant something noble, exciting. And socialist. Remember Jack, when we moved to Montreal? Cousin René was in charge?"

The wooziness caused by the battle of cherries versus chocolate has passed. Myra is looking straight at Paulette's perfect hair, the manicured fingernails and matching toes, dangling jewellery, intensive makeup, taking full measure of a woman who gets up every morning and prepares to be seen in public, an exotic bird, who may or may not be able to fly. Jack produces a fresh bottle of Scotch and three glasses. Feeling the hot scrutiny, Paulette paces against the pastel landscape of a room that has known her total devotion.

"But I don't understand," she insists. "Why would a Canadian be in favour of the independence of Quebec? You want to get rid of Quebec, don't you? You vote Oui to get Quebec out of Canada?"

Not at all, says Myra, "I live in Quebec. I have lived in Quebec for 15 years. My children live there. Je suis québecoise."

Paulette takes the glass Jack is holding out, and shakes her head. "Alors, ça, je comprends pas."

Then Jack hands a glass to Myra, who stares right past him. "I guess you don't follow politics."

"I follow politics all the time!" Paulette shrieks.

"Even out here? That must be difficult. Do they give Quebec much coverage?"

"We get Radio-Canada on the dish."

"Ah huh," says Myra, from her wingback throne. "Well, maybe that's why you can't imagine me voting Oui. I wouldn't exactly call Radio-Canada objective. With all due respect to some very fine journalists, they rarely report anything that doesn't fit in with the nationalist agenda."

"And the CBC? You think les anglais are more objective?"

"No. That's why I watch both."

"Well, to tell you the truth I don't watch either one on the subject of Quebec, because there is never anything new. Rien qui change. Rien qui bouge. Toujours le même blah blah blah."

"You've got a point there," says Myra. It looks like the argument is about to turn a soft corner.

Paulette is numbed by this conflicting information, and shocked by her own anger. Finally she realizes this debate is not with a mysterious woman in Jack's past, it's with her own past. She's boiling, and the feeling is familiar, the same kind of high emotion she knew growing up in Quebec, when suppers were warfare, five brothers fighting each other with as many points of view, jealousy and rivalry and good old-fashioned meanness underneath everything they said. It made her head hurt. Her head is hurting now and she wants to run up to her room and hide, like she used to do back home, while her brothers raged. But she can't move. There is a stone in her throat. Her face is red.

"I just don't . . ."

"What?" Myra presses on, coolly.

"Bien . . . Believe it."

"You don't believe I'll vote Oui?"

She shakes her head, no, feels the stone getting bigger. Now both women are silent and still. Jack has finished his scotch and runs for another.

"Look," he says, whirling the bottle around, "let's not talk politics, okay? It never goes anywhere. People have their views, that's fine. Hey, guess what? *Casablanca*'s on the movie channel. Starts in two minutes. Now that's a movie for you!"

In the pause, both women allow more liquor to be poured into their glasses while the Warner Brothers logo is followed by a black and white map of Africa and a warbly soundtrack brings viewers up to date on events of the Second World War.

"Turn it off," says Myra. "We've all seen *Casablanca*."

He doesn't move. Paulette takes up the channel changer and kills the sound. Jack continues to watch the picture, as Myra takes a sip of scotch and says, "I for one would be interested to hear why Paulette finds it so impossible to believe that someone who has — by choice — lived the better part of her adult life in Quebec would want to vote for the independence of Quebec. Furthermore, I would like to know why you believe my attachment to sovereignty is somehow a violation of your beliefs. As if I have no right to vote Oui."

"I didn't say that."

"You implied it."

"You're hostile to me. You hear what you want to hear."

"I am not hostile. You're hostile," says Myra, struggling to sound calm. "And if I seem somewhat edgy, then I apologize."

"I accept your apology." Paulette gulps the whisky back and traces a pattern in the carpet with her rose-red polished toe. "But, I still do not believe you will vote Oui."

"Why not?"

"Ladies, ladies," Jack throws his arms up in the air like a referee. "In a democracy, voting is a private act. Let's not wash our laundry in public. Casablancaaaaaa!!!"

But the ladies do not find Jack funny, in fact they do not even acknowledge his desperate attempt to lighten the mood, which is now clearly in the red zone of storm warning.

"You won't vote Oui," Paulette declares, hands on her hips, "because people who own big fat pieces of property do not do things that will send the value of their property down. And if the Oui wins this referendum, everybody knows there is going to be a price to pay, for a few years anyway, and les anglais are not going to want to pay it. I am pretty sure we all agree, there will be a price to pay. Right, Jack? There is always a big price for change, no matter how great and beautiful change is. Don't I know that. Ha! Don't I know. Oui. J'ai payé le prix, moi."

Myra tightens the belt on the fluffy bathrobe, and sits up straight. "I certainly don't own any property."

"You own an enormous condominium on l'Avenue de l'Esplanade, with a great view of Parc Jeanne Mance and Mont Royal."

"Me? Ha! I live in a run-down third-floor apartment on Esplanade, where the rent is artificially cheap because I've been there for 15 years. Any day now the landlord's going to kick me out, sand the floors, move himself in for a month and then double the rent on a new tenant."

"The landlord will not kick you out, that's for sure."

"What are you talking about?"

"Tell her, Jack. Jack! You come back here."

Jack was heading for the kitchen but at the sound of his name wrapped in anger, spins around on one heel and shuffles back into the occupied territory of his living room. He wishes he hadn't gotten over his nervous breakdown just yet, but cannot think of a plausible way to dive into a relapse on such short notice. Instead he says, "What?"

"Tell Myra. Every cent you got your hands on for the last ten years went into paying off that maudit mortgage, and that's why we couldn't have kids, until it was too late, and I had to have that operation, and now my maudit ovaries are fried. She — " Paulette points — "is a goddamn rich anglo Péquiste." On the final insult, she hurls her glass at an oversized print of sunflowers, and starts to cry.

Myra looks at Jack, who crawls on all fours toward the heap of broken glass. She calls him by name, with a questioning tone. He shakes his head and moans. Tears streaming down her face, shoulders shaking, Paulette pours herself another scotch in Jack's glass. For an instant, Myra is strongly tempted to go over and put her arms around the shipboard wife: a woman without a child, and all because of some idiotic real estate scheme of Jack's? He always had a handful of excuses for doing exactly what he wanted to do. Then she notices Paulette's earrings, and thinks how great she looks in lavender, and remembers that crazy awful summer of 1980, a certain Saturday morning, when Jack came over to take the kids out and announced he was "seeing someone." He was wearing a crisp white sports shirt — and a tan. He looked great. Paulette still looks good, even in tears. So, instead of following tender instinct, she surprises herself with an explosion of frozen truth.

"Listen, don't you try to make me feel guilty. I was living in that drafty hovel in 1980 when you chose to amuse yourself by lying on a beach blanket with a married man. I was trying to make it as a freelance journalist and cover history and take care of two dripping kids. So if you've wasted your fertile years on home decoration and ironing shirts and staying tanned, don't blame me. Don't even blame Jack. You — you . . . had choices."

More relieved than surprised, Paulette answers calmly, "Sacrament! Now I see why he couldn't stand to live with you." Then without ceremony, warning or remorse, she opens her mouth and out comes one long gush of pulverized shrimp, falling on her bare feet and the cream rug and into a wicker basket full of rose petals sitting on the coffee table. Then she collapses on the sofa and moans.

Jack rolls over on his back and murmurs, "Oh fuck." On the TV screen, the overhead fans are whirling in Rick's Café Americain and the grim-faced man in the white dinner jacket is getting his heart broken one more time, but nobody cares to watch. The homeowners have both passed out.

In the silence of a room destroyed, Myra is visited by lucidity. She goes into the kitchen to get a wet cloth, empties the shrimp-soaked rose petals into the garburator and looks around for the disinfectant. What she finds is a state-of-the-art expanse of white cupboards and stainless steel, ceramic floors and counters, all of it so clean. On the fridge door there are snapshots of Mitch and Sally in the Rocky Mountains, canoeing, swimming, eating barbecued hamburgers. Dozens of pictures, all ages, her children growing up in their secret summer life. Her head aches, thoughts fly — there is so much I don't know. Doors are opened and out comes bile. So Jack dandy secretly bought the apartment on Esplanade? What does that mean? Every month she pays the rent, a cheque to a business bank account, so what? Jack pays his share for Mitch and Sal. That was the deal, once struck, never discussed. The kids said Paulette was an airhead with bad taste and dumb ideas. She is not. The kids told their mom what she wanted to hear.

There are still no signs of life on the living room floor as she tiptoes past the wreckage to climb the broad-loomed staircase. She turns on the water in the guest bathroom's whirlpool tub, and looks at herself in the mirror. The lights are very bright, they drain the colour from her sallow skin. Celtic red pigment doesn't go well with candy pastels. She lets the bathrobe drop and catches herself naked in the full length mirror. Years of hunching over a computer keyboard have given her spine a habitual slump. She inhales, stands straight, examines wrinkles and bulges. Compared to the girl beside Jack in the misty old photo, she looks worn down, as pale as newsprint. Forty-two years old. Exactly the way 42 used to look when she was young and critical and determined never to get old and boring.

The tub fills up. Thinking she might shave her legs, she opens the cabinet drawer in search of a razor, but finds only a pair of scissors. She gathers a handful of hair and examines the split ends, decides to snip off a quarter of an inch. Instead, she cuts high, in mid-ear, and a ten-inch shaft of limp brown weight falls to the floor. The short hair springs out, as if released. It looks ridiculous, but there's no going back, she continues to chop until the line is more or less even and there is a pile of hair at her feet.

Then she steps into the bath. Clear water swallows her tired bones, and she keeps on sinking until her body is entirely submerged, legs and arms floating free. The day's events float too, up past the emerald walls, past the punishing mirror, the blah blah blah of politics and salty taste of tears. Jack, oh dear, Jack. She stays like that, drifting in the dark until the water cools, wishing she had said less, or more.

# IV

◆

The next sound Myra hears is the roar of a lawn mower. It's Saturday morning, sunlight glows through the curtains and a waft of freshly brewed Java beckons from the kitchen. Her skirt is still a little damp, but wearable. Careful to avoid the mirror, she dresses and hurries downstairs to find Jack sitting on a stool by the patio window, smoking one of the forbidden cigars. There are two mugs in the sink and a clean one waiting on a paper towel near the coffee pot. She pours a cup, and for the longest time not a word passes between them, until it's pretty clear the first person who speaks had better say something innocuous, so she says, "Paulette's already up?"

"Yeah, she's gone to choir practice."

"I didn't know she was religious."

"She isn't," Jack snaps. "It's Gregorian chants."

"Ah."

The neighbour is still after his long grass, but mercifully moves around to the streetside so the roar drops to a moan. Jack is wearing his bathrobe and slippers. In the morning light, she notices the skin underneath his chin is slack from rapid weight loss, and the lines in his face are deep. She wants to ask a dozen questions about the breakdown, what medication he's on, what the doctors said and how he feels right now, but he's rubbing his chin with his thumb as if he might be getting ready to say something, so she holds back. Sliding onto a stool by the island counter, she glances down at the front page of the Saturday Globe and Mail, skims the lead story about the new poll, tries to resist peeking under the fold to finish it. She can feel Jack's stare. Reading newspapers at breakfast was something he could never abide. They weren't alone long enough, parenthood overlapped courtship, no time to negotiate a deal on bad habits. She pushes the newspaper out of temptation's way, determined to make conversation. "So, you must have done quite a bit of work on the house?"

"Yeah, a lot," he says in a voice suggesting the subject is closed. She wonders how he survived the noise and inconvenience. There is much about this Calgary life that doesn't seem like Jack. Myra is tempted to ignore the uneasy silence between them and ask whether it just might be the gap that's driving him crazy, but she resists. The high drama of last night has left them both tender. She reaches for a safe subject.

"I guess Sally told you she's thinking about going into art history at McGill?"

At the mention of his daughter's name Jack comes alive. With a familiar mixture of fondness and chagrin, he shakes his head, gets a second coffee and moves to the stool across from her. "McGill?" he winces. "Why academe if she wants to paint? God, I already made that mistake. But then I had no talent, she does."

An ancient theme, Jack's artistic ambitions. That's how they met, at a loft party in the Byward Market, where he and three other painters were showing off their latest creations. At the time, he was into chicken wire and scrap lumber and plaster, transformed into hair-raising installations. Myra had never met an artist before, except a few Sunday barn painters whose precious landscapes adorned the donut shops of Port Hope, and they were all middle-aged women. She didn't know what to think about the art, but the artist made a huge impression. She was disappointed when he gave it up for law school, and didn't resist saying so back then, can't resist now. "I wouldn't say you had no talent, and art history was hardly a mistake."

"I'm a good enough art critic to know I've got no talent. Anyway, it takes something else, which Sally has, in abundance. Okay, this is probably none of my business, but I wonder if she belongs in a classroom, looking at bad slides of Old Masters and pouring over all the gobbledegook that passes for art criticism? Maybe she could come out here for a while. Calgary's got art, and an art college, and there's a spare room upstairs. I've offered. Think she'll consider it?"

The hunger in his eyes is painful, but the answer is obvious. "Sal's pretty loyal to Montreal. Don't take it personally, she doesn't want to live with me either."

Finally, they are walking into familiar territory where conversation never stumbles, arguments and misunderstanding are carefully avoided, ego and edge held firmly in check. Any discussion of Mitch and Sally is a delicate ritual. Jack's views on child-rearing are vigorous and thoughtful, but every statement comes with a subtext: I left, you are raising them, I have no right. Myra's answers always imply variations on the same: you are their father, you belong, you are needed. Still, the final say is hers. They both know this land of parenthood is not a democracy, it is a benevolent monarchy where he is welcome as an intimate advisor, on bended knee. An outsider will never see the bended knee, or the regal pose, only a mysterious web of love and blood, but the bended knee is there, stiff at the joints and weary from the wait. And the regal pose is strained. All this power has frozen Myra in a cold role of goodness. Jack would like the right to intervene without apology, Myra would like Jack to speak from the heart about himself, but they've lost the way to that kind of conversation.

He is about to start on Mitch when Paulette's car pulls into the driveway. He feeds his dry cigar butt to the garburator and starts fanning smoky air with the newspaper.

Myra rinses out their cups in the sink and says, "Look, Jack, I'm totally relieved to see you're getting better, and actually you don't look sick at all, but I've got a huge deadline facing me, so if you don't mind I'll just grab a cab and be off."

"What?" He follows her into the living room. "Don't you want to see anything of Calgary? You might pick up a story or two. I haven't read much on the West Edmonton mall lately. We could drive up."

"I've never been strong on the subject of shopping," she says, picking up her backpack at the bottom of the stairs.

Paulette is coming up the sidewalk with an armload of groceries as Myra rushes out the door. "Bye, thanks so much, I've got to go," she says, striding across the lawn. Stepping over a clump of hydrangeas, she crushes a mound of late-season petunias. She thought the flower bed was beside the sidewalk, but instead, a hedge blocks her exit so she leaps over it, and trips. The clipped branches tear into her bare legs.

Jack remains standing in the doorway as Paulette hurries down the driveway, protesting she's just about to make lunch, but Myra has already stumbled to her feet, picked up her open purse and retrieved a toothbrush from the bushes. The neighbour is quietly gathering up his leaves. He leans on his rake handle and gapes as she tugs at her jean skirt, and she runs like a burglar down the street. Her knee is bleeding, but she skips ahead until the house is out of sight, then slows to a walk. She has no idea how to find the airport, or when the massive suburban compound might give way to a corner store with a phone booth. It seems fairly certain nobody in a station wagon or a land rover will give a bleeding woman a lift.

Not true. A few blocks into her escape, a car pulls up and slows to the speed of her stride. It's Paulette. She has the window rolled down, and is hiding behind sunglasses. "I didn't know your flight left so early," she says. "I could have skipped the choir."

"Oh, that's all right. I've got a deadline."

"Well, get in and I'll drive you to the airport."

There is nothing Myra wants less than to get into a black Japanese hatchback with the memory of last night, but apart from not wanting, there is no logical reason to resist a sensible offer like a drive to the airport. So, being slightly more practical than proud, she gets in.

Paulette power locks the doors, takes off her sunglasses, and as they speed off, asks the obvious: "What did you do to your hair?"

"I only intended to snip off a few split ends. I'll have to get it cut properly." She pulls at the jagged ends around her ears and feels quite naked. Paulette responds by pointing out landmarks along the route, filling her in on how much Calgary has changed over the past decade, how you can now get a cappuccino on every corner, and there's a film club and great theatre and a lot more going on than beer and mountains. For a few miles, they act out the ritual of an ex-Montrealer talking to one who stayed, the message being that it's not as bad out here as you might expect. Then, out of nowhere, Paulette asks Myra how that fellow with the ranch-style steakhouse is doing in Old Montreal.

"Who?"

"They get The Gazette at the public library here. I read an article you wrote about the guy from Calgary who opened an Alberta-style steakhouse. 'Reversing the Flow,' wasn't that the headline?"

"Oh. I'd forgotten. He's still in business, I guess."

They ride up the airport ramp in silence, and as Paulette stops the car, she puts her sunglasses back on, which is an odd gesture since the sun is definitely not a problem now. Myra wonders if the dampness from her skirt has soaked through to the seat. All that hair back in the guest room garbage. And the rug. She hopes somebody remembered to soak those islands of puke in salt. Otherwise, red wine will not wash out. It's too late now. Either they have or they have not been salted. The rug's fate is sealed, and there is no way she can get out of this car without saying, "I'm really sorry about, you know, last night."

Bravely, Paulette takes off the sunglasses, and smiles. "It was fun."

For a split second, Myra is tempted to thank her for looking after poor Jack, but the impulse passes. She gets out of the car and says the things a guest says at the airport and then Paulette speeds off, tooting the horn twice as she disappears down the ramp.

# V

—

The flight back is nearly empty. When the pilot's friendly voice announces they are about to dip over Lake Ontario, Myra leans into the window to catch a glimpse of the bird's-egg-blue water, innocent, like a summer sky.

Port Hope is a great place to come from. That was the quote under her picture in St. Mary's high school yearbook. A town that radiates friendliness, according to the welcome sign back then, when the main employer was Eldorado Nuclear, a uranium refinery. While she was away at university, her mother died of cancer, it came on quickly and got worse fast. One of these days she will look into the connection, Eldorado, radiation, cancer. And other connections, cattails, taillights, moonlight on the silver lake. That Port Hope is long gone now. When her brother graduated and settled in the States, their father sold the house and remarried.

Perched on the northern edge of the lake, the Port set its restless ones on a quest for the centre. Myra fixed on Ottawa, the capital, supposed mecca for people who make things happen. That's where she started drinking black coffee, reading Marx, going to films and concerts with Jack, where finally, life began, night-long discussions, issues, campaigns, speakers, bylines, endless debate over what must be reformed and how. Back then she lived for politics. She did and still does believe in social change and causes.

Passion, conception and marriage — 1976 had it all, but the exclamation marks in Myra's diary fall on November 15, election of René Lévesque as premier of Quebec, with enough Parti Québécois members in the National Assembly to guarantee the question of independence would soon be raised in a referendum. Jack and Myra moved into a basement apartment on O'Connor Street, a few blocks from the Parliament buildings. Sally was born; a year later, Mitch. To his parents' delight, Jack abandoned a masters in art history for law school. Meanwhile, Myra took a double major in journalism and politics — specialty, Quebec, and waged her campaign for the move. More than news, more than politics, in 1980 Quebec was at the centre of history and she could not, would not, be anywhere else. The soul of a country, heart of a nation, yearning, deserving, marching toward independence — everything Port Hope seemed to lack, she felt sure she would find in Quebec. First the news, then the myth, then at last, the real thing.

They arrived amid the deepest snows of February in time to be enumerated for the referendum so Myra could vote Oui, absolutely yes of course, the aspirations of this obviously distinct nation for independence from sprawling, ill-defined Canada being noble and just. He didn't like to talk about it, but Jack voted Non, meaning No, and started to hate politics.

If the outside world offered the swirl of destiny, their home life was a perpetually clogged sink. While Myra set up shop as a freelance journalist, Jack grumbled about articling in a dusty anglo law firm, despised his rinky-dink assignments and prowled around the damp debris of toddlers like a caged bear. It's law school, said Myra, you never should have given up on art. She had no time for his complaints. In Jack's version of that crowded summer, she had no time for him. Too much news to gather, too many phone calls.

When he'd gone, Myra spread her papers out on the double bed, worked until three a.m., met the first deadline and moved on to the next. She sold a feature to The New York Times, another to a small magazine, landed a regular column, tried radio and a little TV, chased stories that mattered and some that just paid the bills, made contacts and lifelong friends, got involved in dramas and caught up in the scene, and when the kids were away with Jack, had lovers and kept odd hours, grew her hair long, learned to speak anglo-French with a Québécois accent and woke up most mornings feeling great to be alive in Montreal. Things just kept happening. Fifteen years, gone by in a blur.

Now the second referendum approaches. On October 30, some five million Quebecers will make their mark beside a convoluted question, each mark meaning something different from the next. Myra leans back, closes her eyes, thoughts flashing backward and ahead in time. In 1980 she knew unquestionably how to vote, who she was and what she wanted. During last night's tango with Paulette, she knew exactly what to say. The old arguments still hold up in debate, but the passion felt misplaced.

Alone, above the lake, she is not so sure about the cause. But she is homesick for the place.

Montreal is Myra's city; the Plateau is her turf. A flat checkerboard of streets stretching east of the Mountain, therefore called the Plateau Mont-Royal, it's less a neighbourhood than a village unto itself. Most blocks are three storeys high with solid greystone facades, winding iron staircases to the second floor, and straight wooden steps inside to the third. The streets are a colourful mix of turrets, gables, slate roofs and ornate moldings, plant-lined balconies, window boxes, tiny flower gardens in front of row houses and apartments.

Bathrooms count as half a room. The quintessential six-and-a-half has a rectangular layout, rooms strung along a central hall that leads straight through from the front door to a kitchen at the back, past a double-arched living room, (sometimes windowless) bath, and bedrooms. The ground floor apartment is dark and easily robbed, the second is cheaper to heat, the third has the best view and skylights, but it's a long way up.

The Plateau, circa 1995, is a grab bag of flush yuppies, crooks and the able-bodied poor. Drug dens and daycares, students on skateboards, movie stars with their Jags, deal-makers, missionaries, madmen, politicians, perverts, the homeless, the hopeless, the hip — ten thousand souls, teetering on the edge. A few are millionaires, many are on welfare, most have come from somewhere else. Incomes zigzag street by street. There's a soup kitchen on Duluth, valet parking at the swanky bistros, low-ceilinged boxes on Henri-Julien parallel elegance on Laval.

The hub of the Plateau is The Main. St. Lawrence Boulevard, also known as le boulevard St-Laurent, depending upon where you're from or when you arrived. Appellation is a serious issue these days. Many streets have two names, the modern militant French version, and an older anglo moniker. For people who've grown used to the latter the frenchification of a place-name can sound pretentious, objectionable. But newcomers tend to embrace the official French, swallow it whole and spit it back out as an English word. *Sanlauron*, St. Lawrence, St-Laurent a.k.a. The Main. Purists claim The Main is only a few blocks around Ste-Catherine, but popular usage has blurred the distinction. Montreal is a city of impure language, fluid and changeable, infinitely supple, maddeningly inconsistent. Like the life it struggles to express.

St. Lawrence/St-Laurent divides and unites. A wide, one-way gutter, it starts in Old Montreal near the river of the same name, and climbs uphill to Autoroute 40, fastest way out of town. Traditionally, English-speakers settled the west side and the French took the east, but now the two spill over, and are outnumbered by newcomers. Gaudy, noisy, seedy, slick, schizophrenic, The Main's face is any colour, the Main's voice a babble of English, French, a warped mixture of the two, and a dozen other languages spoken openly, loudly, persistently. If you hear shouts over the oranges in Quatre Frères, it could be a raving lunatic, there are many on the loose, or an executive with a cell phone, there are many on the loose.

A century ago, the Plateau was a series of tiny villages and fields, a healthy gallop from the cobblestone streets of Old Montreal. Then French-speaking middle-class professionals transformed the villages into a solid residential mass of greystones with basement suites for the servants, and smaller brick duplexes for working people with steady incomes. But the next generation wanted free-standing houses with lawns and malls. As they were leaving, waves of refugees, adventurers, made their way north from the dockyards, transforming the Plateau with their industry and tastes. From Europe, Asia, the Middle East, they opened noodle shops, black bread bakeries, pungent sausage havens, barbecues, cafés, pasta restaurants; sweatshops, warehouses, small factories — the commerce of home. In time, the newcomers made money and most moved on too, though they still come back to eat; food is the Plateau's great unifying attraction, savory, diverse, authentic.

These immigrant stories are testimonies of a world on the move. The minutiae of politics, fallout from events elsewhere. But there is another kind of migrant, numerous, less visible. Self-styled refugees. Internal exiles. WASPs on the lam. No great headlines behind their move, from St. John's to Vancouver, they fled — and still do — the drudgery of careers, the tedium of jobs, the end of U.I., the waste of school, the flatness of home. Anti-American, too poor for Europe, they abandon ROC, the rest of Canada, for a foreign language in a familiar country, the mystery of Quebec. They come here for cheap rent, abundant beer, three a.m. closing time, passion, politics, art, the scene. They come here to breathe. The frenchification that drove so many old anglos out of Quebec is the very reason these almost-ex-pats dig in. They don't want the feeling of home. They are open-minded and excitable.

Desperate, optimistic or both. They are the Divided Empire Loyalists of fin de siècle Montreal.

Welcome or not, they are thrilled to be here, in a city state with the mythical force of a country. A maddening town that dazzles and blinds. A place to be discovered. A time, a beginning. Imagination, soul, heart. The word itself is rock hard sleek magic beautiful blue. Montreal.

# VI

◆

Myra is asleep when the airport bus turns into the Berri Street terminal. At the jolt of brakes and rush of fellow passengers she wakes up, knows where she is all right, but for a moment, the trip behind is blank. A farewell party at This Magazine for the associate publisher who's moving on, coffee with The Globe features' editor, a hand-shaking stroll through the corridors of the CBC — pieces fall into place chronologically until she arrives back at the moment of buying an airline ticket to Calgary. Three days in Toronto to hunt down next month's work, then $1,500 on an impulsive jaunt out West. Never before has she done anything quite that rash. The forthcoming VISA bill looms large, like a hangover. That too. Her mouth is still sour from the night before, although it seems like months ago.

There's a line-up of cabs outside the bus terminal. She's tired and hungry but the thought of spending even more money inspires her to hoof it up the hill. St-Denis Street is just waking up for Saturday night. St-Laurent is crowded, as always. She cuts across at Pine and heads straight for Esplanade. There's a football game going on in Jeanne Mance Park, and lots of slim, middle-aged singles walking high-strung dogs. At the bottom of the staircase, somebody's pet has ripped open a garbage bag, no doubt put out on the wrong day by Mitch. The contents are strung all over the tiny yard.

She calls out his name as she opens the door. No answer. Her newspapers are stacked up in the entrance, beside old shoes and a litter of junk mail. There are noises coming from the kitchen, music blaring from the stereo in his room which she turns down a notch on her way to the bathroom, bringing Mitch shuffling to the door. He is tall and skinny, dressed in a torn T-shirt and jeans with the knee ripped out on purpose, a head of curly hair and a long slim nose, like Jack. He wipes his wet hands on his thighs and says, "Thought you weren't coming home till tomorrow night?"

"Did you talk to Sally?"

"No. She might have called. You've got messages. What happened to your hair?"

"I, ah, left it in Calgary."

"Calgary?"

Before she can explain, Myra hears voices in the kitchen, notices a spicy aroma wafting from the back of the house. "What's that smell?"

"Chili," Mitch replies. The take-out pizza addict might as well have said Argentina. Her face is blank so he explains, "We're making chili. Want some?"

Just then there's a milk-curdling squeal and a small boy slides around the corner, falling flat at her feet.

"Mom, this is James. He's staying over with Mandy. James, this is my mom."

James says nothing until his mother walks into the room and he can hide behind her legs and squeeze out a pleased-to-meet-you. Then Mitch introduces Mandy, a small girl peeking out from a waterfall of long blonde tresses. She mumbles hi and extends a tiny hand. Myra manages a how-do-you-do and in the pause that follows, Mitch says the chili is dynamite, which reminds Mandy that the pot needs a stir, so she and James exit to the kitchen.

When they are out of earshot, Mitch says, "I've told you about Mandy. She's the one who lent me her geography notes."

"When was that?"

"Last year."

Then Myra notices Sally's old room has been occupied, there's a teddy bear sprawled belly up on the floor. The double bed has been lightly slept in by one small person, so she says, "Guess I didn't realize you and Mandy were, well, you know, going out."

"Yeah," says Mitch, head bobbing up and down.

She means she didn't realize her gangly, hitherto largely dateless son was not so much going out but actually staying in with a woman who has a child and cooks. She holds herself back from taking a peek at the single bed in Mitch's room. She thinks of the poster she bought at the airport, a huge map of the world at night, murky seas and continents with the major cities marked by hundreds of neon dots, wonders if the poster should be handed down to James, but before the strangeness of this new situation can settle or overflow, Mandy tells Mitch supper is ready, and they all go into the kitchen where the table has been set for four.

To go with a huge bowl of chili, there's black Russian bread from the St. Lawrence bakery, and salad. James climbs onto a stack of books on his chair, Mandy sits in Sally's old place and to Myra it all starts to feel like she has walked into a page from *Goldilocks and the Three Bears*.

"This is a great flat you've got, Mrs. Grant," Mandy mumbles, and tucks her hair behind her ears to fill their bowls. Myra can't quite place the accent, so she asks, where are you from and the answer is Verdun. "But my mother was English, if that's what you mean. I've still got a bit of an accent."

"Your mother passed away?" Myra doesn't know why she asked such a thing, except maybe for the slight drop in Mandy's voice.

"No. She just left. I mean, ages ago. Split. We're not in touch."

Mitch is deeply into his chili, mopping it up with bread when James begins to sing "Four-And-Twenty-Blackbirds" and Mandy says shh, retreating even further behind her hair. She blushes as easily as her boyfriend, who is suddenly moved to address the situation head-on: "We were going to go out last night, but Mandy couldn't get a sitter so we decided to rent a video and come here. It was raining like hell so they stayed over."

Myra replies, "Sure. And it's okay by me if anybody wants to sing at the table." James looks over at his mother and laughs.

Mitch concentrates on normalcy, "Did you get rain in Toronto?"

"Ah, no. Maybe. Actually, I was in Calgary, briefly. Jack's been kind of sick."

"So I heard." Then he turns to Mandy, "Jack's my dad. He lives out in Calgary."

James interjects, "I don't got a dad," and Mandy corrects him.

"It's 'I don't have,' and yes you do. Everybody has a dad, James. I told you all about that. Remember?"

"Yeah, but I don't have one around the house. He's gone. I think he's in Hollywood." At the mention of such a fate, James doubles up with laughter. He has a great big confident laugh, and it's contagious. They finish the meal talking about all the people James knows in Hollywood, people who live in sitcoms and distinctly adult dramas. Cartoons suck, says James. As Mandy hauls him into the bathroom for a scrubdown, he makes a peace sign at Myra and announces, "We're staying here two nights."

Mitch gathers up the empty bowls and sets about to wash them. "They've got this really small basement apartment. I just thought . . ." and as his sentence trails off, she assures him the guests are perfectly welcome. In fact, this situation is so downright novel she practically bends over backward and touches the floor behind with her short hair, all to let Mitch the blushing host know she is not against novelty. Nobody is fooled, but Mitch is tremendously relieved. Now he doesn't have to announce the news, the news is sliding down the hall in pajamas, with a teddy bear under his arm. If they can make it through breakfast without too many gaps in the conversation, Mitchell Grant will have come of age, officially, and in the privacy of his own home.

Nevertheless, Myra gives him the poster of a twinkling flat earth, and is relieved to see he's genuinely pleased. He moves his Neil Young concert souvenir over to a new spot by the computer, and the night sky goes up over his bed. She watches him make the change, sees that, yes, two people slept there last night. He borrowed a pillow from her room, the feather one with a flowered cover. And tonight, two people will sleep under the world after dark. It's an imaginary image, as Mitch is quick to point out. The entire earth is never dark at once, or entirely lit up to party. But the twinkling thought is beautiful.

When the three bears disappear, Myra retreats to her den, where lights are flashing. There's a message from Sally to her brother on the answering machine; then a garbled burst of French about the toaster, repaired and waiting at the corner hardware store; and four calls from Joey Rosenbaum, each slightly more urgent than the last.

Joey is the founder and artistic director of an alternative theatre company called Off the Main, and when he calls during rehearsals of a new production, it almost always leads to a loan of furniture for the set, or at least a meeting at La Cabane, where Myra plays sounding board to all his frustrations with the labour of pointing ordinary underpaid humans at the divine challenge of the stage.

At least once during rehearsals, Joey will declare he is quitting theatre forever. The only question is timing. Should he do it immediately, in mid-production, when his departure will most hurt the selfish, uncooperative, flamboyantly demanding infantile actors and designers and stage crew who are out to ruin him? Or should he wait until after opening night, when the fickle press and absent audience find the theatre doors bolted shut on a Saturday night, his philosophical suicide note scrawled in blood: you have killed art? Or, should he let the show close and skip out on the deficit, leaving callous arts bureaucrats and usurious creditors holding the bag? Each choice has merit, but Myra, as president of the board of directors, will suggest he wait until, until, until the mood of the moment blows over. If he can survive these three crisis points of theatrical production, close the show as planned and sleep for a month, Off the Main will be safe. Because a month or so later, his inspiration will suggest a new project, then it will be time to write the grants and after that the momentum will carry him along until it is time to start rehearsals, and then it will be too late to quit.

Joey Rosenbaum is an exhausting blend of Sagittarian idealism and Jewish pessimism. As long as he allies himself with someone strong who believes in causes, he could go on like this forever. It's Myra's role, as president of the board, to keep Joey the mule eating straw, and wanting more. In Myra's eyes, Off the Main is one of the enduring reasons for living on or about The Main. It is a cause, and even in his deepest moments of doubt, which can be shrill and mean-spirited and monumentally petty, Joey Rosenbaum is the founder and leader of the cause. He is also Myra's best friend, a thoughtful, well-read, endlessly discursive human being who always has time for La Cabane.

On this particular night, he is waiting for Myra at the Copacabana. The name is somebody's idea of a joke, since apart from palm trees on the sign outside, the

Copa in no way resembles a chi-chi American night club. It's a beer bar pure and simple, with the recently added attraction of Nantha, a superb Malay cook who quit Else's on Roy Street East to set up his kitchen at the Copa. His clientele has followed. Nantha shops at the Jean Talon market and makes fresh curries every evening. He wears a kerchief and a big white apron, does his cooking in a tiny kitchen overlooking the pool table, takes customers' orders himself. Tonight, he has decided Joey is coming down with something and therefore adds a little extra punch to his shrimp. By the time Myra turns up, Joey has nearly finished a pitcher of beer, pours the dregs into her empty glass and waves at the waitress for a refill.

"This is exactly what I need," he says, wiping his brow with his sleeve. "I'm sweating inside and out."

Myra slides into her role. "That's pretty normal for right now, isn't it? How are rehearsals going?"

"The usual."

He brushes his brow again, and when the waitress comes back, whispers a request for cigarettes. She reminds him he has asthma and isn't supposed to smoke, so they agree on one. It strikes Myra as odd that Joey claimed a meeting was urgent, but midway through his glass of beer, hasn't said anything urgent yet. This must be seriously urgent.

"Why are you sweating inside and out?"

"You didn't hear?"

"I've been out of town."

"Where?"

"Toronto, Calgary."

"Calgary, what's it like out there?"

"Oh mountains, sky, money." Enough said about life elsewhere, Joey wants to know it she saw anything in the Toronto papers about Off the Main. Myra wonders what, why.

"We got a letter from Sam Beckett, ordering us to cease and desist with the bilingual Godot."

"Samuel Beckett? He's dead."

"Yes, I am aware of that. His estate. Publishers, whatever."

"You received a letter? Let's see."

"Obviously, it's under lock and key."

"Well what does it say?"

He takes his time, blows smoke up into the air like a man with a valuable secret. "It says, do not do *Waiting for Godot* in English and French, more or less. One language or the other, not both."

"Or else what?"

"Or else five underemployed IRA thugs will break my legs. What? We'll be sued. Well, that's the implication."

Damage control is the board president's specialty, but the possibility of a lawsuit is not something Myra has had to deal with before.

"Joey, disaster! We've already photocopied the flyers. All that rehearsal time, contracts with the actors. I thought you'd signed for the rights long ago. Didn't you tell them you were doing a bilingual version?"

"Of course not."

"Why not?"

"Because it's a well-known fact that Beckett's estate keeps close tabs on all productions. You cannot tamper with the stage directions one iota. A tree, a rock and a pair of boots. They're very strict."

"You knew this, and you went ahead with the bilingual version?"

He smiles. His heavily bearded face wears a weighty layer of rabbinical resignation, as if the most awful prize has come his way. But despite the seriousness of a pending lawsuit, Joey's attitude to this particular crisis includes an unmistakable whiff of glee. This time, he isn't slumped over a beer and obsessing over a particular actor, his eyes are on the ceiling, as though disaster has elevated the mood. Myra starts to draw up a list of high-profile lawyers she has met in the course of gathering news, when a question occurs. "How did Beckett's people find out about the bilingual Godot?"

Despite the warm night and scorching shrimp, Joey is wearing a well-worn green sweater over his T-shirt, and his plumpish shoulders shake with mirth as he leans ahead to confess, in a low voice, "Keep this to yourself, okay? . . . I sent them an unsigned letter."

"What?"

"We need the publicity. It's already been in The Gazette. Entertainment section front, they put it in a box." He pulls a scrap of newsprint out of his pocket and, glancing again at the headline with great satisfaction, sets it down in front of Myra, like it was a winning lottery ticket. Sure enough, the brief news item quotes Joe Rosenbaum as saying, the show must go on.

"You actually used that line?"

He shrugs, "For once it felt appropriate."

Off the Main's mandate is to produce provocative, out-of-the-mainstream work in various locations around the Plateau, featuring English and French actors, mixing the two styles of work. Joey believes theatre has to grab an audience by the balls and shake. If people are sensitive about this English–French thing, then it's the artist's role to flush out all sensitivity and expose the conflict onstage. He's done shows about pretty well every major historical crisis, from the hanging of Louis Riel, to the October Crisis, and a wildly funny satirical piece about Céline Dion's seduction by Mickey Mouse. Politically avant-garde, financially one step ahead of bankruptcy, the company has remained true to its mandate for a decade. But this season, Joey decided to forego the bloody ordeal of collective creation and put on a classic. To Myra, his choice of *Waiting for Godot* seemed to be entirely personal, a cry of despair and an encounter with philosophy, which she agreed might be a sensible choice after all those years of waving red flags at bulls.

The problem is that none of Joey's controversial plays have ever generated any controversy. He gets the usual five hundred fans out to see them, and a range of reviews from mean to patronizing. But after ten years, he has yet to feel the thrill of turning a would-be ticket-buyer away from a full house. Far from it, he's stuck at an audience of five hundred, and it's that particular aspect of failure that grates. He would like a hit, but if not a hit, at least a scandal. After a decade, he is prepared to accept that Off the Main cannot change the world. So, who does? But pissing off a small corner of the world, is that asking too much?

Now he has waved his red flag at the lawyers who take care of a world-famous Nobel Prize–winning author's legacy, and they've paid him the compliment of a warning. Naturally, The Gazette takes notice. Finally, Joey Rosenbaum matters, and he is going to ride this one as far as it goes. Of all the many possible ways of quitting theatre, going out quietly is not one he can seriously consider.

Myra leans forward to glare at his watery blue eyes.

"Are you out of your mind?! What do you hope to achieve by this, this . . . stunt?"

"Stunt! It's not a stunt. It is my duty as an artist to challenge the status quo. If I have to fight Sam Beckett's people, well I'll just have to fight, and put up with headlines and sell a shitload of tickets, which is what happens when major media come rushing at a story. Okay, there is an element of stuntism involved, but I look at it this way: if Montreal wasn't such a pathetic backwater, the very idea of my bilingual Godot would already have attracted national headlines, and somebody at Beckett Inc. would have noticed and I would have got that letter without having to tip them off. All right, I nudged. But the outcome will be the same as if we lived in a regular, healthy intellectual climate. Which alas, we do not."

"And what kind of an outcome do you hope for?"

"International headlines."

"So, you're going ahead with the show?"

"Just watch me."

"Joey, that's what Pierre Trudeau said when they asked him how far he'd go with the War Measures Act against the FLQ. I didn't think you were a Trudeau fan."

"I don't agree with most of his ideas, but maybe any idea needs a heavy-handed dictator. Either that, or a damn brilliant publicity stunt, which we have now got, thank you Sam."

Myra thinks she may be starting to get the picture, although so far it looks more like a Doonesbury cartoon than a serious portrait of artistic success. "So you called me in to start fundraising for the huge deficit you are surely going to rack up when the Beckett estate shuts down the show?"

"There will be no deficit."

"Ho! You're really turning into a political quote book. I suppose this show can no more have a deficit than a man can have a baby? Olympics, Mayor Jean Drapeau? Remember that cartoon of him with a big belly?"

"I did not call this board meeting to talk about money."

"Now it's a board meeting?"

"Yes, and a historic one. Off the Main must rage against the dying of the light. Myra, look at this city, it stinks of decay. We're slugs, clinging to the bottom of society's urinal. The mainstream is so far away there isn't one Plateau rat in a hundred even remembers the smell of water. How could I have been so fucking stupid as to found an alternative theatre company? Alternative to what? This city is a backwater."

"For the English, which is why you wanted to work with French — "

"For everybody! Don't get me started."

"Okay, okay. What do you want me to do?"

Joey is hunched over the table, they are elbow to elbow, eye to eye, only an empty pitcher of beer between them. But before he answers, he realizes it is almost seven p.m., the end of happy hour at La Cabane. They pay the bill and head out into the street.

Saturday night, the bars on St-Laurent are packed, each with a precise clientele matching the decor. Lately the blocks between Sherbrooke and Pine have moved up about ten notches on the trend scale: a couple of high-priced clothing stores, expense account restaurants and a handful of cruising bars, the latter filled with sales clerks and secretaries from the suburbs who spend their meager salaries to dress like hirelings in a fashion shoot. But between Pine and Mont-Royal, smoked meat dominates: the famous Schwartz Deli where at peak mealtimes and after midnight you can't get a seat, and The Main, which is open all night, and you can. Maybe the air of brine-soaked brisket discourages investors, but this stretch of St-Laurent has not been swept up by the taste of money. At least not yet.

La Cabane is a strong hold-out — two desirably dark rooms decorated with beer memorabilia and plastic hanging plants, soaked with stale brew, marinated in tobacco fumes and allowed to stand unchanged for as long as most people can remember, which in a time of constant change, is long enough for a bar to become an institution. Joey's table is along the wall in the south room. When he feels like celebrating he takes the back booth, which is on a raised balcony overlooking the whole room. If he's gregarious he'll agree to a centre table on the other side, but tonight is no time to go public. He nods to the waitress upon entry, the usual, and heads straight for the wall. When they are settled, he starts up again.

"My point is this, once events have been, let's say, nudged, you have to follow up. I know, and you know, lord you of all people know, Off the Main has never relied on publicity. You've said it a million times, 'Get behind the work. Talk to the press.' I hate talking about the work. Maybe it's insecurity. There was too much of me in the earlier shows, I went too close to the bone. That Riel piece — "

"Joey, I don't think we should rehash the past."

"Right. Riel is history. Ha ha. This is the future. A major well-known international classic, featuring absolutely first-rate actors."

"They are."

"One with a brilliant past and the other with a brilliant future."

"I'm glad you're still positive."

"I am. Actually, I'm pretty confident they will start memorizing their lines. Someday. Okay, you don't want to hear about those problems. Agreed. So, I realize I've got to get behind the work and reach out to a public, instead of putting up all kinds of psychological barriers screaming 'stay away from this show.' The international controversy surrounding this Beckett estate thing may be the lost leader, or whatever the supermarkets call it. Smoke screen? Pretext? Ruse?"

"Scam?"

"No."

"In news they call it an angle. The point of the story."

"Exactly. All I want you to do is help me get that angle out to the Toronto press."

"You know I can't write about Off the Main, that would be a huge conflict of interest, especially since I've never written about theatre." Joey's looking smug now, he has her interest. "I don't want you to write about theatre." She waits. "I want you to put me in touch with somebody who will."

A talented director, he's a terrible actor. Myra swiftly figures out what he has in mind, and says, "No."

"Don't say no."

"I already did."

"Well reconsider. Myra, make one phone call. That is all I ask. One measly little call."

"And say what?"

"Hi, how are you doing, remember Joe Rosenbaum? Well he's involved in a pretty amazing controversy and I just thought you might like his phone number, in case there's something in it for The Journal."

"TV? You've got to be joking."

Joey has the television spot already worked out in his mind. He's willing to put Lucky and Pozzo in colourful costumes, if that's what it takes. He's already got a heavy metal guitar solo recorded, and figures it will work splendidly on the box.

"Joey, after all you've said to discourage my interest in that man, I cannot believe you'd be selfish enough to tempt me back into the swamp. You made me swear never to speak to him again, you don't even want to hear his name. You said his name is synonymous with pain."

"Then don't use it. Just call him Mr. Pain, and remember this is a professional call. You're not going back into the swamp, you're proving to yourself you're strong and over all that."

The CD choice at La Cabane is usually palatable, but tonight somebody is spinning Barbra Streisand, and the strains of desperate beauty are dragging the mood down. Myra would like to go home, but she isn't ready to face the nascent Brady Bunch as they curl up for a bedtime tale.

"Mr. Pain. Hmm, yes."

"Just plain Pain. Maybe it's a first name."

She laughs. She hates it when Joey uses his professional creativity in the theatre of life. The name suits her long-lost lover, she's beginning to see it written all over his face. This time last year she swore never to see him again. If his other former girlfriends had been selling T-shirts inscribed with their chagrin, she'd have bought one and worn it night and day. But now.

Time, as they say, wounds all heels.

Joey orders two cognacs to toast the future of Godot, and they agree to talk about something else. Time melts, and conversation flows into the eternal night.

# VII

◆

If cross-examined by Socrates, Myra would say the highest good in life is Freedom. She was born under the sign of water, fire ascending, the eldest of three girls in a family of small-town Catholics. Her father spent his working life at a tool and dye plant, and five years' running, it rained on his measly two weeks off. Burdened with his disappointment, she resolved never to do anything that dangled a fixed vacation over her head, and decided finally on freelance journalism, the consequence being she has never actually had a bona fide vacation. Some deadline always looms; if not, it's the anxious hunt for assignments, appeasement of editors, cultivation of sources, endless clipping from copious newspapers, angles to be looked at, issues to follow. The best stories always end up taking too long, work is never really finished for the day or the week, only suspended while other duties intervene. Her income isn't great and the benefits are nil, but she has never been bored and cannot be fired. Compared to the legions of people who hate their boss and dread the office, Myra considers this a significant achievement.

Born into the whirlwind, Sally rejects the yoke of Freedom. She doesn't see the point of being your own boss if the result is slavery, considers her mother's life a loathsome battle with the clock, detests the adrenaline rush of deadlines, both the nail-biting concentration before, and the delirious exhaustion afterwards. For her, the Summum Bonum is Time. At an early age, she resolved to keep time pure, lie back and let it float like clouds on a summer day. Sally believes in doing what must be done to pay the bills, and if it's mindless, so much the better, you still own your mind. She doesn't follow the news, prefers building snow castles, painting pictures, making music, talking philosophy over café au lait. This luxurious side of time she discovered by way of her grandfather, who was retired when they met and eager to spend every possible moment in the rapturous company of a wide-eyed little girl.

Not that she has grown up frivolous. Like Myra, Sally is frugal, but for different reasons. Starting with nickels and dimes in her piggy bank, she put aside her birthday money, saved the proceeds of babysitting, minimum wage and tips, slid it all into a bank account to be spent in some glorious future, when life begins. Myra has no savings, no retirement plan, no unrequited desire for things, as far as she can tell. She has never had much more than just enough money, and any unexpected windfall is inevitably wiped out by vicious little bills from somewhere. She takes perverse joy from the uncertainty of a freelance income. She associates the constant risk with freedom — tangible proof thereof, the price you pay. Outwardly socialist, she is temperamentally conservative. She balances her books at night in order to sleep soundly. Sally wakes up each morning eager to spend a worthwhile day.

In Sally's adolescence, she and Myra were at opposite ends of an ellipse. They saw each other through inch-thick glass, heard voices under water, touched like sandpaper. But Sally is 19 now, and no longer — in her mother's annoying phrase — "living at home." (Yes, I do live at home, Mom. I just don't live with you.) She has emerged from adolescence into a world of her own, just in time for Jack's mid-life crisis, with a small head start on Myra's.

It's Monday, noon. Sally overslept and missed her morning classes at the CEGEP du Vieux Montréal, Quebec's unique link between high school and work or university, where she studies psychology, film and art history. She's still not sure what she wants to do with her life or where she wants to be. But as they line up at the Commensal, a self-serve health food restaurant on St-Denis Street, and heap their plates with tofu and salad, she is fairly certain there's a reason her mom is paying for lunch. As soon as they've passed through the cash register, Myra says, "So, what's going on with Mitch?"

Sally rolls her eyes, "Let's get a table first."

The ground floor is packed with oatmeal people wearing natural fibres. Nearly everybody here has read the *Celestine Prophecy* and most patrons have heard of Nostradamus, which is one reason Myra is so surprised to bump into Lise Lamotte, a red meat kind of woman who writes a weekly column for Le Devoir and appears regularly on English-language TV, as the CBC's resident indépendantiste.

Devoted to the cause of Quebec with passports, Lise can't make up her mind whether the media podium is preferable to an actual seat in the National Assembly, which is why her columns sometimes read like speeches. Short, plump, formidable in debate, Lise off-camera is mainly interested in men, prefers them as adversaries, be it politics or sport, preferably both. Her most recent challenge was a prominent federal politician. When the affair was at its hottest, they published a series of debates about the constitution in Le Devoir, airing their differences with so much thunder and lightning that a rival columnist in La Presse wrote a hilarious satirical critique exposing the sexual subtext. While Lise basked in the notoriety at parties, her lover found himself locked out of his Westmount mansion, and when he got back in, ended the affair abruptly. After that, Ms Lamotte's interest in constitutional reform took a powerful nose-dive.

She considers Myra one of her contacts in the anglophone milieu, and isn't above calling in the middle of the night to test an idea. Myra cringes at being identified with 600,000 disparate desperate English-speaking Quebecers, most of them raving federalists with little in common, but Lamotte inevitably poses questions an active imagination cannot resist considering. She's strong on mood and never afraid to generalize. Anglo Quebec is a ready reminder of the real menace, the English-speaking world. It's loathsome on principle; but dressed up and available for lunch, that's another story.

She falls upon Myra with double-kiss enthusiasm, introduces the man beside her as Greg Menzie, filmmaker and vegetarian. A gangly fellow in his late twenties, he is clean-shaven and pleased as punch to know a famous older woman. She is wearing the Menzie blue and white plaid kilt, complemented by a T-shirt that stretches a giant blue and white fleur de lys over her breasts. They talk about the startling new referendum poll for a moment — Lise thinks it's the beginning of a bandwagon, but let's not be overconfident — then she wants to know if Myra can identify the tartan, and she gives her a wicked wink.

Being of Irish extraction and from Ontario, Myra's no expert on Scottish clans or their preferences in skirts, but she did get around to reading Lise's magazine profile of an up-and-coming documentary filmmaker named Menzie, and on the basis of the writer's unabashed enthusiasm, quickly pieces together the connection. As he disappears out the door to get his car, Lise giggles, "Il est absolument out of this world, c'est moi qui le dis," and follows him.

"What was that all about?" says Sally, who doesn't read newspapers.

"Lamotte, the journalist? You've seen her on TV."

"Oh yeah, the one who won't let anybody else talk."

"They're paid to be fast. Anyway, she's probably going to be working in documentary film soon."

"What makes you think so?"

Moments like this, when worlds collide, a parent is not supposed to say what she thinks, but Myra blurts out: "Because she's sleeping with a documentary filmmaker and the surest way to predict her next move is to shake hands with the latest conquest."

Sally's mouth drops open. "Mom! That is pretty . . . Oh!"

"Pretty what?"

"Racist. Sexist. Misogynist."

No going back now, Myra presses on, "Wow. Let me think about it. . . . No. It's none of those. Nothing to do with her being a woman, or whatever. Let's just say her mind and body are in perfect synch."

Sally shakes her head, "You are such a prude."

"I'm not a prude. I'm just making an observation. I've known that woman for quite a few years, and her actions are quite inconsistent with her publicly espoused beliefs, which seem to dip and dive according to who she's, ah, dating. Anyway, maybe it's just my mood, doubts, I don't know."

"What do you doubt?"

"The referendum, independence."

"Oh, that." By the look on Sally's face, Myra can see she has raised a non-issue, far less interesting than a kilted journalist's taste in men, and she veers off on a silent side road: Where Have I Gone Wrong? Sally knows the look, and decides to defend herself. "You're beginning to have doubts about Quebec independence?"

"I don't doubt it would be a good move, no, that's obvious. I just . . . well, let's just say a lot of the important players seem . . ."

"What?"

"Crazy. I mean, full of contradictions. So different on TV than off."

"No kidding!" Sally laughs outright. "Mom, TV isn't real life."

"I know, I know, but . . . Whew! What am I saying? Let's change the subject. Some things just do not make sense. Sally, the destiny of Quebec is the most important issue in contemporary Canadian history. It's the reason I — we — are here. To live that destiny. But, lately, I'm beginning to get a feeling that if you stand really close, I mean if you live it and look around the corners and under the mat and behind the scenes, it is so hopelessly hilariously tragically fuzzy that there's no, well, no solution. The drivers of this movement scare me."

While Myra talks, Sally puts both elbows on the table, holds her chin with folded hands and considers the choppy haircut her mother wore back from Calgary. It looks like a worn-out straw hat. Wrinkles around the eyes, still fiery when she gets wound up, but her voice seems odd, kind of high-pitched and her hands are shaking. The hands make Sally nervous. Jack's breakdown was so obvious, he's bored, end of story. But what's going on with Myra? True, she always obsesses on politics. In the middle of a big story like the referendum you can count on her being overtired, overworked, perpetually excited. Still.

Sally desperately wants to light up a cigarette, but this liquorless granola bar is strictly a non-smoking universe. Anyway, Myra would blow if she ever suspected her offspring smoke. (They both smoke.) All right, maybe she suspects, but obviously this is no time to go public with the news. Her mother is staring into a cup of tepid chicory coffee and wondering why you can't believe everything you hear on TV? Of course, it's not as simple as that. She looks at her and thinks, the haircut is a start. Next, cover up the grey and get rid of those washed-out sweaters, work out, get more sleep, sit up straight. Definitely, take a vacation and go to see a few comedies.

Politics? In Sally's world this subject has about as much importance as European soccer. A semi-pro team from Italy came into the Bifteck one night and left gigantic tips. Tried to get the waitresses to go out after the bar closed, but where could they go? The bars were closed. Politics? Make that, less importance than European soccer, semi-pro Italians included. If only she'd had her own place then, she could have invited the whole team back for home-brewed beer.

"Sal, are you even listening to me?" Her mother's question brings her back to the unreality of lunch at the Commensal.

"Oh, sorry."

Myra knows better than to bore Sally with politics, and hopes her digression into Lamotte's love life hasn't rendered any further conversation out of the question. She worries about Sally living on her own, scrambling for rent, spending so much time serving the masses beer in a dingy bar. This is a girl who left teddy bears on her bed, and still owns crayons. Still, behind those penetrating brown eyes is an old soul, a kind of wisdom that's as far from Myra's kind as you can get. The other end of the ellipse, a young woman facing the moon. Right now Myra would like to perform that childish trick, and say let's pretend. When I am 90 you'll be 70, both of us old. Let's pretend we're just women and can say anything. They are almost at this point, Sally is there, but Myra, not quite, so she takes a sip of cold coffee, and asks, meekly, "What's happening with Mitch and Mandy?"

"What do you want to know?" asks Sally, in a tone suggesting she knows all, but will reveal little.

"What have you got? Come on, Sal. I'm the mother. Of course I'm in the dark."

Silence.

"All right, I'll give you five dollars to tell me if she's on the pill."

"Mom!!!!" Sally chokes, then laughs.

"What exactly is so funny? Bribery? You're laughing at bribery?"

"No, at five dollars. I can get that for a couple of cigarettes at closing time."

"This isn't the Bifteck."

Sal stops grinning and leans ahead. "Do you honestly think I'd sell information about my own brother?"

"No. Did you honestly think I'd pay?"

"No."

"Well, is she?"

"Let's just say she's careful. Getting her life together. Far from dumb. The father sends money, off and on. She wants to go back to school and get into physiotherapy. If you ask me, she'll do it. She used to do a few drugs but apparently that's history. Don't worry about Mitch. He can use the experience. God, can he use the experience."

Sally is holding her fingers in a peace sign at her lips, and blows a warm sigh into the vitamin-soaked air. There are brown stains around the first joints of both fingers, and finally, looking straight at those stains, Myra is sure Sally smokes. In fact, she looks like a smoker. Her army bag smells smoky, always has.

She is about to blurt out, look I know you smoke, when Sally gathers up her army bag and says, "By the way, do you think I could borrow twenty bucks? I'm a little short for my bus pass."

Bribery is out of the question. A loan, that's different. Bus pass, sure, necessity. Essential to Freedom. Saves delicious Time.

They leave the restaurant and Sally heads downhill to school. Myra walks toward home, cutting through the leafy oasis of Carré St-Louis, past rubbies on the wooden benches by the fleur de lys–shaped swimming pool, sleeping off their beery lunch in the mid-afternoon heat. Not so long ago this park was a children's playground with swings, slides, sand, full of joyful squeals. When Mitch and Sally were little, they came here often, one on each hand, skipping along Prince Arthur Street, begging for ice cream. No matter what else was happening, on a warm summer afternoon they could sweep her into the moment and hold her there for hours, a bona fide holiday from Self. As she walks home, reeling from the fierce board game of lunch with a savvy young woman, she aches for one of those days, the delicious, mood-floating enthusiasm of childhood.

Whatever Mitch is experiencing in his new-found romance with mother and child, it hasn't affected his study habits. From the bottom of the outside staircase, Myra can hear the blast of a pirated Neil Young concert tape. He is taking the afternoon off from school to work on his geography project. The bedroom door is open; she catches him gazing at a textbook and eating a piece of cold pizza, head bobbing to the music. He turns the pages gingerly, as though they emanated information to be absorbed by breathing. He doesn't hear her knock, and when she touches his shoulder, the pizza flies out of his hand and onto a map of Europe. Mandy made the bed on her way out Sunday, but civilization didn't take hold. Everything Mitch has since touched is on the floor. The room smells of socks and sex. He says hi, and plugs in his earphones. The sudden silence reminds Myra that he, too, is leaving home, in his own sweet way. No sighs and tears like Sally, he is quietly building muscles by lifting weights. The odour of manhood keeps her out of his room, a pungent warning that he will soon be carried away by another woman.

In her dream that night, a pair of giant white horses are galloping down the centre of a highway, bellies bulging with huge, almond-shaped ovaries. No explanation, she just knows they are ovaries. Like most of Myra's dreams, this one is about running and the horses are panting hard against the wind but their stomachs are full of eggs and the weight slows them down. She wakes up suddenly, her heart pounding. She gets up for a glass of water, goes into her tiny office, off the kitchen. The computer screen is still on. The telephone message light is flashing.

It's Joey, reminding her to call "you-know-who." His voice is a late-night plea. "I really really really need this favour. If we go down with Godot, Off the Main is dead." Not exactly subtle.

She notices the message was sent only minutes earlier, without the benefit of a ringing phone. His latest toy. Joey's wardrobe would fit into an overnight bag and his apartment looks like he's already moved, but he always acquires the latest in communication technology, cell phone, computerized agenda, sophisticated answering service. If he sent the message minutes ago, that means he's still up. Myra dials his number. He's wide awake, and answers with a guilty hello.

"It's me."

"What are you doing up at this hour?"

"Checking my messages."

"Right."

The screen gives off a lavender glow. She speaks softly into the darkness. "Joey, I'd just like to remind you that the person you insist I contact has caused me a lot of grief, and probably inflicted lifelong damage on my soul. And you — did you hear the italics in my voice, Joey? — you have spent many long tedious hours convincing me to stay away from him."

"Yeah. And I was right."

"So why have you changed your mind?"

She hears him inhale, and is sorely tempted to mention that an asthmatic should not smoke, but she can also hear him thinking, and that's more interesting. Finally he speaks, the tone is confessional.

"I know, I know, my request is low, very low. I'm a self-serving, weak-willed son-of-a-bitch. I've spent a decade of my adult prime trying to do something artistic for a public consisting of narrow-minded frogs and geriatric anglos who didn't have the grey matter to get off their asses and cut it in Toronto. A small pond full of egotistical toads whose only real concern is how to spread warts. Me, Joseph E. Rosenbaum, sucked in by the stinking joie de fucking vivre. I'm 39 years old in deep debt on the verge of going on welfare hoping like hell that a putrid publicity stunt involving none other than my GOD Sam Beckett will make it possible for me to continue my pathetic existence for one more year. I've got no excuse, except Montreal. This city has me backed up against the wall." He takes another drag, winds up again, "And I have the gall, the slimy, rancid embarrassingly ignoble gall, to call my best friend in the middle of the night and ask —"

"Joey —"

"For a pathetic favour. Prostitute yourself in front of that diseased —"

"Joey!"

"Myra, I'm sorry."

"Thanks. I appreciate your honesty."

Then he starts coughing. "I know — believe me I — know better than — anybody, I am pa-thet-ic."

Joey collapsed in rehearsal once and had to be rushed to the hospital. They clamped an oxygen mask on him at the door, and kept him in bed for three days. He promised the doctor he'd never smoke again, and instructed Myra to slap him hard if he did. So far she has concentrated on lecturing. "You should quit." She is considering a slap.

"I know, I know. Right after this (cough) show."

"Hold on a minute," she says, "I'm moving to the other phone."

On the way to the living room she gets a beer, settles into the sofa and gathers the blanket around her knees before picking up the receiver.

"Still there? . . . Joey? . . ."

He picks up the phone, breathless. "Sorry, I ran to get a beer."

He takes a long drink. She can hear the bubbles, knows he is waiting for her to say something. She says, "So, we're just going to sit here in the dark, and drink over the phone?"

"Now there is a great idea: Télébar, the cinq à sept chat line. Maybe you can get McAuslan Brewery involved.

Fundraising. Everybody who checks in will be drinking one of their beers. Very popular in February, you don't even have to leave the house."

"How do we make money?"

"Details, details."

"Yeah . . . Did I tell you Paulette had her ovaries taken out?"

"Who's Paulette?"

"Jack's — you know — wife."

"Ah, Paulette. The cruise ship. Yeah, you didn't tell me about your trip."

"Your mind was elsewhere."

"Ovaries, eh. You know, I used to think an ovary was one of those large milky-covered marbles. Honest, I thought women had a sack of them under their stomach, and they had something to do with babies. Then I met this nurse, that time I went to Mexico, and she set me straight about a lot of things. Let me tell you, after nurse Jane, my cock felt fragile for months. I mean, that is one complex little vault you women have up there. Dark and warm hardly does it justice. Talk about technical. Ow. Don't tell me more."

"Joey!"

"What?"

The difficult question is hanging in the night air. Myra's had time to prepare an answer.

"I'll make one call, but there's a condition."

"A condition?"

"Remember that comic sketch you wrote about the theatre critic and the Russian whore? Well, you have to stage it as an opening act, before Godot."

"What? Why? Oh."

"Because all those political collective creations you've done, they're important, but you are a very funny writer when you quit grinding axes. I want you to put your comic ass on the line this time. If I'm going to risk humiliation, so are you, Rosenbaum."

"You think I never risk humiliation?! Ha! Humiliation is my life's work!"

"Sure, you risk, but on your own terms. This time I want you to meet mine."

"Ah. . . . Well, I'll give it some thought."

"No sketch, no call."

"Okay, okay."

"Good. Now, tell me how you send a message without ringing somebody's phone."

Pain's number is in an old agenda at the bottom of a box labelled 1993. She rehearses her speech a few times before dialling. Finishes her cognac. The message is brief.

"Hi, it's me. Saw your profile of Don Cherry. Thought it was quite good."

Quite good? It was brilliant but flattery stinks.

"I need to ask you something. Give me a call. Bye."

She's pretty sure he is sitting right there in his big leather chair, drinking whisky and listening to the sound of her voice. He has a loft in Old Montreal with a forty-foot-wide view of the river, stars lighting up the water. She has not seen that view for more than a year, but hanging up the phone she sees it now, twinkling lights in a vast black sky.

# VIII

◆

The trouble with fast-lane communication is that it gives silence an easy excuse. Days go by, Joey says maybe he didn't get the message, maybe his machine is broken, try again. Myra won't do it, regrets she ever sent an idiotic message in the first place — almost as much as she regrets he hasn't called back — and those little drops of regret make their way to a buried sea where the ripple proves that some part of her is still, alas, alive to Pain.

Meanwhile, Joey is immersed in his bilingual *Waiting for Godot*. The first week of rehearsal was buoyant. The actors arrived high on the thrill of beating out the competition in auditions. By week two, they began to realize just how much time would be spent in this drafty third-floor loft, a 1930s sweatshop that rediscovered an old life with the arrival of theatre. According to Union des artistes rules, actors are paid for performances but not rehearsal, so their day jobs take precedence and it's hard to pin them down. Stage manager Noel is strict. Early on, he took a full account of their other commitments and created a complicated schedule running up to opening night. That's what it will take, ladies and gentlemen. Every available moment, within union guidelines, of course.

Now they are midway through the ten-week marathon, and Godot has overtaken all else. Rehearsal means to re-hear. Each word scrutinized, a page can take hours. Myra's been through the cycle enough times to know that however much Joey may protest the tedium, deep rehearsal is the part he loves, when the high anxiety of facing a public hasn't yet taken hold, and everybody is still convinced this play will change their lives.

Only in French Quebec does theatre operate on quasi-monastic principles. A devotional system codified by unions, the spirit of this system is one of the main reasons Joey decided to work in French, because a great play demands long rehearsal, slow cooking. In the rest of the country, actors are paid a small weekly salary throughout the contract, and must commit to a normal eight-hour day, six-day week. They start three weeks before opening night (sometimes less), so there's no time to mull things over, just memorize lines and follow the fluorescent marks on the floor. Developed from the British repertory tradition, Joey says the system is ably suited to the glorified radio plays it was invented to serve, but makes the search for mood, nuance and theme all but impossible.

The match is an odd one. To the French, Joey is English, though he never, ever applies to himself that clumsy techno-ethnic label, anglophone. His father is a Côte St-Luc Jew, his late mother, a fierce Catholic matriarch. Israel Rosenbaum is a practical man, dogmatic but fragile. He believes the Jews have had enough politics for one century. After the 1980 referendum, he threw up his hands and moved to Toronto. Joey stayed in Montreal to open Off the Main. At regular intervals, Rosenbaum père offers to set him up if he'll make the move, but Joey insists he belongs in Montreal. Quebec is finished, says Israel. Kaput, too many politicians, a nation of whiners.

Joey's Quebec is a nation of muses. He believes that the convergence of English and French theatre in the crucible of late twentieth-century Montreal will last much longer than headlines and laws. Politicians coast on the strength of civilization, which is culture, he says. They defend an oppressed nation, claim to be working every day for its survival, but in fact, neither federalists nor indépendantistes would have much grist for their ambition if artists didn't live on brown rice and forego property ownership to keep the mythical state-in-waiting alive. That's Joey's argument for staying in Montreal. He doesn't give a fig about politics. It's the air that counts. In Quebec, art matters.

To which his father replies: "Fine, but how much are you maykink?"

At which point, Joey throws up his hands and shouts, "It's not about money. Ahhhhhh, you belong in Toronto."

And Rosenbaum Sr. shakes his head, "Joey, call your brother in Miami — collect." Then he hangs up the phone.

For a decade now, Joey has been faithful to his muse. His father's opposition has provided regular opportunities to restate the faith. Keeping Off the Main alive has kept Joey alive. But lately, in the privacy of his favourite bar, away from the gang, whose spirits must be kept up, and in the presence of Myra, he will grant the truth. After ten years, staying alive is not enough. Then there are days, like today, when Joey is convinced *Waiting for Godot* is the reason Off the Main exists. This show, this is the one.

The actor playing Estragon is Bill Davies, a stunning wreck of a man who played a dozen seasons of chunky classical roles at the Stratford Festival before heartbreak and drink washed him up on his aged mother's Westmount doorstep. Joey salivated reading Bill's CV and Bill is convinced Joey is the next Robin Phillips. He would love to have slept with Robin and, during auditions, fixed his hopes on Joey and still hasn't given up hope, although there is little evidence that Joey is gay, mainly because Joey isn't gay. On the other hand, he isn't seeing anyone.

At his mother's request, Bill is seeing a therapist, whom she chose and is paying for. Once a week, in a tiny room near the Forum, he gets to lie back and talk about himself for 30 minutes before submitting to a lecture on the importance of long-term goals, delayed gratification, discipline — a kind of 12-step program for contentment. That William F. Davies is an actor and has no use for contentment hasn't occurred to the therapist, or to his mother. But giving them both a crack at saving his soul has bought Bill time to do a great play for a salary that doesn't cover his bar bills. He falls asleep each night to the lull of a French-language tape, and is looking forward to seeing his name on the same bilingual poster as this year's star grad from l'Ecole Nationale de Théâtre. When the postcards are printed, all of his Toronto friends and contacts will get one.

In the role of Vladimir, Bill's co-star is 22-year-old Emmanuel Paré, faintly bilingual and confident that this, his first role in the international tongue, is an important step en route to the U.S. entertainment industry. Of course, Emmanuel intends to vote Oui in the referendum and will be sorely disappointed if he wakes up the next day in Canada. One of about five hundred feverishly ambitious young actors walking around Montreal looking for work, he has no opinion on cultural politics. If wearing long underwear in Joey's loft and mastering the TH is what it takes to make it in America, well then allons-y, let's go. When the postcards are printed, half the film agents in Hollywood will get one.

Two actors from the proverbial two solitudes, they touch, bump and tolerate each other, for love of theatre, in hope of success. That's how Joey ended up with stellar leads in a contemporary classic. If only Sam Beckett could see for himself.

Myra has dropped by the rehearsal hall to bring Joey a budget update, which he promises to look at, soon. She agrees to stay and watch a rehearsal. Emmanuel is warming up. He is wearing spandex, and his thighs figure heavily in Bill's peripheral vision.

"Um-um-um-um-um-um-um-um-ahhhhhhhhhh-um-um-um. Think, thanks, thing, thought, Thursday, this-tel. Ow am I doing, Meera?"

"Fine," she says, "But it's this-el. You don't say the second T."

"Fuck. This language of yours makes no sense. Did you know that?"

"Yeah, well we had it shoved down our throats by muskets, did you know that?"

"Who? Who did that?" He stands on his head in the middle of the room.

"Les anglais."

"I don't follow you up," he says, thumping two feet down hard on the floor.

"I'm Irish, see. Née Myra Mary Callaghan. I'm telling you we had English shoved down our throats, by the English. Who were our enemies from, say, a few hundred years before you Frenchmen set foot on this part of the planet."

Joey loves it when Myra watches him direct, but he has warned her about bringing up politics. Noel is aware of the policy, and scowls as he gives his actors the nod.

"Five minutes, Mr. Paré, Mr. Davies. See Voo Play."

A small, balding youth who hails from New Brunswick, Noel is just bilingual enough to feel part of Montreal. He followed a former girlfriend to the city, and now his rent is so cheap he can't afford to leave. French theatre isn't exactly his cup of tea, he's steeped in the British tradition. Currently reading Sir Peter Hall's *Diaries*, he frequently compares Joey to his mentors at The National, citing incidents from the Olivier production, anecdotes about who said what on the BBC. He treats his actors like exotic inmates of a touring zoo, a species who've given up on reproduction and need to be reminded to breathe. One of Noel's eyebrows is a full centimetre higher than the other; his face, after the first read-through, is fixed in a permanent masthead glare. He occupies an altered state, the film version of *The Dresser* plays on a loop in his head. As opening night approaches, Joey becomes increasingly dependent on

Noel. At least once, Noel will command Joey to postpone suicide until the show is up. But after they go public, it will be Noel's show. He'll make sure everybody turns up dressed, fit and on key. Joey will practically need a letter from the Queen to open his mouth at La Cabane.

But it's many a long day before they face an audience. Bill, suspecting Myra will be watching this rehearsal and eager to get as much attention as possible, takes her aside before they go into the sacred room. A contemporary of Glenn Gould, he is wearing black wool gloves with the fingertips cut off. He nibbles on his cuticles as he talks.

"Tell me," he whispers, "Is Emmanuel gay?"

"You'd be better able to judge than me," says Myra, as she pours them coffee.

"That broad who comes into La Cabane sometimes. Is she . . ."

"I'm not sure the word 'broad' is au courant here, Bill. You mean Francine?"

"If that's her name."

"It's the name we've been given."

"Hmm." Bill pops a breath mint, and looks longingly at his co-star.

Myra can't resist baiting him. "So now it's Emmanuel? I kind of thought you were interested in our director?"

Joey walks by and gives Bill a faintly ominous look. Anything less than a clap on the back and Bill's confidence plummets. "Let's put it this way," he says, watching Joey walk up to Emmanuel. "I am definitely not interested in a boy who is uncertain about his sexuality. Not at my age. No virgins, please." Joey and Emmanuel are talking, laughing, Bill wishes he had studied lip reading.

"So, you've given up on Joey?" says Myra.

Bill smirks, "Have you noticed the way that he dresses?"

"Oh, come on. Love is not about clothes."

"Love? Ha! I'm beginning to suspect he isn't gay."

"What is gay, Bill? It's the end of the Twentieth Century, the age of continuum. Emmanuel, Noel, Francine, Joey. Who can say?"

Bill looks at her with new-found interest. "Are you interested in Francine?"

"I'd be interested to know who does her hair," she says.

"So would I. Definitely, yes, very fine work on the hair."

All this innuendo. Actors are first and foremost bodies. Bill will go into the room and picture everybody naked. It's a trick he's learned to keep himself awake. Heightens the energy level. Joey will think it's something he said, and hope like hell he can say it again in time for the preview.

*A country road. A tree. Evening.*

This afternoon's task is to run the first chunk "off book," actors going through the scene without a script in hand. Two clowns stuck in no man's land, talking of sex and suicide. Davies has more or less decided he's a clown, and is working on two notes — sad and funny. Paré is building his performance on observation, and the subject he has chosen to observe is Bill Davies, the real thing, the wreck of a man. He watches intensely, picking up clues and teaching his body inch by inch how to look like Bill Davies feels. The attention doesn't escape Davies, he thinks it's sexual.

Vladimir and Estragon are both bums, but Paré's bum is the fallen patrician. Besides his study of Davies, there's an echo of the adored Quebec master Jean-Louis Roux in his construction. His Vladimir is a gentleman, a scholar, a tortured intellectual whose superior knowledge of the Bible weighs heavily. A vast contrast from Davies, the emotionally accessible Estragon who tells bad jokes, demands a hug and then complains, you stink of garlic. Estragon needs a laugh.

*Silence. Estragon looks attentively at the tree.*

*Vladimir: What do we do now?*

*Estragon: Nous attendons.*

*Vladimir: Yes but while waiting.*

*Estragon: What about hanging ourselves?*

*Vladimir: Hmmm. It'd give us an* election.

The room breaks up in laughter, Emmanuel doesn't know why. Stone-faced Noel corrects him.

"The word is EE-REC-TION, Mr. Paré."

"No, keep it, keep it," says Joey, slapping the table. "Keep the word election."

The knot in Bill's stomach is getting bigger. He imagines a hundred people laughing uproariously at election, and races ahead in the text to check on his next bon mot.

It's part of the play's power that a slip of the tongue can make the universally pathetic seem locally pathetic. Nobody talks politics in the rehearsal hall, but they are surrounded by it anyway, and the juxtaposition of suicide with election exposes the tension. Joey's adaptation is beginning to work. The carefully constructed mix of English and French heightens the power plays of communication. Estragon struggles limply in French to get into Vladimir's world.

The former Stratford star can't get rid of his bone-deep colonial twitch: he wants to please the audience, and his fellow actor. He'll crawl, he'll ham, he'll snarl. With makeup and work, Paré can convince people he's a spiritual contemporary of the 60-year-old Davies. He will channel his youthful energy and, at chosen moments, play a tragedy by Corneille. French and English are his two swords. He switches languages purposefully. From a strictly personal point of view, Emmanuel's quest is to kill William Davies onstage, all the while loving him most nobly. If all goes well, they will both be rewarded. Paré will land great reviews, and Davies will get many laughs.

Since the two-for-one Happy Hour at La Cabane ends at seven, they knock off at 6:45 and head downstairs. Bill is broke. He has given up making sly remarks about his non-salary, since Noel told him talking about money is a faux pas in French theatre, then rubbed it in by adding, "That's a false step," to which Bill snarled, "I know what a fucking faux pas is. Christmas!"

Now he's settled down to honest begging: "How about a pitcher out of the rehearsal budget, Herr Noel?"

"Only if you promise to bring your own toilet paper from now on."

He promises to bring a case from Westmount, on the bus no less, so Noel orders a St. Ambroise Rousse, and marks it down.

Twenty minutes later, Emmanuel's girlfriend Francine shows up wearing a shiny black raincoat and matching hat. Last week she shot a mutual funds commercial, and was paid as much for two days' work as Emmanuel will make for the entire effort of acting on a play, 15 nights and 2 matinées. She cannot imagine why anybody would willingly choose to hang out at a beer-soaked tav like La Cabane, but she's a fan of this production and fully expects it will launch her man into the big time. As the circle expands to include her chair, she hands Joey a big brown envelope that she found sitting outside the locked door of the rehearsal room. Myra takes it, Joey pours her a beer.

"Notice I haven't asked you about the phone call lately," he says, leaning over to Myra.

"No, it's been hours."

"Forget it. I don't even care any more. We don't need him."

He's so confident, she suspects he is itching to unveil some new scheme, but she has another subject in mind.

"Have you told everybody about opening the show with your sketch?"

"You weren't serious?"

So, she tells the table about his sketch. Joey flees to the washroom as she hands around photocopies from the envelope. Bill groans at the thought of more lines. Emmanuel counts his. Francine thinks adding original work to the evening is truly inspired. She wonders about music. And why not kill the intermission? Intermissions are passé. Fix the public to their seats and don't let them out, that's the French way. High mass. No pee break. Noel points out that Off the Main needs the bar revenues from intermission, a sum of money that normally exceeds box office.

By the time Joey comes back, the two lead actors are reading the sketch out loud, and the whole table is in giggles. Sue and Ann, who work on administration and will also play the smaller but significant parts of Pozzo and Lucky, are quietly worried, since this addition puts even more time in front of their appearance. But, if it gets things off to a good start, they're game. The actors' enthusiasm for the sketch starts to work on Joey's despair; by the time they've talked about it for half an hour, he is scribbling rewrites in the margins.

Bill wonders if there's a homoerotic attraction between the hooker and the critic. Joey says he is prepared to give that one some thought (meaning, no, you asshole). Myra winks at Bill and Bill's smile looks like his tenth breath mint of the day was a rare tropical fish that he just swallowed. Emmanuel can't decide whether he should play the critic or the hooker. Francine thinks it could be funny to have the critic dress like the ubiquitous entertainment columnist/voice, Grimaldi, in flowing African print, a turban and big sunglasses. Myra watches Joey sink into the second pitcher of beer. He regards these brainstorming sessions as a purified form of torture, although the truth is, he frequently picks out little morsels, forgets where they came from and puts them onstage.

Whatever they may think of each other later, right now, in the obsessive present of Godot, cast and crew are as tight as any community on the planet. Like castaways on a desert island, they share an immediate danger. Self-interest demands they pull together. If only some politician could write a giant script with a part for everybody, and get them into rehearsal, revolution would be a snap.

On the way home, Myra wanders into Jeanne Mance Park, through fallen leaves, and thinks about the simple stage directions opening Godot. Joey wants a moment of pitch black silence. He says the play is about loneliness. The city is never dark and quiet, always a million lights under the stars and moon, though the city is often about loneliness. No lights on at home. Mitch must be out with Mandy. Entering an empty house at night is a new and unsettling experience. If there were children sleeping she would listen for their breathing, but now the only sounds are a humming fridge and the creaking floors.

The message light on her phone is flashing. A few words from Pain, the roar of traffic behind his voice. He must have called from a phone booth. Standard style. Makes him sound homeless, women like that sound. When they first met, Myra used to save his messages and play them back, trying to pinpoint the colour of his voice. Something between a dark, hard brown and memorable grey. Walnut. Maple syrup. Lava. None of those words seem to fit now. Mercury, a voice like molten mercury, slippery silver, temperature rising. She erases the message and goes to bed.

It's the middle of the night when the phone rings. Mitch, who got in very late, picks it up on the third ring, just as Myra reaches her office. There's a clumsy moment with the three of them on the line. Myra hears two male voices, like antlers locking in the dark. Hello — Hi Mitch. How are things? — Fine. — Good. — What's up? — Is your mother — Asleep — Oh, well then —

She dives in. "I've got it, Mitch."

Mitch hangs up.

There is no traffic now behind Pain's voice. He sounds a trifle nervous. "Is it too late for a phone call?"

"What time is it?"

"Late. I thought you might be up working on a story, and feel like a break."

"No."

"You're in bed?"

"Yes."

"Alone? Never mind, it's none of my business."

She is awake now, and he says nothing. It's up to Myra to end the conversation or explain why she called him in the first place, but the bed is beginning to float. Moonlight makes the sheets look blue. She can hear music behind the silence, faint voices, brass, jazz. He must be sitting in his leather chair, looking out at the wide-angle river view. She can see the light of a cigarette in his hand, but the outline of his face is in shadow. Maybe he's standing by a window, one long leg supporting his lean body, while the other is curled around the inside of his calf, rubbing up and down in a lazy feline rhythm. Silence sucks the gravity out of her room.

She closes her eyes and tries to remember what he looks like. It's no use. His face is blank. His hair is thin and silver, long enough to be tied back in a ponytail, and his eyes — the colour comes to mind — his eyes are – she remembers the colour but not the eyes — green. The word "green," like an entry on his driver's licence.

"I've been out of town. My mother's in hospital."

"Oh, dear."

"Broken hip. They had to give her a new one."

"I'm sorry to hear that."

"She'll survive."

"Must be painful."

"Yeah. That's why I didn't call back earlier. Just heard your lovely voice message today."

Now the bed is tilting dangerously to one side, and Myra is clutching her pillow in an effort not to slide right out onto the floor and through the window into the blue moonlight. The effort makes her mouth dry, and all she can manage to reply is, "Oh."

"Pardon?"

"I said, oh."

"So, you saw the Don Cherry piece?"

"Yeah, it was funny."

"Thanks. To tell you the truth, he's a bit of an asshole."

"That came across in your piece."

"Really? I thought it was quite flattering."

"Oh yes, it definitely sounded like you approve of his assholiness."

She didn't exactly mean to strip him raw just yet, but he laughs. By now the bed has slipped right up the wall and is resting lightly on the ceiling, and Myra is lying back in the position of an expert swimmer treading water. She catches a glimpse of her nightgown in a heap on the floor, where the bed used to be. She is hanging upside down from the ceiling, her breasts full of moonlight. Maybe Pain can catch a glimpse of moonbreasts in her voice, or maybe he's just plain lonely, because after an ocean of silence he says, "Do you think I should come over there?"

"Not really," she says.

"Maybe I should call you tomorrow."

"That's an idea."

"Bye then."

"Bye."

The line remains open between them for a long moment. Then he hangs up, and there is a most delicious rush of warm blood to the centre of gravity between her thighs, causing the bed to go on turning, until it has completed the cycle. As her mind drifts, she remembers a time in the beginning when they met for lunch in an expensive Italian bistro on Queen Street. He was living in Toronto then, it was summer, she was wearing a grey and white dress with buttons down the front, a bit too small. After they'd ordered, he wanted her to go downstairs with him and semi-disrobe in the washroom. She said no, and cannot now remember why. Probably because he was still living with one of his wives and Myra's moral sense of turf made fornication in Toronto out of the question. But the picture, the dress unbuttoned, the staircase they did not go down, everything about that restaurant has returned to her mind's eye, there is no moral turf, no buttons, no reason not to go everywhere on a floating bed. Only regret. A choppy sea of regrets.

The phone is his instrument. Kingdom of voice. Safe distance. This is the strength and pull and point of Mr. Pain: What he does not say. Where he does not go. Why no woman can ever have him, and why he stays so long. Soon enough, mushy permanent conventional feelings do arise. One is tempted and gives in, kneels down and spells out the tearful word "love," which is the kiss of death. Faced with that kiss, Pain is mystified. Out of reach. At that moment, so familiar, he is gloriously, mistily potent. Seduction is everything. Orgasm, a matter of mechanics.

Afterward, Myra sleeps the sleep of walled gardens, dreamless, safe and locked with a key. So neat and clean, ecstasy of the mind's eye. Still, even for the mind's ecstasy, there is a price to pay.

# IX

◆

*Dear Myra,*
*Thank you for coming to Calgary to see Jack. Your*
*visit was good to him. I'm sorry for bursting out*
*about certain personal details which, as you answered,*
*have nothing to do with anybody. C'est la vie. In two*
*weeks I will be coming to Montreal. Perhaps we can*
*have lunch?*

*Regards,*
*Paulette*

*P.S. I glued the vase and everything came out of the*
*rug!!!*

The handwriting is loose and flowery, scrawled across mauve stationery smelling faintly of perfume. So it wasn't a bad dream after all. The whole escapade happened so fast, Myra can hardly believe it was only a few weeks ago. Now, an apology and an invitation to lunch? Paulette's note arrives the same morning as the VISA bill showing an outstanding balance of almost two thousand dollars, boosted out of sight by the airline ticket.

Unless some easy assignment drops out of the sky, it's going to take months to pay off.

She's still puzzling over the note when Mitch comes into the kitchen. He grunts good morning and pours himself a coffee, fills the cup with milk, stirs in two heaping teaspoons of brown sugar, takes a sip and winces. A man needs habits, if his day's going to start before eight a.m. He is wearing black jeans and a white T-shirt with, miraculously, no advertising. His head is a smooth, mottled globe. If she didn't know better, Myra would swear a strange young man had taken up residence in the broom closet.

"You shaved your head?"

"Yeah." He grins, and runs his hand over the naked crown. "What do you think?"

She thinks the shave makes him look incredibly young, especially when he smiles, the eager grin of a five-year-old, big ears sticking out, pink cheeks. Anything but a tough guy. She says, "Well, it's quite a surprise, good, yeah, amazing. Any particular reason . . . ?"

"James got lice from daycare, so he had to have his curls cut off, then he said he wanted it smooth. Mandy thought it would be fun if we all shaved our heads."

"Mandy shaved her head? Ow! Where'll she hide?"

As it turns out, Myra will soon get an answer. Mitch sits down at the end of the table and explains that on top of the lice fiasco, Mandy's landlord has decided to fumigate their basement apartment for cockroaches. The exterminators say you only have to keep out of the building for an afternoon, but she wonders if it's healthy for a three-year-old to sleep through chemicals strong enough to kill the oldest living creatures on earth. Maybe they could stay over in Sally's old room for a night or two, just to be on the safe side. "James is pretty upset at the news about losing the roaches. He thought of them as pets."

"Sure. Fine by me. What got you up so early?"

"Interview at Euro Deli for a part-time job. I figure, might as well put a little money away. My schedule's pretty easy now that I've dropped that math option. Man, the teacher's an idiot. If I pick it up next term maybe I can get somebody decent. What's the point of failing? Mom?"

"I didn't say a word."

"You had that look of, oh God, Mitch is slacking off again."

"Sudden baldness makes people paranoid. It's a known fact." Myra pours herself a second cup of coffee and offers him a refill, but he's barely touched his. He looks at the stove clock and runs out the door.

Mitch isn't slacking off, so much as he's sliding right out of the system. Good behaviour and a sunny disposition got him through high school with very little work, but now he's at Dawson College, an English-language CEGEP, and hating it. She expected he'd find it easier than French-immersion high school, but no, he's up against a big impersonal regime of crowded lecture halls, and his interest in education has fallen off drastically. Last year he failed two courses; dropping another means this two-year bridge between high school and university will take three years. Mitch flipping pizzas. The thought makes Myra shudder.

A few years ago she wrote a series on Quebec's CEGEP system for The Gazette and turned up the frightening fact that more than half the students drop out before graduation. Large polyglot schools, they were supposed to be a democratic replacement of the old collèges classiques, founded and run by the church for an intellectual élite, but clearly something has gone wrong. Jack thinks Mitch belongs in computer programming and bought him an expensive machine last Christmas, but in Myra's estimation, computer games have overtaken study.

What about Jack? She rereads Paulette's note: your visit was good to him. Sounds warm, if not quite English. Nothing about his health. She can still see him, in his bathrobe, pale and standing at a distance, blowing smoke rings out the patio door. Then the feeling comes over her again, a charge of panic for the future. Mitch, flipping pizza. He's had part-time jobs before, but he never dropped courses to fit them in, never asked to have a woman and child sleep over, or woke up scrubbed at eight a.m., determined to drink coffee. Jack should know about this, he'd have something to say. But Jack's got his own problems, though he protests the contrary. Paulette has erected a wall of cheerfulness around him. The trip was a fiasco. She learned nothing, except that the father of her children is a long way away, in space and time.

Right after he left, Myra moved her end of the kitchen table against the wall, and started sitting in Jack's chair. In no time at all, it became her place, and she is sitting there now, looking at a bread basket hanging on the wall above her old place. It's still early morning but a sudden wave of sadness pulls her down, makes her want to crawl back into bed and sleep for a month. Instead, she pours herself a cold glass of water. In half an hour she's supposed to be at The Gazette for a meeting with the women's editor who wants to talk about an assignment, feature ideas.

On the way out the door, she stops to move the table into the middle of the kitchen, which is large enough, and since Mandy and James are coming over for a few days they'll need all four places. With the table in the middle, the beat-up old kitchen looks almost festive. She takes the bread basket off the wall and throws it in the garbage. Now there's a circle of paint like a halo, about four shades lighter than the dusty beige around it. Fifteen years, she has been sitting in Jack's place, staring at a wall and a bread basket. The question is, why? She is sorely tempted to sit down at the table and think about it, the pit of her stomach is filling up with tears, but she has to leave the house immediately, or be late.

The Gazoo, as the inmates call it, is in a nondescript glass and steel building on St-Antoine. There's a monumental stone facade on St. James, now la rue St-Jacques, a reminder that Montreal's only English-language daily is very much part of the fabled WASP establishment, but the parking situation is dismal, so most people enter from St-Antoine. The walls are glass, the presses are visible from the street. An awesome pair of escalators glide up and down two storeys, connecting the street level to a guarded entrance. The glassed-in reception desk is manned by uniformed guards and about as cheery as the gateway to a maximum security prison. All visitors must sign in and wear a guest pass somewhere prominent on the chest, then be invited upstairs by the person they are summoned to see, who is normally on the phone or in the washroom, so the whole operation usually takes a good 20 minutes.

Myra wonders exactly what kind of unsavory characters this expensive security is designed to keep out. Or is it there to keep people in, make employees feel so privileged to own permanent ID cards that their fragile psyches won't break down under the strain of so little work for so much money, completely lose perspective, start writing stories about the crimes of corporate media, or expose the consummate uselessness of products touted by the advertisers. Having your photo on a badge and striding right by security must make an employee feel good, not to mention the dental plan. Any reasonably competent anthropologist could nail that one.

She is thinking these thoughts as she rides up the escalator, beside a gaggle of bloodhounds from the business section who are gliding down, no doubt on their way to a working breakfast at some posh hotel, where they will be handed annual reports full of first-class fiction, their only apprehension being a seasoned suspicion that the meeting may not be over by noon, which could push lunch into mid-afternoon and pre-empt golf. At least, that's how Myra imagines life in the fast lane of permanent employment.

She had a full-time job once, at The Gazette. She lasted two weeks. Her first assignment was a profile of an English-speaking sheep farmer from the Eastern Townships who also happened to be a card-carrying Péquiste and a Marxist. It was her idea, and she was naturally a little skeptical when the features editor agreed, but went ahead anyway and simply told the man's story. The editor didn't get it. A cigar-smoking former U.S. army major, he had a warm, patronizing manner. He made every effort to blow the smoke away from her face when he said, after the fifth red-pencilled rejection, "Look, Myra, I know what you mean, you know what you mean, but what does this story mean to the reader who, say, just got off a plane from Cincinnati?"

Cincinnati, because he was born in Cincinnati, but Myra failed to see . . .

Finally, he smiled and said, "Look, why don't you just drop the piece and get another subject? You've got a salary now, relax, it doesn't matter." So, she quit. Took a stack of notebooks, pens and paper clips with her, and that stack has been steadily replenished since the damage blew over and she snuck back in the door as a freelancer. Every time Myra meets Sergeant Cincinnati now, he either stares at his shoes or smiles like an ice-pick.

It isn't colour photo badges, she thinks, or even stock options or medical insurance for nose jobs. Most Gazette lifers are there because there's no place else to go — unless you leave town. Most have this much in common with Myra: for a variety of perverse reasons, including Joey's joie de fucking vivre, they want to be in Montreal. But there's no other English-language newspaper, except the freebie entertainment weeklies. No radio and TV jobs left, since the CBC decided to centralize English-language operations in Toronto. No cultural head offices, few permanent news bureaus, nothing about to be launched, or getting bigger, only the status quo, holding on, shrinking, making do, getting used to small-town life.

Since the PQ was first elected in 1976, more than half a million Quebec-born people have left the province, most of them English-speaking. Politics is normally blamed for the exodus, and politics does grate. But a lot of people packed up and left for money and jobs, which are more plentiful at points west and in the States. From the day she arrived, Myra liked this feeling of psychic space. She enjoys being the only person on the escalator gliding up, while other people happily head down.

You would expect, she is thinking, that a place where news is gathered and sometimes even made would hum. But carpets and the glare of computer screens have reduced the newsroom to a silent glow. Open concept had its day, now the desks are surrounded by shoulder-high padded walls. The women's editor is momentarily tied up, so Myra sits down at an empty desk and phones This Magazine in Toronto, following up a pitch she made a week ago.

Both the Cree and Inuit of Quebec are holding independent referenda on whether native peoples want to join the move, should Quebecers vote Oui on October 30. It's an outrageous idea, to ask a simple question of a people who were around long before the 60,000 European-stock residents of la Nouvelle-France were conquered by the English in 1759. Christened Indians and Eskimos by the whites, they've lopped off that misnomer, hired smart lawyers and lobbyists, and are determined to challenge francophone Quebec's 200-year-old role as most powerful Canadian underdog. This Magazine wants a story. Myra is ecstatic, readily agrees to a token fee, tight deadline, and nil on expenses.

As she hangs up the phone, Women's News beckons. Now the pressure is on to get paying work. An anti-consumer who leans left, she doesn't find it easy to come up with story ideas for a section of the paper devoted largely to consumption and health, but lately, soft news is the only freelance growth market. So, she has convinced herself to get interested in the human body and its breakdowns. Her series on breast cancer went over well. Today the editor is offering a stint as food columnist while the regular writer goes off on medical leave. Five weekly columns, for which Myra will be paid $1,500, slightly more than the staff writer gets paid each week, less if benefits are calculated.

"Just between you and me," says the editor, an earnest woman in her fifties, "we could use a few fresh ideas. Harold's getting stale. Maybe when he has his prostrate snipped, he'll get off his fat ass and dig up some interesting copy."

Harold Hand used to be an ace police reporter, but when he decided to get serious about drinking, the brass shipped him over to soft news. Originally, his columns were recipes and chit-chat about the fun of cooking, a novelty item: the hardbitten host wears an apron. But all too often he would forget some essential ingredient and people kept writing in, the worst being his legendary pommes de terre au gratin, baked at 40 degrees for 350 minutes. Some readers actually tried it. After the apology died down, he did a series on the merits of slow cooking. Harold has his following, and a diamond-studded union contract, so nothing much can disturb his sleep until retirement.

Myra assures the editor she is already thinking of colourful food ideas, not too weird, of course. Her reputation as a radical is widespread. In fact, she knows nothing about food. Standard menu in the Montreal Grant household consists of half a dozen lumpy casseroles that take about five minutes to prepare, and the rest is shopping. She has never actually read one of Harold's columns, wouldn't know the man if she fell over him at the laundromat (his column photo is ten years old), but $1,500? Sold. In the euphoria of the moment, she suddenly gets her best idea of the day, week, maybe the month. How about a piece on ovaries?

"Ovaries?" The editor frowns. Myra was hoping she'd be interested, and propose an angle, but no, the pitch still has to be pitched. She starts with a few generalities about how awful it is for women to know they don't have ovaries. Ovaries, those little almond-shaped glands that produce eggs. Is ovary removal really necessary? Out of the blue, she hears herself refer to a recent medical journal report (Reader's Digest, dentist's office), gruesome details of surgery, and within seconds the editor, feeling woozy, agrees it might be worth looking into. Anyway, she has a business lunch.

"Fine," says Myra, "I might stay around for a while and do some research, library, web site, background." The editor has no problem with Myra using her desk, chair, phone, and so the Inuit–Cree referendum story gets underway, with a few dozen long-distance calls to band councils and various honchos in the far north, on The Gazette tab.

At the desk opposite Women's News, page two columnist Moe Mikos is putting the finishing touches on an impressionistic piece about Lucien Bouchard, the former ambassador to Paris, former Conservative Party federalist, who, after a stellar career as a Canadian, woke up one day and found himself veering off onto that fairly well-travelled road to Damascus, Quebec. He became an indépendantiste, more firmly convinced than many a lifelong separatist that Quebec should pull out of Canada. He's leader of the Bloc

Québécois now, the independence party that sits in the House of Commons, but fate and strategy are quickly moving him into the leadership of the referendum campaign.

Officially, the Oui campaign is led by Premier Jacques Parizeau, a portly erudite type who speaks English with a BBC accent acquired at the London School of Economics. But Parizeau has failed to arouse passion, and his campaign is going nowhere. Out of desperation, strategists have taken a cold look at their leader and decided he can't win this one alone. Bouchard at least has the ability to bring a crowd to its feet, and unless the TV cameras get some serious wide-angle shots of a lot of people looking interested in the Oui option, the status quo is going to win hands down. The campaign started to turn in Sorel, Quebec, 50 kilometres northeast of Montreal, headquarters of Hell's Angels, one of two rival motorcycle gangs feuding for control of the underworld. That's where Lucien Bouchard launched his travelling Sermon on the Mount, and his popularity with the press and public is climbing steadily.

Moe Mikos, former freelancer turned staffer, has no natural interest in politics though he does have an eye for colour, and by mid-October the referendum has suddenly become a very colourful story. He went to Sorel for the Bouchard speech, and wants Myra to read a draft of his column, the theme being David and Goliath/Bouchard versus Parizeau. As she sits down at his terminal, he fetches coffee, and talks while she reads.

"So, what's a tie-dyed radical think of the referendum so far? You still one of them? Ah. Finished? What do you think?"

"Hmm." Myra scrolls back to his lead, shakes her head.

"Oh. That bad?"

"I'm not much of a Biblical scholar, Moe, but weren't David and Goliath on different sides?"

"You don't think the analogy works? Aren't they really fighting for power?"

"You know me. I still think some people are fighting for what they believe in. But you're probably onto something with the religious imagery. Once a Catholic, always a Catholic. Sure Quebec is secular, church-going is decidedly unpopular, but the old patterns abide. I'd say Parizeau is the Pope and Bouchard is a parish priest. People believe in the Pope, they even believe he's infallible, but they listen to their parish priest. When they listen, they obey. If they aren't listening, they'll stay home on October 30."

Mikos frowns. "Parish priest. Has that been said before? I mean, did you read it somewhere?"

"Go ahead, Moe. It's all yours," she says. "By the way, did you get a press release from Off the Main?" Moe is itching to get back at the computer screen, but she stays planted in his chair.

"Ah, no," he says.

She hands him another one. He's already well into a rewrite on his column, so she pins it above his computer, and underlines the key words in red. Moe is typing when Myra takes his chin in hand and points his gaze at the release.

"Bilingual play, opens next week, easy story."

"Yeah, yeah. I'll give you a call."

"Great. Mind if I leave a reminder on your answering machine? Moe?"

He's laughing at his lead. "Pope Parizeau. Father Lucien. Yeah, I like it."

# X

◆

The night is warm for October. It's Friday the 13th, and a goodly slice of Bohemian Plateau has decided to spend the risky moon at La Cabane. As Joey tops up his mug of St. Ambroise Rousse, the waitress brings a china plate heaped with fries. She remembered his standing order of triple mayo, six tiny paper tubs, creamy white and bordering on bland. When he asks for a cigarette, she rolls her eyes and reminds him he's supposed to quit. He takes one and vows to quit right after Godot opens, in 13 days.

"Whew, 13 days. So little time, so many words." He wipes his brow on his sweater sleeve. "Any news of Pain?"

Myra hands him the salt. "I called. We met. As per your instructions, I mentioned there might be a TV item in the bilingual Godot."

"And?"

"He laughed."

"Laughed?"

"Yeah, but he took your phone number."

With considerable difficulty, Joey resists the temptation to check his messages immediately.

Myra dips a chip in the mayo, and wonders whether Harold Hand has ever written a column about fries. Having agreed to fill in while he's indisposed, she skimmed a few back issues and noticed Hand claims to prefer a diet of obscure sea creatures, lightly broiled, and near-raw vegetables sprinkled with exotic spices. Given that Harold is about 40 pounds overweight, it's hard to believe he nibbles so wisely. She pictures him at his home computer, wolfing down a box of jelly donuts while he cribs next week's column from a pricey gourmet cookbook. A fantasy, born of guilt. She doesn't cook either, but is determined not to fake, keep it simple, write about the way people eat, not when they're on a diet or out to impress friends, but when they're busy or just plain hungry. Tonight she's thinking, why not start with fries? After all, the column theme is general. Named by the man himself, it's called Hand to Mouth.

"Hello? Hello? Anybody home?" Joey is about to open his briefcase; the prerequisite is Myra's undivided attention.

"Sorry, my mind was wandering."

"You were thinking about Pain. Come on, tell me, what happened?"

"No, actually, I was thinking about fries."

"Fries?" Joey spears three with his fork and twirls them toward his mouth. "You were actually thinking about fries while I was telling you about . . . ?"

"Your great new idea on how to get an audience? See, I was listening too."

"But you were thinking about fries."

"Yeah, I'm filling in for the cooking columnist at The Gazette, and since kitchen stuff is not my line, I've got to do some research, interview a few experts. Watching you eat made me wonder how they make the perfect french fry."

While she talks, Joey eats. His mouth is full of hot potatoes so he shakes his head vigorously and sets the fork down for emphasis.

"Myra, you're always working. I mean, always. Do you get up in the night and write things down?"

"Sometimes."

"That's terrible!"

"Why?"

"It isn't healthy."

"What do you get up in the night and do?"

"Never mind, we're not talking about me. I'm an artist. Artists always have shitty lives, and then they die."

She takes a sip of beer and holds the glass over her mouth, fairly confident he is winding up for a mono-logue on the burden of art, but he does not move off his point. "Why are you running?"

"I have to earn a living."

"You're not starving."

"Ha. You haven't seen my VISA bill. The Calgary trip — "

"Jack's a lawyer, he has tons of money."

"Jack's money is irrelevant. He funds the kids, I take care of myself. Besides, I like work. You work all the time, too. Be honest."

"Not all the time. Sometimes I spend an entire three-day weekend in bed listening to Mozart. Or the whole afternoon walking on the Mountain. Or all night cruising helplessly from one overpriced disco to the next. Yeah, okay, I've been known to exhibit symptoms of desperation, but at least I don't try to cover it up with work. Work, after all, is only work. It is not a life."

"You're saying I have no life?" When he doesn't respond, she says, "What about you? Where's your life? You're a slave to Off the Main, and we spend an incredible amount of our time talking about whether you should fold or to keep on trudging."

His half of the fries is gone, her half remains untouched. He stares at the plate and declares, "Offence is a cowardly defence. I'll say no more."

Joey and Myra have had their heart-to-hearts before, but this time he's gone for the frontal attack. Usually he needs advice, or just wants to air his frustrations. Or they replay favourite scenes from past lives and reveal secrets, shocking little insights into selves and people they both know. Attack is new, and Myra is surprised to feel anger climbing the back of her neck. The waitress arrives with another pitcher of beer, and asks whether there's something wrong with the fries. Myra says no, the fries are fine. The waitress shrugs and reaches to take the plate. Joey pulls it back.

"I'm sorry," he says, "I didn't mean to hurt."

"I'm not hurt. And for your information, at this precise moment, I'm not running."

"Oh yes you are, a hundred miles an hour. Or peddling backwards fast, away from what's really on your mind. Fries? I doubt it. It's Pain, right? Goddamit, I'm responsible for that call, something must have happened. Wait a minute, I need a cigarette. Then I want the truth."

It's hopeless bothering the waitress again, but Joey has noticed someone he knows at a table near the window — Rowan Gaunt, a poet who smokes Du Maurier Kings. They haven't seen each other since Joey convinced Rowan to take part in an all-night cabaret fundraiser for Off the Main. That was ages ago, a memorable event, and they only lost a few hundred dollars. Tonight he is sitting with his back to the wall, surrounded by two women and an older man. One of the women is a tough-looking young thing with half an inch of orange hair and no makeup whatsoever. The other is older, Rowan's age, mid-forties and dressed up for a serious night out. All three seem tense and fairly out of place at his favourite bar.

As Joey approaches the table, conversation stops. Rowan doesn't introduce his friends and it's pretty clear they would not welcome conversation with an outsider. There's a hungry look in his eyes, a look that could be interpreted as a plea. Joey asks if he's still writing and senses the guests are waiting for an answer, but all they get is a shrug and a half smile. Rowan hands over four cigarettes, and Joey says, "Thanks. If you want to join us later on, we're sitting right over there. You know Myra."

Rowan looks over at Myra. They've met. He says nothing, looks back at his friends. For an instant, Joey has the impression this man is trapped at the table and would dearly like to join them, even if it meant having to buy a ticket to *Waiting for Godot*.

"Thanks," he says, and the word comes out in a whisper. The orange-haired girl is tapping a coffee spoon into the palm of her hand.

Joey says goodbye, and they nod him out of the way. He takes a detour to the men's room and checks for messages on his cell. Nothing from Pain.

Back at the table, Myra has ordered another round of coffee. "All right, what's your scheme for packing the house? I know you're dying to tell."

As much as he'd like to get to the bottom of her far-away look, an invitation to talk about his latest idea for rescuing Off the Main from obscurity is irresistible, and Joey opens up his tattered briefcase to take out a colour mock-up of the *Waiting for Godot* poster, which has just been sent to the printers. Late, but it's in. The central image is a photograph of a naked woman hanging on a cross, the word GODOT streaked across her thighs like a censored stamp. Her body seems to be dripping wet, her hair is slicked back, and her facial features are air-brushed beyond recognition.

"What do you think?"

"Well, what does it have to do with *Waiting for Godot*?"

Joey is prepared for that question. A lot of people expect posters to sum up the work, but his taste runs more to the symbolic, which is one of the reasons Off the Main has a collection of beautiful posters for shows nobody saw. "Some people think Godot is God. Some people think God is a woman."

He waits for Myra to get it. All she sees is a cement wall and a faceless woman leaning up against what appears to be graffiti in the shape of a cross.

"Naked God?"

"Jesus! Jesus was, yes, naked on the cross. That towel around his bum was added during the Renaissance. As a

Jew, I'm a little surprised by how many myths you Christians swallow without question. Forget about the symbolism, Myra. We're moving beyond all that. Tell me the truth, this poster is dynamite, don't you think? Everybody's going to be talking about the show. This time I've ordered five thousand copies. They're ready now, and as soon as the printer lets us have them, a gang of professional poster hangers will be splashing this amazing image all over the face of Montreal."

"You've ordered five thousand posters? Joey, that'll cost a fortune."

"I know, I know. Which is why I've got to ask a small favour. Short term, very short term, we need a credit card. I will, of course, pay the interest, if you can see your way clear to lending me a little space. Noel got us a new promotional grant from the City, but it won't be in for a few weeks, you know how bureaucracy works, so if . . ."

As Joey rambles on about the bona fide solidity of his request, Myra sees the familiar fever in his eyes. Two weeks before opening night, every ounce of energy and hope has coalesced into a tremendous adrenaline rush. There is no such thing as an innocent bystander. Anybody who can help push this effort ahead will be called upon to do so. The only way to escape involvement is to run.

For a moment, Myra considers running. Half an hour ago, Joey accused her of being perpetually on the run. He meant it in a general, metaphorical way, as in why doesn't she stop, fall in love, get a life. Joey is a director, he does not teach by example. When his last girlfriend tore up his phone number, she said call if you ever get a divorce from Off the Main. According to Joey, she was jealous of Myra, or at least of the time they spent together, board meetings, strategy, La Cabane. Since Pain disappeared, they've been spending a lot more of it together. She turns the paper placemat over and scribbles a note authorizing Joey Rosenbaum to pay his printer's bill, closes her eyes and slides the plastic card across the table. He nods solemnly, folds the note around her card, and puts the lot into his briefcase.

Across the room at the Gaunt table, conversation has heated up and the once-great poet of St. Cuthbert Street is pinned to the wall, more convincingly crucified than the naked female whose job it is to create notoriety for a play about the forlorn nature of man without God. Rowan feels the nail holes, has felt them for too long now. The purpose of this encounter is to pry his body loose, carry it into a cool, dark cave, where three days later or however long it takes, he will rise from the dead and phone his mother.

The table guests are Rowan's nearest and dearest, an uncle who lives in Pointe Claire, a former girlfriend who keeps in touch, and a fiery-haired fellow poet who believes in "the work." Her name is Gay, and this gathering was her idea. She grew up in New York. It took her ages to convince his uncle and ex that Rowan desperately needed their help, even if their help might look to outsiders like a fairly aggressive assault on the loved one's dignity.

In recognition of a serious mission, they are drinking only coffee, fourth refill. Gay is leading the assault, and the other two are standing by, wide-eyed and terrified. This particular rendezvous has a name, it's called an "intervention," and is normally used on drug addicts during the last lap of a long descent; that is, drug addicts who still have friends who care enough to back them up against the wall. The friends are saying, Wake up R.L. Gaunt. Get a grip on your life.

Gay is holding forth and the other two hang their heads slightly, but not enough to let Rowan imagine they disagree. She is describing in the language of a radical young poet how the mess of his life is a crime against humanity, and the sooner he grabs hold of himself, the better it will be for all concerned. "We love you!" she shouts, and slaps him hard in the face. His uncle winces, and the ex impulsively reaches for Gay's hand.

Myra, Joey and at least two dozen other Cabane patrons stop their conversations to sneak a glance at the altercation. Rowan is oblivious to the attention. He stares up at the ceiling and his clean-shaven cheek hurts like hell. He looks at Gay, realizes she has always been quite mad, it's in everything she writes. And yet, the slap resonates through his body, exactly like Gay's chunky metallic blank verse. These raw young girls, androgynous in their manners and dress, these new girls are scary. He puts a hand to his face and looks at his uncle, who looks away. His uncle drives a soft-drink truck and bowls. Rowan thinks, tomorrow I've got to call my mother.

"What was that?" Myra asks, as the room returns to its beer.

"No idea," says Joey. "I haven't seen Gaunt since we did that all-night Spoken Word marathon. Shit, does he look rough."

"What happened?"

"He used to have tenure at Université de Montréal, teaching English literature. Then he started having an affair with the head of department, who happened to be married. She got pregnant and decided to stay with her husband. Airbrushed Rowan out of the picture. He quit the job and pretty well fell apart. He's only seen his daughter a couple of times, from across the street."

"What about the husband?"

"He's rich, he's gay, and apparently thrilled to be a father."

Myra takes another look at Rowan's table. "Ow. Theft of sperm. You know, that would make a really good story."

Joey smiles a small, wry grin. She sighs, and wishes she hadn't blurted out that thought.

Walking home later that night, Myra is pulled in the direction of a small crowd gathered around a knot of musicians in Jeanne Mance Park, an East Indian on flute, a shaggy-haired drummer and a stunning black vocalist, her eyes closed, chanting an unfamiliar African language. The air has cooled, and the grass is covered with leaves. The midnight breeze hints of fall, summer has gone for good and this delicious reprieve is little more than an echo. People who live with real winter are prone to summer worship, reluctant to admit that fall is more worthy of adulation than fickle June, blistering July, or oven August, because though fall is glorious, it is melancholy. If you are anxious or sad, October is the best month, all those fiery leaves bursting with colour before they let go.

Myra sits down on the fringe of the crowd, and someone passes her a joint. She takes a puff, and leans back on the grass. The night sky glows above with countless stars. She wishes Joey could see her now, not a single story idea in mind. She's glad he didn't squeeze her for details of the meeting with Pain, an oversight, surely. She would have had to confess it went about as well or badly as expected, depending upon which set of expectations apply. Suitable opening to a new round of not getting along. They played telephone tag for a few days, then just as she was rushing out the door, he called and in the space of a few seconds, convinced her to meet him for a drink at Winnie's later in the afternoon. That's Pain's style, same-day service. Having said yes, she was forced to reschedule an interview for the Cree referendum piece, and felt annoyed with herself.

The grass is damp and soft. The international park band is off on a hundred-mile riff, the singer's voice, low and sensuous. She is standing on a wooden platform, her body sways, lost in a song of excruciating ecstasy, swimming in music. Someone offers Myra another toke but she passes, gazes up at the stars and closes her eyes until the song ends on a round of mellow applause.

Then the singer takes a deep bow, stretches out her hand and the flute player helps her down off the box. She is blind. She takes a swig from a bottle of wine and laughs at joke from the drummer, her face wet with exhilaration. She is lost in a moment of bliss and Myra thinks, how beautiful, a blind soul radiant with song. A solitary glowing stranger, a travelling pulse. One more reason to love this big bumpy town. You are never totally alone here. The streets are alive, and green grass breathes.

The concert over, people drift away as the musicians pack up to go. Myra heads across the park, thinking maybe there is something in what Joey said about running. Although he's one to talk.

# XI

◆

They look like cancer patients but the shaved heads have given Mitch and Mandy confidence. James is bolder. He brought his own teddy bear to Sally's old room, and they stayed.

Cockroaches are a sturdy race. The first round of fumigation didn't work, so it had to be repeated. Then the landlord decided to sand the floors. The sander overheated and blew an old circuit so he had to fix the wiring. By the time the electrician had finished, the living room had to be repainted which made the apartment look so good the landlord offered Mandy $500 to sign a paper saying she had no desire whatsoever to live on rue Ste-Anne. She countered by asking for $2,500 cash. He exploded at her in Greek, said he wouldn't pay a penny more than $1,000. Then Mandy said her social worker might not be too happy to hear of a landlord threatening a single mother on welfare, maybe they should phone up the Rental Board, and that's how, in the space of ten days, she ended up with $2,000 in her backpack, but no place to live. Myra agreed they should stay on Esplanade long enough to find an affordable place without cockroaches. Make yourself at home, she said.

The transformation began overnight. Hairballs and dust were the first to go, James being allergic. Then stray clothing, magazines and newspapers started appearing in neat little piles. Picture frames and posters held up with thumbtacks were straightened. Stove grease disappeared from the spice bottles. Knives, forks and spoons no longer floundered randomly in the cutlery drawer, they lay in neat rows on sheets of shelf paper. Tea towels with holes were banished to the newly anointed rag bag, and plump new ones appeared in the designated linen drawer. Empty pickle jars were labelled for lentils, grains and various other staples. Overnight, recycling became an established religion. Myra was so busy scrambling to produce the food column, researching her feature on the native referenda and hunting up items for her regular news program at Radio Centreville that she hardly noticed, until one night she walked in at dinnertime (now a regular event) and thought, this apartment is huge.

Sunday, October 22, a week and a day away from the vote. The latest polls suggest voters are evenly split, and now both sides are operating out of desperation. The campaign is getting dirty. The Oui side has mounted TV ads that seem to ridicule the prime minister's crooked grin, and it continues a deluge of figures showing how unfair federalism is to Quebec. A counterdeluge from the Non tries to prove that Quebecers get far more out of the system than their population and tax base warrant. As usual, proof that federalism is fair and generous falls mainly on federalist ears; voters wanting out of the union are drawn to evidence that lights their view, leaving a tiny, powerful wedge in the middle.

The undecided voter comes in all shapes and sizes. One of them is small, slim, flawlessly bilingual, a smoker (though not in front of her mother), a Plateau rat with a part-time job, a place of her own and secrets to trade. Sally hasn't been back on Esplanade since Mandy and James moved in. She walks through the double living room now as if this were her first trip to the moon.

"Wow. What happened here? Where did all the junk go?"

"Nothing got thrown away," says Mandy, who is just coming out of a kitchen filled with the aroma of simmering couscous.

Myra is standing over the stove, taking notes. Her column on fries didn't fly. As usual, she overresearched and ended up writing about how to make the perfect poutine at home. An authentic Québécois contribution to artery-clogging fast food, the classic poutine has globs of cheese curds and gravy seeping down through a mound of fries. The editor looked faintly disgusted as she read the copy and suggested quietly that Myra "tone it down a little," which under further questioning turned out to mean, "cut out all references to the referendum." That anybody could weave politics into a soft slot like Hand to Mouth, the editor never imagined, but then she'd forgotten who she'd hired. Forced by deadline into a compromise, Myra is counting on couscous from a Sunday night family supper to provide the details for a self-parody — the non-domesticated woman in the presence of a good cook.

Sally breezes into the kitchen in time to catch her mother checking the spelling of turmeric from one of

Mandy's cookbooks, and for one brief moment, assumes she is responsible for the heady smells.

"Damn, I knew I should have brought my camera. This is a historic event. Did you actually make that couscous?"

Myra is about to give Mandy the credit when Mitch says, "You've got to be kidding. Mom, cook? She snared a food column in The Gazette, so she follows Mandy around and copies down the recipes."

Sally dips a spoon into the bubbling pot. "Isn't that like getting somebody to do your homework?"

Myra gives her a welcoming peck on the cheek and says, "Not at all. This is investigative reporting."

"Better watch out, with that new haircut and so much publicity for your cooking, you're going to end up popular, Ma. You might even get a date."

Mitch finds the possibility hilarious, and James joins in the laughter without understanding why. Mandy pretends to concentrate on the salad, Myra winces, and continues to copy down the list of ingredients. "For your information, smarty-asses, I've had dates, within recent history."

Sally won't let go. "Oh yeah, who? When? Do tell. Not that grey-haired hippie who makes you cry. Tell me it isn't him, please."

Myra ignores her.

"Oh sorry, taboo subject," says Sal, turning to Mandy. "Mom never lets her boyfriends sleep over. She thinks it would be a bad influence on Mitch and me."

"That isn't true," Myra protests. Mandy hands Mitch the plates and cutlery, while Sally continues her routine.

"It is true. I grew up thinking you had to be on TV to have sex. Whew, if it hadn't been for that bus trip to

Quebec City when I was 14, I would have gone to Hollywood to lose my virginity."

Myra's mouth drops open. "Bus trip to Quebec City? When was that?"

"Typical," says Mitch, nodding his naked head.

"See? She's shocked," says Sally. "On the outside, she looks like a hippie, but deep down she's a shockable old Catholic."

"I am not shockable!"

"What about drugs? Remember those lectures she gave us against drugs," says Mitch.

"Yeah, we grew up thinking marijuana was a bathroom freshener. The first time somebody handed me a joint at a party, I nearly headed for the can. Well, it's true! She smoked pot in our bathroom and lectured us on the evils."

"The evils of *excess*. I told you to be moderate."

Mandy busies herself cleaning up the counter, but without any hair to hide under, it's clear she's enjoying the tease. Mitch snorts, and uncorks a bottle of dépanneur wine. "Yeah, sure, Ma. Sally used to grow the weed in her closet."

"What!"

"Mitch, don't tell all my secrets," says Sally, taking a glass of wine.

"Okay, I won't mention that guy who used to climb up the balcony after midnight. What was his name? Romeo?"

"Don't tell me you've been reading! Shame on you, little brother. Now zip up."

"One night, he slips and falls right into the lilac bush. Cracked a rib and three branches. Mom doesn't even notice. Next day, we're sitting around the table waiting for the pizza to arrive, typical Grant family scene. Mom's reading the newspaper and listening to the radio, and I can't resist. I say, 'Wonder what happened to that lilac bush? Maybe a semi-naked volleyball player lost his balance, eh Mum?' and she says, 'Ah huh.' Sally starts turning nine shades of purple and waving her hands behind Mom's head. And I end up getting five dollars to shut up."

Sally looks at Myra to see if she believes this outlandish yet true tale. "Yeah, well you wouldn't get a cent out of me now. I have nothing to hide. Whereas Mitch has lots of juicy secrets."

"I have nothing to hide," says Mitch with exaggerated sincerity. "But just in case." He opens his wallet and hands Sally a ten-dollar bill. She takes it, laughing, and says, "Thanks."

Then dinner is served, and everybody sits down at the table except Myra who says, "Whoa, whoa, whoa. What does Mitch have to hide? And, reel back the tape, please. Lilac bush? Semi-naked — Drugs? Quebec City, 14? All this is very funny and I hope you are making it up, because . . ."

Sally casts a smile at Mandy. "Because otherwise you missed our childhood?"

The lightness of banter is starting to disappear as Mitch says, "Oh yeah, she missed it all right. We had the odd personal appearance from the award-winning radical journalist — "

"And we saw her on TV a few times."

"But otherwise, I'd say we pretty well brought ourselves up, right Sal?"

Sally nods, "Definitely. Self-raised kids. But, we turned out very well. Right Mitch?"

"Five stars. We are responsible, well-balanced, moderate dope smokers."

"Mitch can operate a keyboard."

"Sally flosses every day."

"And we both know the Best of the Beatles by heart."

Mitch sighs. "Yeah, that was a Montreal childhood. But, it's not the way I'm going to raise my kids."

Until this moment, the conversation has flown back and forth over Myra's head so fast she could do little more than gasp and enjoy the portrait of home life, apparently staged for Mandy's benefit, the aim, to get laughs. But Mitch's final remark brings the repartee to a halt.

Nobody says anything. Then Sally says, "I'm never going to have kids. No offence, James."

Thinking he's been invited into the conversation, James announces, "I'm having a whole bunch of kids. At my birthday, next year. Right, Mom?" and Mandy says, "Right."

Myra turns to Mitch. "You don't want your kids raised . . . how?"

"With an absent father and a mother who works all the time."

Surprised by the acid in her own voice, Myra replies, "Well then, you'd better find yourself a time capsule and go back to the fifties."

Mitch looks at Mandy, who lowers her eyes, as if to say, shhh.

Sally says, "Mitchy is going to reinvent *Leave It to Beaver*. We watched a few episodes in my sociology of the family class. Better take up the pipe, Mitch. Start reading a newspaper."

"Yeah well, Sally's probably going to turn into a dyke as soon as she's slept with a few hundred more guys."

"Shut up, Mitch."

The air crackles and Myra explodes. "Mitchell! Sally? There's a little boy at this table."

Now James takes offence. "I am not a little boy. I'm a big boy. Right, Mom?"

Mandy says, "Maybe I should give James his bath now. Come on, go get your towel ready, honey."

James grabs his chair, and in anticipation of more fireworks to come, refuses to move. "Sally said shut up. She's going to get in trouble, right, Myra?"

Mandy catches him by the arms, and drags him, howling, away from the delicious possibility that Sal is about to be made to stand in the corner, or worse. On the way out the door, she shoots an embarrassed glance at Myra, then looks at the floor.

"It's none of my business, Mrs. Grant, but I think you've got a really great family here. I mean, the feeling is great. I — I think everybody here probably had a really good, you know, childhood." Then she disappears.

Myra can feel tears pressing behind her eyes, and leaves the table. Sally calls after her, "Sure we did. Mom? Hey, we were only joking."

For a few minutes, she sits in front of the dead computer screen, stunned. Normally, she would have answered back in kind, cutting through any offence by telling just as embarrassing tales from her memories of their childhood, but the words made it through a hole opened up not so long ago, in Calgary, when she caught a glimpse of their secret summer life and wondered why it came as such a surprise. In the darkness of her home office, she suddenly misses them, tiny Sal, baby Mitch. Where have those little people gone?

When she goes back to the kitchen, Mitch and Mandy are clearing the table, and Sally is out on the balcony, watching an impromptu rugby match in Jeanne Mance Park. When her mother appears, she turns and starts into an explanation, but Myra cuts her off. "Sally!"

"What?"

"I know you smoke."

"Oh. . . . Can I then?"

"No."

"Mommmm, you know I didn't mean . . ."

"All right, smoke."

"I don't want to smoke."

"Sally, I command you to light up a cigarette. I've known you smoke for ages. It's your life. Go ahead, smoke!"

"Okay, okay." She takes a cigarette out of her pocket and lights up. Under the circumstances, it's hardly a thrill, but she is a smoker, and the first few puffs do ease the tension. She waves the smoke away from Myra, who sits down, still fuming, in a wobbly lawn chair. She watches the way her daughter handles the fag like a pro, and thinks of her at 14, in the back of a bus to Quebec City. She is wondering how to get into the subject of birth control and sexually transmitted disease, when Sally says, "So, how am I going to vote in this referendum?"

Under normal circumstances, Myra would consider she'd died and gone to heaven if this delicious subject dropped out of the sky, on a Sunday night, after a home-cooked meal. Sal has been adamantly apolitical since she was old enough to notice her mother buried behind newspapers. But tonight, she can only answer weakly, "That's right. You've got the vote."

Sally sits down on the chair beside her, and puts her army boots up on the railing. She takes a long drag, blows a mouthful of smoke that doesn't quite float away in the evening breeze, and says, "I might vote Oui. Yeah, pretty well certain."

"Really?"

"Yeah. Why should we be told what to do by some rubes in Ottawa? If you ask me, Quebec already is pretty independent. I mean, what is Canada, anyway? I go out to Calgary and I feel like I'm in a foreign country. Jack tried to get me to move out there. God! Not on your life. Way too many jocks. Yeah, I'll probably vote Oui, if I get around to voting."

There is a long moment of silence during which Myra tries desperately to become engaged in this first-ever political discussion with her daughter. But no matter how hard she squeezes her brain, she cannot find a significant comment to follow Sally's musings. She tries equally hard to resist blurting out what's really on her mind, but cannot.

"Did I — did I hear you say you are never having children?"

Sally slaps the side of the chair. "Don't listen to Mitch. I'm not a dyke, although so what if I was? He should talk. God, he and Mandy and little piss-pants James are starting to look like some kind of TV sitcom. It's an act I do not find convincing. How long are they staying, anyway? I hope he doesn't wet my bed, I might want to take that bed some day, if we get a bigger place. By the way, did you say I could have the piano?"

"Um, sure. You're moving?"

"Not right now, but soon, probably. I need a bigger place. I might move in with a friend of mine." The word "friend" tingles, and Myra waits for Sal to explain, but she doesn't. She finishes her cigarette, then says she'd better be going. She's got to meet a few people at the Bifteck and to wash her hair first.

"Can't believe I work and drink at the same place. You know what, the Plateau is a fishbowl. One of these days, don't be surprised if I up and take off. No, not Calgary, I mean really take off. What would you think of that?"

She is standing in the door, one hand on her hip, wearing a skimpy T-shirt and ripped jeans, looking to an anxious mother like a juicy young woman who should never, ever, under any circumstances hitchhike or walk home alone.

"Where do you want to go?"

"The moon's a bit too far. Any place else would be just fine."

And with that reassuring comment, she bends down and kisses Myra on the cheek, squeezes her arm and heads out into the night.

When she has gone and the kiss sits there like a sudden pimple, Myra wonders how she will turn this aching dinner into a light Hand to Mouth column. In fact there is no publication in her contact book that would welcome the information she has gathered here tonight, an overwhelming load. Editors want soft news, personal experience and ersatz emotion. They don't want acid moments of truth that completely blot out the memory of what was eaten. They don't want to hear about things a tired parent finds hard to swallow. At least not in a food column. She sits alone on the balcony, watching teenage boys beat each other up for control of a ball, wonders why the innocent search for soft news feels so much like a kick in the chest.

The same night, Paulette checks into the Hotel Armor, a nondescript pension on the corner of Sherbrooke and de Bullion. If she walked north a block, turned onto the pedestrian mall of Prince Arthur Street, continued up The Main past La Cabane, then took a left on Rachel and a right on de l'Esplanade, Paulette would be at Myra's front door. Indeed, that walk is on her itinerary, but not tonight.

Tonight she is taking a modest hotel room in a strange corner of her hometown, where she plans to live like a tourist, think about her life, maybe even change it, and then at the end of the week, cast her ballot in the referendum.

The desk clerk is a tired Polish woman in her mid-fifties. She reads the name on the register and says welcome in English. Used to hearing herself called Mrs. Grant, Paulette makes no effort to correct anybody in Calgary because a pronounceable name is so much easier and she hates what English people do with Chevrier. But tonight, back in Montreal for the first time in years, she feels herself slipping even further back in time. A sudden reflex action, her father's passion, brings the words to mind. She cuts the woman off.

"Vous n'êtes pas capable de m'addresser en français, madame?"

The statement startles Paulette. Like the rat-tat-tat of a woodpecker on glass, a tone she hasn't heard from herself in quite some time.

The clerk apologizes in French with a thick Polish accent, and lowers her head slightly. Her name is Annya and she has been standing behind this counter for a decade, since following her husband from Gdansk. A card-carrying member of Solidarity, he lost his job in medical research over political activity. He drinks all day. She smiles with her lips only. She does not have a vote.

"Bonne nuit, madame. . . . Pardon? . . ."

Madame wants to know if there are telephones in the room. Non, madame, but of course, messages can be left at the desk.

She looks at the leather luggage and expensive clothes and wonders why this well-heeled woman didn't check into the Queen Elizabeth. They have elevators and bellhops. Annya lets her carry two bulky suitcases up the narrow staircase, all the way to the third floor.

The room is a dark, oak-panelled box with high ceilings, old and warm, smelling artificially clean, as if the last guests just stepped out, and their mess has been swept under the carpets. A shower has been jammed into a makeshift corner room, a window overlooks the one-way street.

Paulette drops the suitcases and flops down on the double bed, weary. If the truth were to be said out loud to that chipped mirror hanging at the end of the bed, she's a little confused. The Montreal phone book includes hundreds of Chevriers, a few dozen of whom would be happy to have a surprise visit from a long-lost relative, but she has come home without making promises, checked into a cheap hotel in an unfamiliar part of the city.

She is expecting a phone call from a man named Jacques Laflamme, a building contractor who put up several of those gleaming glass and cement towers, the pride of downtown Calgary. They met at a barbecue in her own backyard. Like Jack, he roots for the Montreal Canadiens. When he came into Jack's office at the Alberta Treasury to answer a few questions about his interprovincial business activities, they got talking about the team's prospects and that's how the building contractor ended up at the Calgary Grants' annual first-day-of-summer celebration.

Jacques and Paulette spoke in French, although not too loud, or too much. She laughed at his jokes, some of which nobody but she and maybe Jack could understand. When the house was empty, Jack said the impromptu guest was a disappointment. Only had a couple of good stories in him. When the house was quiet, she had an attack of homesickness that nearly knocked her over. Her chest throbbed, so real she thought it might be a heart attack, then her whole body felt paralyzed by gloom. She had to lie down. When she closed her eyes and combed the skyline of Montreal, familiar streets, the outside of her family home, each image felt like a knife turning clockwise. In 12 years, she'd never once had it this bad. Mal du pays. Homesickness for country.

A few days later, Jacques called to ask whether by chance he'd forgotten his umbrella. A perfectly cloudless evening, no stray umbrellas. He said he enjoyed meeting her. In spite of making a sinful amount of money in Alberta, he said he missed Montreal too much, and was on the verge of moving back. She said, I know what you mean. Send me a postcard. A few weeks later, he did. Sealed in an envelope, addressed only to her, Place Jacques-Cartier in summer, his office phone number scribbled on the back.

She has the postcard in her purse. Her purse is sitting on the bed in the same hotel Jack and Myra stayed in years ago, when they came to Montreal on a scouting trip before the move from Ottawa. Jack told Paulette all about that trip. As men do, he told the story honestly and it seemed so romantic. The telling left Paulette with the pit of a mystery. She resolved to crack it someday, get to the heart of Jack and Myra, what went wrong.

Paulette believes Jack was jealous of his kids, how much attention they took up. So she put off having any. It's too late to overcome that fear now, but she is stuck on the mystery of Myra, which is what this trip is about. Except that she also has the postcard, and an equally fierce, totally contradictory urge, to forget all about foggy Jack and move back home to Quebec.

Hotel Armor. Not very romantic. Somehow, she always thought he'd said Hotel Amour. Slip of his tongue, or trick of her ear? Might have made a difference, once. But it's too late now. Unfinished business deals with memory, not truth.

# XII

◆

Tuesday night, the 24th of October, Myra's late great lover is on CBC, live from the Verdun auditorium, where twelve thousand passionate federalists have gathered to celebrate the status quo and hear Prime Minister Jean Chrétien promise that if only enough people vote for the status quo, a lot of things are going to change.

A full hall under the hot lights of TV always looks impressive; even the nay-sayers are surprised by their own numbers. Now the campagne is on fire. People are scared. People are excited. The long-time-convinced will be compelled to get off their bums and vote. The unde-cided will be prevailed upon to choose. Finally, every-body remembers why Quebec is still the centre, even with a swampwater economy and no new arguments and few new faces behind the old debate, because the future is open, potent, dangerous. People leave their homes to shout about it.

The camera is close up on Pain who's had his hair trimmed for the occasion, though he refuses to wear a tie. He called Monday night, wondered why he hasn't heard from her, not a trace of irony in his voice. Now Myra watches the twinkling eyes, the serious tilt of the head. He's supposedly talking to Peter Mansbridge, but his real audience is a million thirsty women. He is explaining the mood of the hall to each and every one of them. TV is Pain's medium. High recognition factor, almost no typing required.

As the news moves to the rest of the world, the phone rings. It's him. "Did you happen to be watching TV?"

"As a matter of fact, yes."

"Well?"

"The series has definitely gone downhill this season. Starting to parody itself. *Hill Street Blues* was so much better."

"You were watching an American soap?!"

"Drama."

"Any idea what happened tonight?"

"Oh, you meant Verdun? Yeah, I especially liked the part where you referred to the prime minister as cretin."

"I didn't say cretin."

"Check the instant replay."

"Feel like a beer?" She does, but Joey is into the dark tunnel of tech week, countdown to Godot's premiere on Thursday. She promised to meet him at 11 for a morally supportive pitcher, but Pain doesn't care. "Meet me at Winnie's in ten minutes."

"No, not downtown. Else's, corner of de Bullion and Roy."

"What's that, some kind of milk bar? Elsie the Cow?" Pain hates the Plateau, considers it an unshaven armpit crawling with would-be artists and welfare recipients. Sure, it was great when he lived there 30 years ago, when he was a student at McGill. But since he left, the neighbourhood has gone downhill steadily.

She says, "I'm meeting Joey. Feel free to join us."

Else's is dark green and cozy, with two walls of windows facing quiet streets, ten tables and a clientele that normally arrives around nine and stays put till closing time. When she gets there, Joey and his gang are at a table near the piano, which is not yet being played. There's already a waiting list for the pool table. Pain is sitting at the bar, talking to the waitress. When she touches his shoulder, he throws an arm around her waist and gives her a tug against his thigh, then kisses her on the lips. She doesn't exactly kiss him back and doesn't say hello. Instead, "So, who do you think's going to win?"

He knows what she means but pretends otherwise. "I don't think poor old Joey ever had a chance. Anyway, isn't he gay?"

Never in a million years will Pain be convinced that Joey doesn't have a thing for Myra. He cannot imagine how two people could spend so much time together without getting around to sex. Pain always gets around to sex, but then he gets over it.

From a corner table on the other side of the room, Joey has noticed the kiss/hug and feels confident it means he's going to appear on national TV very soon. It's nice to know people who know people, and who are in the mood to be nice to the people they know. He makes a mental note to do something for Myra as soon as he's famous, to introduce her to a really amazing man, somebody with a lead in a series, or part of the Stratford Company, somebody younger and smarter than Pain.

"I was of course talking about the referendum," says Myra.

"Oh, of course. Cakewalk for the No."

"How can you be so sure?"

"Instinct."

Myra frowns. "Cakewalk? You mean something like 60 per cent?"

"At least. Every ounce of Oui support has already come forward. The last-minute rush will all be Non. I like your haircut."

Pain doesn't think Quebec independence has a snowball's chance in hell. In his opinion, Montreal peaked in the sixties, with Expo, the Quiet Revolution, folk-rock singers, poets and radicals, people like him who took advantage of the bargain-priced elegance of inner Montreal created by the departure of so many normal people for the suburbs. He and his generation of anglo arrivals, dope-smoking fellow travellers, flocked to the McGill Ghetto, a hub of cheap apartments surrounding Montreal's most prestigious bastion of WASP money and power, radicalized in those days by poet/professors. Leonard Cohen lived on the Plateau then, he was taking Suzanne down by the river when Pain was editor of the McGill Daily. F.R. Scott taught him law and Hugh MacLennan, literature. He claims to have attended philosophy of law lectures with future prime minister Pierre Trudeau at the Université de Montréal. He heard Pauline Julien and Gérald Godin recite poetry to a handful of hippies in the Carré St-Louis, and like so many in his generation, became convinced that a Canada without Quebec would be a Canada without a soul.

He is scathing about the petty side of cultural politics in Quebec, headline wars and official harassment over the size of French words on signs, and all of this has given him a huge dose of contempt for the current generation of sovereignists. He thinks independence would be economic suicide for Quebec. It would also be the end of history, at least history that involved Pain. And nobody can take away the memories he and his well-placed Toronto friends accumulated here in the sixties. They'll fight to make sure that personal past remains part of a significant, ongoing history, from sea to shining sea.

Myra thinks he is cynical and addicted to the drug of nostalgia. He thinks she is clinging to a naive dream that died a long time ago. She thinks he is potentially a truly great journalist who should sit down and write something important instead of coasting on hollow TV gigs. He thinks she's a talented reporter whose political blind spot has held her back from moving to Toronto and getting a real job. From time to time, these debates burst into passion. But they always end badly. Which is to say, they never end.

Joey, according to Pain, is a waste of time. If he had any talent at all he would move to Toronto. In fact, anybody with talent should move to Toronto, like he did, 25 years ago, where he landed a string of top media jobs, made money, friends and enemies, before punching out the president of a major television station at a cocktail party. The subject was Canadian content regulations, or the president's trophy wife, or a bit of both. The last of many straws, it got him fired from his high-profile column at the Toronto Star. For a while he tried freelancing, but couldn't abide the fact that people now took half a day instead of half an hour to return his calls. So in 1992 he declared Toronto was on its way down, and fled.

He bought a loft in Old Montreal and got a five-figure advance to write a tell-all book about the Canadian media which, according to the bits Myra has read, should pretty well finish off his once-brilliant career if he ever gets it finished. That's the side of Pain Myra likes, dedication to an ideal, even if it is a fairly fizzy ideal, like revenge. A man in a hole over an ideal. She has a weakness for ideals, and men in holes. What she cannot see in a mirror, she sees in Pain's eyes, or its what she thinks she sees.

He orders another two-for-one scotch and hands her half. "So, is your phoney friend still opening his existential tragedy next week?"

"You mean the bilingual *Waiting for Godot*? Yes, Joey and the cast are sitting right over there."

"I noticed. Have they heard any more from the Beckett estate?"

"Not sure. I know Joey's father has asked his lawyer to look into it." In fact, the estate scandal is going nowhere, not a word out of the great man's people, but Myra doesn't want to be drawn into the demise of Joey's favourite scheme.

Pain glances over at the theatre table, and laughs. "I wouldn't be at all surprised if he cooked up the controversy himself. Were you, by chance, involved?"

"No! Anyway, I don't think a lawsuit over rights is the real story."

"Oh no? What is the real story, Lois Lane?"

"Bilingual *Waiting for Godot* on the eve of the referendum, on The Main, dividing line between English and French. Mood of the moment, could be a great peg for the kind of story you do well."

"You mean a slick, vacuous colour piece that takes one phone call?"

She might have said something to that effect in the past, doesn't deny her sharp tongue, presses on. "You don't even have to make one call. He's right over there."

Watching television may have the effect of saltpetre on civilization, but being on it always puts Pain in an amorous mood. He has known this earnest single mother for three years, thinks she'll be just fine as soon as she gets rid of her obnoxious kids and stops wasting time on fringe journalism. In fact, tonight, under the double-scotch glow of an October night, he is remembering all the things he likes about her, and out of homage to past good times and hope for the night ahead, he agrees to put up with Joey the budding Broadway magnate.

Myra does the introductions, and Noel, the ever-ready stage manager, launches into a glowing assessment of one of Pain's TV columns in The Mirror, a 600-word vehicle for personal grudges that Pain formulates sitting in his big leather chair with a drink while flitting around the multichannel universe. The fee barely covers his weeknight bar bills, but he enjoys the local notoriety. He glows as Noel gushes.

Being francophone, Francine and Emmanuel have never heard of the big Toronto media face, so they ignore his arrival and chat away in French. To Davies, Pain is an important contact. He wiggles into the chair next to him and starts on a string of stories involving himself and other famous people. Joey leans over to Myra and wants to talk about the latest snags in Godot, how Emmanuel is out of control, Davies cannot remember his lines, keeps adding bits of Shakespeare, and Pozzo? Don't ask.

About two minutes into Davies' first anecdote, Pain gets up to leave, but just then the waiter calls Noel's turn at the pool table, and Noel offers a cue to Pain, who takes them both and tosses one to Joey, who nearly misses the toss.

By the flash of his green eyes, Myra knows exactly what Pain has in mind for Joey. "Wait a minute," she says. "It's Noel's turn at the table."

"Oh, that's okay," says the accommodating Noel. "You go ahead. I'll watch."

"How about doubles?" says Pain. "Come on Myra, you and me against art."

"And deny myself the fun of beating you? Ha. No. How about Francine and me against you and Joey?"

Pain looks over at Francine, who, incredibly, he had not noticed until now. She is wearing a tight jersey, and her red hair is slicked back by gel. He agrees. From the moment Francine and Myra pick up their pool cues, it's obvious they're the entertainment, not the competition. The game is still between Joey, who wasted a goodly chunk of his angst-ridden youth in pool rooms, and Pain, who took the trouble to learn a few fancy shots. He does not want to look bad. Joey does not want him to look bad. He wants Pain to feel good and do that TV piece on his show.

On her way to the chalk, Myra leans into Joey's ear and whispers, "If you play anything less than your best game, I will never speak to you again."

"I know," says Joey. He takes off his sweater.

Suddenly in an exuberant mood, Pain buys a round of Scotch for everybody. With the exception of Davies, nobody in the theatre crowd even likes that hairy-chest beverage, but then they weren't given a choice and will never turn down a freebie. The waiter serves and the game begins.

Pain breaks, then stops the game to give Francine some pointers on how to hold her cue. Both ladies miss their first shot, their opponents sink one ball each, albeit Joey's is a difficult back shot which he calls in advance. Noel says, good one, and Pain's concentration soars. He sinks three balls on a single turn, clever shots that bring the game close to a finish. Joey looks faintly relieved. He may yet be on national television and not look like a self-serving wimp to Myra. She's so hard, he's thinking. And at the same time, so innocent.

It's Myra's turn, and she takes her time chalking the end of the pool cue. "By the way," she says to Pain, who is negotiating another scotch, "did you notice Francine's photo in the Godot poster?"

Noel just happens to have one, and unfurls it to show the assembled. No, the TV journalist had not noticed it was her, from this particular angle. He looks at the naked Christ, then at Francine, and smiles. Myra watches for a hairline fracture in his concentration. He lifts his eyes off the table and says, "Vous avez de très beaux seins, mademoiselle."

Francine laughs, leans over to ask Myra who he is. She describes him as a journalist from Toronto, and Francine says, "Ah, bon." Then Myra whispers a plan, and Francine nods yes.

"By the way, is there any rule against combining talents?" Myra directs the question at Noel, who has been watching sagely.

"What do you mean?" he says.

"Could we play together, instead of alternating turns? Double up?"

Noel frowns and says he thinks that's against the rules but Pain overrules. Myra whispers to Joey, who sits down at the piano and begins to play a slow tango. People turn to watch as Myra and Francine approach the table in time to the music, their bodies clamped together around the cue, each with a hand on the end as if they meant to dance the ball into a pocket. They lean on the table, strain to reach for what should be a fairly easy shot, but since neither has popped one in the hole yet, spectator confidence is low. Joey's tango reaches a climax, Pain watches from behind, as both women lift a leg off the floor and stretch out beside each other on the pool table. The whole bar is watching now, a few catcalls and some advice. Noel calls for silence.

Eyes fixed on the ball, Francine and Myra count down in French. At zero, they nudge the cue forward and the ball rolls obediently into a pocket. Half the room has gathered round, and the applause includes cheers. Pain smirks. When she is sure she has his eye, Francine takes Myra's face in her hands and gives her a juicy victory kiss. They throw their arms around each other, happy fists into the air. Then it's Pain's turn.

The fracture in his concentration is wide, but he's confident. It's way too late for a theatrical turn around in this game, with one shot, he can win. Enough people are following now to make his turn a performance. There's an obvious shot, but he picks a long one, and drives the cue hard, sending the intended ball smack into a far pocket. But, the rebound brushes the eight ball and sewers it in the side pocket.

"Eight ball down, game to Francine and Myra!" says Noel, above cheers from the audience.

Pain grins, bows. He hates to lose for any reason, but if he has to lose, will do so with a flourish. He goes over to tell Francine he's seen her in the mutual funds commercial. A friend of his is up from L.A., doing some TV movies, maybe she'd like to meet him? Francine definitely would, and gives him her card. He slaps Joey on the back and suggests they all go back to his loft, claiming the cigarette smoke is making him ill. Emmanuel is tired, insists he and Francine leave, but Joey accepts the invitation. Pain ignores him and follows Myra out the door.

The night air is brisk as they step out onto the street, Myra heads down Roy toward St-Laurent, on her way home. Behind her, Pain jumps around to the curbside and says, "Please, let me play the gentleman. How about a nightcap? I've got a great view of the river. Maybe you don't remember."

"I prefer the Mountain."

"That's a phase. You'll get over it."

"Never."

"Sure you will. Someday you'll wake up and that pathetic excuse for a landform will look like a great big pimple, and you'll take the next plane, train, bus out of here."

She picks up her pace, and declares to the sidewalk, "I'll never leave Montreal. It's the best city in the world."

"How long have you been living here?"

She says, "Fifteen years."

"And still in love. That's impressive."

When they reach St-Laurent, she stops walking to signal goodnight, and shoots straight into his eyes, "I'm not in love, I'm just living, that's all. Anyway, what is love? You once said, never use a word unless you know exactly what it means, and you've checked feeling against reason, a.k.a. the *Oxford English Dictionary*."

For the first time, Pain looks a little sheepish. "I said that?"

She answers softly, "I wrote it down."

"All right then," he says, "love is a disease that makes people blind and deaf. They can't feel pain. You've got it bad, for Montreal. Your life is hard, you aren't making any money or covering any big stories. No man buys you flowers, but you trudge on, volunteering your heart out for asexual Joey and writing earnest pieces for little magazines nobody reads. Why? Because you are in love with the illusion of a city that once was great. You are asleep beside the Mountain."

"I'm sleepy, but not asleep."

He takes her hand. "I say, let me take you down by the river. The river flows west to east."

"Actually, it flows northeast."

Her heels hit the pavement hard. "Why did you come back, if Montreal is dead?"

"I'm not in love. I can leave any time."

"You always make things sound so simple."

"Things always are, when you give up on bullshit."

"Ha! That'll be the day, when *you* give up on bullshit," she says, and turns to go. He still has her by the hand, and follows.

"Why do you always run away from difficult questions, Myra?"

"Because I'm a journalist, I prefer to ask the questions." She keeps walking and he walks beside her, swinging their arms like schoolmates.

"Fair enough. If I walk you home, will you invite me in for a drink?"

"I thought you didn't do domestic scenes. Or don't you remember? Last time you got invited in, when I woke up the next morning, you were gone."

"Oh. I didn't know we were talking breakfast. Okay, I'll make breakfast."

"I think the subject was, the last time we saw each other."

"We saw each other two weeks ago, when you came down to Crescent Street for a drink and tried to talk me into publicizing your friend's play. Although I always enjoy your company, that was not a totally productive end-of-afternoon. All right, let's make a deal. I'll forgive you for trying to use me, if you overlook that, um, middle-of-the-night departure. To tell you the truth, I'd totally forgotten."

By the time they get to her staircase, last year seems like a long time ago.

"Are you inviting me in?" he asks, folding both hands around hers.

When she doesn't answer, he reaches into the bush beside them, snaps off a naked branch, hands her a wintry peace offering. She thinks of Sally's volleyball player, who fell three storeys into the lilacs, smashing ribs and taking half the bush down with him. She thinks of how hard they hit about their endless self-styled childhood, looks at the man standing with one foot on the bottom step, and for the moment, she does not see the angry tracks behind him.

"Leave the twig," she says, and turns to head upstairs.

Paulette is sitting on a bench in Jeanne Mance Park, looking up at the lights in Myra's apartment. She has spent the past two days shopping and walking around familiar landmarks and getting ready to call her family. She visits from every year or so. This time, the city looks run down, defeated, as if paralyzed by some unnamed virus. Montreal is familiar, and at the same time, changed almost beyond memory. Once, she cried openly on the street corner. At other moments, she felt she had never lived here.

Now she watches a man and a woman walk up a staircase, and wonders why should she care what Jack's long-ago wife thinks or does? Myra has a life, children, a view of the Mountain. There are mountains in Alberta, real ones. But every time Paulette looks at the Rockies, she thinks of Montreal. She would like to purge herself of that association. A gust of wind blows leaves around her boots, and suddenly she is homesick for Calgary, for the house they conquered inch by inch, for Jack, who touches her hair in his sleep.

When Myra and Pain reach the door at the top of the inside staircase, they hear African drums and squeals of delight. Inside, the electric lights are out, the room lit by dozens of candles, and the bald trio of Mitch, Mandy and James are dressed in matching boxer shorts and neon T-shirts, dancing up a downpour. James greets them at the door with a shriek. Mitch turns the music down and Mandy stands immobile in the middle of the room.

Pain insists on shaking Mitch's hand. Myra introduces Mandy, who nods shyly and catches James by the elbow to slide him off to bed. Mitch puts all the lights on, starts talking excitedly about his new CD. Pain has heard of the band, and they discuss worldbeat for a few minutes, then Pain says he's got to be going.

Myra walks him down a flight to the door, because it doesn't lock without an inside turn of the key.

When he is outside the door, she says, "Guess you suddenly remembered your curfew, eh?"

He shrugs. "You've got a full house."

"Yeah."

"Look, it's none of my business, but I'd say the little mother in there is high on something serious. Did you notice the eyes?"

Myra has the door closed, all but an inch. "She's always a little dreamy."

"Whatever. Anyway, I'll call you," he says, and heads down the stairs.

She closes the door, and goes back upstairs, where Mitch is scraping candlewax off the hardwood floor.

# XIII

◆

Off the Main's public headquarters is a black box theatre a few blocks east of St-Laurent, formerly the loading shed of a lucrative sweatshop, now a performance co-op. A hundred and six hard-backed seats sit on a steep grid overlooking a cavernous stage with a 20-foot-high ceiling and a handful of temperamental lights. The set for Godot consists of a pile of rocks and a single dead tree, all of it hauled down from the Mountain just after closing time on a rainy night.

Mid-afternoon, a CBC crew has nearly finished packing up, Joey is glowing with a mixture of radiance and panic. He just had his nose professionally powdered and spent ten minutes in front of a camera talking about the socio-political-cultural significance of bilingual theatre on the eve of the referendum. Retelling Off the Main's creation myth has boosted his morale, but tonight is opening night and the idea of facing a public makes him queasy. He's on his tenth cigarette when Myra walks in, carrying an armful of freshly photocopied press kits.

"I owe you big," he whispers, gleefully. "The Pool Shark came through."

"He's here?"

"You just — ah-ough, excuse me — missed him. They've gone off to shoot some pro-federalist rally downtown."

Myra hands Noel the press kits and pours herself a coffee. For about five seconds, her forehead tingles with the absence of Pain, not unlike the sensation of waking up in the morning and finding him gone. Or walking into a room, feeling sure robbers have been there, wondering what's missing. She makes an effort to sound neutral. "So, he's doing an item on Godot?"

"Hard to tell," says Joey. "We talked about the show, then they shot some footage of Francine standing in front of that wall of posters outside. He may not play up the Beckett scandal. But, hey, there's no such thing as bad publicity. Right?"

She shrugs, and goes over to the phone to check her messages. The editor of This Magazine read a wire story about a contingent of Inuit from northern Quebec turning up for the rally and wonders if she could check it out. As predicted, the Cree referendum came down heavily against being part of an independent Quebec, and now the Inuit are on the verge of their vote. She had no plans to attend a whipped-up media opportunity, but the editor says he's holding space in case she wants to add a reference. The November issue goes to print tomorrow.

Around her, the collected talent of Off the Main performs like a small aircraft in freefall, a dozen souls intent on surviving the eight p.m. landing. Actors gurgling, costume designer sewing, lights on, off, up, down; sound levels, same. Davies and Emmanuel are going over their lines, and Noel is prancing around with a clipboard list of things to do, telling everybody to remain calm. The tech crew was supposed to repaint the floor black last night, but somebody forgot to give them the key, so they're about to slap on a quick-drying coat now.

Though it's hot under the stage lights, Bill Davies is wearing a heavy winter coat (his costume) and he smells of booze. There's a couch in the dressing room. Noel suggests he use it but Davies insists he's going down to Place du Canada to show his support for national unity. Anyway, a lot of people from Toronto will be watching the evening news. He plans to be seen.

At the mention of the rally, Emmanuel flops down on the couch, covers his face with a pillow, and groans, "J'en ai assez des fédéralistes," which prompts the unbilingual Davies to inquire whether Emmanuel wants to come with him.

"I think that was a no," says Noel. Then, holding up his index finger thoughtfully, "Remember, we agreed not to talk politics. This is a sensitive time for all of us, but, 'the play's the thing to catch the conscience of the King.'" And he disappears into the washroom.

Emmanuel removes the pillow. "What was it he said?"

"Shakespeare," says Davies, topping up his tea with gin.

"Ah bon."


The sidestreets are jammed with pedestrians when Myra and Davies get to the rally. As the editor predicted, dozens of buses with Ontario plates are parked around the square. For an instant, Myra's reminded of the Port Hope fall fair, swarms of spiffed-up locals heading up to the fairground, wondering whose apple pie and Holstein will take first prize this year. But the curious feature of this crowd is that nearly everybody is either young, or old, about 80 per cent seniors and students, with a small spill-out from nearby offices. The elderly are dutifully well behaved, the young are happy to have an impromptu day off school.

When they reach the square, Davies seeks out a TV camera crew and decides to position himself nearby for the duration. Myra strolls off in the opposite direction, wondering if she'll bump into anybody from Port Hope. Somewhere in the distance on a podium too low to be seen through the crowd, the prime minister is making a speech. She can tell it's him by the jagged boom of his voice, but can't make out the words or even be sure which official language he is speaking.

Later tonight, official estimates of the crowd size will vary wildly. Radio-Canada will put the numbers in the tens of thousands, and offer viewers sparse images, while the CBC camera will sweep by the thickest bulge and estimate six figures. In Myra's reality, this event is the strangest of public gatherings, a protest without a centre. Curiosity, concern, goodwill — these mild sentiments do not a rousing uprising make. And yet, she is drawn by the pensive mood. She was counting on a cheering crowd to boost her energy, make her mad or make her laugh. Instead, the multitude's uneasiness is contagious.

She sits down under a maple tree at the edge of the crowd and closes her eyes, suddenly overcome with fatigue. At the other end of the square, as she drifts toward sleep, there is a cheer from the crowd around the podium. In this semi-conscious state, her limbs seems to float with the clouds, until the light is broken by a shadow and she feels someone watching her. She hears a click, forces her eyes open in time to see a camera lens being pulled back by a man in a blue T-shirt.

"I'm sorry," he says. By now he is standing a couple of yards away. Myra recognizes the face. When she doesn't speak he says, "Rowan Gaunt? Friend of Joey's? We met at the poetry marathon?"

His questions sound like excuses. She sits up straight and says, "Oh, yes."

"Hope the camera doesn't bother you. It's a new toy. I get carried away."

The last time Myra saw Rowan he was slumped over a table at La Cabane, looking like a small-time hood on the lam. She remembers Joey saying he was obsessed by a woman and her campaign to ruin his life, something about a child. She thinks he looks a little better now, like he's had some sleep and a haircut.

"Guess I'd better get a telephoto lens," he says, laughing. "One step at a time."

By now Myra has climbed to her feet and brushed the leaves off her jeans. "Are you covering this for somebody?"

"Oh no, just a hobby." They stand like that for a moment, and for the life of her, Myra cannot think of a thing to say, so she says she'd better be going. Rowan nods. "If you see Joey, tell him I'm having a referendum bash. BYOB. He knows the address. And ah, feel free to drop by."

"Sure," she says, "thanks."

As she walks away, she feels the camera lens aimed at her back, hot like the glare of a thousand eyes. But when she turns around to look, there is no one under the maple tree.

A good 80 people show up for opening night of *Waiting for Godot*, most of them expecting to see a naked woman onstage. A contingent from Emmanuel's theatre class turns out to support him, wildly dressed young grungers whose ebullient voices increase the energy in the lobby by about 300 per cent. Bill Davies' mother has rounded up her entire bridge club. Fierce, grey-haired ladies and a smattering of fragile gents, they arrive together half an hour before curtain time, purses and pockets brimming with hard candy, which they intend to unwrap and suck on as soon as the play begins.

At a quarter to eight, a natty gay couple makes an unscheduled attempt to buy tickets, which throws Nancy, the box office girl, into a tizzy. Everybody else is getting in free. She can't find the roll of tickets they will use once the show is up and running, so she has to call Noel, who has better things to worry about and growls, "Take the money and stamp their hands."

The gents don't much like the idea of having their bodies inked, and shrink toward the door, grumbling. Myra brings them back, suggests Nancy stamp their programs instead, and Noel nods them on through the door.

At one minute to curtain, Pain arrives with a short, bald man, claiming he phoned ahead to reserve two tickets with his credit card. Noel says he didn't get that message, and anyway they don't take cards. Noel's mouth drops open as Myra quotes the price of admission at $25 each, and Pain hands over cash. They go in, and the doors are officially closed. She takes a seat in the back row, beside the booth, and the house lights go to black.

Joey leans over to whisper, "The Gazette is not here."

Myra whispers back, "What about the French critics?"

"Lise Lamotte, Le Devoir. . . . Is she a critic?"

"Sort of."

He whispers, louder, "Is she a *theatre* critic?"

"No."

"Ah!"

"Shhh."

And the show begins. Not *Waiting for Godot*, not yet. First Joey's sketch about the theatre critic and the Russian whore, the price he had to pay for getting Myra onside with her media connections, a price he secretly longed to pay.

Written in the form of a mini film script, the sketch is an ironic tango about art versus criticism, passion versus reason. Art walks onstage in the form of a Russian whore, played by Sue, a nubile young actress who also does administration. Emmanuel is the critic, tall, cold, erudite, desperate. Davies stands by the Godot tree, and in a rich mid-Atlantic Shakespearean voice, reads everything in italics, telling people where the camera travels and how the actors feel. While Sue and Emmanuel trade pithy insults and move slowly toward each other, Davies gets the laughs. Eventually, of course, the combat turns into seduction. Insults become anxious whispers. The whore's blouse melts away, the critic drops his penlight. Just as their thighs are about to touch, the theatre snaps into darkness. A few seconds of silence, then Emmanuel trips over Davies, trying to get offstage. People assume it's part of the show and laugh.

When the lights come back on, the audience applauds loudly. They hadn't expected sex from a familiar comedy of the mind. The applause is too much for Joey, who has to leave the theatre.

Then a pause. Shuffling. And Godot begins.

Enter Davies as Estragon, hopping on one foot, trying to get his boot off. He falls over, and the audience laughs. Enter Emmanuel in the hobo's costume, his cheek smeared with black paint. Unfortunately, the last-minute coat of paint was not quick-drying, and that thump at the end of the sketch was his face hitting the floor. Now every step the actors take is imprinted on their shoes, or on whatever part of their person happens to connect with the floor. People think it's a concept, but Noel is sweating with rage.

Davies speaks first. "Rien à faire."

Emmanuel answers back testily. "I'm beginning to come around to that opinion."

A burst of laughter from the darkness. Nobody knows quite why they are laughing, but from that first moment, Joey Rosenbaum's bilingual Godot is a comedy. It is also a duel. As soon as Emmanuel realizes his co-star is playing for laughs, his actor's instinct sends him in the opposite direction. He is determined to play tragedy, but it's too late. The space between them begins to grow. Emmanuel makes a few quick changes in his movements around the stage, and this throws Davies off, compounding his opening night jitters by real fear that this performance is out of control, not what they rehearsed. He begins to shake, hands first, then voice. The laughter for Davies' mugging turns slightly derisive, then Emmanuel loosens up and it's clear he has control of the evening.

Though audience members don't suspect this performance has turned into a duel of egos between two actors, they cannot help but feel the energy created by the tension onstage. Since the actors are switching back and forth between English and French, according to Joey's adaptation, the audience has to assume this tension has something to do with language. They read the play as a comment on the times. Two testy old friends stuck at a crossroads, hitting each other with words.

By intermission, Davies has sweated off half a litre of gin and throws himself on the dressing room couch.

"Son-of-a-bitch! Creep! Murderer! Pepsi frog killer!" he howls.

Noel tells him to keep it down, the walls are thin, but when he sees Emmanuel he starts up again, and offers to kill him right after act two, unless he agrees to keep to the original blocking as set down by the director.

"You're throwing me off!" he bellows.

"You were never on," says Emmanuel, icily.

Davies beats the pillow. "You're trying to ruin me out there, you goddamn separatist."

Emmanuel sniffs, "C'est quoi ton problème, calisse?"

"How'd you like to get a head butt from a tête carrée? Okay, here you go, tabernac de pepsi!" And at that, Davies attempts to leap off the couch and lands on the floor. Blood gushes from his nose. Joey, who has been hiding out at the bar, rushes into the dressing room. Sue starts crying because she had a good time in the Russian whore sketch and now imagines the worst. Noel fetches ice cubes for Davies' nose while Emmanuel continues to mutter obscenities at him in French and Davies howls about the stain on his costume. The room is a shambles but the normally suicidal Joey has rarely been more calm. The spectre of imminent immolation clears his head, and he drops to his knees on the blood-smeared floor, raises his arms in the air.

"That — what you did out there — on stage — that performance — Emmanuel? William?"

All eyes are on Joey. He lets a stage minute pass.

"That was brilliant. Exactly what we've been groping for these past few weeks. Did you check the audience?"

"Maudit anglais, stuffing their mouths with candies. I hear nothing but the papers coming off," says Emmanuel. "There was snoring in the front row."

Joey ignores him. "They are riveted. Never, ever, in my wildest imagination did I imagine your Godot would be so, so, so . . . right. Now clean up this mess, get out there, and, and, what can I say? Do exactly what you've been doing. Keep it. Keep it. Feel your way. Keep the energy up. You are brilliant. All of you. I'm blown away."

Then he gets up off his knees, leaves the dressing room, shuts the door on a thumbs-up gesture, and bolts for the street, where he starts to hyperventilate. Myra sees him leave and follows. He is gasping for air when she grabs his elbow and starts hitting him on the back. "Joey, what happened?"

"Choked. I'll be fine."

She hands him a Kleenex, and asks, "What do you think of the show so far?"

He blows his nose and spits on the street. "You know I never watch opening nights."

"Right, well get back in there. Pain brought some guy from a film company. He wants to meet you."

As they walk back into the crowded lobby, Joey asks, "How did the first act go?"

She takes her time to answer. "I'd say it was, ah, mysterious. You definitely have everybody's attention."

As Joey goes over to greet the film producer, Myra gets a beer and drifts through the crowd, listening. People are talking about the difficulty of finding a parking spot on the Plateau, about how unseasonably mild it is for October, the merits of hip replacement, and one golden-age gent is telling another about a web site that promotes Russian whores. The French acting students are talking about Emmanuel, about whether he is or is not the best actor in their graduating class, surely the most ambitious, about voice work at Radio-Canada, about who did well at the TNM audition for Hamlet and what Denys Arcand is up to next. Godot and the referendum are nowhere. Some of the other invited guests have good things to say about the play, and a lawyer Myra's trying to get on the board of directors wants to know what time it's over.

Lise Lamotte spies Myra across the room, makes her way over and gives a full account of the documentary she's working on. Then she asks if Davies is Jewish. Myra says no.

"Hmm, that would have been great," Lise says, sotto voice. Noticing Myra's quizzical look she adds, "I'm writing about this for my column. It's . . . interesting."

Noel flashes the lights and Myra goes into the tiny kitchen behind the bar to find Joey and insist he watch the second act.

"They like it," she says. "Your instinct about this show making or breaking the company may have been right. Did you meet that film producer?"

"Yeah, he wanted Francine's agent's number."

"Is that all?"

"He liked the sketch."

As the last of the audience goes back into the theatre, Pain and his producer friend walk out the door. Joey shrugs, and they slip back inside for act two.

The lights go down and nothing happens. At first people think it's a concept. Then a woman in the front row says, what's happening? Candy wrappers rustle and somebody giggles. Joey and Myra look over at the lighting board and notice the operator is frantically pulling switches. He is having a muddled conversation with Noel who is backstage on headphones. The lighting board has broken down. Finally, just as the crowd becomes seriously restless, Emmanuel and Davies begin to speak, in the dark. They get through almost a page of text when first Davies then Emmanuel light a candle. They stop speaking as Noel, walking slowly, like a dreamer, brings another dozen lit candles onstage, and the rhythm of this frantic rescue attempt is so perfect that even Joey can hear the audience sigh.

The wet stage is dry now, and the actors seem to move like ghosts on the moon, so silent is the crowd in front of the candlelit landscape. Act two flies, Davies remembers all his lines and Emmanuel sticks to the original blocking. Then, a few minutes before the end, the lights mysteriously snap on, and Davies is standing looking out at the audience, his face and hands covered with blood. A woman screams. He doesn't know that his nosebleed continued to leak, and is stunned to see blood on his hands. Emmanuel hands him a cloth handkerchief. He whispers, merci, and the play continues.

When it is finally well done and over, the theatre school crowd breaks into wild applause that sweeps the senior citizens into a standing ovation. As people leave their seats to eat the free sandwiches and drink complimentary wine from plastic cups, they are all talking about the play. The Russian web-site man thinks darkness was an accident, but the woman beside him is convinced it was planned. Emmanuel and Davies emerge from the dressing room wet with champagne, a gift from Francine. They have their arms around each other and Davies is bleeding on Emmanuel's Stones T-shirt, but neither of them seems to care.

Joey hands Myra a glass of wine. She smiles and shakes her head. Their plastic glasses touch, a toast. All he can think of is a line from the play, "To every man his little cross."

# XIV

◆

Paulette's voice on the answering machine is as smooth as Chanel No. 5 and her message is entirely in French. She hopes Myra got her note, wonders if she might like to have lunch at L'Express on Sunday. The number to call back is an 844 exchange, which means she's staying somewhere on the Plateau. Myra plays the message over a few times, listening for a clue to the mystery of this sudden camaraderie, but there is none. The voice is cheerful, confident, not quite old friend, but friendly acquaintance.

She climbs into bed and turns out the light, wonders if Jack is in Montreal too, whether she'll bump into them on the street, and realizes how much she dreads that moment. It was a relief when they moved away, as if finally, Montreal belonged to her. All the confusion, suppressed jealousy and well-managed anger lifted and she could walk down any street safely. Now the city is crowded again.

She stares at the ceiling and thinks it's time to get serious about that ovaries piece for The Gaz. Work, yes.

Work is the answer. Impossible to sleep, the day's events still whirling through her head, the rally, Joey's hectic opening night of Godot, Pain's sudden interest in theatre. Then she remembers the query from This Magazine, the editor is expecting a call. She saw no sign of the native contingent, nothing to add to her story, but it's best to leave a message on his machine and avoid an expensive conversation tomorrow. She tiptoes into her study and dials Toronto.

By the time that's done she is far too wide awake for sleep, and wanders into the kitchen for a cup of tea. When she turns on the light, James is sitting on a recycling box, holding a pillow on his knee. He squints, and she hears herself talking like a parent. "Hey, what are you doing up at this hour?"

"My tummy growled. It woke me up." He looks up at her through sleepy eyes.

She bends over to touch his forehead. "Does that mean you don't feel well?"

"It means I need toast."

"Well, I can make toast."

"With cocoa?"

"I guess so. As a matter of fact, guess I'll make myself some, too."

James takes this offer as a sign they are going to stay up, pulls out his chair and climbs up onto the pile of books, suddenly enthusiastic for a good time. He reminds her which mug is his and where to find the cocoa. The kitchen is a model of domestic organization, bread in the breadbox, half-a-dozen used yogurt containers with various leftovers in the fridge. Since Mandy and James moved in, the chaos of light housekeeping has given way to a cozy rhythm of hot meals and chores. She always resented time spent on housework, but Myra has to admit the effect is delicious. Maybe she should have gone in for all this organization when the kids were little, but she assumed kids didn't notice details. Now, she wonders, how could they not notice? Mandy's motherly touch has transformed the beat-up kitchen. Switch on the light and the room glows with her presence. No wonder Mitch is in a permanent swoon. The transformation is seductive.

As if he's reading her mind, James says, "Are we going to stay here forever?" He's sitting with an elbow on the table, head in one hand, dipping toast into cocoa. She looks at him, big eyes on the central question, and is tempted to say, yes, of course you can stay forever. Instead, she gives him a kiss, tousles his hair and answers honestly.

"I really don't know, James. We'll just have to see what happens."

But he's not like Sally and Mitch, he doesn't mistake the firm adult tone for an answer, he persists. "I know we have to wait and see. But what do you say? It's your house."

"Yeah, but it's not just up to me. Other people have plans. Your mom, for example."

"She'd stay. All you have to do is tell her to stay."

"Well, let's not worry about forever right now. Let's just go back into bed and get a good night's sleep, okay?"

He slides down off his chair and wraps his arms around her leg. They walk like that into Sally's old room and Myra tucks him in. As she turns out the light, he says, "I wish you'd tell my mom to stay. She doesn't listen to me. She does whatever she wants. Bad girl." As she tiptoes out of the room, Myra shivers for the boy-man in Sally's bed, nearly four, already working on his future.

The floor in Paulette's room at the Hotel Armor is covered with shopping bags and fashion magazines, empty pop cans and leftover St-Hubert chicken boxes. On her first-ever vacation without Jack, she's done everything he habitually resists, and loved it. Finally she gave in to a pungent mixture of guilt and curiosity and called her mother, which led to the predictable command visit. Now it's after midnight, and she's back on the firm ground of this familiar room, relieved to have survived a fiery encounter with the Chevrier clan.

Four brothers, four pairs of eyes scrutinizing her (the fifth is Georges, Quebec City notary, he couldn't get away). They see their little sister through severe, protective eyes, but they never listen to what she has to say. As boys, they were pushed into lucrative professions; she was expected to get married, nothing more. Even when she announced she was moving to Calgary with an anglais, nobody believed she'd go, or stay. Now she's back and wants to vote in the referendum, having called her brother Charles two weeks ago wondering if he could use his connections to get her on a voting list. A little bit illegal, he chuckled, but not immoral. His Jesuit education established that distinction long ago. "You'll always be a Québécoise." The subtext was clear: you're on your way back home.

From the moment she walked through the door of the tiny Rosemont apartment, she felt the heavy presence of their past. Four small rooms, big enough for a widow who lives to travel, overstuffed with furniture and pictures and keepsakes from family life in a bigger house. The table was spread for supper, four portly brothers and two wives wedged tightly, looking her way, as if they were posing for a frosty family portrait.

Looks like a jury, Paulette snapped as she tossed her purse on the sofa. Knowing she'd be facing them, she couldn't resist wearing something a little on the racy side, just to annoy. A leopard-print skirt and tight black sweater, matching purse. She had fun shopping for this look, no intention of showing the vigilant warriors their little sister has become a well-behaved Calgary suburbanite. The shopping worked, they seemed uneasy.

At the head of the table, helmsman Marc, a highly paid labour lobbyist married to a doctor, both of them active Péquistes. Beside him, Charles, a cop with friends in high places, Gilles, the CEGEP math teacher and his wife Lucia, Italian, a nurse. None of them except Lucia speaks much English, nor cares to. They all earn considerably more than their late father, whose memory they hold sacred, ever did. Now that he's dead, they've happily forgotten how they once looked down on the patriarchal bon vivant, a man for whom politics and tavern life were linked. The Chevrier brothers take their politics as seriously as Jeanette Chevrier once took religion. Their ambition comes from her, a tiny, dynamic woman who is cheerfully spending a wealthy aunt's legacy on guided tours of the world. She is pleased her sons are doing well, relieved her daughter has snagged a lawyer, secretly proud he is English.

Only Frédéric, who's gay and runs an art gallery, appreciated the leopard-print joke. Of the five, he's the only one who ever understood Paulette's contempt for their heavy-handed conformity. Growing up, they argued politics constantly, Charles even went through a federalist phase when he started police college. They've been through every colour of the political rainbow, but now Paulette thinks the palette has merged into a hard, dull brown. A colour that sucks the air out of a room, makes her want to flee. Even Frédéric has made his pact with convention; although he's critical behind their backs, he insists Paulette should try to get along. Why? says Paulette. I don't like to be told how to think. Frédéric says, because Mom deserves peace in her old age. He'd saved her a chair beside him, leaned over for a kiss and sighed, "Chanel, lovely."

"You look pale," her mother said, hopeful that it might mean a grandchild. "You should eat more."

"I'm on a diet," Paulette replied, and noticed her brothers suck in their stomachs.

The meal itself went smoothly enough, an elaborate spread from Chinatown inspired by Jeanette's recent 15-day trip to Taiwan. But before anybody could crack open a fortune cookie, Marc launched into a speech about the miracle of Lucien Bouchard, former Canadian ambassador to Paris, former federal Conservative, now head of the indépendantiste Bloc Québécois in Ottawa and for the past few weeks, de facto leader of the Oui campaign.

Like a chapter from the *Lives of the Saints*, Bouchard's story. A fiftyish small-town lawyer who found his way into a jet-set lifestyle via politics, he married a perky young American who quickly produced two photogenic boys. Then fate struck him down. A deadly flesh-eating disease attacked his leg. But, defying statistics, he survived. Now he hobbles valiantly with a cane, thousands of candles burning for his health beneath the secular surface of Quebec.

But Marc wasn't talking about Bouchard's death-defying powers. He praised the leader's ability to remind Quebecers of what's at stake on October 30. Once Bouchard took over the referendum campaign, support for independence soared. Four days before the vote, Bouchard has made a Oui win seem possible. *Our liberation possible*. Marc's voice rose to a pitch, then he stopped talking. Paulette watched all eyes turn her way, and realized finally, why the room felt so crowded. Her brothers believe she has come home to vote No.

Charles said Paulette will always be a Québécoise.

"Mais oui," she nodded.

And then Marc cleared his throat and said, how *are* you going to vote? Paulette answered evenly, she would vote according to her conscience, which he took as a No, and threw up his hands. What do you expect, after 12 years in Calgary? La mère Chevrier advised him to mind his manners, and Marc's wife chimed in on behalf of Paulette's right to live wherever she wanted to live. Frédéric got up to make coffee, but before long the entire table was talking all at once, until Paulette snatched up the leopard purse and said, bonsoir. She slammed the door on her way out.

Now she is lying on the chenille bedspread at the Hotel Armor, barefoot and aching and lonesome, wishing to God she had not booked into this idiotic Plateau hotel with a hot winding staircase and no phone in the room. She needs to talk to Jack, but before she can summon the energy to put on shoes and go down to the lobby, there's a knock at the door. Must be one of her heavy-handed brothers, come to talk sense. She ignores the second knock, but then a female voice calls out her name. She opens the door to find the Polish concierge standing there with a pink piece of paper.

"Vous avez un message, madame." Annya hands her the memo slip on which she has carefully printed the name Jacques, a phone number and a message in quotation marks: "I've been out of town, please call, any time." Paulette can feel her cheeks turn hot. Except for a sparkle in the eyes, Annya's Slav expression remains placid as she hands her a cell phone, explaining, please press this button when you're finished. Taking the phone, Paulette whispers merci and closes the door.

Mid-morning, the house is empty when Myra finally gets up. Mandy left early with James to help paint the daycare co-op extension, and Mitch is working all day. She stays in her pajamas, makes a few changes in the Hand to Mouth column about meatless meatloaf, feels remotely guilty for having cribbed another of Mandy's recipes, but the days flew by and the deadline loomed and every time she went into Warshaw's hoping to be inspired by food, she came down with a headache. The feeling made her think of Jack. Maybe that's how his breakdown started, destiny pushed him flat against undesirable duty and something snapped.

She is still in her bathrobe at four when a high-pitched child's voice fills the stairwell, and James comes striding into the room. When he sees her, he squeals, "Hey, Grandma's ready for bed and we haven't even had supper yet!" Mandy blushes and tells him to say Mrs. Grant.

"No, no. My name's Myra," she corrects.

"Gran-myra," says James, grabbing her with both arms. Myra can't help smiling at Mandy's obvious embarrassment. Maybe she and Mitch have been scheming and James overheard. Whatever the cause, the tiny home-hunter has clearly decided to advance his case with all the charm at his disposal. By five o'clock she decides to take her column down to The Gazette and dig around in the library archives for a while.

The St-Urbain bus is pulling away from the curb as Myra gets to the stop. It's raining slightly, a soft mist wrapped around the approach of evening, cool fog rising from the sidewalk, mysterious, tender. She decides to walk but as she nears Place des Arts the mist turns into solid drops. She is carrying her favourite umbrella, rescued from a church rummage sale years ago, a Montreal icon. Those vast black domes once hid nuns as they scurried along the street in twos, secretive and purposeful. Never lost in thought, always in a hurry. It's ancient, but the spring still works and at a touch of the button, the umbrella flies open like a bird taking flight.

Walking under the glistening black dome makes her think of high school in Port Hope, the smell of nuns, a musty mixture of cornstarch and holy water and skin. She never quite understood the anger Quebec women harbour for the religious life. In Port Hope, the nuns had degrees from impressive universities. They quoted T.S. Eliot and explained the theory of relativity in simple

179

English. Against the sound of bouncing raindrops, she feels light, thinks, I could have been a nun, if not for the tiny problem of belief. Women with jobs, in a hurry. Nobody expects them to cook.

By the time she gets to rue St-Antoine, it is raining hard. Her shoulders are dry, but her shoes are soaked. She decides to drop her column at the security desk and catch a bus back home, but just as the guard is taking her envelope, the elevator doors open, Moe Mikos steps out, and beside him, Pain. They are sharing a joke and don't notice Myra, who keeps her eyes on the envelope. At least they decide not to notice, and continue talking as they sink out of sight down the escalator. Unwilling to risk conversation, she convinces the security guard to let her pass through the building, to take the St-Jacques exit. She waits for the downpour to subside, but it doesn't. She steps out into the rain.

Rush hour, office workers run for cover and cars are piling up outside The Gazette's big glass doors. Once known across the country as St. James Street, the principal financial artery of Canada, la rue St-Jacques is now a gloomy back street, but still one of Myra's favourites. It leads onto Place d'Armes, one of the oldest town squares in North America, paved in cobblestones and soaked in history. The centrepiece is Notre Dame Basilica, an imposing structure that always makes her think of Paris. She went to Paris once, the tender summer after her mother died, and promised herself never to live anywhere without scent of human history. She is thinking of Paris as she crosses the street, dodging sheets of cold rain, and crashes into Pain, who is about to climb into a taxi.

"See, it doesn't work when you try to avoid me," he says, picking up her purse from a fresh puddle of rainwater.

"Sorry, I can't see much under this umbrella."

"Good policy for a dark and stormy night," he says. "Care to join me for a beer at Winnie's? Or the hangout of your choice? I'll pay."

She lets his questions hang in the air for few seconds, then says, "Maybe some other time. I'm in a bit of a rush."

"Get in, I'll cab you home," he says, holding the door.

"No thanks, I've got to, ah, do something first."

He looks at her, soaked from the knees down, at the rain falling hard around their feet, and reaches out to raise her hand high enough so they both fit under the umbrella. "You know, I've always wanted to kiss a woman under an umbrella like this. Like in a French movie."

She steps back and lets the rain fall full force on his face, lit now by a streetlamp. "Well, I wish you luck," she says, turns, and walks purposefully toward the open doors of Notre Dame.

He lied. Jacques Laflamme wasn't out of town all week, but he knows better than to return a woman's call the same day she makes it. A woman who'd follow a tight-assed anglo lawyer to Calgary deserves a four-day wait. But a woman with juicy breasts and good taste in perfume also deserves to be shown a good time. His secretary made the call to the Polish concierge and took the return call, confirming that Paulette would meet him for lunch in front of the Queen Elizabeth Hotel. L'Hôtel le Reine-Elizabeth. Jacques peppers his French with anglicisms, but he never, ever refers to a landmark in English. Le territoire est français.

Paulette remembered him as a small bulky man with poutine tastes. When the white stretch limo pulled up and he peered out over a tinted window, she ignored the whistle at first, thinking it was some smart ass, or meant for somebody else. Then he got out and opened the door for her, with a bow, and she got in. The back seat felt like a cosy room. Jacques had a bottle of champagne waiting on ice.

He seemed like a different character in Montreal, cruder but also more interesting. In Calgary he'd worn khaki shorts, a polo shirt and a baseball cap. He fit right in with the barbecue set, and when he spoke to her in French he seemed to speak for the entire planet of Quebec, everything she missed about that glow on the horizon. Now, he was barking out instructions to his driver in a French that somehow managed to be both pretentious and endearingly rough and tumble, joual with new money, quickly made. They were on the Laurentian autoroute, speeding out of Montreal before she finished the first glass of bubbly.

As the skyline disappears behind them, Jacques Laflamme is telling an anecdote about a private dinner he attended with Lucien Bouchard and Audrey, who Jacques says is no fool. She comes from California and speaks French, with an American accent of course, but Parisian French. Bouchard is not much of a conversationalist up close, at least not with ordinary millionaires, but he had a few good lines and Jacques was more than happy to scribble out a five-figure cheque, for the cause. He's impressed that Paulette has flown all the way back from Calgary to vote in the referendum. He puts his hand on her knee and says, "We need you, baby. We need everybody. The goddamn English will try everything to stop what has to happen." Then he winces. "Of course, I don't count your husband."

She says, "He's not my husband."

He smiles, pours another round of champagne, and says, "Félicitations."

She drinks the second glass very slowly, and cannot imagine why she denied being Jack's wife — except that it's true. They aren't really married.

The limo driver takes them to a swank restaurant near Ste-Agathe, where the chef has prepared a table for two overlooking a private lake. The leaves are a gorgeous blaze of red and gold, past their prime, but still a stunning view. The dining room is lined with natural pine, their table crowded with china, silver and linen.

From the moment she saw his ruddy face peeking over the edge of a smoky window, Paulette had started to think she'd made a ridiculous mistake to take his phone number, but midway through the meal, as he is telling her how he made it from tenth kid in a tenement family to a multimillionaire, outlining his dreams for a new Quebec, something clicks. She has no attraction to this man, but she is starting to like him. He's earnest, scrubbed, honest. Well, probably monumentally dishonest, at least in business, but straightforward. Tangible, like a freshly hewn log. Surely not an intellectual, but a man with strong convictions. She can even imagine taking him home to meet her brothers, and knows that with their snobbishness arising from a little hard-earned education, they would be full of scorn, but forced by shared conviction to listen. That would be fun.

As they ride back to Montreal in the late afternoon, it is raining. She has been careful to take one sip for every five of his. Now he opens a bottle of cognac and tells the driver to slow down.

We're not in a hurry, he says, smiling fondly in her direction. He assumes she is staying at the Queen Elizabeth. When they pull up outside, he pushes a button that closes the window between them and the driver, then draws a curtain. This is it, she thinks. Here we go. How many ways to say Non?

He leans over, stares straight into her eyes. "I had a wonderful time," he says. "Can I see you again before you go back to Calgary?"

The politeness of the question takes her by surprise. She says, of course. I leave Monday.

Too, he has to be in Chicoutimi tomorrow morning, till Monday evening. Gets back just in time to vote. That's terrible. Always work, work. He wanted to take her to the Opera. Do you like Opera?

She likes opera.

He wanted to show her some of his art. He collects art. Riopelle, Borduas, he's even got a very expensive Lemieux.

Ah, here it comes. The etchings in his penthouse apartment.

He asks, "Do you like art?"

She laughs, "Of course."

"Merde," he mutters, looking at his Rolex. Too late to see anything today. They're closed. His art is all locked up.

She says, "What do you mean?" and he says, "Okay, you're going to laugh. But, all my art is in museums. I buy it and give it to the public. Because I'm never home. And I don't care about making money on art, I just want people to be able to look at it and say, that is Québécois art. La patrimoine. So, all my art is in museums, and all the museums are closed. Except, one. Do you have time? I want you to see one work of art, purchased by Jacques Laflamme, crazy son-of-a bitch slob who speaks French like a bullfrog. I would like to show you the most beautiful saint in all Quebec. If we go right now, she might still be awake."

Paulette hasn't even a vague idea what he's talking about, but she shrugs and says, sure.

"Okay, allons-y." But he has one more tiny question, and if she wants to say no, okay, he'll forget about it. She notices he is looking boyish, and she likes the look.

No harm in asking.

"Could I kiss you, in front of the most beautiful saint in Quebec?"

She laughs.


The five-thirty mass at Notre Dame had just ended as Myra stepped through the wooden doors, the faithful long gone, with the exception of a few desperate souls who stayed late to petition the Lord in solitude. The janitor had turned off the main lights, and the basilica was lit by hundreds of small candles, each one representing private agony, a fervent hope. Though she stopped going to mass ages ago, annoyed by the puerile sermons, she sometimes slips into a church after hours. An empty church is an ideal place to think or just sit with an empty mind and breathe in the vastness. The building is magnificent.

Tonight she wanders along the side pews, past a statue of St-Joseph, the model father, and a faintly disturbing painting of Ste-Marguerite Bourgeoys sitting beside lusty-eyed native children. She kneels to light a candle at the shrine of St-Jude, patron saint of hopeless causes, closes her eyes and feels her speeding heart grow calm. There need not be a God to make this landmark a sacred place. There need only be people gathered together in search of something, a feeling they've lost or suspect they have missed.

She can sit in silence, but kneeling, that's a problem. Every time Myra kneels in a prayerful position, a strange reflex takes hold. While she has no anger against nuns, this church is a strangely powerful tomb of truth into which she enters fearfully, for every time she kneels in prayer, wicked thoughts begin to seep into her mind. Sometimes the thoughts are silly, sometimes perverse fantasies. Sexual thoughts, ribald, and she has to admit, not very original. Sometimes she is filled with anger. Like right now, she would like to see the big tease elusive Pain fall on a pitchfork and have to wear his dick bandaged around a splint for about a month and a half. She would like to see Jack —

The only way to stop the flood of wicked thoughts is to get up off the padded bench and move on. Walking in the cool dark of an empty church, Myra thinks, these wicked thoughts are not from the devil, they're from deep within some private prison. So many demons lurk below the busy blur of life. Some day they will have to be let out. Joey is right, the running has to stop. Someday.

Her clothes are clammy against her body. She has reached the altar now, and out of habit, genuflects before the Blessed Sacrament, walks in front of the altar railing and heads down the other side, toward the street, planning to take a taxi. At the back of the church, dominating a corner just before the door, there is a statue of Ste-Brigitte des Champs, a small porcelain figure painted in delicate earth tones, brushed from nose to toe with gold leaf and lit from below, so the ridges on her dress and the lines on her adolescent face are radiant. She can't take her eyes off the statue, it is so pure and beautiful, obviously superior to the rest of the kitsch collection, which looks fine in the context of a cathedral, but cannot seriously be called art.

There is a small confessional beside the statue. As she approaches, she can hear the moans. A woman's voice, as though she is struggling. The velvet curtain waves slightly and she can see the heel of a man's shoe. She is standing close enough to hear the whispers but not the words. No, not struggling, breathy sighs. Pleasure. She is embarrassed, but cannot walk by. Impulsively, she peeks through a gap in the curtain and the candlelight illuminates a woman's hair. Myra screams, not loud enough to fill a cathedral, but the man turns around and the curtain opens and suddenly, she is eyeball to eyeball with Ste-Brigitte des Champs, and Paulette, who is holding a leopard-print purse in her left hand. Her blouse is unbuttoned and one breast has sprung out of a black lace bra. Her cheeks are red, flushed and smeared with lipstick. When she sees Myra, her eyes are wide.

For a moment, Myra thinks she might faint. Or laugh. The moment seems to last an hour, and by the last quarter she knows the only polite and sensible thing to do is turn and run. But she doesn't.

She says, bonsoir. Then she turns and runs.

When she is outside and the huge wooden door closes behind her, she notices the rain has stopped, leans on a pillar, catches her breath. Then she hears the doors open, footsteps, Paulette and the man with the shoes. Hand in hand, they are leaping down the stone steps, coats flying in the wet wind, like fugitives from the top layer of a wedding cake. There is a white limo parked in front of the church. As they approach, the man shouts and the back door opens. They climb in and the limo door slams shut.

As they drive away, Myra begins to laugh. She laughs so hard she doubles up and the nun's umbrella falls over on the cobblestones. Falling triggers the spring, it opens and is carried away by a sudden gust of wind. She runs down the cathedral steps after the black umbrella, dodging puddles, still laughing.

# XV

◆

*Do you agree that Quebec should become sovereign, after having made a formal offer to Canada for a new economic and political partnership within the scope of the Bill respecting the future of Quebec and the agreement signed on June 12, 1995?*

The question facing five million voters is a question designed by people for whom the correct answer is Oui, people who believe the dignity and survival of Quebec depend on achieving independence within the span of their lifetime, but who know their fellow countrymen will never be tempted by rash action. Reason over passion. The sanctity of parliamentary procedure. Faith in negotiation. With hindsight, the question will seem quintessentially, even excessively, Canadian. But on Monday morning, October 30, 1995, the words count for less than hope and fear. Today is referendum day, a tightrope walk to the future.

When the phone rings, Myra is pouring herself a second cup of coffee. It's Joey, a voice she never hears before noon, wide awake and furious. "Have you seen the paper?"

"I've got it right here. Let me get some milk. . . . There, okay. What's up?"

"Turn to page 38. My obituary."

"Oh dear. I thought The Gazette didn't show up?"

"Oh yeah, oh yeah. She came the next night after we opened, worst performance of any run, no energy, no audience. Davies forgot half of his lines and his nose started bleeding again, right onstage. A nightmare. What could I do? Deny her a ticket? Get this: she brought her kid, a six-year-old kid! With that opening sketch? When she covered his eyes with her purse I knew we were dead."

"Oh come on, kids see far worse on TV."

"He cried in the first act and slept through the second."

"Wait, I'm reading. . . . What are you talking about? It's not so bad. 'Once again, Off the Main steps into the fire, this time with a bold reinterpretation of Samuel Beckett's *Waiting for Godot*, in English and French, and casting which seems to capture the essence of our current political conundrum.' That's good."

"Read on," Joey says, ominously.

"'William Davies, former Stratford luminary . . . hammish comedy . . . mugging for laughs.' Oh dear. '. . . sidekick Emmanuel Paré . . . in a totally different play . . . tragedy by Racine.'"

"Here it comes."

"Oh! 'If a critic can be permitted a personal reflection on this day of soul-searching, Joe Rosenbaum's bicultural existentialism leaves one with the sinking feeling that this larger bicultural experiment on the banks of the St. Lawrence has, finally, outlived its time. I left the theatre feeling Godot has come and gone. The clowns in waiting may stand at a crossroads, but spiritually, they have long since gone their separate ways. These clowns don't talk to each other, they talk to the audience. How Canadian. Ultimately, who cares?'"

"Ow. Ow, ow, ow." Joey bleeds, Myra takes another sip of coffee.

"That's cynical bordering on sick," she says. "What's this got to do with art? What does it mean?"

"It means 'don't see this play.'"

"Hmm. No. Your obsession with the box office has blinded you to the positive aspects of this review. It made her think. Better still, it made her feel something. Look, she linked the show to the wider political issue. Isn't that what you wanted? I mean, you've always said you weren't out to teach people, only to make them ask questions. Hey, hold on. You're in Le Devoir. Lise Lamotte. Op-ed page. Wow, great play."

"She says that? Great play?"

"No, I meant good positioning in the paper. Op-ed page. Serious reader stuff."

"What's the headline?"

"En attendant Godot: un pays se fait."

"Waiting for Godot: A Country in the Making?"

"First two paragraphs on the theatre, intermission, atmosphere. Good, good. She had a fun time. Background on Davies and Paré. Candlelit second act, she loved it. Oh!" A few long seconds tick by as Myra reads to herself and Joey perspires.

"What? What did she say? She killed me, right?"

"Not at all. She says Off the Main's *Waiting for Godot* proves Quebec's maturity and sophistication of culture. Roughly translated: 'The interplay of language . . . natural and potent. Nothing small or simple about this tale. . . . Metaphor for Quebec. . . . A country whose time has come.' Well! There you go, a positive reaction, if not quite a theatre review. Definitely good publicity."

There is silence on the line. Myra can hear Joey puffing away, then a muffled cough. More silence. For a moment she thinks he's disappeared.

"Hello? Are you there?"

"I'm here."

"Well, what do you think?"

"She's using Godot to make a pitch for independence."

"At least they're paying attention. Remember, Joey, you've always said, the only death for an artist is obscurity. Well, the Beckett estate finally didn't sue, and nobody raised an eyebrow over your scandalous nude female Jesus. By the way, where's Pain's famous TV spot? At least this is coverage, and not exactly flagellation either."

"No whip. Still . . ."

"What?"

With a voice that confirms it, Joey says, "I feel like I've been mauled by politicians. You know, handled. Indelicately. From behind."

"Now now, don't get hysterical. You should be laughing. This is so ironic. Two journalists come on different nights, and see a completely different play. They see what they want to see. I'd say you've scraped a layer of muck off this crazy, neurotic town, and found the truth."

"Maybe."

After a long sigh, Myra attempts to change the subject. "You are going to vote, aren't you?"

"I'm thinking of folding Off the Main."

"You always say that when the reviews come out."

"This time I'm serious."

"You're always serious. Come on, Joey. Vote, then —"

"Vote! I'm supposed to express an opinion on a greasy ghost of a question about what? About who runs nothing? When my work is being chewed up by a pair of hobby horses and ignored by everybody else? How am I supposed to —"

"Calm down, and don't forget about Rowan's party."

"Rowan's party? Oh god. Rowan."

"Meet me outside La Cabane at seven. We'll get the bus."

"No, too early. I'll meet you there."

Monday morning, Paulette drags her suitcases down the narrow stairway at the Hotel Armor and asks the desk clerk if it's okay to leave them behind for a few hours. She has an airplane to catch at noon, an appointment to keep first.

"Bien sûr, madame," Annya replies, with a sweet smile. She opens the door to a small closet and watches while the departing guest struggles to stack three bulging bags beside a vacuum cleaner.

Paulette's name is on the voter's list in her mother's riding, Rosemont, a quiet neighbourhood of tiny brick apartments rented by working stiffs, immigrants, most of whom have lived there for years. She gets into a taxi and sends the driver north on St-Denis Street, past L'Express, where less than 24 hours ago she and Myra ate a memorable lunch. The time and place had been set before they eyeballed each other at Notre Dame. Thinking about it now still makes her head spin.

L'Express is a French-style bistro frequented by salaried intellectuals and artsy types, the kind of place Paulette felt sure a journalist would appreciate. She imagined they would talk about politics, and she'd been reading newspapers all week, even the Globe and Mail, ready to be on top of the conversation. After Notre Dame, she thought about cancelling or not showing up, but in the end curiosity overcame embarrassment. At least until she walked through the door.

Her guest was already there, sitting at a table along the wall.

When Paulette pulled out her chair and said, "Hi, how are you?" she surprised Myra, who blurted back, "Bonjour." She was wearing a severe black suit and dangling earrings. Must be for an important meeting after this, thought Paulette. She intended to ask about the Lévesque connection, whether Myra was in touch with her Quebec relatives. She expected they would talk about the referendum, and was prepared to explain why she had decided to vote Non, but first the waiter came to take their order and then Myra said something about the mess of her hair. They both took the soupe au pistou but before their wine even arrived, Paulette caught herself telling Myra about a coiffeur on Laurier, an anglais, who used to be fantastic, maybe he's still there. He was the one who suggested she go with blonde highlights and stay away from brassy reds. Then Myra took out a note-

book to write down his name and Paulette was morti-
fied that they should have veered off onto a subject like
hair, but it was Myra who brought it up, and by then, it
was too late to mention Lévesque. Somehow, she could
not fit him in.

Myra got there early. Not for the world would she miss
this rendezvous. She even went to the trouble of dragging
out a skirt and jacket for the occasion, clip-on earrings
and lipstick. She hated to admit that Paulette's love of
superficial things like clothes set the tone, but she didn't
want to sit across from a woman who perfumes her envelopes and reek of one of Mandy's spicy dishes. She decided this lunch on her territory would be in French, but
Paulette surprised her, started off in English, and before
they even glanced at a menu she knew she was both over-
dressed and underprepared for this one. She caught a
glimpse of her hair in the reflection of the window and
thought, oh my god. The earrings hurt. She took them off.

She hardly touched the soup, which Paulette thought
was quite good, for a pistou. Then their salads came and
Myra wondered what was in it, which reminded Paulette
to mention how much she enjoyed Hand to Mouth, and
that led to the story of Mandy and James. Before long
they were chatting on about Mitch and Sally, a once-
touchy piece of the past that somehow seemed quite
harmless, at L'Express, after Notre Dame. It's an olive
paste in the dressing, Paulette ventured. Tapenade. The
waiter confirmed it.

Then suddenly, apropos nothing in particular, Myra
started on about Jack. She said she hoped he was getting
better, and Paulette said, "Oh he is, much better." To

which Myra replied, "I'm glad to hear that. I would never wish Jack . . ." And there she stopped, looked right past Paulette, out the window, as if something had caught her eye. By the time her attention returned, the word seemed to float, as if it had come unattached from the previous thought.

*I would never wish Jack trouble.*

The tone was unmistakable. A scolding tone. Possibly even a subtle threat. Be good or I will tell Jack on you. Outrageous, and yet there was no way to protest, because the reproach wasn't in the words, it was in the air between them. Now Paulette wanted to rip into Myra in French. She could talk politics in English and have fun, but . . . Hein, qu'est-ce que tu veux dire? Dis-le-moi. Too late. Even though the French language would have given her the power of nuance, she knew that turning back now would be an admission of weakness. Her face burned. She could not speak, sat there in the awkward silence, frantically searching for a way into the real subject. A way to say, Jack and I are . . .

What?

Jack and I are fine. Very happy.

In French it would sound all right but formulating the sentence in English, she knew it would come out sounding like a lie. She took a deep breath, stared at the earrings on the table, little iron spirals, like twisted question marks.

Just then the waiter appeared and started rhyming off the dessert menu. They savored the list. Myra said, "Non, merci. Pas pour moi," and Paulette, without stopping to think, said "J'vais prendre le gâteau au chocolat, s'il vous plaît."

When he'd disappeared, they sat in silence. Myra glanced at her watch. Paulette knew she wanted to leave, but wouldn't, until the cake had come and gone. Les anglais are so polite. Then the cake arrived, it was an enormous piece. Paulette pushed the plate toward her, and said, "Vas-y, prends-en la moitié." Myra answered her in French, and told her a funny story about James and a mousse, how disappointed he was to find out it was only pudding and not a pet, and a few minutes later, they'd finished the whole piece.

When the taxi pulls up outside Rosemont secondary school, there is already a crowd outside. Paulette follows the signs to the gymnasium, converted into a polling station, where a few dozen people are waiting in line, surprisingly quiet, almost sombre. Maybe it's too early in the morning for excitement. Still, she feels her stomach flip, gets in line behind an old woman who is leaning on a cane, holding a yappy little dog with her other hand. His leash is elastic, and she lets the dog roam as they wait. Paulette eyes her watch as the minutes tick by. She hadn't calculated waiting, doesn't want to miss the flight. Finally, she taps the woman on the shoulder and asks if she might go in ahead. The woman's pinched face cracks into a smile.

"Allez-y, chérie. Mais, il faut prendre patience."

Paulette takes her ballot and heads behind the cardboard booth. She did not come back here with the intention of voting for her brothers' side, for independence, not at all. Nine days ago she landed at Dorval airport convinced that Quebec should stay exactly as it is, as it was when she left. Now the words are in front of her, a blur. She marks a solid, unequivocal X beside Oui.

Oui, meaning okay let's go. Meaning, I should have spoken French to Myra. Should have played the game with my own language, instead of demonstrating ease with English, thereby handing victory to the other side of the table. The arrogance of accommodation is a mistake. A lecture about Jack! How dare she? Paulette feels ashamed of herself, ashamed of her shame. And shame, like guilt, makes her angry. Anger makes her bold. Suddenly, it all becomes so clear. A country is an institution that protects poor mortals from these endless tests of courage. A country does matter. So does marriage, yes, the same. Institutions matter, because they tell the world who you are. They tell you who you are.

Paulette folds her ballot and drops it into the box, hurries by the old lady, smiling — merci — and steps out into the morning sunlight. All that remains is one more taxi, luggage, airport and up in the air.

Up in the air, the steward brings her a gin and tonic. She unfastens her seatbelt and leans back, eyes closed, happy as hell to be going home to Jack.


Most elections have trouble getting half the eligible voters out. The much-debated question, downright incomprehensible to anyone who hasn't been following the news for months, is no longer the issue. Everybody knows what this choice is all about. Like the final game in the Stanley Cup playoffs, this referendum has grabbed the attention of even casual citizens. An astounding 4.7 million people, 94 per cent of eligible voters, are casting ballots, most according to ancient allegiance. A solid majority of anglophones and immigrants will vote Non; the majority of French-speaking Quebecers will vote Oui. All of this is known in advance, still the outcome remains open, to be determined by a few thousand, the undecided.

Fate, fluke, weather will all play a part in the outcome, and it has always been this way, from the beginning. In 1759, Scottish Highland soldiers under British command fought the French from France and Canadiens on the Plains of Abraham, a 15-minute skirmish that ended with generals on both sides, Montcalm and Wolfe, dead. The British fired the last shot, then settled in for a long winter of occupation, half expecting the French to counterattack from Montreal, unsure of what spring would make of their victory, since neither imperial power really wanted the snowy northern settlements. As the ice finally broke on the St. Lawrence, a fleet of ships appeared on the horizon, and for one chilling hour neither side could be sure whose flag was flying on the mastheads. When it turned out to be the British Ensign, the real history of these parallel peoples began: a history without much bloodshed and few rousing anthems, a history of tall ships on the horizon, compromise, backroom deals and tie games hanging on the final face-off. This referendum is a tie game. When the ballots are counted, many words will be spent on the meaning of victory and defeat, far too few on the power of fate, fluke and weather.

By the time Myra gets over to the polling station at Bancroft school, it's after six and the line-up stretches the length of one entire corridor. All day she has been putting off this civic duty, fighting an impulse that began in her dreams last night. A dare, from the demons inside. Keep moving. She dreamed of a pencil that would not touch paper, it danced in the air and lifted her right off the sidewalk. After a while her body felt weak, like a swimmer growing tired, so she lay back and floated, no effort at all. Still, her fingers gripped the pencil. Or the pencil held her fingers. Either way, there was no letting go.

Now she is standing in line, fighting an urge to bolt. For a few seconds, she doesn't recognize the young woman walking toward her. Her eyes go first to the grey-haired man who is holding Sally's hand, a slim fellow with thinning curls and a white scarf slung over his corduroy jacket. For the first time since Myra can remember, Sally is wearing a skirt and a necklace over her T-shirt.

She says, "Hi, Mom!" and soon Myra is shaking the man's hand and having a three-way conversation in French. His name is Pierre-Marie, he teaches art, taught Sally painting and sculpture last year. He was called something else then, Monsieur Lacoursière. As they stand chatting, they are no longer holding hands and Pierre-Marie looks vaguely embarrassed to be meeting a mother. Eyes shining, Sally slips a Oui button out of her pocket, announces they've just voted and now they're off to the Palais des Congrès to join several thousand hopeful Péquistes gathering to wait for the result. Gradually, as Myra looks at Pierre-Marie she remembers the mysterious shadow over Sally's expression that night on the balcony, like there was something she wanted to talk about, but they never quite got to the point. The point must have been Pierre-Marie.

"Mom, guess what?" She looks over at the professor. "Je peux le dire?"

He shrugs, "Pourquoi pas?"

"Remember that painting I did last year? The woman and the Mountain, sleeping giantess? For school? Well, Pierre-Marie's curating a group show and I'm in. Isn't that just unbelievably outstanding? December 1. Put the date down."

Myra looks over at Pierre-Marie who is as proud as a new father, and says, "Really? That's . . . well, unbelievably outstanding!" Minutes later, they are out of the building, leaving Myra a few feet away from decision. As the long line moves forward, she is still floating. In spite of profound historic personal conviction, she has not, this time round, made up her mind. She struggles to touch the floor, as if to slow the advance of time. But it passes anyway, and soon she is standing in the cardboard confessional, alone with a question. The words stare back at her. Clear-eyed words, waiting for an answer.

# XVI

◆

Rowan Gaunt has lived in a six-and-a-half on Park Avenue for almost a decade, but he's clearing out tomorrow. His walls are bare, the hallway crammed with boxes, furniture down to a minimum, just the few wrecked pieces he has decided to abandon. The so-called referendum party is actually his farewell, but he's keeping that part quiet, doesn't care to let everybody know he's leaving town. They think he's relocating to Old Montreal, which is true, but only temporarily. Rowan can't stand attention right now, and besides, he has attended too many going-away parties in recent years. They're all the same. Gripped by the presence of so many friends he or she never before counted, the departing soul inevitably feels ill with nostalgia. Then a surge of panic. The mood of friends ranges from jealousy to vague anxiety, but mostly these friends are absorbed by the whirl and gloom of their own lives.

Though it doesn't look that way, Rowan isn't leaving by choice. Desperation is driving him out. He's fed up. Overtired. Since a woman stole his sperm and closed the door on a pair of shining infant eyes, he has quit a tenured teaching job, stopped writing poetry and gone to work renovating houses; he's changed everything about his life except the city, and still it isn't enough. His body now feels strong enough for the final push, though his spirit is so low he can hardly speak. He did not vote today. He'll leave that to people who are willing to live with the consequences. Instead, he took five boxes of old clothes to the Salvation Army, bought a gallon of red wine, 24 bottles of beer, and made three kinds of dip for the post-vote party. Guacamole. Sour cream and dill. Chili sauce with chives and garlic. A former girlfriend and a fellow poet named Gay are bringing chips and pita bread.

By the time Myra rings his doorbell, a dozen people have gathered around two TV sets, one tuned into French, the other English. Joey is nowhere in sight, late as usual. Myra gives Rowan a frozen zucchini loaf wrapped in a tea towel. He recognizes the subject of her most recent Hand to Mouth column, which he cut out and clipped to the fridge door. She is about to give Mandy the credit, when new guests at the door distract his attention.

Looking around the room, Myra realizes she knows almost everybody: a couple who make independent films; three Dawson College teachers, one a union activist; Seamus Farley, a taxi driver and singer for a Celtic folk group; Anne Hanks, the woman who runs the daycare where Mitch and Sally went years ago; a fellow from the freelancers' association; a musician who helped paint the set of Godot. Least of all, she knows Rowan, his former girlfriend and his young protégé, but she feels fairly confident of knowing many people he knows, which is the way the tiny community of Plateau English Montreal works. Seldom more than two degrees of separation. Now they are gathered around the TV sets and Seamus Farley, who is bordering on drunk, has decided that everybody must have Scotch.

And then there it is, the verdict. Non. No. But very close. So close that it will take some time before an official declaration that 50.56 per cent of votes were against independence, and 49.44 were in favour. There are no cheers or caustic remarks in the room, only a wordless wave of relief, followed up sharply by a gust of disappointment. A vote this close settles nothing. It means no more than history suspended.

Farley insists on his toast, "To the future — whatever," which elicits a few chuckles, but for the most part his audience prefers TV. As Rowan unwraps enough water glasses to pour a round of whisky, the premier of Quebec fills both screens. Like two eyes, suddenly in focus, the two TV sets finally agree. Somebody tells Farley to hold off on the toast. All conversation stops.

Jacques Parizeau's eyes are snapping. Later, people will say he was drunk. For the moment he appears to be in charge. Like a general conceding defeat, he speaks directly to his wounded soldiers, and not even a cool medium like TV can miss the pulse of hot blood in his voice. There are reasons for our defeat, he tells his side of the campaign. Money and the ethnic vote. There's an audible gasp in the room. Farley says, "Jesus Christ!" And somebody replies, "No, more like St. Peter." So rarely do politicians dare to say what they feel that

Parizeau's outburst temporarily stuns the tiny clutch of TV watchers. Fifty thousand voters decided the outcome of this referendum. Logically, any 50,000 would have made the difference — French, English, immigrant, rich, poor, or a mixture, a few more Oui from anywhere in Quebec. But no, the pain of losing is too great for logic. Parizeau's moment in history has just been written. Defeat. Bloody raw emotion splattered on the TV screen makes this room shiver.

Rowan is standing beside Myra when everybody begins to talk at once about the speech. For a long moment they stand fixed to the screen, aware that neither is moving or speaking, until Rowan says, "You can't help but admire him."

He reels back as Myra fires: "What? You admire Parizeau?"

"Sure," he says, looking away. "He's going down in flames. Tomorrow, he'll either resign or get pushed out for losing the referendum. In the meantime, he's taking the trouble to piss people off. That's guts."

"Well he succeeded, then." Myra twirls the scotch in her glass, and finishes the shot.

"So, you're offended. What are you, ethnic or money?"

"Neither. And I'm not offended, just really, very, miserably disappointed. From the beginning this whole campaign smelled bad. The people in charge are desperate, mean-spirited, small-minded, and this moment pretty well sums it all up. Think of the 1980 referendum. A much bigger loss, but somehow Lévesque made it feel like a victory. Remember what he said on TV: à la prochaine. Till the next time. Who can ever forget the sight of

René Lévesque that night? He knew how to catch the spirit of a moment. He said what he felt, and it wasn't full of hatred. Words matter, you know. At a time like this, they count for a lot more than numbers. They hang around and inspire people or worse. I'd like to climb right into that TV and strangle him."

Not since his former mistress started hurling potted plants off her balcony at him, before the police arrived, has Rowan faced the ferocity of female wrath, and his scars are still a little tender. Six months ago, he would have fled to the bathroom, but that was before he stared reading books on how to hold your ground. Ready to test the literature, he replies softly, "He's being honest, that's all."

"Honest? Well then he's honestly a creep! That speech made my skin crawl. I'd like to stick my fingers down my throat and puke."

Rowan hands her a plastic bowl, and says, "No offence, but I just mopped the floor."

"Metaphorically, puke. I'm sorry, I don't mean to yell at you. I feel like standing on a streetcorner and yelling my head off."

And that's when Rowan realizes his ground is firm enough to let him see right beyond the face of politics and into the fiery eyes of desperation. Yelling on a streetcorner: the literature talks about that impulse. This woman is a kindred spirit. There are days when he thinks he should actually become a therapist, except that he can't stand hearing about other people's problems.

"I've got a better idea," he says, and reaches into a cardboard box at his elbow to produce two long-stemmed crystal goblets wrapped in newspaper. He fills the glasses with screw-top Hungarian red, and hands one to Myra.

"I really shouldn't be mixing drinks," she says, taking a long sip. A rough-and-tumble house wine, it lurches down her throat like an old jalopy. For a second, she is reminded of Calgary, and the contrast stings.

Rowan watches her expression, wishes to God he'd reached for Farley's Scotch, but it's too late now. Screw politics, he is thinking. This woman is out of control. He decides to encourage the outer limits. "If you're going to denounce the PQ on a streetcorner tonight," he says, "I think you should mix your drinks."

"I'm not denouncing the PQ! I mean . . . I voted . . ."

She doesn't finish her sentence. He waits, she stares gloomily into the wine.

With a grimace of incredulity, he says, "You voted Oui?"

Myra glares at him, doesn't answer. Instead, she fires. "Did you vote?"

"No."

"How could you not vote?!"

"Because I'm leaving. The rest of you will have to deal with the future."

"You're leaving Montreal? When?"

"Very soon," he says, and refills the glasses.

Before Myra has time to ask the inevitable questions, he heads her off by changing the subject. "Remember those pictures I took of you, at the rally? A few of them were pretty good. Are you interested in taking a look?" She is, vaguely, and follows him to the storeroom. Like everything else in the apartment, Rowan's photos are wrapped for moving. The tiny room behind the kitchen is dark and unheated, empty except for a column of cardboard boxes. He rummages through the largest and lifts out a slide projector. Myra protests, too much trouble, but he persists, and a few seconds later the wall is filled with colour. Red-and-white maple leaf flags, teenagers with signs and big grins, an ocean of cheering faces, a baby eating ice cream, dogs engaged in sex and finally, Myra, curled up against a tree in the middle of a crowded park, asleep. Myra in the distance. Myra closer, the contours of her face, filling the screen.

She laughs nervously. "Yikes! This is definitely not going to get me nominated Journalist of the Year. Actually, that rally felt artificial, dead. But look at the pictures! Where was I? Sleeping through the whole event, I mean, even when I was walking around, I didn't see half of this . . ."

When his shots of the rally are gone, he slides in another tray, this one containing images of the city from all angles, day and night. The Mountain, stone and steel, history, gleaming glass and gloriously gorgeous people, some memorable beauties, many more surpassing beauty with original faces and bodies, lumpy, thin, wired. Bag ladies and transvestites. Slick dudes and dogs. He flicks the photos by quickly, lingering a few seconds longer on a night sky over water, an old couple at the bus terminal, and then the screen goes pure white. They are sitting on the floor, in the black room, staring at an empty wall. He flicks off the projector, and the darkness is broken only by a distant street light. The city has vanished. The city is in their heads.

Finally, Myra says, "Why are you leaving?"

"Time for change."

"Where are you going?"

"Well, I'm loft-sitting for a while. Then probably Toronto. My brother lives there."

"Oh." Her oh is another whole conversation. The rivalry between the two cities is ancient, the truth about their respective merits all mixed up with emotion, including pride. You can either be commended or condemned for moving to Toronto, but Montrealers do it all the time.

She takes a fairly neutral position: "Toronto has changed."

Rowan appreciates the eagerness of her voice in the dark. He says, "I know, I know."

Without speaking, he flips back through the slides to find a shot of Myra sleeping under the maple tree. She tells him, enough. But he lets the motor hum.

Finally, there's a knock at the door. It's Farley. By the jocular tone of his voice, it seems the drink is gone. "Rowan, you son-of-a-bitch. There's a party at your place tonight. Any chance of you showing up?"

Watching politics on TV turned out to be a very bad idea for a party, and the half-dozen people who've lingered are determined to find a public place with life. Farley suggests Au Cepage, in Old Montreal, chief watering hole for Gazette types. He's married to the assistant news editor, expects to meet up with her there, and offers to take everybody in his taxi. Myra wonders about Joey, who still hasn't arrived, so Rowan leaves a note on the door and they head out into the street, in search of a reason to believe this is not the most dismal night of the year.

An icy breeze sweeps down Park Avenue as they huddle near a bank machine, waiting. When Farley arrives in the taxi, it is a beat-up Toyota, with three cases of empty beer bottles in the back seat and a full trunk. There is no way five people can fit in. Somebody suggests they get a "real cab," which makes Farley howl, but Rowan says, "Don't worry about it. I'll take my bike. You want to come with me, Myra?"

She is wearing a heavy sweater, hugging it close across her chest. Rowan is looking straight into her eyes, waiting for a yes.

"You're riding your bike?" she asks.

"Yeah."

"Can it move two of us?"

"Sure."

"Well, okay."

"Wait here, I'll get it," he says. The Toyota taxi roars off and Rowan disappears into the alley behind his building.


On the night of the vote, Jack had to work late. He kept calling home, expecting Paulette to pick up the phone. Her flight got in from Montreal at five p.m. but by seven there was still no answer and he'd started to worry. Nine days alone in an empty house; at first it seemed delicious, but after a while just plain pointless. When he opened the front door and saw a purse on the coffee table, he called out her name. No answer. Going upstairs he noticed she had emptied her suitcase and put a load of laundry into the machine. It was still on the last spin. Finally, he found a note on the fridge door, reminding him about the choir fundraiser she'd promised to attend. He poured himself a scotch, flicked on the TV and settled down to wait.

Eight p.m. Mountain Time. Ten o'clock in Quebec. The referendum is all over, a narrow win for the No.

Parizeau faced the cameras conceding defeat in his own memorable style. After flipping back and forth between Le Point and the CBC for a few minutes, he turns the sound off and goes over to his massive music library for a little background comfort. Commander Cody and the Lost Planet Airmen hippie country rock. Watching the vinyl spin, he thinks, CDs are fine but nothing beats the juicy geography of a good old record, hills and valleys, grooves that seem to capture the sweat of warm skin working the instruments. He pours himself a second drink and starts dancing around the coffee table, talking heads in Quebec still blathering away soundlessly. Where the hell's Paulette? He says it out loud, and as if by way of answer, hears the sound of tires on gravel. He picks up the newspaper and pretends to read.

"Bonsoir, mon amour."

She always sings in cheerful French when something's up. He turns to the stock market report and tiny numbers swim in front of his eyes. She walks straight over to him, lifts the paper out of his hands and sits on his knee, lick of a kiss before he can say anything. She tastes like booze.

"Tu m'as beaucoup manqué. Beaucoup. Beaucoup. Beaucoup." She kisses him again with each repetition of the word, but all he can think of is how strange the expression sounds in French. Translated literally, you missed me very much. Meaning I missed you. Or, you were missing in me. Never in a million years would he get used to tu m'as manqué.

"So, did you catch the referendum results?" he asks. She's brought an order of Chinese food and leaps up to take it into the kitchen.

"Ben oui, I heard on the car radio."

"Well?" He follows, glass in hand.

"Well, we're having another referendum, that's all."

"So you voted?"

"I voted."

"How?"

"Hein, it's a secret. Anyway, I'm tired. I don't want to talk about politics. I want to talk about Chinese food, and a few other things."

"Oh dear, sounds serious," he says. "Let me top up this Scotch first." Before he can reach the bottle, Paulette takes his glass and puts it into the dishwasher. He can tell by the way she closes the door, firmly, that the rest of the evening could be long.

"Chéri, you're drinking too much. It doesn't go with your medication. Come on, get yourself a mineral water and set the table."

He suspects her nine-day waltz with the indomitable Chevrier clan is responsible for this mood. Thinking about that impenetrable feud, he reaches for the plates, hopes to change the subject, makes a big mistake.

"Did you happen to bump into Myra?"

Her eyes blazed as she repeats the key word, "Myra!"

From then on, there is no going back. By the time Jack dips the last deep fried shrimp into hot sauce, the subject matter will have been well and clearly defined: Jack-Myra-Paulette. He will manage to put his foot down and get the top off a fresh bottle of Scotch, but he cannot change the subject.

Why now, after all these years? Something must have happened. By morning, tears and stored-up truths will be unleashed into the autumn air. Some things will be clear and others that once were clear will be forever muddy in Jack's mind. But at least he'll know what to do next.

Myra is waiting for Rowan at the corner of Park and Bernard. Her mouth is gritty with the combination of good spirit, cheap wine and a chaser of disappointment. A streetcorner, the perfect opportunity to yell her head off, yes, a good long loud belly scream might be just the thing, followed up by barks and foot stomping. Boo hoo Parizeau, something like that. Standing there, in the perfect spot, she can picture herself yelling, she can even explain the reasons why, but she doesn't feel like it any more. The night sky is heavy. Too much emptiness. Hearing people talk about leaving Montreal always makes her sad. She chose this city. She loves this city, after Mitch and Sal, maybe more than anybody on the planet. This city and self-made Myra are one and the same. The cause that brought her here was never her cause, though it was the context for her life during many fine, hard years. She cannot honestly say the loss tonight, or the temporary setback, is a setback for her Self, still she takes it personally. She can sympathize with the premier's disappointment, but his attack hurts. Rowan is right. In his own perverse way, Parizeau is right. What will happen to passion now is anybody's guess. Winter is at hand.

She dreads the thought of sliding downtown on the back of a bicycle and talking politics with fellow anglo journalists. She does not want to be in a room full of a small feeling, like relief. She would rather be with Sally and Pierre-Marie, where people are angry and tearful.

Then she hears a roar, and turns around to see Rowan nosing a beastly big motor cycle into the gutter. He is wearing a jacket and helmet, and hands her a second set.

"I thought you meant bicycle," she says.

"I know," he says, grinning. "You in a hurry to get there?"

"No."

"Good."

So, she zips into the jacket, straps on the helmet and slides onto the seat behind him. They take the long route, over the Mountain. It's freezing and scary and too loud to talk, but the night air tastes like well water. They stop on the slope of Mount Royal for a better look at the city Rowan is about to leave. They can see a million lights, and more. They can see the silver river. It flows around the island and beyond, all the way to the ocean.

# ANSWER

# I

◆

November, a month of record snowfall, a blizzard of melancholy editorials. Nowhere to hide. Snow covered Myra's lilac bush and clung to the rickety staircase. Newspapers piled up inside the door, unread. By silent consent across Montreal, citizens from all shades of the rainbow let go, let fall the will to shovel and read about politics, and when the sun came back to melt the snow, they had either decided to forget about politics, or plunge back in, or they were gone.

There was no consensus about where to go, except that everybody knew something fundamental had snapped. The referendum had changed nothing, and yet everything changed.

Having said exactly what he felt about the results on TV, Jacques Parizeau woke up the next morning and resigned as premier of Quebec. Those who despised what he said thereby got the impression a drunken slip of the tongue had ruined a brilliant career, and let out yelps of bitter joy. Those who thought he was right were glad he'd spoken out, expected he'd remain powerful behind the scenes. Strategists and pundits were convinced Lucien Bouchard had saved the PQ from abject humiliation. Parizeau was blamed for the Oui's defeat, Bouchard reaped the rewards of victory.

And now he made them wait — the better part of three weeks to decide whether he even wanted to be premier of Quebec. First, he took a vacation in California to think it over, promising an answer on his return. But nobody who followed that story imagined his trip was all piña colada. His mission was dealing with Audrey Best, 37, dark and lovely, mother of their two young sons, Simon aged four, and Alexandre, almost six. Published rumours claimed their marriage had been shaken by the pressure of politics. But when the vacation ended, Audrey came back to Quebec with an official smile and Bouchard said Oui to the dismal chore of assuaging widespread regret and balancing a huge provincial debt. To a nation facing winter like a flare-up of some genetically embedded virus, his conjugal victory counted for something. A man who can charm a blooming American away from perpetual summer, get her to smile at snow and a 66-cent dollar — everybody agreed, that man deserved respect.

It was Pain's choice of movie. Previous roles had endeared him to Michael Douglas, which is how he and Myra ended up sitting side by side at a Hollywood schlockfest called *The American President*, at least until a few minutes before the end when he couldn't take any more and stormed out. Totally forgettable plot except that an ordinary woman with savvy played by a stunning actress (who looks like Audrey Best) winds up dancing with the president. And true to the genre, they do dazzle. When Myra met up with him out in the street, he was still fuming, said the movie revealed an important truth about Quebec.

"Picture Audrey dancing with Bill Clinton," he said, stopping on the crowded sidewalk so he could capture her eyes. "Now, tell me, what would be her chances of dancing with the president if she said goodbye to Bouchard and settled into life around a pool in California?"

"Ah, zero?" Myra answered while stomping her feet.

"Right."

"Let's keep walking, I'm freezing."

As they turned toward Crescent Street, Pain developed his theory of the American domination of Quebec, how language is a tinfoil shield against imperialism, and nobody should count on the Americans giving a damn about the French language, culture or politics. "Quebecers are in love with the drama and culture of the U.S. of A. They went for free trade when everyone in the Rest of Canada knew it would be fatal. Their desperation to break up this country includes a fierce desire to dance with the president. So, Quebecers are getting the premier they want, and the premier has hung on to the wife Quebecers want."

Later, at Winnie's, they circled round the subject, poked at it from all angles. Then he ran home and pounded out his column for The Mirror. Emboldened by his lifelong animosity to America, he dressed his opinion in enough outrage to set the editor's computer screen on fire. It was Pain's column on The American President that finally got him fired, not the content so much as the fistfight that erupted when his editor, a young, nautilus-friendly journalism grad, suggested that the line, "Quebecers are tarts when it comes to power" be, "Ah, reworded."

Pain exploded, said the publication lacked balls. No, said the editor, the publication lacks money. He pointed out that last summer, when a Quebec City talk-show host broadcast rumours that the Bouchard–Best marriage was on the rocks, the station was slapped with a $1.4-million lawsuit, still before the courts. "Right or wrong, a give-away entertainment weekly cannot afford that kind of, hum, debate," he said.

"You're scared of the truth," bellowed Pain.

"Not at all," the editor sneered, dropping the column into the wastebasket. "I'm just not going to go down over this belch of gossip you're trying to pass off as political insight."

Seconds later, he was sprawled out on his desk, blood all over his keyboard, and before it dried, the police were at the door. In the end, Pain ate enough humble pie to keep out of jail, but decided to visit his mom for a week or two before dropping by The Mirror's competition with a new column idea.

Meanwhile, in a high-rise living room overlooking Lake Ontario, Israel Rosenbaum clicked on his TV at bedtime and found a news item about his son's theatre troupe. He called immediately with congratulations, at least his version of them.

"So, you have fin-a-lly voken up." Those were Israel's first words and they were, literally, true. Joey had fallen asleep on the couch after microwaving a cup-a-soup for dinner, and as he fumbled in the dark for the phone, thought he must still be having a bad dream. The setting was hell, the voice appropriate.

"Papa, is that you?"

"Of course it's me. Who else calls from Toronto? Everybody is here, but they don't call you, do they?"

"Not everybody is in Toronto."

"They can't afford it."

"Papa, why did you call?"

Rosenbaum senior took his time recounting The Journal item, most of which he had on tape and replayed over the phone, complete with his own commentary on the visuals. "And fin-a-lly you have taken my advice and chosen a voman for the play who is good to look at. Is she in the play? What is the play? They don't mention the play! What, this is the poster? This poster is supposed to sell tickets? The voman, she sells tickets, but the poster! Yosef, you are still so very very far from sane."

As Israel rambled over a background of Pain's sonorous tones and Francine's breathless giggles, Joey began to piece together what he'd missed by not having a TV. The item had been mainly about Francine's struggle as a young, gorgeous bilingual actor in referendum-soaked Quebec, the theme being, The Morning After — Work Goes On. Nowhere was Off the Main mentioned by name, though footage from a rehearsal implied Francine was the star of *Waiting for Godot*.

As soon as Israel had finished giving familiar advice and hung up, Joey called Myra. She wasn't home.

Mitch and Sally were at home, brother and sister revisiting a childhood ritual, and loving it. Mitch held the rickety stepladder while Sally rummaged through the closet in Myra's bedroom.

"What do you want with baby pictures?" he demanded.

"Art," she answered. Stretching to reach the back of the top shelf, she laid hands on a large cardboard box labelled "odds and ends 1980–90." "Hold on, this could be it." She handed the beat-up box down to him and stuffed a ball of rumpled summer clothes back on top of file folders and worn-out shoes. The pile didn't hold, came tumbling down on James, who was helping steady the ladder. He fished out a string of Christmas lights and dragged them off to the living room.

"Are you sure you should be going through Mom's stuff when she's not here?" Mitch held the box gingerly, peering at the top layer of old phone bills and photos and scraps of paper as if he could hardly wait to start the rummage. A ritual they'd played since they were old enough to get into trouble: Sally the instigator gets an idea and Mitch the accomplice holds the ladder, meanwhile building his defence for the inevitable moment when Myra walks in and catches them.

"I'm just looking for pictures, that's all," said Sally, taking the box. "Get me a diet Coke and we'll have a look."

By the time the phone rang, James had plugged in the lights to create a twinkling halo around a mound of pillows in the living room. He put his teddy bears and himself on top, and declared that nobody could come into the fort without paying a dollar.

"A dollar! James, you are one ferocious little capitalist," Sally teased. "How much does it cost to get out?"

"Another dollar."

"Ow."

It was Joey calling for Myra, with the sound of bar babble in the background. Mitch said he didn't know when she'd be in, went to a movie or something, left right after supper. By the time he came back into the living room, Sally had emptied the contents of the box on the floor and was deeply engrossed in the search for photos of herself as a baby, research for a new art project.

Mitch discovered it first. He wasn't looking for anything in particular, and felt vaguely uneasy sifting through the pile of papers, but the large manila envelope was hard to miss. Sealed shut, unlabelled, clean brown surface both sides, not a recycled envelope, which was Myra's habit.

"Wonder what this is?" he mumbled, but Sally had bought her way into the fort and was busy showing James pictures of herself in cute dresses.

He'd always wondered if you really could steam an envelope open without tearing the paper, the way they do in the movies. He figured this was a pretty good opportunity to find out, so without attracting attention, slipped into the kitchen to put on the kettle. It worked, although the paper got hopelessly soggy. The envelope was pretty standard, easy to replace. What he wasn't prepared for was the contents. Pages and pages of Myra's wobbly handwriting, some on fine stationery, others scribbled on lined sheets ripped from Gazette notebooks. A few pages were folded carefully and slipped into envelopes, others stapled together.

At first he thought it must be a diary, but no, the pages were letters — addressed to Jack. Unsent letters. His heart pounded as his eyes picked out phrases, salutations like bells. Dearest Jack. My Darling. Jack! Love letters, hate letters. They started around the time of the breakup and continued intensely for months, a couple of dozen from that period, full of anger and love. Wailing, weeping, sobbing letters, soaked with recrimination and regret. Gradually, the tide seemed to change, and the salutations said simply, Dear Jack. Later letters were full of news about the kids, incidents from daily life, and as Mitch sat rigid on the kitchen chair, peering into his mother's soul, he could not for the life of him understand why she hadn't sent these letters. The early rage and ranting — he could imagine she wouldn't want those words in Jack's hands. But the night he won the hockey trophy? What was wrong with that letter?

"What's with Joey?" Sally asked, walking into the kitchen. He startled her. The pile of letters slid to the floor. "He called again. Hey, what are you doing? Reading Mom's old love letters?"

"Not really."

"Well, put them away. How would you like it if somebody snooped into your stuff? Anyway, she's gonna walk in here and you will be in deep shit."

He stuffed the letters back into the envelope and glued the flap shut. Somewhere, he thought, there must be another envelope because this one ends in 1990. Unless she gave up on her secret unsent conversations. He resolved to have a thorough search someday soon. As he slid the letters back into the bottom of the box, under old bills and photos, his chest hurt. He wished his mother would walk in right now and catch him. Then he'd make her explain. So many words, written down but never sent. Why not?

By the time he'd stuffed the box back into the closet and put the ladder away, Mandy had come out of her after-supper nap and was wandering amid the ruins of James's Christmas fort in the living room, trying to get him to go to bed. He didn't want to go to bed. Sally put on a new CD and turned it up loud, so naturally, James wanted to dance. The phone rang again and Mandy yelled, "James Go To Bed NOW."

James said, "I'll get it," and dove for the phone.

"She's not here," he roared, over the music. "She's gone to Toronto. But she'll be back in time for Christmas." Then he slammed down the receiver.

"Who was that?" Sally asked.

"It was a man," he said, mischievously. Then he heard footsteps on the stairs, and Myra opened the door.

James bit his lip and told the truth, quietly, so nobody paid attention. "Oops, guess she's not gone to Toronto. Or else it's Christmas."

# II

◆

Failing to find Myra at home, Joey spent a beer-soaked night alone at La Cabane, wrestling with his furies. As the days passed, anger over Pain's TV piece was absorbed into the greater gloom of pitiful box office receipts, muddled reviews and the inevitable dip in adrenaline after the premiere. On a chilly Wednesday night midway through the run, he walked down St-Laurent and felt little rivulets of personal gloom flow naturally into the massive collective hangover of post-referendum Montreal. The street seemed deserted, except for a few desperate panhandlers and worse — people having fun. *This city is killing me*. He exhaled the words like a mantra, resolved to hold that mood, face up to the reality of Off the Main's complete planetary irrelevance, and act.

When he got to the theatre, Noel was sweeping the stage. Emmanuel had just finished his warm-up; Davies was nowhere to be seen.

"He'll be here," Noel pronounced, keeping his eyes on the broom. "His mother called. She's putting him into a taxi."

Joey decided to ignore the ominous tone and get himself a beer. He wasn't expecting Myra to show up. Seeing her walk thought the door, he felt better. In that hour before a performance, the risk of live actors holding up an evening produced a knot of anxiety in his stomach that could only be dissolved by their flesh-and-blood presence onstage. Perverse but true, he secretly loved that hour. Must love it or could not endure. Feeds on the necessity of endurance, yet does not like to endure alone. He grimaced, he seethed, he perspired. He handed Myra a beer.

"What did you want the other night?" she asked, as they sat down at a corner table. "Mitch said you called a few times. Sorry, I got in late."

"Nothing. Ancient history." He hated to use up sympathy on last week's woes, but she insisted, so he said, "I just wondered if you'd seen Pain's TV piece."

"Oh, that." She grimaced. "I was out but I taped it. Did you want a copy?" He didn't find the offer amusing. "Well? I warned you, there's no point in trying to manipulate the news. It always backfires."

"Wrong. A lot of people know how to manipulate the news. You have to be powerful, and obviously I'm not," he snapped. A long pause ensued during which Myra wondered what she could say by way of consolation that would not lead to a protracted conversation about Pain, wherein Joey would find out they'd been seeing each other again and have comments to make. She decided to change the subject. "Remember that night you borrowed my credit card? I was just wondering . . ."

"Didn't Noel talk to you?"

"No."

"Shit. He is so evasive. Where is he? Noel!" He started pawing through his jacket pockets for a cigarette, and Myra knew the news was not good. Then he went into the kitchen to rifle through a few drawers. "It's like this," he said, reaching for a two-inch butt in the ashtray, "The grant didn't come through. Noel was absolutely certain. He spoke with the jury president's secretary. We were highly recommended. Don't ask me what happened."

"You mean that $3,000 debt on my credit card . . ."

He turned on the gas burner and leaned his face in to light the butt, drawing heavily on the stale remains of hand-rolled tobacco, the sign by which an abandoned butt could be identified as his, cast-off in better times. Like, last week. Myra sighed. "What are you saying?"

"You'll have to wait. Of course I'll pay the interest."

"Interest!?"

"Shh. I've got to see the actors. Are you staying for the show? I want to talk to you about something afterwards. Fate has handed me a tempting moral dilemma, and I need advice. Don't worry about the credit card. You know I'm good for it. Stay right here, I'll be back." And with that he disappeared into the dressing room, leaving Myra to cope with the rush of theatre-goers.

Except that the rush amounted to even less than a trickle. Twelve minutes before eight, Davies turned up breathless and wet-haired, having been hastily fortified by black coffee and a lecture from his mother. With a guilty nod, he rushed straight on by to leap into his costume, exchanging one broken-down ensemble for another. The box office attendant sat hunched over a hefty paperback. Myra glanced at her watch, then at the empty lobby. "Nancy, how does the house look tonight?"

Nancy looked up from her saga, clearly lost in the dream of some other drama. "We've got one reservation. But I'm sure quite a few people will come at the last minute," she said, with the calm of one whose salary does not depend on box office returns.

"This is pretty well the last minute," Myra mumbled. But just then the doors opened and in walked a small, elderly man. He was wearing a rumpled suit and a narrow navy tie. He carried a grey trench coat over his arm and leaned on an umbrella cane. A battered fedora topped off the outfit. It struck her that if this man could walk onstage and if he knew the lines, no one in the audience would even blink. A seamless match between play and public.

"Good evening," he confided. "I have a reservation for two. Errrtzberrrgh."

Myra stifled a giggle when Nancy replied, without the hint of a smile, "How do you spell it?" Hertzberg spelled his name, and sure enough, it was written in the book.

"The problem is my friend is late. Perhaps not coming," he said, reducing his voice to a whisper that nevertheless carried across the empty room and made her reply sound like a shout.

"No problem, sir. Just give me twenty bucks for two tickets and go on in. If he shows up, we'll take care of him. If not, you can get your money back when it's over."

The man smiled. "Thank you. He is never late. Something may have happened." Then he handed over a twenty-dollar bill, and after establishing that there was no coat check, followed her into the darkened theatre. Hardly had the door closed when Noel came bounding out of the dressing room, rubbing his hands. "How's the house look tonight?"

Nancy surveyed the reservation book and crossed off the name Hertzberg. "So far, one. His friend is late."

"One?!"

Myra could feel the $3,000 credit-card debt setting, like cement. By two minutes after eight, Herr Hertzberg was still sitting alone, his coat holding a seat to the left. When cast members outnumber the audience, the usual procedure is to cancel the performance, but Noel's ritual conference resulted in a unanimous decision. Emmanuel was thoroughly warmed up and ready to go. Now relatively sober, Davies protested he'd paid for a long cab ride. Sue and Anne were adamant, they'd appreciate the experience. The play must be played. But, given the unusual circumstances, they decided to skip Joey's sketch and get right into Beckett, there being nothing worse than comedy without laughs.

The night outside was cold and wet. The theatre felt as warm as a Dublin pub. Myra entered the darkened room, the door clanked behind her, and she tiptoed up to the back row, where Joey waited in a transcendent state of despair. As she sat down, he shook his head and his shoulders heaved with silent laughter. A pragmatist, an irrepressible optimist, even Myra had to admit, with a credit-card debt poking at her conscience, this one-member audience constituted a new and terrifying low.

"He bought two tickets," she whispered as the preset lights dimmed.

"Yeah, Nancy offered a refund," Joey replied. Then the hobo clowns appeared, and Estragon announced, "Nothing to be done," and from then on they sat in silence. From then on, Herr Hertzberg owned the night. Nothing to be done.

For the first eternal five minutes the actors were stiff and embarrassed. A couple of times Hertzberg glanced toward the door, as though hopeful his friend might still turn up. Finally, he gave up and settled back. He chuckled. Once, he wiped an eye. Sam Beckett's worthy defenders cast a spell over the cavernous room, and the magic held like a silver spider's web, filling in the space between stage and audience until the two became part of a single action.

At intermission he reluctantly broke away from the play, read the clippings on the lobby wall, and stayed in the washroom until Noel flicked the lights. By the second act, the web was complete. Hungry Emmanuel attached by an invisible vein to Davies the ham, a clown who'd lost heart. His irrepressible desire for laughter provided Emmanuel's studied seriousness with balance, and in the absence of an anonymous crowd, they had no one to talk to but each other. The pace was steady, the lines potent, the moon a most forlorn blue.

From the back row, Myra and Joey watched this new play, a play about one man watching a performance of *Waiting for Godot*. This was a play they'd never seen before and probably would not again, a great play about the glory and humiliation of poor humanity's desperate search for connection, a hymn to trust and hope. The actors were asked to fill the stage with life, Hertzberg to fill the empty theatre, and they both succeeded. They played to one set of eyes. To one man, more anonymous in his solitude than a crowd of thousands.

When the performance was over, he stood to applaud. The cast applauded back and Bill Davies wept. Then he fumbled into his coat (Noel forgot to turn on the house lights, or didn't dare) and nodded to Nancy on the way out the door. In a mad burst of gratitude, Joey ran after him insisting he take back ten dollars for the unused ticket, but Herr Hertzberg declined.

By the time Joey got back, the actors had resolved to celebrate. "Ladies and gentlemen," Davies announced, in his best head-table voice, "that was our finest perform-ance thus far," and commanded a round of applause, ostensibly for Sam Beckett. As they trooped off into a gust of freezing rain, Joey stayed behind to lock up, and Myra stayed too, eager to hear about the "tempting moral dilemma" fate had handed him.

At the edge of the set, Joey slipped off his boots and padded over to the lone tree in his sock feet, slid his hand behind a branch and extracted a small plastic pouch held firm and out of sight with duct tape. They sat on their coats facing the empty seats while Joey rolled a joint. Noel had turned the furnace down, but the heat of the performance lights lingered. They stretched out, as comfortable as lizards, rehashing the night's perform-ance as they smoked, comparing favourite moments and savouring the blessed inanity of it all. Finally, in a natural pause, Myra mentioned the fateful dilemma.

"All right, it's this," he began, handing her the toke. "I've been offered an opportunity to sell out. Should I take it?"

"What's the offer?"

"Hollywood, via Pain. Remember Rowan's party?"

"The night of the referendum. You didn't show up."

"Right, because I bumped into Pain on Crescent Street, and he said his friend the L.A. producer was going to be at the Cépage, so why not drop by. Actually, he asked about you. Are you two . . . ?"

"Joey, focus."

"Okay, it turns out the producer'd been meaning to call me since opening night. In brief, he liked my sketch. He wants to hire me to write for his TV series. Twenty-five thou for a half-hour script. It should take about three weeks to write. Apparently they pretty well put a gun to your head. Anybody can write one of those suckers."

"So, what's the story?"

"Well, I go down to L.A. — "

"No, I mean what'll you be writing about?"

The blue light of a theatrical moon cast its glow through the dead tree, throwing shadows of twigs across Joey's face. The light made him look pale and young. He lay stretched out, hands folded Buddha-like on his plump beetle belly, feet crossed. Both big toes peeked out through holes in his socks. He pondered the question, then with some difficulty rolled over on his side to answer.

"Basically, ah, sex."

Dope does it to some people, makes them laugh hysterically at the slightest provocation, and Myra's laughter crowded the night like a mischievous attack of Celtic fairies. Laughter got her up off her coat and made her choke, brought tears into her eyes, until she took a deep breath and then laughter came at her again from the other side, it rolled her over and over on the matte black floor until her head hit the rock and she said, "Ow!" and coughed laughter, wiped her eyes with the back of her hands.

"I'm sorry, but — " Then it got her again, so she stood up to take a deep breath and blamed the dope.

Joey chuckled weakly. "I presume you're laughing at the combination of me and sex."

"No, no, not at all," she said, now quite composed. "It's been a long night and — I mean, this is great news. An L.A. producer. Wow. . . . Don't they have a lot of writers down there?"

"Oh, insult after insult. It's a Quebec co-production, so they're forced to hire local talent. People who officially reside here and write in English. There aren't that many of us. So, ergo, my golden opportunity."

"That's excellent. I told you that sketch was damn funny. And sexy, too. Sizzling, in its own offbeat way."

"So you think I should sell out?"

"Well, give it a whirl. It's only three weeks. If you don't like it — "

He sat up now and faced her, legs crossed, rolled another joint and looked thoroughly resolute. "No. This is it. If I take that contract I am going to move down to L.A. and not come back. No halfway measures. Don't believe in dabbling. If I go, I stay."

"I thought they wanted you because you're a Quebec resident?"

"Yeah, yeah, which I will still be on paper. But in order to take full advantage of selling out, my mind must move to L.A. The body goes first, as soon as Godot closes."

"You're leaving Montreal?"

Now her urge to laugh was swallowed up by a wave of something cold and unpleasant. A thousand times he'd threatened to give up on theatre, this could be one of them.

"Call it escape. I'm fed up. I'm 38 years old and the woman I confide in finds it uproariously funny that anybody would hire me to write about sex. Doesn't that say something?"

He reached down and tore at the holes in his socks, letting the big toes out completely. "I do go to the odd R-rated movie, you know." He continued in a delicate voice. "I mean, do you even consider me a sexual being?"

Given the phraseology, it took her a moment to realize this was a personal question, considerably far off the subject of L.A. and giving up on Montreal. Although, she thought, maybe not.

"Me?" she said, stymied.

"Who else is in the room? Of course, you." He groaned.

"Of course I . . . consider you a sexual being. Assuming I know what you mean. It says something that you even have to ask."

He looked at her, "What does it say?"

She shrugged.

He wiggled his two bare toes at the heavens, and she knew he did it to make her laugh. For one long moment, the room seemed more crowded than a full house on opening night. The empty seats were watching, waiting for something to happen. Neither of them knew what lines should come next. They lay beside each other, lazy with dope, waiting.

Finally, Myra said, "You wanted advice?"

"Should I do it?"

"What, write for TV?"

"Go to L.A. forever."

"I wish you wouldn't be so dramatic, Joey. Chances of you never ever coming back are pretty slim. I mean, why make pronouncements?"

"IF I come back it WILL NOT BE to Off the Main."

"If, if, if. Why not just go and see what happens?"

"You don't understand." He gathered up his coat, exasperated. She did understand that she was being called on to put firm, warm words after all these questions. All she could think to say was, please don't go, but she didn't say it.

She slipped into her coat. Joey laced up his boots, puffing with effort. "It doesn't matter," he said. "Nothing matters."

"Everything matters," she said, quietly. "But what can we do about it?"

By now they were standing next to each other beside the door, in coats thick enough to protect them from the onslaught of winter and the burning chore of truthful conversation. Joey said, "I'm sure we're doing something every single moment, but we just don't know what to do."

Myra sighed, and looked away.

He said, "What?"

She said, "We've spent too long in Mr. Beckett's head. We're starting to sound like his characters."

"Hmmm."

"Hmmm."

Then, matching high-pitched dope-dazed belly laughs seized them both, and Joey said, "Et alors, let us

seek out human company at the fountain of El Cabana."
His soulmate concurred, and as they walked out of the
empty temple of art, they fell back on Beckett as a shield
against the frozen rain.

*"We can still part if you think it would be better."*

*"It's not worthwhile now."*

*Silence.*

*"No, it's not worthwhile now."*

*Silence.*

*"Well, shall we go?"*

*"Yes, let's go."*

*They do not move.*

A few days later, *Waiting for Godot* closed with one of the
worst box office tallies in Off the Main's history, but Joey
floated through the final toasts on a cloud of good cheer.
Suitcases packed for L.A., he nevertheless downplayed
his departure to the troops, preferring to rally sentiment
around the epiphany of Hertzberg's Godot, as that legendary night came to be called. As for their final pay-
cheques, he said, "Off the Main does not take charity. We
simply ask for your time and patience." On the subject
of money, he always used the first person plural, the
presence of stalwarts Noel and Myra acting as silent pil-
lars under his reasonable request. The word was out
about Myra's credit-card guarantee, so nobody had the
nerve to whine about a couple of hundred dollars. They
saw the empty seats. They all knew Joey the sunbound
stone had no blood to give.

After a final kissy-kissy with the actors, Myra and
Noel hung back, and the three of them huddled outside
La Cabane, bludgeoned by gusts of snow that seemed to

come down between the rows of buildings from odd angles. Joey said all the things a good friend says when he doesn't know how to say goodbye. Then he said he didn't have time for the Metro-bus trek to N-D-G. By the easy way he flagged the cab and waved from the back window, they could tell the surf was up in J.I. Rosenbaum's oceanic ambitions.

When he was gone, Noel took a chestful of frosty air and assured Myra she would always be an integral part of the company. He made it sound as if they'd just witnessed the merciful end of great suffering.

"If he doesn't come back," he said, hugging a briefcase full of important papers, "I get to take over the company. In which case this town can expect more musicals and a few laughs. Not that I don't think Joey wasn't a great artist and everything. He was. Is. But people have been through enough. They don't necessarily want *that* kind of art."

"What do they want?" said Myra.

"They want what everybody wants," Noel said confidently. Myra knew she was supposed to swallow the bait, so she resisted the obvious.

"All right then, oh wise one. Tell me, why is Joey going to L.A.?"

"For the same reason everybody goes to L.A. To get laid. Which I can identify with. Frankly. Can't we all? Ha ha. Well, I don't mean you, of course, directly."

He put his briefcase between his knees, whipped a toque out of his jacket pocket and jammed it down over his ears, as if to close the doors on a potentially sharp comeback. Then the bus arrived. He hopped on, and as it pulled away, stuck his head out the window to shout,

"I'll fax you figures on the final damage Monday. Don't worry, he'll be back."

Myra didn't doubt it for a minute, but as the bus lumbered out of sight, she felt sad, as if some important bit of conversation had been tossed to the wind.

# III

◆

Morning broke with a blinding sun. As Myra went to the door for the newspapers, the mailman was about to ring the bell. He'd already slipped a handful of bills through the letter slot but an oversized envelope wouldn't fit. She glanced at the postmark, Calgary, with a return address to the Alberta Treasury, and registered the natural shiver of anxiety that comes with any government missile. Noticing the black letters J.W. Grant, didn't make the whole thing any less mysterious. She decided to start a new pot of coffee first, check the headlines, then sit down, relax, and slice it open with a knife.

Inside was a thick formal document bearing a seal and pink cardboard corners holding the legal-sized pages together. The text was in French — day, month, year, written out in words, her street address, her name and a black line waiting for her to sign; the same for Jack, his runny signature scrawled across the page. Two copies, and a return envelope postmarked Calgary, his office address. Another letter from a downtown Montreal bank about a mortgage. Still mystified, she checked the padded package again and found a single sheet, folded, typed on Alberta Treasury letterhead:

*Dear Myra,*
*Enclosed please find the deed to the condominium on Esplanade, and documents concerning the discharge of the mortgage. As you know, I have purchased the property, and am now turning it over to you. If you have any questions regarding taxes or other aspects of ownership, we can discuss them when I am in Montreal for Sally's exhibition. Anyway, we need to talk about another matter. Until then,*

*Jack.*

As she stared at the paper, Myra thought, a secretary wrote this from dictation. A Montreal notary had prepared the legal work, showing Jack owned the property and was selling it to her for the nominal sum of one dollar, which was marked "paid in full." She hadn't paid anything, or been asked to pay. She felt her spine stiffen with cold, fast rage. Just as the knot seized her brain, she heard an explosion, so loud it made her leap toward the door, scared by the noise, instinctively ducking hot black mist. The espresso pot, spewing coffee grounds.

This has happened before: she forgets to put the stainless steel filter between the twist-together halves of the pot, so the grounds shoot up like a volcano through the lid and land everywhere, walls, cupboards, ceiling. It takes a good two hours to clean up the mess. When she realized it was only coffee and not the roof, she felt weak with a mixture of relief and self-reproach.

Wearing oven mitts, she carried the growling pot out to the balcony, pulled out a clean chair and sat down. Watery brown stains had left the first page of the deed limp. She wiped it off on her bathrobe, but the page stayed translucent. She could see the look on Jack's face when he found a legal document ruined by a spill, a look she always dreaded; it made her feel small and stupid. So sorry! A gush of tears blew up like the coffee pot and were over just as fast. Then she felt mad. So what? Who cares about the look on Jack's face?

The documents were as potent as a death announcement. She held them tight with both hands, letting the blurry words settle. Then she reread everything carefully, and took up Jack's letter, thinking, this page cannot accurately be called a letter. She looked at the terse legal sentences and wondered if they'd been distilled from a much longer version, but rereading, thought, no. It's a note, written on the fly, doesn't say or mean anything. Cold formality. Office language. The enormity of his shrunken gesture lay like a sharp knife on the table.

She slipped the pages back into the envelope and hid them under towels in the linen drawer. Then she fled to the living room for a breath of air.

The morning sun had melted the ice on the big bay window and the warmth felt good. Her head stopped pounding. Staring into the shrivelled remnant of fall that was Jeanne Mance Park, she wondered how an envelope could have the power to knock her down. After all, the news was hardly a surprise. Paulette blurted it out in Calgary, blamed Myra because all their money had gone into the mortgage until it was too late to have kids. She sounded angry all right, but the words didn't mean anything. More like a vase or something sharp you hurl during an argument, and anyway, Myra could not for a moment believe a mere mortgage stopped them from having kids. People make up excuses, but when it comes to decisions like kids, if you want them, you have them. Even if you don't, sometimes you still do. Children will be born.

She turned and looked at what now, apparently, belonged to her. Eight-and-a-half ample rooms sloping ever so slightly toward the St. Lawrence River. Thirty-six walls standing against the slide, lightening cracks where they couldn't bear the strain any more. Plaster held tight by decades of wallpaper. High ceilings ringed with ornate moldings, lit by dangling brass fixtures that flickered with the tentative juice of ancient wiring. Lace curtains covering the milky glass of big, old windows, their painted sills chipped down to the original wood by seasons of rolled plastic, stapled and taped to the frames each November, ritually ripped off on the first warm day of March. A massive oak fireplace that never worked. Half-a-dozen closets with porcelain doorknobs that will not stay shut. A big bathroom with a tiny, low sink and heavy tub, as white and porous as an old person's skin, too fragile to scrub clean, rust marks like habitual drools under the taps. Bedrooms painted impulsively, the colours demanded by burgeoning teenage personalities. Two balconies, clay pots full of dying plants, stacks of beer cases, recycling plans, rusty bike parts and things nobody remembers saving. Familiar rooms, stretching out from a splendid view of the Mountain at one end, to a cluttered cubbyhole of books and old newspapers, where she went to work each day. Rooms she once thought of tentatively, even contemptuously, as "the landlord's." Rooms she might have despised, if the rent hadn't been so unbelievably cheap. Now, those rooms seemed to look back at her. Almost alive. Like an image in a mirror, if you move, the image moves.

"The property now belongs to you. I sincerely hope this will be satisfactory." She recalled the stilted tone of Jack's memo and might have laughed, but the stare of the rooms made her uneasy. She decided to clean up the coffee grounds and give Sally a call. Surely Sal would have heard something about this latest installment in Jack Grant's rainbow crackup.

Until now, Sally's forthcoming exhibition had consisted of one or two paintings in a group show organized by her professor, mentioned in passing with a dismissive tone. If not for the reference in Jack's legal correspondence, the event might have gone by with a hum. When Myra called, fishing for information, Sal let all hints pass unnoticed but she did concede reluctantly that the exhibition featured only three students, and there were posters and a reception and yes, of course the family is invited.

"I'm sure I mentioned it, Mom. Okay, this is your formal invitation. I hope you'll be there. Jeeze! It's no big deal, really. Don't get your expectations up or anything."

Ships are launched, plays have premieres. Art, in French, gets a vernissage, from vernis, meaning polish or gloss, dating from times when oil paintings were finished with a coat of varnish, applied in public. In the far-flung Grant family, Sally's vernissage did just that, lined up everybody's boots on the stairwell for a good coat of spit and shine.

Chief among the bakers of vernissage sweetmeats was Mandy, who insisted James be outfitted in new togs for the evening and that she wear a freshly sewn dress. First, she cleaned the house from stair to ceiling, blushing as she pointed Myra at four green garbage bags full of stuff, which she suggested, "well, um, might not be, like, needed any more?"

The prospect of meeting "Mr. Grant" loomed huge. She insisted Mitch tell her all about him, which netted her little more than a list of hobbies and tics, such as Jack's lamentable performance at card games, his unfamiliarity with the rules of football, intolerance for mess, fondness for old cars and prowess at chess. As for what's he like? "Well," said Mitch, quietly, "He's quiet." He still glanced nervously at Myra when the talk was of Jack. "He likes scotch. He's a pretty good story-teller, when you get him going."

Myra noticed he said nothing about Jack's so-called nervous breakdown, and wondered if he'd even registered the news.

While Mandy's anxiety, disguised as enthusiasm, bathed the days in pre-Christmas-like excitement, James translated her mood into a full-blown case of kid hysteria. By the time the day of the vernissage rolled around, he had managed to leverage the promise of a new video game if he behaved in public.

Except for important deadlines, Myra left everything till the last minute. Finally, Saturday, the day of the vernissage, she took out the phone number Paulette had given her, and booked into a swanky Laurier Street hair salon, called enigmatically, Click.

First, she decided to find something to wear. She didn't quite know what to expect, how to prepare. Sally's friends would be young and unmatchable, the art crowd, meaning you could get away with turning up in anything. Jack would likely wear a three-piece suit; she resolved for once to dress for Jack, hand herself over to a sensible department store, and suspend judgment.

Riding up the escalator at Eaton's, away from the perfume stalls and stockings, she followed her reflection in the wall of mirrors: choppy hair the colour of bark, pale jeans, a flannel shirt at least a decade old (worn through some excruciating deadlines), navy mellon coat, warm but that reeks of must when wet. Somewhere in this jungle of smart-smelling clothes, she hoped to find something fresh and sure, a look that would hide her anxiety and encourage others to do the talking.

The first saleslady she met was French-speaking but had never heard of a vernissage. Finally, they came up with "un cocktail," and she hurried off to gather up a few suggestions. The season's colours seemed to be beige and a dusty shade of purple, which Myra pegged as maroon and the saleslady called marron. She liked the double entendre of maroon, savoured the idea of herself, marooned in a sea of art and unpredictable family currents. What difference does it make who owns the house, she thought. The heat, lights, water and now taxes still have to be paid. Taxes could be the killer, not to mention upkeep. The "landlord" had the good years, now that third-storey ramshackle was probably sliding into an era of high maintenance. She tried on a maroon dress but it made her feel ancient. Beige might be all right for a wallflower but she would never wear it afterwards.

Something a little more, ah, vivante. Myra explained this to her in French, but even as she persisted, French still did not work at Chez Eaton. "Ow much did you want to spend?" the saleslady asked.

When Myra shrugged, she smiled, convinced a fat sale was in the bag, and wandered off in the direction of designer labels.

Trapped before a full-length mirror view of herself in wrinkled undies and a bra held together by safety pins, she took a deep breath and stood unnaturally straight, sucked in her cheeks and pushed the hair back away from her face. She looked at her body coldly, and thought how much it looks like the house, sloping unconsciously, resisting the drift, barely. Neglected, ignored. A place where things happen, but unremarkable in itself.

The saleslady appeared with an armful of clothes, suits, pants, dresses, weird colours and cozy fabrics, grey, brown, rust. She tried on everything, began to despair and after despair to change her mind and go with wearing something familiar, until the saleslady handed her a black knit dress with a slit up the back, elbow-length sleeves and a boat neck. She pulled her hair back and stood on tiptoe. The black dress was simple, a pillar of severe homespun wool, a dress you could hide in, walk beside a pin-stripped lawyer and not stand out. The price was double what she was prepared to spend, but she knew she couldn't stand another minute of shopping. "D'accord," she nodded, pulled on her old jeans as the saleslady, smiling, loaded up an armful of discards.

Taking one last look in the mirror, she resolved to stand up straight, and get a pair of high heels. Nothing like walking on heels to remind you there is more than one way to walk. On the way out, she stopped at the ladies' lingerie department long enough to pick up everything that goes under a body-hugging dress, and then headed toward the Metro.

Paulette's hairdresser's name was Barry, and even after 12 years, he was still happily on the job, introduced by the front-desk clerk as "your colourist." Barry's assistant Chantal came downstairs to greet Myra. Bon, alors, this way, s'il vous plaît. No squabbles with language at Click, all conversation takes place in a fluid mixture of English and French, often within the same sentence. From the moment she left her clothes in the dressing room and wrapped herself in the pumpkin-coloured hospital gown, Myra was under Barry's care. Examining the shafts of hair, he nodded gravely and recommended a severe-sounding product to the assistant. Catching their exchange, Myra got the impression her hair represented a formidable challenge to the world of professional grooming, but Barry and Chantal seemed ready to proceed with confidence. They left her out of it.

Even Chantal had an assistant, an eager young girl working her way up from floor-sweeper. She directed Myra to the row of black sinks and helped her up onto what looked like a padded operating table, eased her head back onto the sink rest, then offered her a choice of cappuccino or orange juice. "I'm only here for a haircut," she felt like saying, but under the sepia lights with zenlike music muffling the splash of water and snip snip snips, she could only nod and mumble, "Juice, fine, merci. "

Then Chantal appeared, and with deft fingers, delivered a scalp massage that travelled down her spine and almost put her to sleep. Finally, head wrapped in an oversized towel, she was pointed in the direction of Barry, who stood chatting to a pencil-thin girl in a tube top and tube shirt, her meaty legs ending in open-toed shoes with soles as thick as phone books. At the sight of Myra, Barry stopped smiling, whirled a chair around, indicated she should sit down. Then he took off the towel and peered at her wet hair ominously.

Sensing a crucial moment, Myra said, "I thought it might be — "

But Barry cut her off with a tch tch tch and said, "Don't cross your legs, please." Then he wrapped a black plastic apron around her neck, and proceeded with the briskness of a surgeon who had already diagnosed the problem. She sat up straight, and he began to drag a comb through the tangles, starting from the base of her neck. She closed her eyes and heard fierce snipping, peeked once and saw chunks falling on the floor. Finally, he took her chin firmly in both hands, pointed her face at the mirror, and disappeared behind a velvet curtain. A large glass of fresh squeezed orange juice had appeared on the counter. She reached out and took it, noticing that every other patient along the rows of mirrored counters seemed similarly submissive, wrapped in plastic and ugly, with their head under construction.

Finally, Barry returned with a plastic cup, stirring the mixture furiously. By the resolute set of his jaw, she figured it was probably too late to question his plan, so she uncrossed her legs and closed her eyes again, hoping her face projected a meditative air. She could feel him pulling on little bites of hair and painting the shafts with a brush. When he'd covered her whole head, he wrapped the hair in plastic and said "20 minutes," then spun around and disappeared. She wondered if it was up to her to watch the clock.

Not even during childbirth had she submitted to a taciturn professional this way, but something in the decor and clipped banter of the lean, dervish staff took away her ability to intervene. She felt out of control, but was surprised to find it wasn't an entirely unpleasant feeling.

Chantal kept an eye on the clock, and as she led Myra back to the sinks to wash off the dye, her cheery expression eased the tension a little. While Myra sat for another 15 minutes, Barry counselled a 20-something fellow whose mass of braids hardly seemed in need of help. Finally, he pointed a roaring hairdryer at her head and when he was finished, her hair was streaked blonde and coaxed straight up and out, like a frightened cat, screaming.

She looked at herself in the mirror, at Barry, at the head she would have to carry around in public for months. She looked like somebody else. Like a stranger. No, she looked like Barry. Same colour, same style, same everything except the age, sex, face and life.

"Well!" said Barry, and it wasn't a question.

"I'm blonde," said Myra.

"No no no. You're golden brown. Fabulous. Fabulous."

And thus he pronounced the transformation a success, held an oval mirror to the back of her neck and gave her a brisk peek at the windswept look from behind. Too late to panic, she thought. But panic crept up her spine anyway. He handed her the bill and recommended a few of the hair products available at the front counter. "Don't forget to have them touch up your makeup downstairs," he said, winking. "It's included. Tch tch. Magnifique."

She moved her lips for what she hoped looked like a smile and mumbled, thank you. Chantal floated by, and Myra asked if there might be a washroom on the premises. She took her clothes from the dressing room and locked herself in the powder room, determined to stay there until the shock waves stopped slapping against her eyelids and she could cope with this startling new self.

She thought of Paulette — the impulsive act of chopping off a foot of dead hair in her guest bathroom had been one thing, a personal gesture, response to Calgary. All that hair, for so long, a heavy appendage that got caught in zippers and tangled by wind and pinned out of the way while she worked. The first cut left her naked, now she felt raw. And scarcely four hours until the vernissage. She forced herself to get dressed, thinking, it's too late to find a wig.

Downstairs the receptionist cooed, "Hein, c'est cute!" as she took her bank card and pointed Myra at the makeup tables, where yet another image expert was waiting to touch up the damage to her makeup done by Chantal's shampoo, the point being to demonstrate products and thereby encourage sales.

Myra was about to say, I never wear makeup, when the makeup man pointed to a chair, and she sat down. By the time she walked out half an hour later, she'd bought one of everything he used to bring her face into the new universe of golden Barry's spiked hair.

# IV

◆

Saturday morning, Jack checked into the Queen Elizabeth Hotel and prepared to spend the afternoon strolling through the streets of Montreal. He'd considered taking the kids for lunch, but decided instead to go slowly, let the city settle into his bones. He was wearing an old pair of jeans and a Canadiens T-shirt under a down-filled parka, carrying only a battered gym bag, not much more inside than a toothbrush and a change of underwear. The desk clerk eyed him, asked coolly, "May I take your luggage, monsieur?"

"Nope," he said. "This is it. I'm only here overnight."

When she asked for a credit card, he had one but pulled a fat roll of bills out of his jacket pocket. She looked dismayed, as if cash put a man in a bad light. He enjoyed that reaction. Lately, he'd begun to take immense pleasure out of watching people play their roles. Looked at a certain way, it's pretty obvious that everybody's in a movie, they dress for the part each morning and go out on location and try to stick to the story. If you doubt the story for a moment, you lose your place in the script and somebody steps out from behind the camera and taps you on the shoulder. That's what Jack Grant learned from his foggy nightmare of a so-called breakdown. It wasn't a breakdown, he told the psychiatrist. It was a breakout. Now it's over, he has stepped back into the light, script firmly in hand. But now he knows it's all unreal, and knowing that, he cannot resist a little improvisation.

On the phone, Sally had tried to make the vernissage sound insignificant, but he recognized the tone of voice. She's serious about art, so she cannot bear to let anybody know how much it all means. That's why he decided not to drag her out to a restaurant for one of those phoney family meals, when the poor kid's stomach would be a fist of terror. He planned to walk into the gallery looking like he'd just been strolling by the door and happened to spot her name on the poster. In fact, he was as nervous as if the vernissage was his. "Shit," he swore to himself and decided to get a drink before taking the grand soul-satisfying tour of Montreal, city of choices, site of pivotal scenes from his past.

He hadn't come back to Montreal much since leaving, didn't miss it. But Sally and Mitch — the city that held them burned like a light in the back of his mind, 24 hours a day.

Walking down Ste-Catherine, his leather boots began to soak up the slush, the sting of winter seeping into his socks. The street seemed battered and grey, too many stores boarded up, à louer signs everywhere. Shabby. He thought, it's true what they say, politics has put Montreal on hold. He bought a Gazette, turned into Winnie's, took a window seat. When the waitress went off to get his drink, he opened up the sports section and spotted a columnist howling over the forthcoming closing of the Forum. Signs of the times — constipated referendum result, city on the skids, and the greatest hockey arena in the country goes out of business, killed off by the billion-dollar ambitions of speculators who control the game. He couldn't finish the column, didn't want to slide into a nostalgic mood with a long night in the family-knot stretching ahead. His psychiatrist said something about a lot of people his age suddenly feeling the world does not make sense any more. Jack didn't say anything; he didn't want to encourage the man's expensive bullshit. But he thought, that's not my problem. My problem is, everything makes sense. Never did before, but it does now.

The Gazette's art section had a big piece about a controversial acquisition by the National Gallery. Is it art? The pig farmers of Saskatchewan think not. These same arguments have been going on for years. The very thought of art and art talk made him weary, but the bad mood went away when he thought of Sally and the intensity she poured onto a page or a canvas. He hoped she could go on believing in art until the life of art had settled into her bones. Then it would be possible to continue, because then the arguments won't be with pig farmers or critics, the only arguments that count would be within herself. Her life, her movie. He wondered if he could say that to his daughter and be understood. He wished to God she'd come out to Calgary, and give him a chance to say things.

Walking, walking, his feet started to grow numb with cold. What an idiot, he thought. Not even a dry pair of socks. Coming here without luggage was a bad idea and 100 per cent his own. Paulette packed a bagful of clean, pressed winter clothes, but he left it in a locker at the airport in Calgary. Noticing Eaton's coming up ahead, he decided to buy himself a pair of socks, and that's when he saw Myra, picking through a sale bin in ladies' lingerie.

His first thought was to go over and say hi, but she'd already moved to the checkout counter and seemed to be in a hurry. Watching her walk out of the store, he was glad he let the impulse slip. She'd want to know why he didn't call, why he didn't fly in Friday night, and what about this business with the house. What does it mean, she'll want to know. The minute he dropped the envelope into the mailbox, he knew it was one more step over the line. He wanted to cross the line. Paulette's right, ultimately, life has to be pushed and pulled toward resolution, otherwise we just drift. Still, he dreaded the next 24 hours, wished he had the almighty script in hand and knew exactly what was going to happen next.

He decided to wander around the store for a while, put a little distance between himself and the possibility of bumping into Myra. The perfume stalls and stocking displays reminded him of airports. He started to feel grubby in his parka and beat-up old cowboy boots, and began to wonder if maybe he shouldn't pick up a shirt. Then he thought of Myra, her granola politics and well-informed intensity, and he let the revolving doors toss him right back out into the street again. No way was he going to play the pin-striped suit, symbol of suburban comfort, and watch the take-out earth mother of Esplanade shake her head with disapproval. Not this time.

He saw a phone booth and decided to call Sally. The sound of her voice always made him feel good, especially the first milk-pure rustle of hello.

Mitch thought he'd never get an hour alone in the house again, so constantly present had everyone suddenly become since the day he stumbled across Myra's unsent letters to Jack. He had not dared to open up the envelope again — anyway, he didn't really want to read them, he just wanted to know if she'd stopped writing in 1990. Or was there another bundle somewhere? Saturday afternoon, finally, the house was quiet. Everybody out shopping for Sally's damn ver-nee-sawwwge. He opened the door to Myra's study, and looked with dismay at the mounds of paper. He was still poking through the filing cabinet when Mandy called his name. He decided to hold off answering till he'd finished the search.

Finding the house empty, Mandy went into the kitchen to put away the yogurt she'd picked up after dropping James at a friend's birthday party. She dreaded the thought of how wound up he'd be after all that sugar, and with Sally's vernissage starting just before bedtime. Maybe she should have booked a sitter, but he really wanted to go.

So quiet, she could hear the clock tick. She opened the fridge door, felt the whirl of cool air blasting against white light. She loved staring into the white light, it was something she got out of a book once, about mind control. You stare into a small complex shape and let your thoughts go blank. Staring at a light up close long enough can make you go temporarily blind. That wasn't in the book, it was something she learned on her own.

Staring into the light, she started to dread the night ahead, though for weeks she'd been looking forward to it. Getting to meet Mitch's father, the mysterious Mr. Grant. She wondered how Myra could have let that one fall apart, him a lawyer and everything. People who have it good don't realize how easily it can fall apart. You have to try really hard to put even the simplest of lives together. Kids help. Still, the white light is so so bright. She couldn't take her eyes off the light, and just at the moment when her mind normally started to empty out, she thought, just this once. One more time. She kept a little box of the white stuff right up there in the spice rack, as a reminder that being strong is a day-by-day effort. Anybody can be strong, in jail. But real strength is in the mind. It would be so so great to know that tonight'll float by and be great. Mitch is such a great guy. James is so goddamn lucky, we're both lucky, she thought, taking the little tin box off the shelf. Maybe not lucky, maybe blessed. Living under a white light blessed star. Just in case, she took the tin box into the bathroom and locked the door, thinking, Mitch must be at the library.

He couldn't find the proof, at least not in the paper-packed den where Myra wrote her stories and spent the day on the phone, yet he felt positive proof did exist, somewhere. Ever since he could remember, Mitch had wanted to kick the old man's ass for taking off like that and starting over. They had pictures of them all as a family, mother, father, cute girl, baby, and they looked pretty happy. Jack never seemed happy when cute girl and boy turned up in Calgary with their suitcases, he acted like a scout leader and the way everything was set up for them, rooms and places at the table, they felt away from home. He thought his dad felt away from home, too. Why didn't he just come home? Mitch wanted to kick his ass, and say, get home.

But Myra's unsent letters told another story. She had things to say but didn't say them. Maybe if they'd yelled at each other and thrown a few plates, Jack would have known what to do. At least that's how Mitch put the story together as he sat in Myra's swivel chair and tried to figure out why this big dark home always feels half-empty, no matter how many people crawl under the covers and fall asleep each night. Something missing. He always thought it was Dad. He blamed Dad. Now he had the proof it was her fault. Behind a closed door, boy did she type away, night and day. News. And what was the news? Letters, kept in a sealed envelope. 1980–1990. Maybe even longer.

The sound of his daughter's voice cheered Jack up, even if she had to run. That's to be expected. He was right not to drag them through a family lunch before the vernissage. He felt exuberant, as he put the phone down and headed back out onto the street.

Five minutes later he was at Birks talking to a sales clerk, a smooth, well-kept woman about Paulette's age, both of them looking down at a tray covered with fine gold chains. She glowed when he said, "It's for my daughter. She's an artist." Women love the kind of love that leaps right over sex and beatifies their entire sex. Unless they have good reason to be jealous, for example, the father-daughter thing, then watch out. Jack handed over his credit card and scrawled his name across four figures for Sally's present. He wasn't the kind of man who fell into a swoon every other day, but he had to admit that as the seasons passed and Sally turned into a woman, in his mind she had become the paragon of womanhood, the most beautiful, mysterious, untouchable female ever. Knowing Paulette would be jealous, he felt vaguely, deliciously guilty.

He tucked the velvet box into his jacket pocket and headed back to the hotel for a change of socks and a bite to eat. The woeful November sun had slipped behind the Mountain; the slush was colder than ever. His toes were beyond numb, his ankles clammy, but the fingers around that blue box burned with anticipation. As he dodged the twinkle of street lights and bumper-to-bumper traffic, he thought, this shabby old city still aches with magic.

For an instant, the far-off sound of her father's voice made Sally think he was calling from Calgary, and her voice snapped with accusation. "Where are you?"

When he said, "I'm standing in slush on the corner of Ste-Catherine and St-Somethingerother," it felt like the street lights had just come on downtown, that moment you so rarely notice, when light suddenly burns dusk into evening, yet it happens every night.

"Just checking in," he said. "Are you ready?"

"I'm ready. Don't know about the rest of you . . ." She laughed, the ever-confident Sally chortle.

He faked nonchalance. "What time is this thing, anyway?"

"Daddy! You wrote it down. Seven."

"Just checking. Seven on the dot, or fashionably late?"

"For you, on the dot. It's going to be awful at first. Come early so you can make your comments before the snacks are all gone."

"Snacks, eh? Must be a high-class event."

"Don't get your hopes up."

Sally hung up the phone and felt the day's excitement inch her nerves a little further up the scale toward panic. For a long time, putting paint on paper and fooling around with clay had seemed like play, but lately, since she moved out on her own and into a place where you could do anything you want any time of the night or day, the paint and clay thing had started to feel more like escape. She'd go into her makeshift studio whenever she wanted to get away and think. Once her hands made contact with the materials, her mind became colour and clay. Sometimes she worked all night, swinging back and forth from one piece to another. Deep into clay and colour, whatever it was that made her head churn disappeared. Or came out someplace else. In colour or clay.

When the van came to load up her three paintings and two sculptures for the exhibition, she'd felt weird, like a box of secrets was leaving home. Now her parents, both of them, plus gawky Brady Bunch Mitch and his tweeky little kitchen slave, were going to mill around with drinks in their hands and see all of her secrets. Too late now to call the whole thing off. When she thought about her father standing in front of some of those images, she felt sick, like staying away. But where? The only thing worse than facing this music would be killing the agonizing hours somewhere else, knowing they'd all be waiting, blind to the work, asking, "Where's Sally?"

She wondered if all artists felt this way, whether a major attack of regret happens every time you expose yourself. Je m'expose. The French have it right, she thought, stepping into the shower. Now the proverbial shit is about to hit the proverbial fan.

# V

◆

At five minutes to seven, Jack made his way through the cement bowels of Place des Arts and emerged from the parking garage within sight of the warehouse, corner of Ontario and Clark. On the door, a poster welcoming people to La Planète de Saturne, vernissage de nouvelles oeuvres listed three artists, but made no mention of Sally. Odd, he thought, trudging up grimy stairs to the third floor. Must be some mistake.

She was waiting for him outside the gallery door, kissed him on both cheeks while he reached out to give her a big bear hug that lifted her right off the floor, clunky shoes and all. "Hey, you don't look so crazy," she said. "I mean, no worse than usual."

"Who told you I was crazy?"

"You did! Remember that letter? Oh dear, you are."

He hated losing the first blushing round of repartee, so before she could say more, dropped the velvet box into her hand. She gasped when she saw the gold chain, put it on immediately and asked him to hold on to the box, because in all the excitement, she'd forgotten to bring a purse. Against her pale skin the necklace looked like finely woven baby hair, and he thought, pure gold is one particular earthbound substance that is not a whit overvalued.

Then she kissed him on the cheek, close to his ear, and whispered, "I am never, ever going to take this off, Daddy. Thank you. Come on, there's somebody I want you to meet."

Mandy and Mitch had to drop by a little kid's birthday party and pick up James. They seemed to be in the middle of a fight, angry whispers floating from the bathroom, so Myra decided to stay out of the way, hide in the back room office till she heard the front door close.

Despite a day's preparation, she was not exactly looking forward to the evening. It was Sally's night. She could happily play invisible, but she had an uneasy feeling, as though the tremor of Jack's breakdown were moving east. The feeling had forced its way to the surface, already come out in her hair, left her as self-conscious as a 15-year-old. If not for the anxiety of being in the same room with Jack, she never would have bothered with a new hairdo, or thought twice about what to wear.

At the last minute, she almost decided against the black dress, so hopelessly awkward did it feel to be wearing something unfamiliar, but everything in the closet was old and limp. Heading down the slippery outdoor staircase in new high-heeled shoes, she felt silly. She hadn't thought about how a well-worn three-quarters coat and sensible three-year-old waterproof boots would look with a dress that's slit up the back. Winter boots were clumsy; she resolved to persevere with the high-heeled shoes, get a cab if necessary.

By the time she got to the warehouse, no cabs had appeared and the backs of her heels were raw. She wiped salt off the leather with a Kleenex and tiptoed through the door, hoping there would be an elevator, but there wasn't.

The first person Myra saw as she entered the crowded gallery was Jack, in a Montreal Canadiens sweater made for a bigger man, jeans tucked into cowboy boots. He was standing beside Sally and the new boyfriend, both men gripping plastic wine glasses, and he did not look happy. Pierre-Marie seemed to be doing a lot of talking, gesticulating with his wine-bearing hand. Jack's lips formed that tight little line he tries to pass off as a smile whenever he's resisting an urge to run.

Sally saw Myra first, came over to the door and peeled her coat off, turned her mother a full 360 degrees and said, "Wow! You look amazing. Mom, what happened?"

"Not amazing," said Myra, ever the fount of abnegation. "I tried to fix up that suicidal haircut from Calgary, and this is the result. It'll grow out." She tugged at the dress, which had ridden up slightly during the walk.

"No, it's a vast improvement. Trust me. Just try to keep it up." Sally tossed the coat in the storage room and led Myra toward the men. Despite the confident tone, Sally seemed nervous. Pierre-Marie showed no inhibition at all as he filled Jack in on the merits of the National Gallery's latest controversial acquisition, delivering a monologue without much punctuation. She knew how Jack loathed art talk, but surely an unfortunate choice of subject matter could not fully explain the lobster hue of his ears. Pierre-Marie greeted Myra with two kisses, as if they were old friends. When he and Sally had gone off to get more wine, Jack growled, "Who's that?"

"He's a professor of art," Myra said, cheerfully. "And a friend of Sally's."

"Friend?"

"Well, boyfriend."

"Boy? How old is he, 50?"

"The grey is premature," said Myra. "He must be somewhere in his late thirties. Anyway, I thought you'd be more likely to choke on the word 'friend.'"

Jack looked over at the bar where the professor and Sally stood in giddy conversation. He watched how he touched Sally's arm, the way she leaned into his ear to whisper something that made him nod in agreement. He thought about the baby-fine gold chain around her neck, her promise never to take it off, and with a heave in his throat that made him put a hand to his mouth, he imagined his daughter lying on top of that hairy-chested blabbermouth, or worse, pinned under the son-of-a-bitch, and he had to hold himself back from going over there and ripping the goddamn thing off her neck and shoving it down the toad's throat.

Instead, he turned to Myra. "What have you done to your hair?"

"You've seen my hair like this!" she said, clapping her hands over her ears.

"Not blonde."

"It's not blonde," she stammered. "It's, you know, light brown. Why, is it that bad?"

Suddenly realizing what he had done, Jack said, "It's actually kind of cute. Who is this fellow that Sally's, ah . . ."

"Seeing? Oh, he's recent. She's into art these days, he's an artist, at least he teaches at the CEGEP du Vieux-

Montréal. Naturally, a girl like Sal is going to fall in love with a few professors. Don't worry about it. "

A few professors. Hearing it put that way, Jack started to feel a little better. He could see a line of grateful middle-aged men slipping in the mud of all that beauty before they even got to first base. Look at this exhibition. Not bad for a 19-year-old. She's not stupid, that's for sure. He watched the professor walk toward them, a glass of wine in each hand, noticed his lopsided grin and the way his glasses sat on his somewhat crooked nose, absent-mindedly. How clichéd. Of course he'd be wearing a black shirt and black blazer, the uniform of every fake *artiste* in Montreal. But obviously he'd moved his tight little ass and made this exhibition happen for a talented young woman. Those who can, do, and the rest teach. Who said that? Jack took a second glass of wine from the *teacher of art* and remarked how easily the slippery cad seemed to wrap Myra around his little finger, gaping at her hair and dress like he was hoping to score a two-for-one. Ha. Little does he know, Myra's got his number. Sally is going to fall in love with *a few professors*! Fall in and then walk right back out again. Jack watched calmly as the aging kicker struggled to make conversation — in his second language — with the parents of an up-and-coming young genius, and for a moment he felt almost sorry for Pierre-Marie. Then he thought about the poster and reminded himself to have a word with the professor. Where was Sally's name?

As the conversation turned to hockey, inspired by Jack's choice of sweaters, Myra slid away to look at the exhibition. The room had filled up with parents and friends of parents who looked flush enough to buy something. Way down the age scale was a young, colourful, buzzing art crowd, most of them hanging close to the bar. The four walls were lit with spots, and the centre of the room where people stood to talk was kept in the shadows.

Myra's attention was drawn to a large rectangular canvas along the far wall, full of dark blues and blacks, a busy collage of cityscape with the cross on Mount Royal providing the main source of light. As she got closer, she saw the skyline was actually a naked woman stretched out on her back, with bits of the city growing up from the crevices, orifices and folds of her body. At first she thought the pose might be languorous, but looking closer, she noticed a grimace on the woman's face, the arms and feet twisted awkwardly. A woman in pain. Her hair was as long as her body and flowed to the forefront of the picture until it became the St. Lawrence River and disappeared off the canvas. All this you could only pick out from the shadows, since the first impression was that of a fluid landscape. She leaned in to look at the signature, Alexis Meilleur. Then Sally was standing at her side.

"Well, what do you think?"

"Who's Alexis Meilleur?" Myra asked.

"Mom! It's me. Can't you recognize my style? . . . Alexandra Grant, a.k.a. nickname at home, Sally, turned into Alexis. It's my professional name. You know, freedom. A new name helped me let go."

"What happened to Grant?"

"You can't get far in Quebec with a name like Grant. Pierre-Marie and I were brainstorming one day, looking for something better than boring old Grant. We tried translation. Accorder? Octroyer? Dumb. Something better. So, finally we came up with meilleur. Isn't it great? A name that's on the move."

She didn't go as far as saying, "on the move, like me," but the shine in Sally's eyes left no doubt about her intentions. Myra turned back to the painting for another look, this time searching for a sign of the old Sally, some reassurance that she still knew this heady young woman now dancing beside her. The contrast was stunning. In the picture, the woman's body was writhing with agony, her womb thrust toward an empty night sky. A tiny figure of a man had thrown himself against her breast, in a Christ-like pose of flagellation; he seemed to slide down helplessly, pulling the skin with him. The city growing out of her body included vague photos of familiar buildings and angry newspaper headlines in both languages. The overall theme, visually and in the texts, was aggression and lament.

Sally was waiting for a comment, and Myra tried desperately to think of something intelligent to say. "Did you give it a name?" she asked, by way of stalling.

Impatient, Sally pointed at a tiny white card on the wall beside the paintings. Myra leaned closer, and read, beside the new name and date, "Maman."

"This is me?"

Sally rocked on her heels. "Well, it's an image of mother. I'd say it's pretty general. Pierre-Marie says I should have called this one Montreal. But I found that too vague. Don't you think? I mean, calling a painting Montreal? A little pretentious?"

Myra looked at the painting again and took a step back. Then she looked at Sally, who was fingering a chain around her neck, and she thought, who are you? Really? What woman is this, I need to know. But she said nothing. Sally shrugged. "I gotta talk to a few people, okay?" She squeezed her mother's hand and walked away.

The shoes had already worn rips in Myra's stockings, and she thought, any minute my heels are going to start bleeding. She took a few careful steps to the next work, and noticed it was a sculpture from the hands of Alexis Meilleur, entitled Le Couple. The same fluid lines and tortured expressions on the figures, but this time, a man and woman engaged in what looked like mortal combat, or sex. Peering down from the top, she noticed Sal had somehow managed to chisel out all the vital sexual parts, and her first thought was how to prevent dear Jack from attaining this perspective. Mercifully, the male was not wearing glasses, but nevertheless the two figures looked familiar. As she stood studying the sculpture, wondering if other people found it as unsettling, she heard a familiar squeal and James grabbed her by the legs. Mitch pulled him off, barked a command, "Be good." Mandy was nowhere in sight.

"We're not staying," said Mitch.

Grateful for this burst of arrowroot-scented reality, Myra picked James up and hugged him. He took a big bite of lipstick with his kiss, directly on her lips, and announced, "Granmyra's hair turned all yellow!" In a minute Jack was at her side, looking six degrees more friendly, as if he'd downed a half-a-dozen glasses of wine. James caught his eye, and pointed down into the erotic bundle of clay, standing on a pedestal between them.

"Look, that man's got his thingy out," he said, and Jack leaned over obediently to follow the little finger.

Mitch, with no reason under heaven to mitigate his sister's impending scandal, leaned over too, and when their heads came back up it looked like the apple bob had been gloriously successful. Mouths full. Speechless. Eyes big.

"Well, surely you boys have all seen a thingy before," Myra said, hoping to keep the tone nice and light. "Right, James? All boys have one."

James covered his mouth and giggled. Jack and Mitch played deaf.

Mitch said, "Hi, Dad. How's it going?"

Jack said "Great," and stuck out his hand. When they shook they seemed to shake all the tension out of the air, and Mitch said, "How was the flight out?"

"Painless," Jack replied. "One of those little four row things, but smooth."

"Oh yeah. Air Canada?"

"Yeah."


Myra figured it was time to slip away and look for Mandy before the small talk petered out. James insisted on walking, which was a relief, because her heels didn't appreciate the extra weight. She couldn't find Mandy, but managed to get a look at the rest of Sally's creations, which consisted of a second female nude, this one in happier shades of greens and greys. It showed a young woman sprawled out beside a lake, Mount Royal in the distance. Her hair was entwined in a rose bush, and she cradled a child in her arms. Her transparent womb held an unborn baby and another slipped happily from between her thighs. Eyes closed, her face bore an expression of orgiastic abandon. The title was Jeune Femme.

Beside the painting was a second sculpture, a couple in what looked like a post-coital swoon, bodies wound together, legs and arms fused into a single form. Their eyes were closed. The man's face was rough with age lines and troubled dreams, the woman's, smooth and almost featureless. One could say, blank.

Five works, Sally had said. Myra hunted around for the last one, and found it in the corner, barely six inches square, framed and hanging on the wall, but closer to sculpture than a painting. Bits of broken mirror, titled L'Avenir. The future.

Mitch came and took James by the hand. "Mandy's waiting outside," he said.

There were a few people present Myra knew, and she made an effort at conversation but her mind rang with vibrations from the world of female bliss and pain. She wanted to grab Sally and say, "You've got it all wrong," but she wasn't sure. Maybe childbirth is blind bliss, and sex is anesthetized pain. Sex and birth. Woman's eyes, closed. The vision of life Alexis Meilleur had unveiled tonight did nothing to dissolve a sensation she'd had for months. The known world has begun to tilt ever so slowly, and if people/places/things are not nailed/glued/held down, they will soon give in to the slide.

A few minutes later, Jack reappeared. "Looks like Sally's busy with her friends," he said. "My feet are freezing."

"In other words, let's go?"

"Right," he said.

Feeling his hand under her elbow was a relief. She thought, I have known this man forever.

# VI

◆

On the postcards, Montreal under winter looks icy and white, but people who live there year in year out know it's not the cold or even the dark that gets you, it's the swings. How, suddenly, in the middle of a wintry month everything melts and the streets are awash with salty mush, rightly called slush. Then either the slush evaporates, leaving sidewalks bare and people who've known Toronto winters feeling right at home, or it freezes hard at dusk, turning the downtown core into one big ice floe. Sometimes, when the temperature hangs a breath away from zero, snow starts falling and if you go into a movie, when you come out, the city is white and the way home takes forever.

Snow had started to fall as Rowan Gaunt nosed his van along the narrow streets of Old Montreal, searching for a legal rest. Finally he gave up, decided to risk an alley near L'Air du Temps, where the Curly Qs were booked in for the weekend. They called Rowan at the last minute when the horn player came down with strep throat. He hadn't played in public for years and said no at first but

Clancy, the boss, insisted. Their one and only rehearsal seemed to go okay, at least Clancy thought so. Rowan's hands shook when he touched the old sax. For the first couple of numbers he kept his eyes closed. Later, his chest hurt but he felt good.

How could a handful of grown men in their right minds form a jazz band called the Curly Qs, he wondered, as he tossed a blanket over his camera equipment and slammed the van door shut. Maybe all the good names had been taken. Clancy's no poet. The snowflakes were big and soft, they seemed to come down and go right back up again. Rowan unbuttoned his coat and slipped the cold sax under his sweater, giving a rueful sigh. Everything starts happening once you decide to leave town.

As the snow fell in dizzy sheets across the plate glass windows of Ben's Delicatessen, the waiter brought Jack his second smoked meat platter of the day.

"Aren't you worried about putting that weight back on?" Myra asked.

He stared at the sandwich, a few inches from his mouth, and said, "You can't get this in Calgary."

She emptied a creamer into watery coffee and watched him eat, glanced at the snow coming down outside and decided this was going to be a one-night stand for the painful shoes. Tomorrow, the garbage. On their way out of the gallery, Jack had noticed her limping and insisted they look for Band-Aids. Her feet felt better now with the heels taped, but on the walk back from the pharmacy, fresh snow had wilted the highly acclaimed hairdo. She felt like she was wearing a wet dishcloth. She tugged at her dress, wrapped the skirt tighter around her legs. "Was there much talk about the referendum out in Calgary?" she asked, more to make conversion than anything.

"No," Jack replied. "People are sick of it."

"I can imagine."

"Paulette flew all the way out here to vote," he said, with a trace of sarcasm. "Illegally, of course."

"Yeah, I bumped into her. We had lunch."

"She mentioned that."

Myra watched his face for a clue to Paulette's account of their meeting, but the subject didn't seem to carry significance. When he finished the sandwich, he pushed the plate to the side of the table and centred the coffee cup. The gesture had definite deliberation, and Myra thought, here we go. Who starts first? She'd prepared a long speech about the apartment and how she didn't really need charity, anyway wasn't it something they might have discussed together, and it's not my business but postponing children for the sake of a mortgage? Surely you don't blame me? Paulette said — But the speech did not have a solid opening line, so instead she said, "What do you think of Sally's work?"

He shrugged. "Interesting, for a 19-year-old. The sculptures are a little derivative."

"Derivative?"

"Half-baked Rodin."

"I don't think so."

"The kiss? Every museum on the planet has one. Even Montreal."

"That wasn't exactly a kiss," she laughed. As soon as the words were out of her mouth, she knew they'd been aimed at Jack's soft side, and hit. Sally wrapped in carnal combat with a man only slightly younger than her father: she could tell the picture hurt. Jack slumped in his chair.

"I'm no art critic," she continued, "but I thought the paintings were wonderful. The woman asleep, giving birth, it says something about the swoon of maternal instinct, but I know what you're going to say. Pictures aren't necessarily supposed to say anything. Still, they moved me. Her art seems, I don't know, a lot darker and more complicated than, well, than Sally."

Jack looked sharply at her. "I've always found Sally deep."

"Sure, she's deep, but . . ."

She stared at him, and the silence between them carried a dozen drops of too-familiar poison. According to their ritual, Jack would now decode the silence and administer the antidote all by himself. *I know, I know, I haven't been there, but nevertheless I do know Sally, she confides in me. Sometimes.* Of course he won't stoop to plea, but his every thought will plead not guilty, and colour the rest of the evening.

At L'Air du Temps the Curly Qs broke into a soulful version of "Summertime." Surrounded by whirling gusts of snow, wrapped in melody, melted by the heat of a few drinks, players and public fused, delighted by the irony of the opening tune. Meanwhile, in a nearby alley, two red-toqued members of the City's snow-removal squad struggled to fit a chain around the back axle of Rowan's van. Before the Curly Qs had finished their first set, the van lurched unhappily toward a far-off corner of Montreal.

Oblivious, Rowan closed his eyes and blew an old Earl Hines tune called "Ridin' A Riff" and thought, maybe my luck has changed. It hadn't changed yet, but the ache in his chest was better than luck.

Ben's Deli on a stormy Saturday night was hardly a mecca for goodtime seekers. While Myra and Jack sat at a corner table it was pretty well empty except for a few seedy types with nowhere else to go. They wished to God they'd thought to go somewhere else, but it was too late now. Jack pried out the story of Mitch and Mandy, managing to convey his disapproval along with a sense that he had, of course, no right to disapprove, and the words hung over them like the smell of liver when you've already finished dessert. Everything Jack had planned to say got said out of order, and the list ended up sounding like an argument. Before he even arrived at the big thick envelope full of paperwork, he handed Myra a roll of bills covering her airline ticket to Calgary, which he'd said he would pay. Of course she said you don't need to do this, but she also said it's pretty stupid to be walking around downtown Montreal with that much cash on you.

"I could give you a cheque," he said, curtly. She looked at him and said, "What would that change? Then you'd be carrying the cash. Either one of us could be robbed."

This from someone who regularly loses keys, but Jack said nothing.

"Speaking of money," she lunged, "what in the name of God possessed you to buy that apartment? Have you gone completely crazy?"

For the second time in one day, a female had called him crazy. He took a deep breath.

"Why did you do that?" she asked.

"It was a good investment."

"That's not what I mean."

"What do you mean?"

"I mean, why did you give it to me?"

He said nothing.

"Is it for the kids?"

"No," he said.

Myra was tempted to throw out guesses, but lately her clear-eyed approach to the world had begun to flounder and she could now imagine there might not be a right answer to the question. So why guess. What mattered was Jack's answer, and at the moment, he seemed to have none.

The truth was a spectrum including guilt, pride, generosity, concern, affection, even love. But now that he was sitting across from Myra, none of the noble shades seemed real any more. Jack could feel his throat clench, as if his brain would not send enough words down to keep the conversation flowing. This is what happens when you step over the line, he thought. Grey and black. Nothing to do or say but take another step.

"Speaking of paperwork," he said, "we should probably get around to a divorce. All things considered."

His tone was light, all the couching phrases light. Still, he feared her reaction. A year after they split up, when the break felt permanent and the child management lunches had become routine, he slid the paperwork for divorce across a restaurant table and she slid it right back, unopened. Not much more was said, but he felt oddly grateful at the time, as if they had just agreed to live beyond the failure of a marriage, on a higher level. Compared to other people, Jack had it good. A friendly divorce and reasonably priced too, although in the absence of a fixed rate he had paid his share, and more.

Finally after 12 years, he couldn't stand the effort of rising above failure, the air was too thin. In every conversation, subtext outweighed actual words by a thousand to one, and he was exhausted trying to figure it all out. Now he wanted what everybody else wanted, resolution. Clarity. He wanted to know how much he had to pay and for how long. At least once every day, he thought of death. He needed the lightness. He was counting on divorce to make him feel light again.

"I have no objection to divorce," Myra replied calmly. "Is that why you're giving me the apartment? Because if it is, don't bother."

"No," he said, "There's no relation."

She watched him, slumped in a hard chair under the white light, and thought how far this middle-aged man seemed to be from the Jack in her mind, the face in a photograph taken in front of Niagara Falls. He seemed neither familiar nor strange, no more like someone she knew than an icon, yet as sacred and numinous as an icon: "Your father," J.W. Grant, Jack of Calgary, his power was greater from a distance. The real Jack up close at Ben's on a nasty Saturday night seemed pale and grey. Not the man she had dressed for, surely not the man from whom she needed kind words.

The only kind words Jack could think of to say were thank you. And those words were not what she needed to hear, not what he could bear to say. All the wrong words.

He offered to get her a cab home, but she said no, she wanted to drop by Multimags for the Sunday papers first. It was almost 11 and the Sunday Times might be in by now. He said, "Fine, then I'll see you tomorrow morning. I'm taking the kids to lunch. If you want to . . ."

As he paid the bill, he noticed she did not move, stayed sitting in front of an empty coffee cup while he headed out into the storm.

# VII

◆

The storm had turned soggy by the time Myra stood on the corner of de Maisonneuve and Guy with an armful of newspapers, sports section balanced on her head, waiting for a taxi. Jack would probably catch up with Sally and the celebratory dinner, but all she wanted was a hot bath and toast, then to crawl into bed and dream whatever dreams could be conjured from this muddled day.

The taximan who stopped was a Haitian with a bounteous head of dreadlocks. He looked too young for the old jazz coming out of his stereo, and he spoke like the words were sweet candies waiting in his mouth.

"Où va-t'on, madame?"

"Chez moi," she said, and gave him the address.

"Ah, mais c'est trop tôt pour rentrer à la maison." Too early to go home. She hoped it wasn't going to be one of those rides where the driver keeps up a steady patter of pointless conversation, not tonight, please. With one hand in her pocket, she gripped the 15 one-hundred-dollar bills, but the car was luxuriously warm, and as they headed up the hill, she started to relax. The

282

driver beat his fingers on the steering wheel in time with the music. She watched him turn the mirror to catch her eyes, and thought, here we go. But he must have noticed her shrink back into the seat. He didn't say anything and the silence suddenly felt rude.

"Oscar Peterson, il est né à Montréal," she said. For a second he didn't catch on, then his eyes lit up and he turned up the music. "Oui, oui, Peterson! Montréal. Is very fine city! Festival of Jazz, I go there. Me, I take Charlie Biddle in my car last week." She smiled at him in the rearview mirror, wasn't paying attention as he sped past Jeanne Mance and signalled to turn up St-Laurent, which was jammed. A city of nighthawks, or at least enough of them to keep certain corners alive at midnight. Should have told him to take Park, she thought. Now we'll sit here listening to jazz while the meter presses on.

The taxi was a red Lincoln with plush seats, warm, enveloping. She watched the maze of neon and brake-lights outside, thought of cold coffee at Ben's, the zigzag of words that had made a precious night drag and then end with a crack. Since the fiasco in Calgary, she'd ached to be alone with Jack, wanted to ask a million questions, how do you feel and what do you mean? Longed for reassurance that the Western pillar of existence was safe and sound. He seemed so far away and nothing she said brought him closer. Now he was gone, the chance to be alone with Jack was gone. He walked away two minutes after casually dropping an ugly word. Fine, obvious, after all, why not. Still the word made her shiver, despite the passage of time, it stung like a slap. She'd gotten used to his absence, now she would have to get used to the word "divorce."

She felt bruised but, suddenly, not at all tired. Her mind was racing. Toast and a hot bath seemed like a very bad idea. The driver's right, it's too early to go home. In this jazzmobile heading for a jam on the Main, she felt ready to burst, and when it was their turn to catch the green light, she leaned ahead to give him a new address. He chuckled, nodded approval.

"Ben oui, madame. Ça c'est meilleur."

Horns around them blew furiously as he lunged into the forward traffic.

The streets of Old Montreal had taken only a few inches of snow but the plows were out anyway, prepared for a deluge. She walked along St-Paul, past L'Air du Temps and Stash's Café, continued on down the dark side of the street and around the corner to an iron door that opened on a wall of buzzers. Not all occupants listed their names. The first one she pushed answered with a sleepy growl. Finally, trial and error ended in an airless, "What?"

"It's me."

Nothing. Then a buzz and the inside door clicked open.

She wondered if he was still up, alone or entertaining, but it was past the time for turning back. The lateness of the day and the day itself merged into a reckless blur, as the freight elevator clanked up four floors, toward a view of the river she had seen before and sworn never, under any circumstances, to see from that particular perspective again. Bad news, definitely. But after jazz and rainy snow, tight-lipped Jack and all that parenting, she was beginning to remember why bad news sells newspapers. Because bad news keeps your eyes open, makes the next five minutes seem dangerously important, blots out the last five hours, five days. Five years, if it's very bad news.

She caught herself tiptoeing toward his door, smiled at the pointless trepidation. Who along this solitary row of wharf rats could be home and up at this hour? At the door, she reached under the black dress and tugged her slip down, smoothed the skirt around her legs and was glad, after all, to be wearing high heels. She knocked and heard the shuffle of slippers.

He was wearing a purple bathrobe over nothing; a cigarette dangled from his lips. She half-suspected he'd changed into this outfit while she managed the elevator, and felt privileged. This was Pain at his B-movie best, the lone river-watcher, presiding over a vast room full of darkness. The glossy expanse of hardwood floor was dominated by a green leather chair beside an ashtray full of butts and a half-empty glass, all of it facing a wall of windows, looking out at the night.

"Well, to what do I owe?" he said, as she peeled off her coat and threw it on a stack of newspapers, tossing her wet Sunday Times on top.

"I was in the neighbourhood."

"Catching a little jazz?"

"Not really. Sally had her paintings at an exhibition near here. Jack's in town."

"Say no more," he said, going to the kitchen area for a second glass. He dragged a bar stool to the middle of the room, pointed at the leather chair, and handed her a whisky. The chair was still warm. The springs were shot so she sank way down. He looked awkward, a six-foot-plus man perched on a bar stool.

When she told him about Jack's gift, a deed to the apartment on Esplanade, he whistled. "So, you're sitting on two hundred thou," he said. "That's quite a windfall."

"What, for that drafty barn?"

"Location, square footage, location."

"But, why would he do that?"

"Obvious. He feels guilty. He's paying you off."

"Jack has no reason to feel guilty, I've never asked for anything," she said, watching as he swayed, his bare toes gripping the bar-stool rungs. Must have kicked his slippers off at the door, she thought. The middle toe was long and skinny, taller than the others. Same on both feet.

He snorted. "Right, if you'd retained a lady lawyer and twisted his balls, he'd have earned the luxury of hate. But you did not twist. You live like a pauper while he makes gobs of money and travels around with his twitty housekeeper-cum-mistress. Talk about guilt. Ow. It's so obvious."

"Is it? Well, she's not a twit."

While he rambled, she was looking at his bathrobe, a deep mulberry velour, that soft, expensive towel material that looks like velvet under the lights of night. The hair on his chest was sprinkled with grey but still dark brown on his legs. Why is it, she wondered, that the hair on heads, beards and chests goes grey while legs and groins so often get by untouched?

She always liked the way he said her name. "Myra, face it, you've poured your youth into raising Jack's kids, and never used them in a fight. He owes you big."

"My youth. Thanks a lot," she said.

"It's true."

"Jack's kids? They're my kids, too."

"How old are you?"

"Forty-two."

He got up and walked into the bathroom, leaving the door open so the sound of hot urine pouring into the bowl filled the loft. Pulling herself up out of the chair, she felt her limbs ache.

The single room that now held all of Pain's worldly possessions included a ceiling-to-floor bookcase on one wall, with a shelf for his stereo and pared-down library of CDs. She chose Billie Holiday, and the lady's sad orchid voice muffled the belch of a toilet flushing. Mainly the library contained books about power, timely titles by people he knew, intimate portraits of public figures, including a biography of de Gaulle in French and Conrad Black's two-volume portrait of Maurice Duplessis. On the bottom shelves were signed first editions by famous Canadian novelists and a few self-help tomes with pungent dedications from women. It was a good ten minutes between the flush and Pain's reappearance at her side, time enough to wonder whether this visit might be a mistake, but not enough time to answer yes, and leave.

"Can I top up your drink?" he asked.

"No, I've had enough for tonight. All that cheap red wine at the vernissage made my head ache. Whisky gives me heartburn."

"You're definitely getting old," he said.

"Everybody's getting old," she answered. "You've got a head start."

"Okay, I deserved that." As he said it, he stayed planted beside her. She took down a volume by Pierre Elliott Trudeau, *Federalism and the French Canadians*, and noticed the former prime minister had signed an inscription, dated 1968. It was a quote from Francis Bacon, "Knowledge is power."

He glanced down at the open book and said, "Is it just me, or does that statement sound incredibly naive?"

Myra put the book back. "I used to think knowledge was everything, and you only had so many hours in the day to get it, so wake up early and don't be lazy."

"And you were wrong?"

He leaned his arm on the bookshelf. She felt she should step away, put a little more distance between herself and the hairs of his chest which the loose-fitting bathrobe let show, so close she could smell the warmth of his skin, too close to permit significant conversation. But she didn't move, didn't look him in the eye either. They stood that way for an unnaturally long time, in full knowledge of what the next move should be, aware that whoever acted on knowledge would lose power. She'd rung the bell; Pain only answered the door. He expected she would reach out and untie the belt of his bathrobe, and he was old enough to wait for it.

"I should be going," she said.

"As you wish," he said.

"Could I use the bathroom first?"

"Sure."

The walls were exposed brick, the lighting, soft. A large mirror framed in oak hung over the sink and Myra was surprised to see she didn't look as bad as she thought. The medicine cabinet contained a few prescription bottles, essential toiletries and a flowered makeup bag. She touched up her eyes and powdered her nose, stalled briefly over a tube of wine-coloured lipstick. Why be squeamish about lips, she thought. Makes no sense at all. Like a kiss. The idea of wearing another woman's lipstick was amusing. An expensive brand, it tasted faintly sweet, one of those fruit flavours concocted from chemicals.

When she came out, he was sitting in the chair and had poured fresh glasses of whisky. She took a glass, climbed up on the bar stool.

"I saw your piece on the theatre," she said.

"Oh, yeah that. They liked it in Toronto," he replied, sounding ever so finely defensive.

"I'm sure they did. And I'm sure you know what I thought about it."

"Not really."

"Well, never mind."

He laughed a little meanly.

She took a good gulp and looked at the door, thinking it isn't far away, time to cover the distance. With nowhere to lean, her back hurt. Pain sat with his glass balanced on his belly, and looked like he might fall asleep, swallowed up by the room's one comfortable rest, except for a man-sized bed that occupied the far corner, low and covered with big pillows.

"How's work going?" she asked. It sounded like manufactured conversation.

"Actually, it doesn't pay me to work any more," he replied, taking a vengeful gulp of liquor. "I am a free man, in the monastic sense. There is nothing left of me for lawyers or women to take. What a relief. The next stop is starvation and abject solitude, but so far neither one of those doggies has come sniffing at my the door.

In many ways, I'm a fortunate man. At least tonight."
He smiled.

Myra knew she had just been accused of attempted salvation, and slid down off the stool. She wandered over to the window for a look at the river. "The view up here is definitely worth the trouble of your elevator," she said.

"So you've come for the view?"

She turned around, and leaning against the window, looked straight at him. "I came up here to see you," she said.

If he doesn't come over here in the next five minutes, I'm going home, she vowed silently.

"Lucky I was home," he said. In his voice, there was no taste of the maple syrup warmth that always proceeds an ice-breaking gesture.

"I came because . . . I missed you," she said, softly.

"What part did you miss?" His tone was ironic, but the question seemed to deserve an answer.

She spoke slowly. "I missed the part of you that stays alive after I've forgotten your voice. How you always say sharp things with a hungry voice."

He leaned forward and put his head in his hands. She could no longer see his face, but could feel him listening.

"Most of all, I missed a certain kind of truth."

She thought, after I've seen you, I always feel like running again, and that's good. That's what I need.

She said, "You are the loneliest human being I have ever gotten to know. You remind me — " She stopped.

"What?" he said.

"Well, that I am, too. Lonely. It isn't something I'd want to be reminded of all the time. But sometimes, yeah, I really miss you."

He looked up, and she thought, he's going to cry. The hardness in his eyes had disappeared, as if the legendary contempt that made it possible to face the world had been sucked right out of his repertoire. Under the mask, there was only more Pain. So aptly named by a man who needed Pain. Or thought he did.

Okay, the door, she vowed to herself. But just then he got up and came over to her, took her hand and kissed it.

"Myra, you know I can't give you what you want. I'm —"

She reached up and put her hand over his mouth. "If you say anything bullshitty, I am going to walk right out the door. So, if you want me to stay, I strongly suggest you say nothing."

She gave him a few seconds to reflect before taking her hand off his mouth. His eyes were smiling as he undid the knot in his bathrobe, all by himself. This is good, she thought. After Billie Holiday comes Tom Waits, and then some cigarette-smoking jazz. This is good.

# VIII

◆

The celebratory dinner scheduled for Le Continental Bistro Américain on St-Denis Street was a little beyond the reach of Sally's crowd, but Pierre-Marie had made the plans. Jack carried the address in his pocket as he left Ben's. He decided to walk, work off the smoked meat, prepare himself for the excruciating chore of making conversation with Professor Boyfriend. Climbing the stretch of St-Laurent below Sherbrooke left him out of breath. Not surprising, he thought, after everything that's happened. In the middle of his bout with doctors he had resolved to start working out, but then a guy at the office dropped dead while out jogging and he'd been running three times a week for years. So Jack decided to go slowly. He picked up a book on breathing exercises, and started doing them after dinner.

On the corner of Pine, he stopped, took a few deep gulps of night air and filled his lungs with the sweet salty aroma of sizzling chicken wafting out of a Lebanese take-out. Shish taouk, he'd never seen it in Calgary — strips of sizzling chicken, raw onion, thick yogurt, lettuce, tomato and red turnip pickle, all of it wrapped in pita bread, not greasy, either. He thought of treating himself, they aren't very big, but figured the juice would drip all over his shirt. Considering the professor's desire to impress, he was probably gravely underdressed, as is, for the Continental Bistro Américain. At the corner of Rachel, he looked at his watch, decided there was still time to swing past the choice piece of real estate that until a few weeks ago had been his. The company he hired to keep an eye claimed it was still in pretty good shape. He'd head out into Jeanne Mance Park and have a look from afar, thereby lowering the risk of running into Myra.

He saw the flashing lights from the corner, a police cruiser and an ambulance. Didn't know it was that kind of a neighbourhood, he thought, and edged along the park side of the street, nosy, as anybody would be in the presence of disaster. Two large men were coming down the staircase with a body strapped to a stretcher. He recognized the figure behind them right away — Mitch, grave-faced and carrying a small suitcase. He stood back and watched as his son spoke to an elderly foreign-looking woman huddled in a bulky coat. He recognized the face — Mrs. Pagnos, their neighbour. She headed up the staircase as the men loaded the stretcher into the back of the ambulance.

"Mitch!" Jack heard his own voice, desperate and distant.

"Dad, what are you doing here?"

"What's going on?" He hadn't meant to sound accusing.

"Shit," said Mitch. "Shit, shit, shit."

"Tu viens, toé?" the ambulance driver snapped. "Faut se dépêcher, hein?"

"Oui, j'arrive," Mitch replied. "Dad, I gotta go."

Mitch climbed up into the ambulance and Jack followed him.

Bad weather and a relatively unknown band could be blamed for the slim turnout at the Curly Qs' debut at L'Air du Temps. And competition, Saturday night in Montreal, it's ferocious. Rowan was doing Clancy a favour so it didn't really matter if their split of the door was pathetic. Besides he was too strung out to notice how many eyes watched his fingers in the dark. The sensation of his breath transformed by the instrument and blasted into the dark was enough. A thousand people or one, infinitely more than nobody.

The Qs stayed behind drinking while the bar staff cleaned up. Rowan headed home. He was loft-sitting a few blocks from the bar and didn't give a thought to his van. He whistled as he walked down the street, "Some Enchanted Evening." What if the Qs' horn man develops permanent throat paralysis? Or signs up with a band that's going somewhere? Don't even think about it, he told himself. You don't want to know. Lately Rowan had begun to — not exactly talk to himself — but think in the second person, and it seemed to make a difference. Whereas before his mind used to bounce back and forth between wildly conflicting desires and opinions, now he simply agreed to disagree. At least it kept his feet moving.

Old Montreal has grown so dingy and dead, he thought, fumbling for the key to the front door. Who'd want to live here? A tenured university poet, friend of his, sort of, was on sabbatical in Costa Rica, so the loft was free. Otherwise he'd never have paid the price. The freight elevator clanged ominously. He could well imagine the door refusing to open and he'd have to spend the night stuck inside, while Art went without supper. Art, the squawking caged one, reason for Rowan's tenure in the loft. Just look after Art, the man said. Who would name a bird Art? A pretentious dude named Arthur, that's who. The elevator stopped at the top floor, he waited for the door to open. Please. So far things have gone relatively —

"Hell!" He swore out loud as the iron door clanked open. The van! Too late now, it's either gone or safe. You asshole, he said to himself, took the abuse and shook his head, kicked his left foot with his right, and felt better already. Opening the door to temporary digs, he could hear Billie Holiday moaning from the loft next door. He stopped for a minute to catch the horn solo. That's good, he thought. That's good.

On the edge of sunrise, Myra put her key in the lock and was surprised to find the door open. Must have been Mitch, she thought, he should know better. She tossed her newspapers on the pile inside the door, and kicked her shoes off beside a pair of unfamiliar cowboy boots. Jack was slumped on the couch, covered up with his coat. He heard the rattle of her keys and dragged himself into consciousness but could not find the energy to speak.

"Jack?" She stood staring helplessly, as if he was an intruder or an apparition.

He yawned and sat up, rubbing his bloodshot eyes. "What time is it?"

"Quarter to six," she said.

"In the morning?"

"If you don't mind me asking . . ." Myra took her coat off as she let the question trail and walked into the kitchen. He followed. She went about making coffee, figuring he needed a few minutes to wake up. She checked the espresso pot for all the necessary parts and turned on the flame. He leaned against the table with his arms folded, as if he was working himself up to something. Finally, he said, "How long has this drug addict been living here?"

"What are you talking about?"

"Mindy."

"Mandy. Why?"

"She OD'ed last night and had to be rushed to hospital. I spent the night at the Royal Vic with Mitch. Looks like she's going to pull through. Just."

Much as the news was shocking, Myra was stunned by the tone, cold, accusing and he did not stop. Jack could hear the words hit the air. Could not hold back, didn't want to.

"Really, Myra. I know you're busy, but it might pay to keep an eye on the kids. It's a dangerous world out there. So easy for a kid like Mitch to get mixed up with the wrong kind, and right under your nose? Didn't you notice anything? I thought reporters had an eye for detail. Isn't that what you do for a — I mean, your profession?"

The coffee pot gushed and she let it gurgle for a few seconds before filling two cups. Jack dropped three lumps of sugar and stirred absent-mindedly.

"What about Sal?" He shook his head sadly. "You say this thing with the professor is only temporary. I wonder. Have you spoken to her? I know, she's 19, I'm not saying we have any right to tell her how to live her life. Nobody could tell us, although I sometimes wish to God they had. Huh. Anyway, she's sensible. I know this sort of thing has to be prevented along the way, and yeah, some of the blame lies with me. But you can only go so far with that line of thought. By the way, some — " he spit out the word like it was a dead bug in his coffee — "some man called for you a few minutes ago. Left a message. I couldn't find a pen." He looked down at his damp sock feet.

When it was clear he wasn't going to say more, she said, "What was the message, approximately?"

His answer was soaked in acid, "He said to tell you it's rude to split before daybreak. Also painful. Have a nice day."

She studied Jack's face for a trace of humour, but found only smothered triumph.

"Did he happen to leave a name?" she asked.

He glared at her, deaf to the intended joke.

"A little humour, Jack. I know his name. So do you."

She used Pain's name and Jack snorted. "Am I supposed to be impressed because you're sleeping with somebody famous? Anyway, didn't he get in trouble for punching out some CBC honcho?"

She took a sip of coffee. "Let's go back to my failures as a mother. Where were we? Or maybe my nightlife isn't off topic."

"I don't know why you're making a joke of this, Myra. Mitch and Sally are in big trouble."

"They are not," she said. "You've been up all night. So have I — "

"I had some sleep."

"Well so did I. But not enough, obviously." She was so tired she felt like crying. "Let's start with Mitch," she said. "Where is he?"

"At the hospital."

"How's Mandy?"

"She'll live."

"What was it she took?"

"A mixture. I don't have the details. But this is far from the first time she's fallen off the wagon, or whatever they call it with drugs."

She got up to make a second round of coffee. "I know that, but it has never happened under this roof, for your information. She's a wonderful girl, a very domestic, caring, great mother, and Mitchell adores her. I could say she's turned him around from being a lazy video-crazed teenager into a responsible, hard-working young man. Wait till you see his marks this term, he's going to have an A in math, I'll bet you anything. Mandy's trying, that I have noticed. If she slipped, well then she's got all of us behind her and we won't let it happen again." She felt his eyes on her back, crawling with reproach. To Myra this seemed like nothing more than another new phase in the ongoing hurdles of raising kids. Poor distant Jack, she thought. He's out of the loop. Using this night as ammunition in some strange new war of nerves.

While the coffee pot simmered, Jack stared at the floor. He was sitting in his old place at the table, although it hadn't been the obvious choice of chairs. Force of habit, despite the years. He noticed a halo of light-blue paint where the bread basket had been taken down off the wall, but otherwise the kitchen looked exactly as it had when he left, paint faded and a little shabby, but the same. As if time had stopped and here they were, sitting at the kitchen table, worrying about the kids.

Myra busied herself at the counter. She wanted to open the door and toss his boots down the staircase. Had to remind herself that wouldn't be fair. Jack's last real taste of domestic trauma had been croup and runny noses underfoot, and he hadn't weathered that phase very well either. The coffee was ready. She poured two more cups.

"Jack, you've had an awful night," she said, trying to sound sympathetic. "But things aren't that bad. We'll manage."

"Mitch is coming out to Calgary, with me," he said.

"What?"

His voice was cold. "We talked about it last night. I can get him a job with a landscaping firm, friend of mine from the golf club. He'll do some night classes and try for law school after he gets a B.A."

He wasn't looking at his socks any more, he turned to clock Myra's reaction. She stammered, "When?"

"As soon as his exams are over here. Couple of weeks."

"What about Mandy and James?" She could hear the quiver in her own voice, and gripped the counter for support.

"Please God, they will be history." He added a few lumps of sugar to his coffee and started stirring.

"I'll have to talk to Mitch about this," she said, then caught herself and wished that thought had not slipped out. He answered firmly, "Mitch and I have talked."

"I know you have, Jack. And if it's all decided, well then fine by me. He's a big boy."

"He is just that. A big boy. He needs some kind of guidance, Myra."

"Guidance from whom? A fog-bound, half-crazy, semi-alcoholic bureaucrat and his slut of a girlfriend?"

"Excuse me?"

Jack stood up, his hands were shaking.

"I'm tired," she said. "We both need sleep."

"My hearing is just fine, thank you."

"Well, I'm sorry. I mean, sorry about, you know, the crazy bit."

"Slut?"

"That, too."

He walked over to the kitchen window and leaned on the sill. Staring into the slim reserves of his patience, he wondered if this sudden shortness of breath could be the first signs of heart attack. Or a simple case of unrequited desire to strangle. The book of breathing exercises recommended two deep ones and a series of short puffs. He followed the book, then continued calmly.

"Myra, you have hated Paulette from the moment she walked into the picture. I can sort of understand why, although the truth is she had nothing at all to do with what happened between us. Still, you have shown profound contempt for her values and taste."

"Or the lack thereof."

"Right, still bitter." He kept staring at the sill and resolved to be reasonable. "She's a good person, a kind, loving person. And Mitch likes her. As for you, you've always had your agenda, your goals. And woe to the family member who got in the way."

"What were my goals, Jack? I tried to keep the god-damn household together and running, and still — make a contribution to — society. Somehow. Even though the result was earning a pittance and constantly scrambling to keep my name — *your* name — in print." She sobbed as she spoke, he hung his head.

"I know you've worked hard," he said, trying to be soft but aware that he wasn't soft. "Everybody admires you. Paulette thinks you're some kind of great writer. But — I don't mean but, I mean — and — the consequences are . . . all around us."

As quickly as the tears had come on, Myra could feel them dry up, and in the place that ached, a rush of blood.

"What was it you wanted from me, Jack? A good, kind, loving wife who baked cakes and ironed your shirts personally and took singing lessons on the side for amusement? Is that what you wanted? Well, I'll tell you where those kind of women end up. In Notre Dame Cathedral with their lipstick smudged and damp cheeks. Panting for a strange man. At least strange to me, you may know him. Why? Because they get bored, Jacko. A life of service is boring. And boredom leads a woman to do things when she's away from home."

He turned to stare at her. "Like what?"

"Paulette cruise ship Grant is having an affair in Montreal. I saw them. She didn't tell you?"

They were standing close enough, she could see his eyelashes flicker.

He said, "I heard."

She picked up a dishcloth and started wiping the counter. Then she twisted the espresso pot apart and emptied the grounds. As if the iron doors of coupledom had slammed shut, he said nothing. She was furious with herself for hurling the information at him, wished she could take the moment back, at least explain, hurt me I bleed, then fight back. But all she could think to say was, "I'm sorry. It's none of my business."

"No, it isn't," he replied.

She folded the dishcloth and wiped her hands on her bathrobe. "Why don't you go in there and get some sleep?"

"I will," he said, but he didn't move.

She put her hands in her pockets, looked at the floor. "Is lunch with the kids still on?"

"Of course."

"Fine, well."

Still, he stood as if frozen, the kitchen seemed crowded. She said, "Where's James?"

Faced with an easy question, he seemed to revive slightly. "Mrs. Pagnos came over from next door and got him. So, she's still alive?"

"I hope so," said Myra. "The dead don't make great sitters." She let out a tiny nervous giggle.

Jack reached down and took her hand, held it with both of his. For a moment she thought he was going to start talking. About what? Paulette, Notre Dame? Oh please no, she thought. Please, let's not talk it over. She waited a moment, then slid her hand out of his and turned away, began tying up the garbage.

"Things blow over," she said.

"It has," he said.

"Good."

Then she took the garbage out to the balcony, and decided to hide out in her study for a while.

Jack wandered into Mitch's room, closed the door and dropped onto the bed. Deep breathing, he thought. Take a few deep ones. The pillow smelled of perfume. He brushed it onto the floor, buried his face in the crook of his arm, and inhaled the warm, safe nest of a night's sweat. In a few minutes his aching body was paralyzed by sleep.

# IX

◆

As soon as the referendum was over and everybody got a good night's sleep, the next campaign began. That's not how it looked from the streets — the streets were empty. Montrealers hunkered down to a season of record snowfall and the kind of cold that only summer could make them forget. As Christmas drew near, people were grumpy and blamed the weather, but the hair's-breadth vote was part of the mood. Like a bad dream clinging to the border of consciousness, the narrow outcome proved that nothing had been decided. Faint celebration among the winners, soft despair among the losers, because everybody knew the referendum result meant little more than a delay. Both sides included a goodly number of people who longed to think of something else.

Jacques Parizeau's angry words were soon echoed by more angry words from desperate federalists, and a new theme entered the political vocabulary: partition. If Quebec can leave Canada, then why can't the parts of Quebec that want to stay Canadian leave Quebec? The partitionists produced maps showing vast territories inhabited by the Cree and Inuit, who had affirmed their federalist leanings in separate referenda. Combined with the western, largely anglophone municipalities of Montreal and swaths of English-speaking areas in the Eastern Townships, the partition campaign made the face of Quebec look hopelessly blotchy. Subliminal metaphor, illness. If media coverage was any indication, the partition movement gathered momentum quickly. Myra covered some of the early meetings for a radio documentary, and came home convinced there was far more madness out there than anyone had guessed. Beirut, Berlin, Montreal? Suddenly the boast of cosmopolitan city status seemed more like a danger than a point of pride.

A phone call from the other side of the continent forced Myra to admit anxiety.

"They're doing what?" It was Joey, calling from his producer's office, somewhere in the sprawl of Los Angeles.

Myra stared at the Gazette, which had just published a potential map of the future showing newly independent Quebec as a tiny strip along the St. Lawrence River. "Who's talking about partition?" Joey demanded. "A handful of quacks?"

"As a matter of fact, some serious people are behind this one," she replied. "Kind of makes me nervous. You know, most really hideous ideas start out with one or two articulate fools. Then it catches on, and before long . . ."

"Oh God, I'm glad I'm not there," he said. "It's 82 degrees outside. Remember Fahrenheit, remember 'in the eighties'? Doing a hundred miles an hour in a convertible?"

"Don't torture me," she said. "Anyway, you'll probably come crawling back with skin cancer and I'll have to nurse you into an early grave."

"Relax," he said. "I'm quite capable of thwarting happiness and success without the intervention of gratuitous illness. What else is happening?"

"Well, let's see," she said, turning the pages of the newspaper.

"I mean, what's happening to you?"

"Oh, the usual. Wrote my last Hand to Mouth column yesterday. Things to do with apples, and I'm glad it's over. Food isn't my forte . . ."

He could hear her swallow, the line was so clear. She'd left him three messages over the last few days. He figured she had a reason for calling, but now that she had him, and on a free long-distance line, all he could hear was breathing.

"Look, if it's about that credit-card stuff," he began, without a single idea of where to go next.

"No, it isn't," she said. "Mitch is moving out to Calgary with Jack. We're getting around to a divorce. Sally's in love with a 39-year-old professor and she changed her name to Alexis Meilleur."

"Wow."

"Yeah, wow."

Joey put his feet up on the desk and swivelled around to look out at the oceanfront view, but all he could see was the inside of La Cabane, an empty table and a pitcher of beer. He said, "Hey, you guys have been split up forever. . . . Mitch and Sal are pretty well grown up."

"Are they?" She sighed, "Yeah, yeah. In general, I'm fine. You know, I just really wish you were back here, at least tonight, until say, closing time."

"Jesus, me too," he said.

"Are you thinking of coming back?"

"Not really. At least not right away. I'm in the middle of the script and —"

"I know, I know," she brushed the mood away. "Did Noel send you those financial statements?"

"Listen, Off the Main's accumulated debt weighs in at less than the fruit-juice bill for a half-hour of TV down here." He waited for a chuckle but didn't get one.

"Are you going to let Noel have the company?"

Just then the producer's secretary came back from lunch, so Joey swung his feet off the desk and gave her the one-more-minute finger.

"Possibly," he said.

"He's determined to do musicals and mindless comedy."

"I've got to go. I'll call you tomorrow, all right?"

"I've got meetings and stuff all day," she said. "Maybe later on. Thanks. Bye. Good to hear your voice and Joey, wear a hat."


Mandy was peeling apples when Myra walked into the kitchen. Since coming home from the hospital, thinner and with eyes drooping, she hadn't spoken much but the smells coming out of the kitchen were heavenly.

Mitch's imminent departure for Calgary and his sudden interest in the law had been the subject of several pots of tea. Thanks in large part to the cockroach fiasco with Mandy's last landlord, their combined savings now totalled nearly $3,000. Mitch was convinced Jack's landscaping connection combined with night school was going to be a far more inspiring future than the midnight shift flipping pizza, followed by flabby days at a school full of wasters. Since he and Jack spent their night together in the waiting room at the Royal Victoria, Mitch seemed smitten with the idea of the West. He read everything about Alberta he could find, and if oil or wheat came up on TV, he turned up the volume.

On the subject of Mandy and James, he remained adamant: they were going too. Myra walked by the phone when he was talking to Jack, heard him confirm the plans, then stand there while the caller drowned in silence. She hadn't noticed before, maybe it was just happening now, but Mitch was becoming a lot like Jack, fond of silence, full of determination, hidden currents and corners.

One night, he opened up and talked about why it's so important for Mandy to get away from people and places that remind her of bad times. He'd like to get his hands on a few pushers. It's the pushers, he insisted. They should have tougher laws, at least enforce existing laws. Mitch, embracing a cause? His shaved head had grown back to a respectable, law-abiding length and Myra thought yes, a cause and a law degree, the combination makes sense.

Regarding Mandy, all she said was, are you sure? Mitch shot back, "Were you and Dad sure?" When she shrugged, he said, "We're not exactly getting married, just going out West." She wondered if Mandy was his lifelong love or his first cause, and whether there was anything she could say that mattered. The new Mitch left so little room.

The kitchen was full of sweet, warm cinnamon. Mandy was wearing an apron and the pot under the tea cozy was still warm. Myra poured herself a cup and scraped a layer of frost off the windowpane, but the transparent glass fogged up again. Mandy set a plate of apple tarts on the table and mumbled, "Oh, excuse me."

Since the night of the overdose, Myra couldn't remember them looking each other in the eye. Now the suitcases were packed and in less than 24 hours this stretch of home cooking would be history. For days, she'd felt a choking sensation in her throat every time she thought about them driving off in a $900 Jetta — one of the reasons nobody looked each other in the eye any more. But just one reason. The other was a mutual fear that some kind of thick gloom or heavy judgment would seep out if they ever started to talk. If they didn't talk, it would soon be way too late, so Myra said, "Would you like a cup of tea?"

"Sure," said Mandy, with a nervous little smile.

"Would it be okay if I had one of those tarts?" Myra asked.

"Oh! I'm sorry! Of course." Mandy's apologetic reaction seemed way too big for an apple tart.

Myra said, "Sit down here a minute." As she spoke, the already tiny girl seemed to shrink. She slid onto a chair and gripped her tea mug with both hands.

"First, you've got nothing to be sorry about. Second, these tarts are delicious, and I only hope my column in today's paper did them justice. You know, several cute guys have written in asking to meet me, and all on the basis of your cooking. So if things don't work out with Mitchy, I want you to know I'm keeping their names and numbers for you. Just say the word."

Mandy giggled. Then she said, "You can have the cute guys, Mrs. Grant."

"Thanks. I'll give you three weeks."

The banter had worked all right, till that point, but at the mention of a time limit, her eyes darted up to catch Myra's. She swallowed, but the tightness was still in her throat when she said, "I'm sure you're all really, you know, wondering. About drugs and everything. I did have a problem, but it was mainly because of, well, I guess it's not fair to blame him. But James's father. They say it isn't hereditary or anything, and I pretty well have it under control. Finally! I guess."

Myra sat frozen while Mandy stumbled, then stopped talking, closed her eyes. Tears began to leak out. Myra went over and put her arms around her. Mandy seemed to collapse. She could feel the tiny frame shake, and thought, there's nothing to this girl. Her bones are twigs. Myra said, "I'd say you've pretty well got most of the important things in life under control, Mandy. Don't be too hard on yourself. And you are totally, totally welcome in this crazy family."

Mitch came in then, and flung the keys to his newly acquired car on the table. "Passed the safety check with only a bit of muffler work," he said, proudly. ". . . Oh."

Mandy and Myra took separate chairs, as if they'd been caught, red-handed. Mitch decided he was supposed to ignore the moment. Mandy blew her nose.

"I told them we're taking it out to Alberta and the guy looked at me as if I'm crazy," he said. "Damn frog. Suppose he's anti-West."

Before Myra could answer, Mandy whispered, "Maybe he just meant it's a long drive for an old car, Mitchy."

The recently mobilized driver snorted and plopped an apple tart into his mouth. It was hot and he did a little dance. They laughed. Then Sally was at the door, James woke up from his nap and by the time the chilly sun had set behind the Mountain, Mandy's plate of warm desserts had completely disappeared.

Later that night, when the last supper had come and gone, Sal and Myra sat huddled under a blanket, warming their hands on Chinese tea mugs, candles all around. Taking advantage of a benevolent glow created by the occasion, Sal asked whether — just this once — she could avoid catching an early death on the balcony and smoke inside. One cigarette. So they sat together, feet meeting in the middle of the couch but not touching. Myra held a corner of the blanket over her nostrils and Sal puffed away confidently.

"You're taking this really well, Mom," she said.

"What do you mean?"

"Mitch leaving. Sure he'll be back, but, Mandy and everything."

Myra wanted to say, I'm not taking it so well. Sometimes I'm numb and sad and pissed off at myself for not putting my foot down, but all she said was, "There comes a time."

"There does," said Sal, as if that settled the matter. Myra watched her smoke, noticed how she handled the cigarette, like a stage prop. Nineteen, going on 30, she had her hair held up by little butterfly barrettes that caught the candlelight. A flawlessly bilingual product of the francophone school system, a natural Oui vote, confident, ambitious, driven. Dating a grown man and lord knows what else. Faintly scary.

"What did you think of the other two artists in our exhibition?" she asked.

311

Myra tried to remember. "Colourful. I didn't really notice."

"That's the trouble with these loft exhibitions. You don't get a real gallery public."

A whiff of sweet lethal smoke drifted by, and out of respect for the mood, Myra took a sip of tea to avoid coughing.

"Dad was sure pissed off about my name," Sal said.

"Really? What did he say?"

"Oh, stuff like, why did you do it — don't you care about — that name belonged to — of course you're free — did your mother — why oh why oh — egcetera egcetra egcetra. Whew! I didn't know he was so attached to the damn name. Did you? I mean, did you expect he'd throw a fit?"

"I didn't have time to think," said Myra. "We just walked in and there was this strange name. By the way, it's 'et cetera,' Latin."

"Yeah, et cetera."

An easy silence prevailed. They could hear the clatter of dishes being washed and stacked, Mitch's low voice, from the kitchen. There were moments, like this, when she thought, I might get to like this new phase of adult children. She felt a burden lifting, not only the obvious responsibilities, no, greater still, the weight of silence behind the title Mom.

"Tell me," she ventured. "Do you think I've been too permissive, as a parent?"

"No," said Sally, without a even a brief pause for credibility's sake. "You are, sometimes, how can I put this? Secretive."

"Really? When?"

"When you seemed to be open and easy going and a 'get yourself a sandwich' kind of mother, *et cetera*, but behind the scenes, stuff was going on that, you know, maybe somebody should have known about."

"Such as?"

Sal actually butted out her cigarette, as though the conversation was about to exceed the bounds of this occasion's benevolent glow. She gathered the blanket around her shoulders, and said, "Promise you won't get mad?"

"Sally!"

"Okay, Mitch found a whole box of letters you wrote to Dad. He didn't read them, but he noticed they went on for years, and you never sent them. Did you?"

"No."

"Well, he figures maybe if you had expressed yourself, you know, directly, over the years, he might have come back home."

The candle sputtered, and Myra was grateful for the darkness. She could hear the floor creak as Mitch and Mandy went into their room, voices full of excited energy. He'd taken all the posters off the walls, even the map of the world at night. It was rolled up somewhere and carefully stuffed into an empty foilwrap tube, labelled by Mandy, "map of the world at night." She saw the label and wondered if Mandy realized it is never dark everywhere at the same time. She thought of the map now, the twinkling distance between Calgary and Montreal, and the gap of time, infinitely greater, infinitely more mysterious.

"It wouldn't have made a difference, Sally. I'm sorry — "

"I know that, I guess," she said, briskly. "That's what I told Mitch. I'm only telling you because maybe you deserve to know the real reason he's going to Calgary."

"What do you mean?"

Sally shivered, and under the blanket, moved her sock feet over to tuck them under Myra's. Then she said, "He's going out there to give Jack his chance."

"Oh." Myra's answer was a moan.

Sally leaned forward and continued in a soft, honey voice. "You don't have to explain anything to me, Mom. You and Jack are night and day. Mitchy's young, he's got a lot to learn."

The new day broke, cold and crisp. Snow underfoot squeaked like chalk. James resembled a tiny mummy in a snowsuit big enough to get him through another year. The going-away presents Myra had assembled made the travellers laugh and cry: enough candles and snacks to last out the winter in the car, if it came down to that. A dozen stamped, self-addressed envelopes for James so he wouldn't have to rely on grown-ups to keep in touch. A teddy bear for Mitch. A blank notebook for Mandy so she could jot down her recipes and eventually turn them into a book.

When he'd been settled into the back seat and his seatbelt secured, James said, "Sit here, Granmyra. Right by me." He hadn't fully grasped the implications of goodbye, and when Mandy explained, his eyes grew big with anger.

"No!" he said. "That's not fair." His howls extracted a round of promises that nobody'd thought to make until then. The $300 airline voucher in Myra's top desk drawer would be used before spring, and as soon as school got out they'd make the trek back East — all the things people say when kids put their foot down.

Mandy looked mildly terrified. Mitch was fully absorbed by the thrill of driving his own car. The atmosphere around this departure resembled a vacation or an adventure, and Myra thought, it's just as well. Denial is a wonderful state of mind. Then they were off.

She went back upstairs to make a cup of coffee and check for messages. There were none.

# X

◆

In the dream she is naked and flying through the night sky. The Mountain is thick with shaggy pines and barren maples. Below a luminous cross, the city is dark, so she follows the silver river, effortlessly, as if she has always known but somehow forgotten how to fly. Waist-length hair waving along her back, she turns, like turning over in bed, and suddenly the air is water, cold but not unpleasant. Sleek as a fish, she glides past rocks and bones, hands pointed ahead, steering through the current, a dangerous, exhilarating blur. Then the river narrows down to nothing more than a cement tunnel, and rushing towards her, she sees a black stone like a devil's head, about to crash. She closes her eyes, hugs her breasts in panic, but just as the stone should hit, she feels the air again, opens her eyes and is surrounded by the night sky. Now she is drifting downward, to a clearing in the pines. She lands bum first and the ground gives way, like a pillow.

A telephone is ringing, in the distance.

By the time Myra got to it, the answering machine had kicked in. "Hold on a minute," she said, as the voice message rolled on, then, "sorry, hello?"

"Hi. It's Rowan Gaunt. You were sleeping." The voice startled her. "Must be later than I thought. Is it too late?"

She looked at her watch, 9 p.m. "No, I dozed off. It's not late." As she spoke, the memory of his face came to mind and she thought, no, not late in the day, but still pretty late to be calling after a motorbike tour of Montreal and a club sandwich at Beautys, what was it, six, seven weeks ago? Definitely, a friend of Joey's.

"So you're back from Toronto?" he said.

"Toronto?"

"I called, right after the party. Your son said you wouldn't be back until just before Christmas."

"My son?"

"He sounded, I don't know, about eight or nine."

"Oh. That would have been James, he's four. My son's friend's child. But I haven't been in Toronto."

"Well, then, I'm sorry I didn't call back." He sounded genuinely sorry.

"It wasn't your fault," she said.

He wondered if she'd like to get together and she said sure, but it would have to be after Christmas now, because every night was booked and she was taking off for Port Hope on Christmas Eve.

"My father and stepmother always have a houseful, turkey and all that. We go every year."

"That must be nice," he said.

"Yeah, it is."

Then he said he had a small renovation job in the Townships, starting right after New Year's, but would probably be back and forth and if so, why don't they get together.

"Fine," she said. "Merry Christmas, then."

"Same to you." Then he hung up.

She put the receiver down and looked at her watch. Just after nine. She thought about calling him back and saying, what about right now? But remembered he'd moved into somebody's loft and hadn't given her the number.

As she stepped into a hot bath, the sensations of the dream returned, image by image, flying and falling. The thrill was still vivid, but recalling the dream now, she saw herself from the outside, as her body, the size of a small statue, flew through the night, and was pulled by the current. The dream looked like one of Sally's paintings.


In Pain's opinion, the partition movement was a mark of genius. "Fucking brilliant," he said, yanking on his skate laces before winding them into a double knot. "Where do I sign?"

Myra was still trying to work up enough courage to take her snowboots off and slip sock feet into cold skates. She took his outrageous statement as an excuse to delay, and stood glowering. "You mean you actually think a country can exist as little patches of territory?"

"Look at Indonesia. Thousands of islands."

"With water in between. And hardly a tribute to democracy!"

"Westmount exists as a separate city, surrounded by Montreal. Different taxes, mayor, whatnot." He stood up and grabbed his hockey stick. "Are you going to skate or watch?"

As he slid onto the ice, she called out after him, "Westmount is a municipality, not a country," but he was too busy slapping the puck back and forth to hear, and she sat down in the snow to tackle the chore of lacing up.

Normally, the skating pond was behind the Chalet on the top of Mount Royal, but this year the City snow crew had plowed a swath of ice on Beaver Lake. Myra wished she'd thought to bring a thicker hat, night air is cruellest to the extremities. When she had finished changing, he circled back and grabbed her hands, pulled her onto the ice, then took off again, this time after an imaginary puck against a phantom team. A skater since the age of two, he played Junior B as a teenager and kept it up as a hobby, a weekly chance to let off steam and stay in touch with one of the central ritual forces against winter and TV. He thought everybody should skate, or at least watch other people do it.

She pressed one foot forward, pushed the other from behind, then further forward until the added height and sense of sliding ceased to feel unnatural. Then she went for speed, making her way around the edges of the pond. The ice surface had been hacked up by the afternoon crowd, and a maintenance man was spraying the far end with water.

It was cold and late, so the only people left on the rink were serious sports types, a gang of youths and two other middle-aged men playing with hockey sticks, a friendly exercise in puck snatching. When one of them lost control, Pain slid in and grabbed the puck away, and then the exercise became a game that wanted a winner. The other two men were smaller than him, one looked plump under his down jacket, but they were fast. Their bodies seemed to tense with the excitement. She noticed how they skirted around his height and slammed each other. The puck was now travelling fast.

Myra skated around the edge of the pond to where the gang was standing, a mixture of girls and guys, huddled together, smoking. Seemed like an odd way to spend a cold night, watching other people play. But as the game heated up, one of the young onlookers tossed his smoke into the snowbank and hurled himself out into the action. He was grinning, leaning on an imaginary stick, itching to play. Pain howled, "Toé et moé, contre ces deux patates?"

One of the potatoes shouted back an equally friendly insult. After they'd kicked hunks of snow from the sidelines and improvised two goalposts, the game began in earnest, all non-players relegated to audience membership.

The young stickless one quickly adapted a tactic of interference, and it was pretty obvious the absence of contact with the puck would in no way prevent him from having a great time. Myra heard one of the girls say, Michel always plays to kill, and the others laughed. But they also kept back. She looked over and saw that the man with the hose was watching, too.

For the first few minutes the game looked more like an awkward skirmish than a demonstration of poetry on ice. Finally, one of the potatoes whipped the puck away from Pain and shot it between the goalposts. They cheered and a girl yelled, "Pas juste." The stickless partner and Pain exchanged a few words and then went back at it again.

320

Suddenly, the younger player had Pain's stick. He surprised the others by snatching the puck away and in about five seconds, scored. They all had a good laugh, then Pain got his stick back and started gliding innocently along the side of the pond, slapping the puck gently from side to side as if he was contemplating strategy but hadn't found one yet. The potatoes stood leaning on their sticks, defending their goal and waiting for an advance. The stickless one skated in from the side, and before anybody could tell what happened, they were fighting over the puck, a hard knot of struggle, angry and real. Then a thud. Pain went down and red blood splattered the ice. The skirmish stopped. He lay face down. Myra skated over, and one of the girls started yelling at the stickless one, something about how they never go anywhere without seeing blood. But the stickless one was bent over in agony, clutching his ribs. He dropped to his knees, gasping.

As Pain got up on all fours, blood continued to pour from his nose. Somebody gave him a Kleenex, he tried to tilt his head back but choked as blood poured into his throat. Myra handed him her hat and said, "Use this, and hold your nose with your fingers, higher."

The young player was helped off the ice. His girl-friend ran with his boots, said they'd better take him to a hospital, sorry, bye, and as quick as the fight started, they were gone.

As Myra and Pain changed out of their skates, she noticed the rink man spraying the bloodied ice with water. In about ten seconds it was white again. Pain swung his head back. The bleeding had stopped. She took him by the arm and they headed toward the car.

"What happened back there?" she asked, when the heater was running.

"Testosterone," he said.

She laughed, "I thought it was some form of hockey."

"Wherever man doth gather together, there is the fucking hunger for blood. I'm sick of it."

"It was an accident," she said.

"It was not an accident. The point of that game was to damage each other. Fucking perverse humanity, bloody-minded men on ice and hysterical women cheering them on. Hockey is a metaphor for life, and life stinks."

He jammed the car in reverse and spun back into a snowbank. Trying to move ahead, all he got was the spin of tires, and the spinning got faster the more he tried to move ahead. Myra suggested he get out and push while she handled the wheel, but he leapt out and slammed the door so hard the window cracked. She heard a thunderous crash against the back fender, and silence. He got back into the car.

"What was that?" she asked. "Did I just hear you kick the fender with your boot?"

"You did," he said.

"You are a goddamn idiot."

He turned to her with a look in his eyes that was neither friendly, nor unfamiliar.

"You knew that," he said. He gripped the steering wheel, hands red with rage. He leaned his head on the wheel for a few seconds, then tried to move the car ahead, but the wheels spun worse than ever. His nose started bleeding again, and he wiped it on his coat sleeve.

"Let me dr— "

"No," he snapped. "Give it time to cool down."

Give what time to cool down, she wondered. You. There was nothing to do but sit. The heater was blasting out hot, stuffy air but her hands, feet and nose were freezing. Car heat always made her slightly sick, and the feeling was expanding quickly toward nausea. She noticed he had blood in his hair and under his fingernails. His hands had loosened on the wheel, he seemed to be calmer.

She wondered when it would be safe to make another suggestion about how to resolve the hardly original dilemma of tires spinning on ice. She thought of Joey, and all her resolutions against getting into these familiar moments, Joey at 82 degrees Fahrenheit. She put her hands into her pockets and was surprised to feel the roll of hundred-dollar bills from Jack, completely forgotten. How could anybody forget $1,500 cash? She almost laughed out loud. The times they are a changin'.

Just then they heard a tap on glass, Myra's side, and saw through the ice the bundled up face of the rink man. She eased her window down half an inch and he said, "J'peux vous aider?"

"Oui, merci." She opened her door and got out. The rink man told her to get behind the wheel and they'd both push. Five minutes later the car was rolling out of the parking lot, Pain sitting on the passenger's side, holding his broken nose wrapped in her blood-soaked hat.

He refused to drop by a hospital, said he didn't want to sit in a waiting room all night, and if it was broken then a new direction could only improve his appearance. Nor would he agree to go home and take a handful of aspirin. Instead, they took a back booth at Grumpy's and talked the bartender into making hot toddies. After washing much of the blood off in the washroom, he looked a little less like a freshly escaped convict.

"As I was saying about partition," he began.

"Look," said Myra, still confident after the snow-bank rescue. "Why don't we just lay off politics for the rest of the night? I think partition is a hideous idea because it is one baby step away from violence and we've had enough of that tonight! Okay?"

She was shouting. He raised his palms in a gesture of whoa, and whispered, "That was exactly my point. Violence. Of course I was being ironic."

She glared at him, "How are the Habs doing?"

"Don't talk about the Habs," he muttered, shaking his head.

Topic after topic pushed off limits. They sat in silence for a few minutes, until he reached out to take her hand. Then he noticed the blood-caked fingernails and with-drew.

She shrugged.

"Quite a memorable date," he said.

She had to smile. "You sure know how to show a girl a good time."

He waved at the waiter for another round, and clar-ified, "Don't heat mine, Jake. Hold the lemon and honey, Just bring me room temperature scotch. Doubles. Two."

When the glasses had arrived, he said, "Don't quote me, but as a matter of fact, for the record, I'm sorry."

"About what?" she asked.

"My black mood tonight. I should have stayed home. But you so desperately did want to skate. Anyway, my mood." He drained a glass and leaned forward on the table, covered both her hands with his bloody fingers, clamped his green eyes on her startled expression and before she could protest said, "Two of my ex-wives are getting married on Christmas Eve, meaning my son and daughter will now be raised by other men."

"What?" She wanted to move her hands out of his grip, but it was firm, and warm.

"I told you about them. Well, not exactly wives. One is, was. The two women I, you know, impregnated in the same week. They gave birth nine months later, one a boy the other a girl, same day. Now, they are each getting married, on the same day. Night. Christmas! Isn't that just fucking uncanny?"

She broke up with laughter, but he wouldn't let her hands go. She found it very awkward to be laughing and imprisoned between bloody fingernails at a table full of glasses with a lean young waiter keeping an eye out. Finally, she swallowed the last of the mirth and said, "Could I please drink my still-warm toddy?"

He released one hand and held the glass to her lips. She smiled but refused to open her mouth, so he let her hands go. She took a sip and leaned back, rested her arms on the back of the booth. Just in case.

"I've forgotten," she said. "How old are the twins?"

"Very funny. Seven."

"Well rejoice, they need fathers."

"They have a goddamn father," he howled. "They have goddamn me."

She lowered her voice. "You live in Montreal. They live, where?"

"Toronto and Vancouver."

"Do these women know each other?"

"Only through their lawyers," he said.

She sighed, "Well, you're not there. They have to get on with their lives. And I'm pretty sure nobody can actually replace you. In a sense. I mean, there aren't that many people like you. At least not in Canada."

He was staring into his drink and didn't seem to acknowledge the fact that she was biting her lip to avoid laughing. He said, "Yeah, I guess you're right. Still, this means I have to face the fact that we won't be getting back together."

"Who?" she asked, genuinely lost.

"Kit and I. Or Rita and I. Rita's in Vancouver, Kit lives in Toronto."

"You mean you seriously think of getting back together with . . . both of them?"

"Well, with Rita it wouldn't really be getting back together. What we had was more like a fling. Still, if they're getting married, that means they could be tied up for months, years. Christ, fucking forever. I'm out of the picture, more or less."

Myra caught the waiter's eye and ordered herself a cup of coffee while Pain contemplated the universe in his last double.


Later that night, she climbed into bed and thought of Mitch, little Mitchy, slipping and sliding on the figure skater's pond in Carré St-Louis, and James, whose first letter said they were living in a house under ground, with a dog named Montreal. He drew the pictures, Mitch took notes. She re-read the letter and slipped it under her pillow, thinking, ah Mankind, the universal hockey team of Mankind.

# XI

◆

Myra M. Callaghan. M for Mary. Two days before Christmas she was looking for a suitcase and came across an old diary with her name scrawled across the cover, a flowery scrawl in indelible blue ink.

Patrick had wanted to call the baby Mary, after his mother, but his wife said it's too common. According to the oft-told story, with so few relatives of her own, only a great-aunt in Toronto and a brother somewhere in Poland, Isabel had faced their wedding day with trepidation, half-expecting the groom's side of the church to sink from the weight of his clan and fall right into Lake Ontario. When it came to naming children, she wanted some sign of her ancient Jewish heritage, so they called the first-born Myra and her brother Jake.

Myra kept the M in her schoolgirl signature, until she had become Myra Grant. Then the signature became a stiff, hurried scratch on the page, letters rushing to the left. The tails of y in Mary and g in Grant were completely closed. Only a broad slash through the t suggested flight.

Leafing through the pages of her high-school diary, she noticed all the tails were fat and optimistic, as befit the times. August 1972, she was packing suitcases, about to leave for the big city of Ottawa, a four-hour train ride, a lifetime away. The entries ended with summer, a door closed. Isabel died, and the past disappeared.

She put the diary back into a cardboard box labelled "high school," returned it to the top shelf, beside another one labelled "1980-1990." That one contained the unsent letters that had set Mitch on his quest for fatherhood. She wondered how much he'd read, and why she even bothered to save them. They were, in a sense, the substitute for a diary. When the kids were small there was no time to record intimate thoughts, no energy at the end of a day. But sometimes a burst of anger or longing or a dozen other contradictory emotions would make her think of Jack, something she had to say and couldn't get out of her mind. Once set down on paper, another equally fierce feeling, pride or practicality, would rise up and check the impulse. Still, she couldn't bring herself to throw the letters away, had tossed them into a box, and the box became a real place until eventually the exercise started to feel absurd. Giving up the letters was her New Year's resolution, 1989.

Beginning with the new decade, she resolved to keep a real diary, but couldn't seem to get started. The first entry looked artificial, self-conscious; she ripped the page out, tried again, still could not read what she wrote. Finally, she gave up, bought a fat daily agenda, and began filling the pages with lists and detailed notes of appointments, chores, interviews, books read, movies and plays seen, phone calls, important mail. Year by year, these hardback agendas accumulated, serious tomes on her office shelf, comprehensive archives including money earned and spent, doctor and dentist appointments, prescriptions, milestones in the kids' school years. Five years' running, Myra could account for practically every day of her existence.

Nor did the milestones of childhood escape her urge to document. Thick binders full of drawings, school stories, old tests, report cards; boxes full of photographs, schoolbooks, old clothes and toys, the archives of Mitch and Sally filled one entire walk-in closet, along with out-of-season clothes and empty suitcases.

Now, two days before Christmas, with everybody gone and the house so empty, she knew better than to start flipping through old pictures, reading diaries, or even thinking about the past. But the ritual trip to Port Hope required a suitcase. She found one, an ancient box-like valise, heavy even when empty, and gave it a dusting. As she tossed in enough clothes for the two-day visit, she was still thinking about the flowery signature. Unfamiliar at first, instantly pleasant, it felt like an old sweater, packed away for ages, then suddenly it turns up, looking fresh and familiar, just the thing to wear.

The M is pretentious, she thought. But Myra Callaghan. The name sounded familiar, and fresh.

Men disappear after marriage. They keep their own name and spread it among wife and children, but that's only a concession to the fact that a man typically joins his wife's family. It didn't happen with Patrick Callaghan and Isabel Schapiro because she had no clan to take him in and then the winter Myra started university, Isabel got cancer. With

Isabel gone, it seemed Patrick would die of solitude and leave Jake to raise himself. Then, when Myra was busy with university, Patrick met a sympathetic woman with grown-up children and a house of her own, and around the time Myra graduated they got married. Jake went off to school in the States, made money, gave birth to Americans.

The second Mrs. Callaghan had a knack for detail, so the birthday cards kept coming and the families started a tradition of getting together at Christmas. It was lovely when the kids were little, to be welcome in a house with tree and trimmings. Myra still likes being swallowed up by Christmas in Port Hope. For more than 20 years she has watched as familiar characters bloomed, flowered, bore fruit, caused trouble and got over it. The politics, too — she enjoys representing Quebec at a small-town Ontario dinner table, shocking the entire stepclan by defending the PQ and demolishing conservative Ontario politics. During two decades of mistletoe and turkey, she has charted the waves of curiosity, shock, enthusiasm and dis-enchantment, as goodwilled Ontario flirted with the French Fact, sent their little ones into French immersion, then reeled, hurt and angry, when Quebecers sneered at their bilingual ambitions. Every year, extended family members draw names for the exchange of gifts, and every year she wraps up a CD by a new Québécois musician. They may be diehard federalists, but they are humming Michel Rivard. These trips to Southern Ontario are a lit-mus test of where they've gone, and where she has come.

The post-referendum Christmas would surely be a lively one. She could picture her stepmother tiptoeing around with sherry while the opinionated sons swill rye as they goad Myra about another defeat for "separatism." They will never accept the term "independence," never mind the softer euphemism, "sovereignty."

She put her suitcase by the door, beside the traditional Christmastime presents, a few quart bottles of Molson's and a bundle of Hoffner's sausage, with smoked meat and bagels to be picked up later. Things you can't get in Ontario, the exotica of Quebec. She was thinking about cleaning up the house when the phone rang.

A husky female voice introduced herself as Anne Hiller, an old friend of The Gazette's living editor.

"She speaks very highly of you, Ms Grant."

Anne Hiller, award-winning investigative reporter, first editor of a glossy new magazine called Canadian Life, scheduled to hit the stands nationally next spring and be delivered to the doorstep of every household earning $60,000 or more.

Hiller had read Myra's Hand to Mouth columns and she liked the attitude. Buying, cooking, eating food, anybody can do that, she said. But good writing with humour and flair is much harder to find. Myra could hear Ms Hiller smoking as she rambled, a seamless caffeine monologue about how Canadian Life was going to reshape the personal habits and tastes of a nation, kind of a northern Martha Stewart concept without the — "well, I'm sure you know what I mean," she said.

Myra didn't, exactly, but she said ah and Hiller went right on. "My point, yes get to my point, how would you like to be part of the action?"

Anne Hiller hadn't actually said she was calling from Toronto, but the names she dropped made that pretty clear. The Gazette editor had given Myra a great build-up in the categories of writing to deadline, copy editing, versatility and coming up with story ideas. The staff of the new magazine would be small, the pace hellish. She made it sound like a guarantee, not a warning. And the money. Hiller sucked back smoke, allowed herself the time to exhale. "We are entering a golden age of news publication, my dear. Don't ask me how long it will last. But some people with piles of money and huge egos are willing to spend the former on the latter and I say bravo. While it lasts. You will be well paid. Buy blue chip."

In another pause that did not seemed to be smoke-filled, Myra thought maybe she was supposed to ask how much, but Hiller leapt back in. "I won't risk launching your first heart attack by talking figures over the phone, but I'll have my assistant book you a flight for right after the holidays. Do I hear a yes?"

She heard an I'll get back to you, which Myra hoped contained sufficient enthusiasm. Hanging up the phone, she looked at the room and laughed out loud. A slick lifestyle magazine wants to hire a woman whose house looks as if vandals have come and gone, taking their time.

As soon as Mitch and Mandy had driven off, she had come back upstairs and started moving furniture. Desk and phone into the living room, table facing the Mountain, stacks of newspapers by the desk, a printer table and bulletin board and filing cabinets within easy reach. Before long, the entire double living room looked like one big sprawling office. Once there was no longer anyone wanting or preparing meals, she discovered just how arbitrary a convention were the customary hours of eating. A couple of pieces of toast with cheese three or four times a day, a bit of yogurt and a few cookies in between, not only saved a lot of time, but also reduced the garbage to almost nothing. Old rituals died and new ones took their place. Some of the new ones felt faintly indulgent, like two hot baths a day and one so-called meal in bed, but it took about two weeks for Myra to realize she had probably always harboured the soul of a spinster.

Now that solitary Self had begun to flourish. When she wasn't tearfully lonesome and temporarily blinded by an unexpected flash of self-pity, she was cheerfully busy and, reluctant to admit it, quite excited by the novelty of privacy in all eight-and-a-half rooms. Wandering around in her bathrobe one day at noon, she thought, this must be the life of people who write books. I could possibly write a book. I could bear the relentless solitude.

In the dream, she is fumbling with a clutch of keys at the door, hands stiff with cold, none of them seems to fit. Finally the door gives way and she is standing in the living room and everything has changed. The furniture is gone, closet doors swing open. Somehow there are many more rooms off the hall and a lot of people standing around in groups with drinks, as if a party is going on. She recognizes a few faces but there are just as many strangers, music from the stereo. Then she notices it isn't Esplanade after all, but the house on Bronson Avenue in Ottawa, the house she shared with three others so many years ago, and she's in the kitchen where someone is handing out beers. Everybody seems to be student age and she thinks, how odd, they haven't changed at all. There's another room behind the kitchen, it's confusing, the rooms seem to go on forever.

Suddenly she is sitting on a saggy couch in the living room, beside Jack. He's drinking a beer and their legs are touching — his leg against hers feels warm. Seems like they just met. Then she is standing beside a closed door in a completely different room, and all the people at the party seem to be watching. Jacques Parizeau is there, drinking a beer from a bottle, watching her. She turns her back on them and reaches for the door handle. It isn't locked but her hand is shaking. Then she is back sitting beside Jack and their arms are touching too, but he won't look at her, keeps staring straight ahead. Turning to catch his eye, she realizes why he isn't looking. The other side of his body is nothing but dry white bone. He is dead, she knows it now, and an overwhelming rush of sadness seizes her body, like a drug. With all the strength that is left, she tries to hold him, but the minute she moves, his bones and flesh disintegrate. When she touches him his bones crumble and fall through her fingers like sand, until there is nothing at all left of Jack.

She woke up aching with sadness, relieved to know she'd been dreaming, lay curled under a mound of blankets, too warm to move. Random images came floating into consciousness, the intensity of feeling too, as if the dream walls and doors had been attached to her body by nerve ends, each room living the mystery and loss as if it were a person, as if the rooms were part of her. She remembered party music in the background, and the insistent ringing of a phone, but no one seemed to pay attention. No, the phone wasn't in the dream, she thought, it was real. Now the silence of an empty house seemed to contain a lingering ring. It made her uneasy, this connection of the dream with a real event. She got up to check the phone, bare feet on the cold floor.

A light was on in every room, a new habit, an unconscious decision. The lamp on her desk was hot, too old for an all-night light. The answering machine had recorded a call just after midnight, minutes ago, no message, but listening to the empty space between the beep and a click of someone hanging up, she knew who it was. His signature, the empty pause where he did not say, it's me.

She made a cup of tea and crawled back into bed, letting the moist fumes warm a breathing space under the covers. She drank the tea, then tried to sleep. Red minutes flicked by on a digital clock. When zero blinked into one, she turned her back. By two, she gave up.

Three layers of sweaters, tights under jeans, she dressed for the brutal night, wrapped her face in a thick scarf and took out a pair of snow goggles, just in case. The outside steps were slippery. She sat down and took them one at a time. The sidewalk was glassy, she picked out a crunchy route along the peak of a small snowbank. St-Urbain was empty. She kept to the salted edges, hoping for a taxi, walking anyway. None passed until she was nearly at Place des Arts and then it was too late to bother.

She could hear the sirens from Place d'Armes. A minor traffic jam had already collected along Notre

Dame, and the street had been blocked off. The flames were visible from St-Jacques, the night air rancid with smoke. Police had barricaded the building so she couldn't get any further than the corner of Saint François-Xavier and Saint-Sacrement, where a crowd had gathered, some people holding bundles of clothing, coats and boots thrown hastily over their nightwear. Three fire trucks attended the blaze, one with a huge crane and a hose gushing water down into the flaming roof. She made her way past the barricade to a policeman who was standing beside an ambulance. His face was smudged with soot, and he shouted at her to get back behind the barricade. She said she knew someone who lives there, and had to find out if —

He said the building was empty now. An explosion.

"Quel étage?"

"Ecoutez — "

"Please!!!"

When he told her, she said, "Oh my God." He put his hand on her shoulder. Four ambulances had already left for the Royal Vic.

Arriving at emergency, she had prepared a little story in case there was some rule against giving out information, but as soon as she mentioned his name, the nurse said, "Oh! You must be Mrs. Grant. We've been trying to call you." She must have looked puzzled because the nurse continued, "Your name and number were written on a piece of paper in his pocket. I think the police want to speak with you. Hold on." Then she picked up the phone and asked another nurse to take Myra to his room.

When they got there, a doctor was just coming out. The nurse introduced them and before Myra could ask, how is he? she wrinkled her eyebrows together and said, "Was your friend on any kind of drugs?"

Myra shrugged, aware that she'd probably have to repeat this conversation to the police. "He was going through a lot, but I don't know what specific medication . . ."

"I wasn't referring to medication," the doctor said, curtly. She was young and petite, with fiercely short hair.

"I wouldn't know," Myra replied. "Is he hurt badly?"

"He'll survive. But he's got a lot to answer for."

"What do you mean?"

The doctor's frown deepened. "A woman next door wasn't so lucky. The blast knocked her wall down. And at least 25 people are homeless."

"Are you saying he did it on purpose?" Myra angrily demanded.

A police officer wheeled around the corner and said he had a few questions.

"Look," she said. "I'm ready to co-operate here, but I'd like five minutes alone." After an exchange of nods, the doctor disappeared and the cop took a chair in the hall.

Pain's head, arms and hands were covered with bandages. His torso was raised by pillows, and half a dozen wires were attached to his body, fluids going in, data coming out. He seemed to be sleeping, but when she got to the bed and said his name, he opened his eyes.

"Can you talk?"

"I can," he said.

"What happened?"

He turned his head away. Between the bandages on his swollen face, she could see bruised lips stretched tight. His eyes were glassy and full of bitterness. His body seemed huge, stretched out on a hospital bed, strapped down. She waited for him to look her way. When a few minutes passed and he had not moved, she reached out and took one of his fingers, peeking through the bandages. He pulled his hand away angrily and closed his eyes.

"My name and phone number were written on a piece of paper in your shirt pocket," she said. He looked up with an expression that suggested he'd forgotten all about that part.

"Would you like a cup of coffee?" she asked, thinking she'd love one herself.

His dry lips formed the word scotch, without much sound.

"I don't think the machine downstairs does hard liquor," she said.

Then she sat up on the bed and leaned in to his ear. He acted as if the move hurt, and she said, "Shhhhh. I've got a cop out there wants an interview. What do I say?"

"Say the suspect is an asshole," he replied.

"I don't think that's the kind of information he needs right now."

He raised his eyebrows and closed his eyes. "I'm tired. Go home and have a nice life."

"I'm not going anywhere," she said. "I want to know what happened, and why."

He sighed, as if annoyed by the conversation. "A little fireworks. I did not plan to be here answering all these goddamn questions."

"Where did you plan to be?"

He closed his eyes before answering, "Hell, if there is one."

When the blast hit just after midnight, Rowan Gaunt had already packed his van with enough work clothes to get through the month of January, emphasis on flannel shirts and long johns, a box of most-important papers, a slim selection of indispensable CDs, and his saxophone. The loft he had agreed to keep an eye on was way too intensely decorated for his taste, at least too decorated with somebody else's taste. Original art works that made you wonder how some people keep a straight face. Cold leather chairs reminiscent of a trip to the dentist. Kitchen gadgets so numerous and complex that making a cup of coffee required an engineering degree. He'd been living on bread, cheese and instant. He was glad to see the last of Arthur's classy living for a while. Tired of his glossy magazines and thoroughly sick of his budgie bird, named, egotistically, Art. Nobody ever thought to call Arthur Art, because Arthur had tenure and family money. Enough to live tastefully and spend a sabbatical in Costa Rica.

Not that Rowan envied Arthur. He didn't. Driving across the Champlain Bridge, Rowan thought, I don't really envy anybody. If anything, I envy my former self, the one who was happy. I would like to be a wise, old man, with certain people and events just a hazy memory, somewhere back there, in a long-lost life.

He reached inside his pocket and checked for the keys to the chalet on Lake Memphremagog. Keys accounted for, perfect. Art, the bird, asleep in his cage, snug under a pile of blankets. He flicked on the radio and was hit with a blast of Hallelujah. Why not, he thought, smiling.

Hallelujah!

# XII

◆

As it turned out, the bruises under Pain's mummy costume were less serious than they appeared at three a.m. and by the time the nurse had come around with his poached egg, he was well enough to take note of her first name. He sounded almost cheerful when he called Myra mid-morning, with an invitation to join him for coffee.

"I thought you didn't want to see me last night?"

"Untrue. I need to explain a few things," he said.

When she arrived with a bag from Second Cup, he was reading the sports section, fuming.

"Have you seen what Patric Roy's doing for Colorado? Fuck! I still cannot believe they traded the golden goose. The Habs are finished. And what a team they used to be. They can't call it hockey? Ha! It's TV, that's all. Bad TV. Does this town have a death wish or not?"

She pulled up a chair and handed him a cappuccino.

"Sports are the litmus test," he continued. "Montreal is headed for bleak times. Chaos, violence, destruction. Armageddon. Remember, I said it first."

"No you didn't," she said. Taking a slow, warm milky sip through the white foam, she looked at him. Under one eye was a huge red gash and the skin around it was purple. They'd shaved his hair back around another cut and soaked it with antiseptic. His arms were still bandaged, but the scrapes on his hands were exposed. He looked as if he'd been beaten up.

After their encounter last night, she'd had to deal with the police, who were treating the blast as a criminal offence. The clumsy attempted suicide ended up seriously wounding a woman whose bed touched the wall of his bathroom, and it caused hundreds of thousands of dollars of damage to the building's top floor. Four lofts were completely gutted by the fire resulting from the explosion.

Myra argued fiercely that a man desperate enough to take his own life could hardly be blamed, because the state of mind in which a man faces death is not a state that includes compassion for other people or their property. He still wants to be dead, she told the police, and suggested they guard him against himself. The cop shrugged, said he was investigating the case as attempted manslaughter. She looked at his snapping black eyes, a hungry young man in his thirties, and wondered what kind of a charmed life he must live that would let him be so cold in the face of self-destruction. That was last night, the cusp of crisis.

Now she watched the Desperate One cradling his cappuccino, seriously churned up about hockey, and the night before was beginning to look like a mysterious hybrid of nightmare and television.

"I would have thought after yesterday, hockey would be the last thing on your mind," she said.

"Hockey is not on my mind," he replied, putting aside the newspaper. "My mind is dormant."

"Why did you do it?"

He folded his arms and winced, unfolded them, and with a gesture of helplessness, laid his hands on the sheet, palms open to heaven. When he did not answer, she repeated the main point.

"Why?"

"Because it's Christmas, I'm alone, and completely finished with my life," he said.

"You're alone because you want it that way," she said.

He snorted. "I see why you never went into social work."

"I've done a fair amount of freelancing," she said.

He laughed. "Tough love, eh? That's your policy?"

Gazing at him, stretched out under a grey hospital blanket, she kept up her end of the match, but wondered what it would take to get beyond banter and onto a subject where the skating would be smooth. They'd known each other for three years, and yet conversation was still a mind game, never a flow, always the uneasy exchange of barbs with an edge that sometimes led to passion, but passion never led to easier conversation. The next day, it was as if the most intimate act possible between two people had been, after all, part of the game. She complained when he would not stay all night, but once rendered naked and snug in his bed, she waited until he fell asleep, then left. Pain always led the dance. She would like it, just once, if they could stop the music and hold each other. She half-agreed with the black-eyed cop — the botched suicide was the ultimate selfish act. And yet she knew him well enough to know that the mood had been real. He wanted to die, he got it wrong. That, too.

She said, "I've got a train to catch at five, I should be going."

He reached out and took her hand. "Please stay, I'll buy you lunch."

"Impossible," she said. "You get the free lunch. I hate machine food."

"I'll fast. You can eat my mush."

Not like last night, now the anger was gone. That's a start, she thought. When she settled back, he started talking about his children, wondering if they'd like what he sent for Christmas. Maybe the husbands weren't such a bad idea after all, maybe they would demand quality romance time and he could pick up the slack, take the kids to Disneyland. His dream was one kid on each arm, balloons, Mickey, junk food. Maybe even someday, when the time is right, no pressure, of course, a playoff game. He looked rough, his face a mass of bruises. She thought, the beaten look suits him. Now the wounds are on the outside, spirit made manifest.

"You know," he said, "I named both of them. My choice of names. That was a coup, believe me." When he said their names, his face softened. It is possible, she thought, that this man is better at fatherhood than his life with women will allow, the essence of the tragedy being that vice cancels virtue.

He wanted to talk. Since the subject was children, she found herself telling him about Mitch and Mandy, all the funny things James said. For once, he seemed genuinely interested, not cynical or defensive.

"You know something? You're a hell of a fine mother," he said. "You miss James even more than Mitch. He's the child you lost when the others grew up."

Impossible to resist, the tears welled up in her eyes and his eyes went wet, too.

"I'd like to have a child with you," he said. "Really." That made her laugh, dried up the gush.

"Do I take it the feeling isn't mutual?" he asked.

"Well, it's a totally novel hypothetical conundrum," she said, "Considering we've never even had breakfast together."

"Waiter! Eggs and bacon, sunny side up," he said, snapping his fingers.

"I've got to go."

"Okay, here's what you do. Run home and get your stuff. Pack a small snifter of whatever you've got. Swing round here for a Christmas Eve drink, and then I will lie back and think of you pregnant, I mean down in Port Hope, tucking into a family turkey."

"I can't miss that train," she said.

"I won't let you miss it."

She thought about him spending Christmas alone in the hospital, after all that had happened. She thought about traffic and hassle and a dozen things she had to do. Then she ran down the hall and waved at a taxi, jumped in and told the driver to wait outside her door. There was half a mickey of cognac and a bottle of red wine in the kitchen cupboard. Good wine, a birthday gift from Joey, saved for a special occasion. She grabbed them both, suitcase, sausage, beer, bagels, an extra scarf, ran back out and sped off.

He was dozing when she got back to the hospital. It was three-thirty, just enough time for a toast and goodbye.

Somehow, he had managed to find two clean glasses. They pulled the privacy curtain around his bed so as not to unduly punish the man next to him, forced to listen. He toasted her health and held her hand and made her promise to have dinner the minute she got back to Montreal. At five minutes after four, she gave him the red wine and a corkscrew, kissed him on the cheek. He grabbed her arm and made her redo goodbye on the lips.

"You taste like blood and cognac," she said.

"I take that as a compliment," he said, reaching for her bum. Then she flew out of the room and into a taxi, astonished to find it was the same driver who had taken her to Old Montreal the night of Sally's vernissage. When she said bonjour and smiled, he flashed a broad grin. "Ah oui, vous avez changé d'avis. Oui, oui. Joyeux Noël."

Yes, yes, Merry Christmas. It had started to snow, and the traffic downtown was bad, as she'd expected, but they had plenty of time. Everything was falling into place. She loved how at heady moments, some coincidence always seems to happen that reminds you there is probably more to life than material reality. Some kind of higher power, if not in charge of destiny, at least connecting the dots. Coincidence could become the basis of a modern religion. A minor miracle, but it happens all the time. She thought of the Christmas Eve party ahead, kind of wished she'd kept the birthday wine, but hey, it's the season of good deeds.

When the car turned the corner of de la Gauchetière, she reached for her wallet and felt a thud. No purse. Suddenly, she remembered hanging it on the back of the hospital chair, looked at her watch — still 35 minutes before the train left. No choice, her ticket, money and credit card were in that purse. With luck.

At the entrance to the hospital, she told the driver to turn around and be ready to roar, ran to the elevator that was mercifully waiting, leapt in and counted the floors. The skeptical short-haired doctor was walking down the hall ready for conversation, but she brushed by, ran into the room and flung open the curtain around Pain's bed.

He was sitting up. Francine was sitting on the bed beside him, very close. Francine, the star of Joey's Godot TV coverage, who had never even appeared onstage. Francine of the naked Jesus poster. She had her shoes off and one leg flung over his lap. They were just starting to drink the red wine, a Château Lafitte, 1989. He had a hand on her leg. Their faces bore the wide-eyed stare of people who've just been photographed with a powerful flash.

Her first impulse was to say I'm sorry, but she swallowed it and grabbed the purse, a small black bag with a long shoulder strap, recently acquired to wean herself away from the ache of a too-heavy briefcase. Now the purse swung loose, and her second impulse was to swing it right by Pain's head. She had no time to swallow. The purse, which was leather but purchased on sale, hit Pain in the middle of a bandage and he howled like a skewered bear. Francine dove out of the way and spilled her Bordeaux all over his hospital gown. Lipstick and Tampax and small change flew everywhere. Myra swooped to pick up the pieces and when she resurfaced, the freshly opened bottle of wine fell over on the floor and broke.

Then the nurse appeared and demanded to know what was going on. The man in the next bed was frantically ringing his buzzer. She checked to see that her ticket and wallet were accounted for, then with Pain still howling and bleeding and Francine babbling in French, she fled.

The elevator was not waiting. It took a good five minutes to arrive, and it stopped at every floor on the way down. The driver had misunderstood. He had not turned the red Lincoln around, ready to bolt. He had the motor running all right, but was deep into a Bob Marley tribute tape, turned up full blast. She piled into the car and shouted, "La gare centrale."

"Ho-kay," he said, and shoved the car into drive. It stalled.

They continued the rhythm, lurching behind slow-moving trucks and illegal pedestrians, sliding into amber lights and blasting at lazy drivers, and finally, when it seemed like hours had passed, arrived at the train station. She had nothing but one of the godforsaken hundred-dollar bills in her wallet. Now convinced of the emergency, the driver leapt out to get change, but the hour was desperate. She told him to keep it. Ow. "Joyeux Noël." As she grabbed the luggage, he blew her a big kiss.

Too late. The train had just pulled out when she arrived, breathless, at the empty lineup. She begged the steward to let her run downstairs anyway, on the off chance that it might be moving slowly enough, but no. He said, "It's gone. Next one tomorrow."

She had to wait 45 minutes at the bus stop while a dog on a leash pined over the sausage. It was dark and cold as she rummaged through her purse at the door, to no avail. The house keys must have stayed under Pain's bed, because she couldn't find them and had to call a locksmith. He took another hour and charged overtime, company policy. She gave him a quart of Blue and said I'm sorry. Put a sausage on to boil, ripped open a beer. By nine o'clock, the Christmas Eve party in Port Hope was in full swing as she called to say don't bother meeting the train. Sally was already there, she'd taken the noon train. Myra would have taken it too, if not for . . .

But she didn't dare tell the truth, could not with a Christmas sausage boiling away bear to hear Sally's inevitable critique, so she said simply, "My watch stopped. Kaput. It was old."

"Oh Mom, that is so weird," said Sally. "I bought you a watch for Christmas. Oh, if only, if only."

"Sal, never say If Only. Save me some turkey. I'll take the first train out tomorrow."

She could hear laughter and somebody playing the piano in the background. The party was in full swing, Sally had to raise her voice to be heard, "I almost forgot. Dad called here looking for you about half an hour ago. When he calls back I'll tell him you're in Montreal. See you tomorrow, bye, kisses."

She hung up the phone, surveyed the shambles of spinster life. Newspapers, dried coffee cups and disgarded layers of clothes, a stellar mess. No one to blame but myself, she thought.

At nine o'clock, Paulette put a turkey full of chestnut stuffing in the oven and sprinkled the breast with wild rosemary, set the timer to be sure it would be cooked for the next day's Christmas dinner. Mandy was bringing dessert. Edith had condescended to forego her perpetual bridge party for the afternoon, so it was shaping up to be a regular family reunion. She made a tourtière for supper, her mother's recipe, set the table in the kitchen, and went about washing up pots and pans while Jack made his ritual phone calls.

He phoned from the den, had a chat with Sally who, he was pleased to find out, had not taken Professor Boyfriend to her Grandpa's for the holiday. Maybe it would blow over. Maybe Myra was right. But not for a second did he believe that cockamamie story about the dead watch leading to a missed train, not on Christmas Eve. I know her better than that, he thought. As the phone rang on Esplanade, he pictured her curled up in front of the fire with the famous obnoxious journalist, or worse.

Then he remembered the fireplace wasn't working, and wondered whether he should maybe offer to get it fixed, as a Christmas present. Definitely added value. Then again, she might take it the wrong way. After the vernissage fiasco, he'd begun to wonder whether she wasn't headed for some kind of breakdown. The signs were there, she seemed to explode over the smallest irritation. The phone rang six, seven times, he stopped counting, told himself he'd try once more and that was it. Then she picked it up and said, breathlessly, "Hello."

"Oh, you are there," he said.

"Jack?"

He could hear a roar in the background, like a snowplow. She said, "Just a minute," and the noise stopped.

He was tempted to say, what was that sound, but figured it was none of his business. She said, "Well, Merry Christmas. I guess Sal told you I missed the train."

"Yeah," he said. "That's too bad." Might as well play along.

Myra said, "C'est la vie."

From the tone of her voice he was beginning to think she might be alone. It surprised him to find out he preferred to think of her alone. In his pocket was a small velvet box with a diamond ring inside. Paulette picked it out, and Jack had to go back later and pay. Tonight, they were formally getting engaged, and a few weeks later, they were going down to City Hall, where a woman judge would take them through the 15-minute procedure of marriage. Somehow, he still wasn't quite sure how, Paulette had managed to link her confession about screwing some building contractor with the need for marriage, real marriage, not some shipboard act. He hadn't quite followed the logic, but his arguments for the other side didn't amount to a hill of beans. He'd said things like, why bother?

Now he was standing in the den looking out on a sparkling tree, one hand squeezing the velvet box, the other holding the phone, and for some pathetically insane reason, tears were streaming down his face. He swallowed and said, "Yeah, c'est la vie."

There was a long pause, during which either one of them could have been thinking, we have nothing more to say to each other, but both knew that wasn't true.

Myra said, "Jack?" And then she caught a wrenlike gasp in his voice and he coughed to cover it up. The years of knowing silent Jack had taught her a thing or two about the various shades of silence. She didn't need to look into his eyes to know this one was blue.

"Okay," she said, "I know you're going to say the goddamn shopping season makes people sickeningly sentimental, but while I've got you on the phone, and you're picking up the tab, I just want to say — Well . . . I don't ever, ever want to lose touch with you. And I'm not talking about the kids either."

She could feel him floundering on the other end of the line. He coughed again, and said hoarsely, "Me too."

She knew it would be cruel to pry more words out of a broken voice, so she said cheerily, "I've gotta go now, but merry merry to all of you, and take care of that cough, eh?"

Then she hung up the phone and turned the vacuum cleaner back on. To the music of Vivaldi's "Four Seasons" full blast, she went back to cleaning the house. By midnight, a huge mound of paper and useless junk dominated the middle of the living room floor, and bed looked as good as trifle and cranberries. The mound was still there next morning when she left, in plenty of time to catch the noon train. By New Year's, it was gone.

# XIII

◆

When the mound of papers and useless junk disappeared, she realized that was only the beginning. She did not want a new life as a childless homeowner.

Jack said, you'll never sell a mountainview condo with Montreal on its knees. Sally said, go for it, Mom. Mitch said, why? As it turned out, Pain was right. She got $202,000 for 3,000 square feet plus parking, off the alley. The roof was practically new and once all the junk had been cleared out, a coat of white paint worked wonders. Three weeks from the day the sign went up, it sold. Then Jack said, why did you take the first offer? You should have held out for more.

She let Barry have another go at her hair and bought a new coat for the job interview. Anne Hiller turned out to be mad all right; she weighed about 95 pounds and seemed to exist on a diet of muffins and Happy Hour snacks. But the offices of Canadian Living have a view of Lake Ontario and Myra decided it might be just fine to look out on water. She might employ Mandy on retainer, if her own non-interest in things domestic turned out to be a problem. Sally thought it was just plain exciting and took her shopping for clothes on Laurier because, "People in Toronto expect women from Montreal to look a certain way."

"I am not *from* Montreal," Myra insisted. "I am *of* Montreal, temporarily out of Montreal, spending a year or two away in order to get perspective and write a book about Quebec. That job is only a pretext to keep me sane."

"When are you going to write this book?" Sally wanted to know.

"In my spare time."

"Mom," she said, shaking her head over a pricey plate of curried chicken salad, "People making that much money don't have spare time."

"You'll see," said Myra. "I will write the book." The book would be an answer to Jacques Parizeau's referendum-night outburst, his whisky-sodden slam that ethnics and money had provided a fatal obstacle to the forward momentum of an independent Quebec. Her thesis: Parizeau was right. People whose names did not figure on the list of two hundred founding families of la nouvelle France, or at least slide easily off the French tongue, the people of the funny names had definitely voted Non, en masse, because nothing and nobody in the independence movement circa 1995 gave them the faintest reason to believe this tumultuous project in any way concerned them, or even wanted them aboard. And until the would-be leaders of an independent Quebec came up with a future-leaning vision that believed in a pluralistic state, then nobody but vieille souche Québécois would pay the slightest attention. Furthermore, if it was only a project for one thick-blooded slice of the population, then it was a grievance-based howl and would blow over, like the rest of the rhetoric of political correctness.

While Myra outlined her thesis, they were sitting in a non-smoking section, where Sally found it hard to concentrate on politics. Myra agreed to move for dessert because, "This is important. I'm going to run this book by you, chapter by chapter. I want it to come out in English and French and I want young people to buy it."

After lighting up a cigarette, Sally ordered an espresso. "Okay, write up a few chapters and send them to me," she said, perusing the dessert menu.

"I will. On Parizeau's second point, money, I think I can make a good argument that international money would not logically be against an independent Quebec. Mel Watkins wrote a piece in This Magazine, published October 30, and spelled it all out. You know, Watkins, the respected economist?"

"Mom?"

"One more thing, do you realize that more than half the countries in the world today are smaller than Quebec, with fewer people? Fifty years ago there were 74 countries in the world. Today there are 193, and the list is growing, not shrinking. Technology, free trade, globalization — I'm not flinging these words around like they are all good news, but they're facts of the 21st century, which is what makes small countries more viable than ever before. The imperial state conglomerate is withering. Small states can specialize and — "

Sally was nodding in all the right places, but Myra could see she wasn't exactly taking notes. "You wanted to say . . ."

"It's not really on topic," said Sally.

"Go ahead."

"Where are you going to get the recipes?"

"What?"

"The job. Won't you have to write stuff about home life and all that? I know you're a damn good reporter, but how are you going to keep interested?"

Myra leaned over the table. Her eyes glowed like somebody drunk on a scheme. "I'm not interested, and that gives me confidence. If I was slightly interested, I might lose interest, and that would be dangerous."

Sally scowled. "Better have a fallback position."

"I do," Myra said, "If they fire me, I'll write the book full-time. That's one of the reasons I sold the house. Half the money is stashed away for you and Mick. With the rest, I'll write the book."

Sally held her head in her hands and groaned. The waiter was standing over them. Myra ordered crème brulée.

Only Mitch's question remained unanswered: Why? By the middle of February, he'd pretty well decided Calgary was nice enough but a little cow-poky. Mandy liked it but said she'd probably like Vancouver too, at least for a while. He applied to pre-law, and hoped Jack's interest stayed high because it looked pretty expensive. Assured that all household effects would be boxed, labelled and put in storage, waiting for the great return, he came down in favour of change. "You don't need to explain yourself to me, Mom, I know it must be lonely without all of us."

True, she smiled, and yet not quite the entire truth. All empty nests smell lonely, but often, so do crowded nests. The beginning of the big move had come with a crack on Christmas Eve, full of fury and resolution. Once resolution became action, it generated new energy, and she was high on the drug of change.

Still smarting from Sally's yuppie-toned analysis of the situation, she made one resolution and wrote it down in her diary, which she now found easy to keep since so much was happening that deserved to be written down. The resolution was: take one carload of stuff to Toronto, and do not acquire more. All she needed was a room with a plug for her computer. At least a dozen good friends had settled there, some with rooms to rent. That would suffice, at least until such time as the resolution might be amended, should noise became a problem.

Everything seemed so logical. She ran her fingers through her golden hair one morning and thought, this is easier than I imagined. She felt surprisingly little emotion as a Chinese-American computer nerd wandered through the empty white halls and nodded, saying how lovely it could be if he spent some money. It was a steal, in U.S. dollars. Let him take it, she prayed. The feelings of this house are in boxes and hearts. Mitch was right about that.

When the papers were signed and boxes packed, she bought a medium-sized black car with a big trunk. The job with a view would start March 4. She looked at the calendar, and decided it made sense to implement this change with a touch of symbolism, head westward on February 29, leap day of leap year.

Two days before the leap, Joey came back to Montreal, unannounced. His script had been written, rewritten and completely garbled by a flank of story editors and other highly paid non-writers until it bore little resemblance to his original idea, which was fine, he said. Any two-bit book on screenwriting will prepare you for that. But in the middle of coping with suntanned cannibals, he had fallen in love with a stunning and "really nice" actress, or so she seemed at first. As it turned out, Sherry had expensive tastes and wild habits. They ended up doing stuff, going places, barely escaping things he swore would make a hell of a movie.

Joey closed his eyes when he spoke her name, Sherry. He rolled the word around in his mouth, as if the entire escapade had been one long delicious fiery banquet of experience. He couldn't stop talking about Sherry, though he made it clear there were things he could never reveal.

"So, why did you break up?" Myra asked.

"We didn't exactly break up," he said. "She took off with this, this . . ."

"Another guy," Noel prompted.

Joey glared. "Barely human."

It was the night before Myra left for Toronto, and they met at La Cabane. After the Fahrenheit marathon of L.A., formerly plump Joey was thin and tanned. He wore a pale lemon suit that fit like scales on a fish. He looked great, at least perfect for Hollywood, a place he swore on a pitcher of beer would never again see his face. Joey was furious to find out Myra's mutterings about a possible move had been thoroughly acted upon. Noel looked understandably downcast. His bilingual production of *South Pacific* had been put on hold. ("It's in the text! The guy who goes for the nurse is French!")

Having thought the whole thing through, Joey had decided to cease and desist with bilingual anything. He was planning a strictly English adaptation of Proust, probably scenes from *Swann's Way*.

"Proust is French!" Noel roared, slamming the table. In the absence of Joey, he had become much more assertive, a common side effect of hope. Joey unbuttoned his lemon jacket to protect it from mayo, should a fry slip off his fork.

"I know Marcel Proust is French, as does everybody. But an English-speaking artist has every right to embrace the greats in his mother tongue. Although English isn't mine, but anyway. We'll do Cervantes next, in Spanish. From now on, only the greats."

Noel predicted it was bound to fail and Joey said so has everything else. But now, tanned and broke and so much wiser, he was ready to pick up the torch again. When they had settled on the next production and closed the business end of the meeting, Joey and Noel set out in unison to convince Myra that Toronto was a very bad idea.

"Shut up, Noel," Joey said, when the world's-best-smoked-meat argument came out. "It's like this. I have been to L.A. which is in some respects Toronto writ large, if not the world." He raised a hand against Noel's bubbling intervention. "I can assure you Montreal is the finest city on the planet. Go, I say go. Because you will come back, and you will kiss the ground this city allows you to walk on. Because this city is real. Politics? No! I'm all through being vulgar, though the subjects of politics makes it hard. Never mind. Whatever happens, this city will survive and remain great because Montreal has spirit, soul. You'll see. Give her a month, Noel. She'll be back. *Swann*, then *South Pacific*. That's a promise."

There was, of course, no question of paying off the credit card just yet, but Noel suggested they either put the debt on a monthly long-term basis, or write it off immediately and let Myra have the full value of an income tax deduction in the current tax year. She said she'd have to think through the options. "Talk to my people." Ha ha. There was no hesitation when the bill came. Joey snatched it up, handed it to Noel. They embraced her in the street. "This will never happen to you in Toronto," said Joey.

She said, "Come and visit, we'll see."

# XIV

◆

So painless, so logical. Except that time ran out on the 29th of February. It was mid-afternoon before Myra got served at the Fairmont Bagel Factory and headed north to Autoroute 40. The day was mild. Around noon it had started to snow. Nothing serious, the streets were still bare. By the time she was free and clear on the 401, a cold orange sun was sinking fast on the horizon, snow falling lightly, swirling above the highway.

The Macdonald-Cartier Freeway is an independent climate zone, a gale-force strip that can suddenly turn ugly, but a storm will often retreat as quickly as it hits. Weather always comes from the west, and as Myra was heading in that direction, she half-expected to drive right out of this one. West-bound traffic thinned out after Dorion. Across the meridian, the two lanes going east were almost empty. Nothing on the radio yet to make it sound serious. Still, she felt anxious inside a ton of steel and glass; the steering wheel seemed to tremble in her hands.

Car culture. In calm daylight, the freedom of turning a key and flying had seemed miraculous. Now, as a train rushed past she caught the yellow glow of coddled travellers and wished to be on it, settling back into a tepid coffee and newspaper while other people's headlights fought the elements.

It was almost five by the time she passed Cornwall. The gloom of dusk turned into pure night, easier on the eyes, safer. But now the snow was really blowing, and there was a lot more of it in the ditches than she'd noticed in Montreal. Sensible drivers were slowing down; trucks and maniacs ignored the blizzard, hurling by the crawlers at a terrifying speed. The highway still seemed wet, no freezing yet. But when a passing car cut in front of her, she hit the brakes and felt the tires slide, a sign that the road was slippery under the fresh snow. Likely patches of the dreaded black ice.

Finally, there it was, first car in the ditch. Flares, police. She slowed to a crawl and resolved to pull over at the next service centre. Should have played it safe, she thought, stopped in Cornwall, checked into a hotel. No reason to rush. While the flakes danced frantically in the headlight beams, she tried to focus on the road ahead. The hypnosis of swirling snow was hard to resist.

Most of the 401 is straight and as boring as a dialtone, but just after Cornwall there's a scenic bend where the highway cuts through rocks. While the two westbound lanes keep right, the eastbound ones disappear out of sight. After the rocks they meet again beside a marshy stretch, and the glare of oncoming traffic is surprising.

Myra rounded the bend of rocks and braked slightly as a maniac transport driver insisted on passing. She was careful, knew how dangerous it is to brake in a storm, knew there would be ice. But the transport driver seemed oblivious. He cut in front and the transport started to slide, sliding right on by, off the side of the road and plunging snout-first into the marsh. In a matter of seconds, the monstrous cargo flipped over on its side, and the wheels spun in the air like big ugly paws.

She gripped the wheel and fought against closing her eyes, signalled right and let the car slow down naturally, glide onto the shoulder until it was well off the highway. Most dangerous place to be, stopped on the highway. Oncoming cars can mistake you for moving traffic. She put on her blinkers, slid over to the passenger side door.

She hesitated getting out, scared the transport might blow up, half-expecting to face a mangled body. Then the transport door opened skyward and a man crawled out. By the time she got to him, he was on his cell phone and shouting for help. A blustery fellow with a big belly, he hauled off his glove and thrust a sandpaper hand at her. "Thibeault, bonsoir." He seemed more excited than bruised.

They'd hardly had time to denounce the night when a blast of car horns filled the air. Over the snowy meridian, in the eastbound lane, a passenger bus had tried to overtake a van and started skidding, swerving in zigzags like an airplane struggling with the currents. The van made a wide swing to avoid the slide but was going too fast, did not stop, plunged straight into the rock face, followed hard on by a half-ton truck, which skidded up onto the snowbank, nose in the air. The warning horns were soon drowned out by a terrifying clap, like thunder, the crash of steel and shattered glass. Headlights flashed and died, then came the awful silence, as if all that moved had suddenly been frozen.

Myra shuddered, turned away, felt her entire body gripped by the sudden reality of a premonition of disaster that had been with her since the first flurries in downtown Montreal. Thibeault stepped in front of her, swore under his breath.

The bus had pulled over to the side of the road, the lights had been turned on inside. She could see it was full of people who couldn't take their eyes off the crumpled van. When the bus driver got out to surround the area with flares, she could hear a child screaming, inconsolably. A few people opened their windows to gape at the smoldering ruin.

Thibeault appeared with a first-aid kit and crowbar. "What if it blows up?" she asked. He said that was unlikely, anyway, sometimes you can do things in the first minutes that save a life.

He handed her a spare flashlight and they headed toward the crumpled vehicles. Her feet and hands felt numb, so did her head. She was sure some gruesome discovery awaited them. The driver of the pickup was already out, uninjured and jumping mad. He blamed the bus. Thibeault started shouting at him that this was no time to be shouting. "Get over to the goddamn van. Somebody could be hurt."

As they got closer, their panic tempers were quelled by the obvious. The van had been totalled, the short front hood completely smashed. The entire right side had collapsed under the impact of rock.

"She's old, she might blow," said the pickup driver, suddenly calm and determined to take charge. He heaved on the driver's side door but it was jammed shut. Thibeault elbowed past with his crowbar, smashed the window and leaned in to unfasten the driver's seatbelt. He was able to unlock the door, and gave it a yank.

Together, they dragged the driver out into the snow. His face was bloody, he seemed to be unconscious, but when his head hit the snow, he opened his eyes and shouted, "Art."

He kept repeating it, "Art, art, art, what about art?"

"What's he talking about?" barked the pickup driver, who was French and assumed he'd missed something.

"Maybe there's somebody else in the van," said Myra. Realizing any other passengers would feel trapped, they hauled open the side door and peered in, but found only a battered bird cage covered in blankets. When they ripped off the cover, the bird gave out a fierce, rusty squawk. The cage door swung open, the bird flew out and began circling frantically above their heads.

The van driver was standing up now and he started leaping at the bird, trying to grab it. The bird gave another squawk, this time more frantic, and flapped higher, above the rocky bluff where the van lay impaled. The driver followed the flapping bird, shouting, "Art. Goddamn you, Art."

Myra thought, at least he seems to have recovered.

"Il est fou," growled Thibeault, slapping his head to emphasize the point. He and the pickup driver took off after the van man, whose gashed forehead left spots of blood in the snow. A crowd from the bus had gathered at the roadside, and a few people wandered over to investigate the skirmish. Police sirens screamed in the distance. The bus driver was shouting at passengers to get back inside, and the child was still howling. Despite the conflagration of wreckage and flares, cars still whipped by them on both sides. Myra thought, this could get worse, much worse.

Finally, the van man reappeared, held ever so kindly by the two Samaritans who were, by now, convinced they had rescued a madman. He whipped off his toque and wiped the blood off his forehead. Only then did Myra recognize Rowan Gaunt. She was wearing a thick wool hat and heavy layers of scarf. When she said, "Hi, Rowan," he looked astounded.

"Myra Grant!"

"No, Callaghan," she said. "It's a long story."

By the time the police arrived, the bus driver had been able to get everybody back inside and head off to Montreal. After considerable shoving and spinning, the pickup man was able to drive off, and soon after, help arrived for the transport driver. Given the miracle of the night and his courage in the face of possible carnage, Myra decided to support Thibeault's story that ice, not speed, had put him in the ditch. When the police were out of earshot, she leaned over and shouted, "Moins vite!" He threw up his hands and dove into the warm company car that had come from Montreal to fetch him.

Rowan insisted the blood on his coat was nothing. He insisted on inspecting the remains of his van, which would clearly never move again, except to the wreckers. And he insisted on looking for Art. They spent a good half-hour combing the area. Finally, Myra said she honestly did not believe a tropical bird could last any longer in the subzero weather, although it's a terrible way to go, and she could see why he felt so bad.

"I was supposed to be looking after that wretched bird for somebody else," Rowan said grimly. "He will not be amused."

Myra said, "I can vouch for you. It was definitely an accident."

"Sure, the accident was an accident," he moaned. "But I have to admit, I've been living in a chalet in the woods with Art for the past two months. He lost half his feathers over the noise from my electric screwdriver. He lost a lot of weight on a steady diet of toast crumbs. Then, oh! I never should have taken him to that poetry reading at Harbourfront. People kept poking at him. God, people are stupid. Maybe it's just the poetry crowd."

"Harbourfront. When was this?" she said.

"Yesterday, I was testing the waters in Toronto."

"Oh yeah," she said. "Toronto."

Rowan was on his way back to Montreal, at least temporarily, and Myra volunteered to give him a lift. But tonight, they agreed, was no time to travel in any direction. The safest bet was to crawl into Cornwall and turn off at the first motel. Wait till daylight, then see.

The first available bed was the Starcrest Rodeo Motor Inn, where luckily, the vacancy sign was still lit up. Rowan said they could get two rooms if she thought it was necessary but they'd have to take off early if she was going to make it all the way to Toronto. Myra insisted on paying for her own room, then Rowan insisted on paying for them both. So Myra said all right, one room is probably enough, it's a shame to waste all that money.

Luckily, the kitchen was still open. They slid into a leatherette booth, ordered hot chicken sandwiches on brown bread, smothered with gravy, canned peas and a mound of fries on the side. Despite the storm, the diner was packed with people drinking beer and picking at phoney little nibblies. "Ontario liquor laws," Rowan groaned. "If you don't pretend to eat something you can't get a beer. No dancing either. Or cards."

The warmth of the diner felt glorious, the low mumble of small-town talk, unimaginably hospitable. She was shattered by the highway ordeal, grateful to be resting on firm ground. The waitress brought two drafts. Rowan looked dazed and emptied half his glass. He seemed to study his fries, avoiding her eyes. She thought, he's pretty shy for a photographer.

Then she asked about the Harbourfront reading, "Pretty prestigious, isn't it?"

He shrugged, "Five Governor-General winners in one room? Yikes. Anyway, I went because they let me read new stuff." His latest tome was an epic-in-progress called *Angel of Death*. So chaotic had life become that he'd hired a post office box and now mailed himself each day's work, just in case.

"I know it sounds morbid, or religious. But it isn't either," he said. "Actually, *Angel of Death* is hopeful. People laughed. Well, I've been through quite a few deaths over the past few years, Art being the latest in a string, real and metaphorical. After a while, you start to see another side to misery. I mean, you've got to."

He was wearing a thick oatmeal sweater. As he talked he hauled it over his shoulders. A couple of days without a shave, his ruddy face was covered with stubble. His eyes were still a little bloodshot from the freezing quest to find Art. She noticed the irises were an earthy shade of brown.

As he talked about the *Angel of Death*, he sounded far from miserable. He talked like a man who was carrying some important revelation around in his belly, nothing to do with religion, per se.

Dessert was a choice of lemon or apple pie. The apples were canned so they took the lemon, which is never real anyway. When the waitress came with coffee, he sat straddling the corner of the booth, as if talking out into the crowd, stealing the odd glance her way while she told him about the new job. Listening to the description, she thought she sounded quite enthusiastic, but Rowan only frowned and said nothing. When she finished, he started telling her about the fiasco of Arthur's loft being gutted by fire, the very night he took off for the country.

She said, "I know somebody else who was involved in that fire. Oh, this is, oh. Awful."

"See what I mean?" he said, suddenly turning to reach for her eyes. "Three times in the last few months, I should have died. Last month, my bike was stolen, snatched right out of my hands at gunpoint. If not for that renovation job on Lake Memphremagog, I would have been killed by a blast Christmas Eve. And tonight, you saw the van, I should be dead. Everything I've ever owned is gone now, except this backpack, a change of socks and underwear, and my sax. I'm still here, which is a miracle."

He leaned across the arborite table. "At the risk of sounding totally flaky, I'm starting to believe in coincidence. Well, fate. I mean, being open to events and working with them. I've totally given up planning and tossing all night trying to figure things out."

He leaned back and stared out into the storm. "I still can't believe it, though. Much and all as it fits."

"Believe what?" she asked.

"That you came along out there. I mean, *you*." Being shy, like being bold, is faintly contagious. She looked down at her coffee cup and shrugged.

As they headed back outside to room 27 at the Rodeo, Rowan said, "Look at that sign, don't you just hate it the way everything in this country is a little bit of something else? I mean, Rodeo?"

"Yes," said Myra. "But that's changing, gradually."

"True," he said.

Since they hadn't asked for single beds it was hardly a surprise not to get them, though Rowan acted surprised. It was late. They were both very tired, and far too old to feel awkward. Myra took the bathroom first, took a shower while Rowan fiddled with the thermostat. When she came out, he went in and started fiddling with the dripping shower nozzle. While he was gone, she slipped into a nightgown and got under the covers, closed her eyes. He sat down on the side of the bed with the weary nonchalance of a man who has sat on that bed a thousand times before, unlaced his construction boots, peeled down to his thermal underwear, piled in under the covers. He yawned, and turned out the light.

The neon Rodeo sign cast a blinking red shadow over their faces, and Rowan said, "Why do they do that? I mean, think about it. People come here to sleep."

He got up to pull the drapes shut. After that, it was so dark he couldn't see the bedpost, and crashed his knee.

"Ow," he said, "Right on the bruise."

Myra giggled. "I'm sorry." Then she started laughing and had to bury her face in the pillow.

"Am I missing something?" he said.

"Art — Art — Art. Excuse me, but the sight of you galloping off into the snowstorm, and the look on those guys' faces. Please, don't be mad. Sorry, sometimes I get the giggles when I'm scared, or really nervous."

"Which is it this time?" he said.

"Bit of both," she replied, softly.

He reached out and turned on the lamp, which was a poodle on its hind legs holding the bulb in its mouth. He lay on his side, watching her concentrate on the ceiling. She noticed he was smiling, and there was nothing of the bashful poet left in his expression. No tears for Art, or Arthur. He had the look of a man who has just waltzed a woman into his bed, who knows there is nothing left to do but smile. Yes, he was thinking, the new religion of coincidence has delivered up one more miracle.

She looked back at the ceiling, then at his earth-brown eyes. He was not exactly waiting, but not sleeping either. So, she kissed him. And while the night outside still raged white, the Rodeo room glowed soft and warm, like summertime.

# XV

◆

For a long time afterwards, Myra wondered why she did what she did on October 30. Between the phone call to Jack and the day that a small press in Winnipeg said yes, they had read and would happily publish her book about the future of Quebec, quite a few things happened that made her feel she was standing outside herself.

But October 30 remains a mystery.

The day after the referendum she was ashamed of herself, and when Catholics feel guilty they have to confess and make good or the feeling gnaws and will not go away. You can dispense with official religion but its patterns hold, so she confessed to Lise Lamotte, "I wimped out. Spoiled my ballot."

Lise laughed, "Don't worry. From what I hear, your vote was counted."

As the day drew near, she'd been having weird dreams about a floating pencil. When she stood facing the unmarked ballot, the pencil felt quite solid but her mind was floating, and for the first time since the idea of

Quebec lodged itself in her life, she was paralyzed by uncertainty. Sure, she'd had doubts before. But doubts that could be quelled by facts and debate. Now she was standing on a precipice, expected to leap, everybody shouting —

But she couldn't. After 15 years of Quebec up close, she could not with solid conviction say Oui. And yet to vote Non was definitely not an option. The honest act would have been to turn and leave the polling station and let other people decide. But she couldn't do that, would not be left out. Finally, she took the pencil and marked a question mark beside Oui, handed over the folded ballot and went home.

The morning after the snowstorm, Myra told all this to Rowan over steak and eggs at the Starcrest Rodeo diner. He said he'd been reading Lamotte's column in the Gazette. Could you believe a card-carrying separatist writing for the Gaz? Yes, said Myra, she's walking that tightrope now. He shook his head. "There's so much about this place that makes no sense whatsoever."

"That place," she corrected. "We're in Ontario now."

They talked all morning, no repartee, not a single barb, only the story of their lives. Myra told him about Paulette, admitted she actually admired that leap into the limo at Notre Dame. She talked about the transformation of Mitch, and the latest news about Sally. Six months in Europe with the boy-friend, starting after the end of term. Jack was crushed, but agreed to pay for her ticket.

Rowan talked about his fiasco with the married literature prof, an expert on Emile Nelligan, the mad-brilliant Irish-Québécois poet. He described how they'd met at a

crosscultural poetry reading and disagreed about Gins-
berg, how right it had seemed until everything went
wrong, and how his child was then born and swallowed
up by somebody else's marriage.

"Seems strange. She'll grow up speaking perfect
Québécois French. Fine, it's her mother tongue, but she'll
never know I exist."

"Don't count on the last part," said Myra. "Stories
have a way of circling around and sweeping you up again,
in another time." Rowan said that was a good way to
look at it. Then he said he could understand why Myra
wanted to leave Quebec, with her son gone out West and
Sally about to take off for Europe.

"No, it's not just that," she said. "I have to get my
certainty back."

"Certainty is overrated," said Rowan. "In some
ways it's downright immature."

She thought, I know what you mean. Stridency and
glassy-eyed conviction — but this is not the same.
Certainty is when you're standing on the edge of a
precipice and the leap is scary, yet necessary. You do it,
you do not have to think things over. That's the way it will
be someday with Quebec, maybe the next referendum —

Referring obliquely to his disasterous last love affair,
Rowan wondered if Myra would mind not talking about
politics at this particular moment, and she said, "Actually,
I've more or less decided to give the subject a good six
months on ice."

He laughed. "Six months? Count me in."


Then it was time to check out. The day was clear but they
kept on talking, and he talked her into spending all

afternoon and another night at the Starcrest Rodeo, which turned out not to be so hopelessly Americanized after all. The owner was once a well-known country and western singer, born and raised in Lac-St-Jean. He'd written a few songs that were still being sung wherever men sang of horses and heartbreak, in French.

By the following morning, the sky was a sober grey. A scrapdealer came and took Rowan's van away. He rescued a box of manuscripts and books, a suitcase full of summer clothes and sandals. "I hope to need these very soon," he said.

The back seat of Myra's car was loaded with boxes and office equipment. She tightened up the load to make space for his stuff, but when they were ready to roll, Rowan noticed he'd forgotten to give the motel key back, so they had to turn off again. The Starcrest Rodeo diner was in full lunch mode, a hive of truckers. Rowan said he could use another coffee, so they slid into the familiar corner booth.

"You two can't get enough of this place," the waitress grinned, as she filled their cups.

"So far, so good," said Rowan, winking her way.

They drank the coffee slowly, and Myra thought, this diner feels like a world under glass, as if we've been here for years. No longer marked by lists of things to do, time had melted, reconfigured as a curve-bottomed vessel holding fluid thoughts, liquid confession, warm silence. Now the flow was coming to an end, and Rowan rested both arms on the table, folded his hands and looked straight at her.

Apropos of nothing special, but well within the spirit of their night-and day-long talks, he said, "I've never actually done anything that I completely regret. Sure, at the time, but not looking back. No, my big regrets are all things I didn't do."

Myra said she'd have to think about that. Then she said, "I've written a few letters maybe I should have sent."

"Oh yes, letters. I've sent a few that should have been burned."

"Everybody has," she said.

"Doesn't count," he said. "That's a fiery impulse. I'm talking about things you should have got up and actually done. Taken the steps. For example, that job in Toronto. Do you think you'd regret saying no?"

Without hesitation she said, "No, I could live without that job."

"Then why are you going?" She saw the flicker of shyness in his eyes, and it struck her that they weren't mulling over the contingencies of Life any more. They were talking about something real, immediate.

"I'm going," she started, avoiding his eyes, "because it's the right thing, at this time."

"Why?"

"Well, the book. I need distance. The book cannot be written in Montreal."

"Okay," he said, "let's go," as he knocked back the rest of his cold coffee, tossed a toonie on the table and headed for the door. She was a little taken aback by his briskness. She went to the ladies room, washed her hands, spent the full regulation time under the hand blowdryer, checked her hair and cleaned out her purse. When she got back to the parking lot, Rowan was standing beside the driver's door, arms folded.

"Sky's clear," he said. "Do you still want me to drive?"

"Sure," she said. "If you don't mind."

He didn't move. Then she remembered the keys and fished them out of her purse. She held them out, but he kept his arms folded, just stood looking at her, as if on the verge of speaking.

She said, "Were you about to say something?"

"Yes," he said. "It's none of my business, but, you'd be better off with me."

"What?"

"Sure, I could say things like 'what a wonderful snowstorm,' et cetera. I could talk like one of my goddamn poems. What I mean is, why don't we just get into the car and drive off? Place a few calls and liberate yourself from that job you don't want and . . . you know, see."

He had that smile again, as if he'd already made all the right moves and now she was either going to have to drive the car out of the parking lot, or come up with an alternative plan.

"Where?" she said.

He found hope in the question. "A guy I used to know from the music business bought a small hotel in Cuernevaca, just outside Mexico City. It's got a restaurant and a bar, and he's putting together a blues band for the season. He gave me a call. Nothing permanent, of course. But I was toying with the idea of checking it out. Maybe you'd like to go along."

"Mexico?" She said the word like it was a new-found planet.

"Don't think of it as Mexico," he said. "Think of it as a warm place to write a kick-ass book about Quebec."

She folded her hand around the keys, looked at him, at his familiar velour shirt, familiar brown eyes, familiar dear tousled hair. She reached out and put her arms around him. He hugged her back, and whispered in her ear, "I didn't want to do that. Could be considered unfair persuasion."

"Let me think," she said. Then she reached down to unlock the door, and said, "I'll drive."

On the way back to Montreal, the car seemed to fly like a glider. She watched the speedometer ooze upwards, 120 km/h and not the slightest hesitation. No shimmy at 130. Powerful heater, air conditioning, AM/FM. This beast was worth every penny, she thought.

As they soared toward the city skyline, Rowan the passenger seemed to read her mind. He rambled, she watched the road.

"To be perfectly honest, despite everything that's happened, I can't see myself leaving Montreal forever. All it takes is a flash of that skyline, reality or dream, and my chest feels squeezed. I was born here, left half a dozen times, swore never again. But it isn't an easy city to leave. Maybe it's love, but what does that mean? I've been in love, with Jacqueline — we were 19 and 20. Ten years later she died and I thought, there will never be another woman like Jacqueline, and there never was. Then, you know the story. All right, this may sound cruel, and no doubt open to debate. But it seems to me you can get over most people, eventually. A place? Never. At least not Montreal. Places don't die. And deep down, they don't change. Something familiar always remains, and it does not let go."

It was the middle of the afternoon, too early for rush hour. The expressway was empty as they swung around a wide arc and glided down Décarie. A mile of silence had passed when Rowan added, "I could be wrong. Sometimes I get so furious with — ahhhh. The never-ending debate."

They stopped at a phone booth in Verdun, after Myra got seriously mixed up on a network of one-way streets. Sally was home when the phone rang. She thought the idea of Mexico was a good one, but wouldn't it be wise to stick around for a few days and —

"Think it over? Sal, if I think it over, I won't go."

"Yeah, I know what you mean. Well, then, go."

"You think I should?"

"It's your decision."

The infuriating truth. Myra said, "Okay. Sorry. I mean, goodbye. And take care of yourself."

"Ha! You too."

"I'll write Mitch a letter. Don't say anything. Oh dear!"

"Mom, go. You can always come back."

"True enough. Well."

"Bye."

"Bye."

A silent moment passed between them. Then Myra hung up, the shiver passed, and she thought, yes, this is it. Certainty.

Rowan drove the first lap. He brought maps, a thermos and a cooler. On a sparkling blue-sky day, the St. Lawrence disappeared behind, and the dream river narrowed down to nothing more mysterious than a silver high-way, straight south. She could feel the Mountain grow smaller, out of sight. Eyes closed on the winter sun, sleek as a fish, she soared.